Step by Ste[barcode sticker] 版

圖解 狄克生片語

一本學會470個
關鍵日常英文片語

作者 Matt Coler　譯者 李盈瑩　審訂 Judy Majewski

DIXON'S IDIOMS

如何下載 MP3 音檔

❶ 寂天雲 APP 聆聽：掃描書上 QR Code 下載「寂天雲－英日語學習隨身聽」APP。加入會員後，用 APP 內建掃描器再次掃描書上 QR Code，即可使用 APP 聆聽音檔。

❷ 官網下載音檔：請上「寂天閱讀網」（www.icosmos.com.tw），註冊會員／登入後，搜尋本書，進入本書頁面，點選「MP3下載」下載音檔，存於電腦等其他播放器聆聽使用。

Contents

UNIT

Introduction 片語動詞

本書分成 39 單元，整理共 470 個狄克生片語，並逐一拆解結構，全方位講解片語的詞性、特性、用法、同反義語、例句等。本書收錄的片語中，有許多為「片語動詞」(Phrasal Verb)。片語動詞由「**動詞＋介副詞**」所組成，英文母語人士在日常生活中也經常使用片語動詞，例如同樣要表達「考慮」，口語上會使用片語動詞 think over，consider 則更常用在書面上。

○ 片語動詞的動詞與介副詞

片語動詞裡的**動詞**多為**意義簡單的詞語**，常見的有 take、get、break、bring 等；**介副詞**則多能表示**方向**與**意象**，如 on、in、up、down、over 等。兩者加在一起時，**介副詞**會賦予片語動詞**核心意義**。

舉例來說，介副詞 over 有「跨過」、「越過」的意象，含有 over 的片語動詞就會隱含 over 本身的涵義：

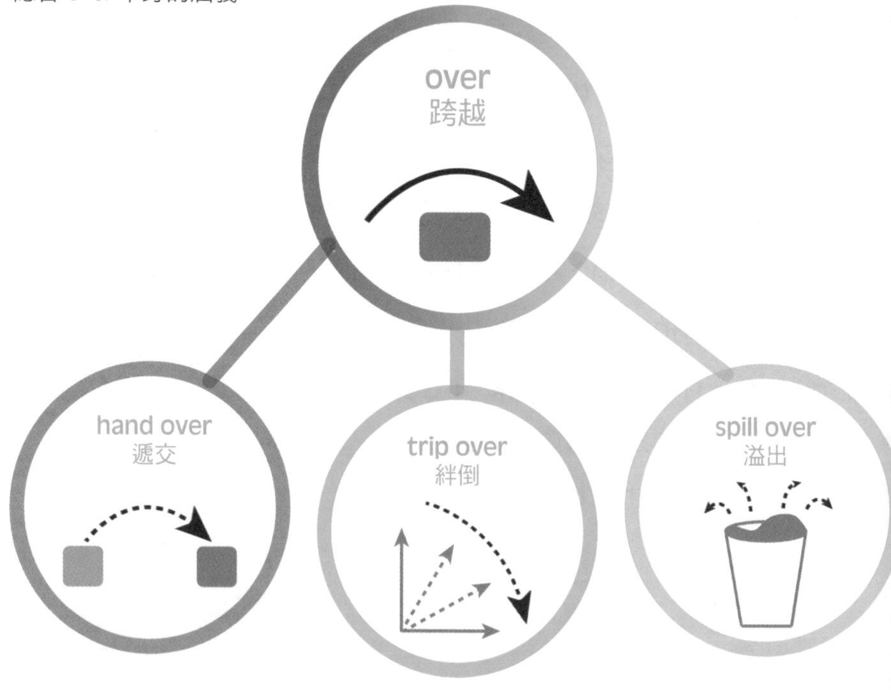

❍ 片語動詞的特性

1 多種涵義：

一個片語動詞，可以有多達五種以上的意思，因此片語動詞真正的涵義得由句中的上下文來判斷，如：

pick up	
❶ 拾起	❶ John **picked up** the kitten and took it to its mother.
❷ 購買	❷ We can **pick up** some food on the way to the library.
❸ 汽車接送某人	❸ I have to **pick up** my sister from soccer practice.

2 分成「及物」或「不及物」：

及物的片語動詞後面要接受詞；不及物的片語動詞後面則不可接受詞。如：

- Derek **made up** the story. 德瑞克**瞎掰**了這件事。
  → **make up** 及物，後面要接受詞
- Jessica didn't **show up**. 潔西卡並未**現身**。
  → **show up** 不及物，後面不可直接加受詞

3 分成「要分開」、「不可分開」或「分不分開都可以」：

❶ 要分開與不可分開

	要分開的片語動詞	不可分開的片語動詞
規則	受詞置於動詞和介副詞之間	受詞置於介副詞之後
例句	I **talked** my father **into** letting me buy the computer. 我**說服**我爸讓我買電腦。	They are **looking into** the problem. 他們正在**研究**那個問題。

❷ 分不分開都可以

有些片語動詞兼具兩種特性，既可以分開使用，讓受詞夾在動詞與介副詞之間，也可以合在一起，受詞放在介副詞後面。**唯獨當受詞為**代名詞（**如 he、she、it 等）時**，一定要分開使用，如：

- Gary **tore** the letter **up**. 蓋瑞把信**撕**了。
- Gary **tore up** the letter. 蓋瑞**撕**了信。
- Gary **tore** it **up**. 蓋瑞把它給**撕**了。
  → **tear up** 的意思是「撕毀」，可以分開，也可以不分開；
  但受詞若為代名詞，則代名詞一定要放在 **tear** 和 **up** 的中間。

The School Test
學校考試

Sandra and Nick talk about their history test.
珊卓拉和尼克在談論歷史考試。

001

Sandra: Hey Nick, where have you been? I've been trying to **call** you **up**[1] for a few hours, but you never answered your phone! Did you just **get up**[2]?

Nick: No, I've been awake for a few hours now. I think I forgot to **turn on**[3] my cell phone this morning. Come in and **take off**[4] your jacket. Make yourself comfortable.

Sandra: We don't have time to chat here. **Put on**[5] your jacket and let's go!

Nick: Why?

Sandra: We have that big history test to study for.

Nick: I'll study for it **sooner or later**[6]. What's the rush?

Sandra: The test is in three hours!

Nick: Yikes! I forgot! We'd better get started **right away**[7]. Let me call my mom to **pick** us **up**[8] and take us to the library.

珊卓： 嘿，尼克，你到哪去了？我**打電話**找你找了好幾個小時，你都沒接電話！你才剛**起床**嗎？

尼克： 不，我醒來好幾個小時了。我想我早上忘記**開機**了。進來**脫下**夾克，別拘束。

珊卓： 我們沒時間在這裡聊天了。把夾克**穿上**，我們快走吧！

尼克： 為什麼？

珊卓： 我們要準備歷史大考了。

尼克： 我**遲早**會準備的，急什麼呢？

珊卓： 考試再過三個小時就要開始了！

尼克： 天啊！我都忘了！我們最好**馬上**出門。我要叫我媽來**接**我們，送我們到圖書館。

turn on the TV 打開電視

take off 脫下

002

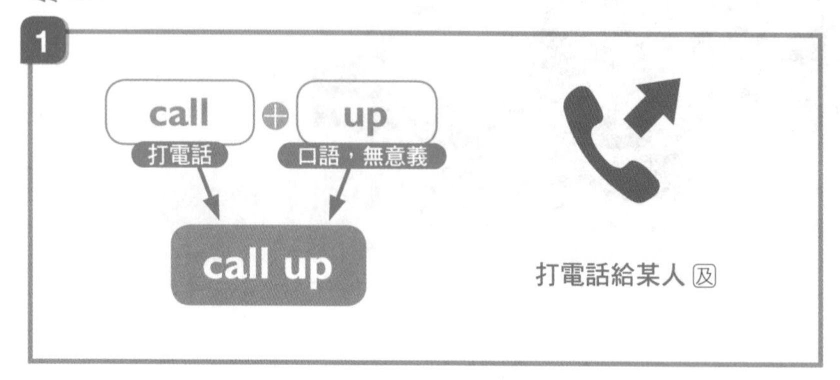

- I was bored Friday night, so I **called up** some old friends and organized a party. 星期五晚上我很無聊，就**打電話**給幾個老朋友，籌劃開一個派對。
- Derek told the pretty girl she could **call** him **up** sometime, but she never did.
  德瑞克告訴那個漂亮女孩改天可以**打電話**給他，但她從未打過。

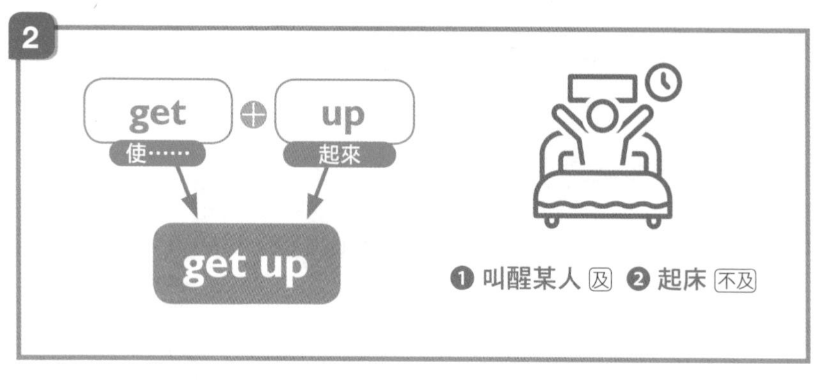

❶ My mom **gets** me **up** every day before school.
我媽媽每天上學前會**叫我起床**。

❷ I brush my teeth twice a day: when I **get up** and before I go to bed.
我每天刷兩次牙：**起床**後和上床前。

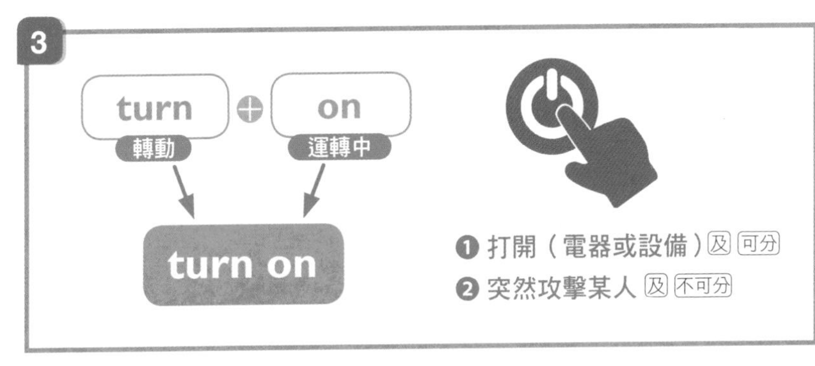

❶ Hey, **turn** the TV **on**, or we'll miss the game!
嘿，**打開**電視，否則我們就要錯過比賽了！

❶ Frank couldn't figure out why his dinner was still cold until he saw that he had forgotten to **turn on** the oven.
法蘭克想不透為何晚餐還是冷的，直到他發現忘了把烤箱**打開**。

❷ I tried to help her stand up, but she **turned on** me, shouting, "Get off!"
我想扶她站好，但她**突然**吼我說：「滾開！」

❶ When entering an official building in America, a male should **take off** his hat.
在美國，進入講究門面的大樓時，男士一定要**脫**帽。

❶ It was cloudy out, so Jen **took** her sunglasses **off** and put them in her pocket.
外面天空陰陰的，所以珍**摘下**太陽眼鏡放在口袋。

003

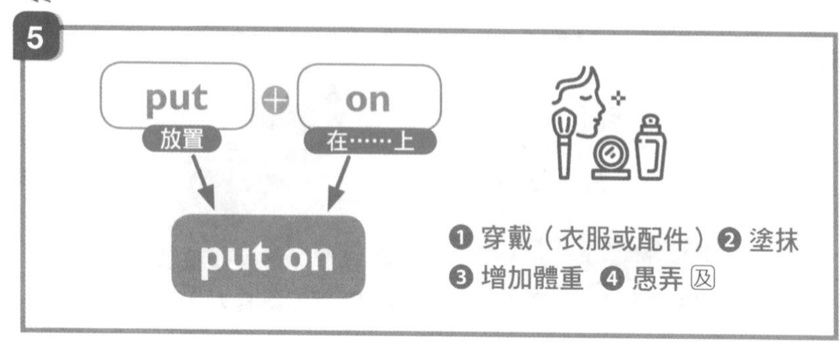

❶ I **put on** my watch every morning before work.
我每天早上上班前會**戴上**手錶。

❶ Tim **put** his winter hat **on** before he went out to play in the snow. 提姆在出去玩雪前，把冬帽**戴上**。

❷ Is there a mirror somewhere? I need to **put** my makeup **on**. 這裡有鏡子嗎？我得**補**個妝。

❸ He's **put on** a lot of weight since he gave up smoking.
他戒菸後**胖**了好多。

❹ You didn't believe him, did you? He was just **putting** you **on**. 你沒有把他當真對吧？他只是在**耍**你耶。

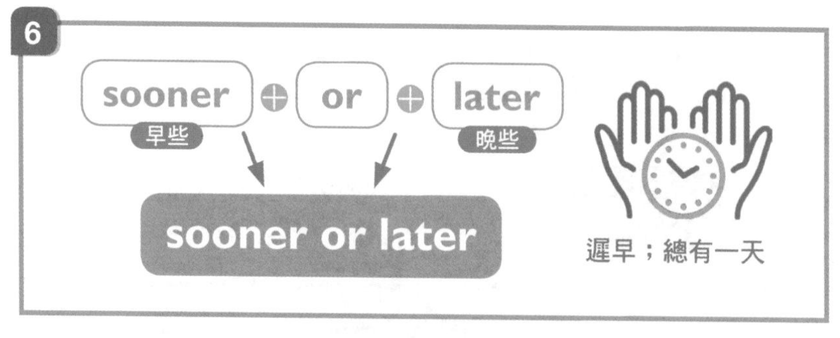

- Jay isn't sure when he'll finish his paper, but he's convinced he'll complete it **sooner or later**.
傑不確定何時會完成論文，但他相信他**遲早**會完成的。
- Life may be difficult for you now, but **sooner or later** it has to get better.
現在生活對你來說也許很困難，但情況**總有一天**會好轉。

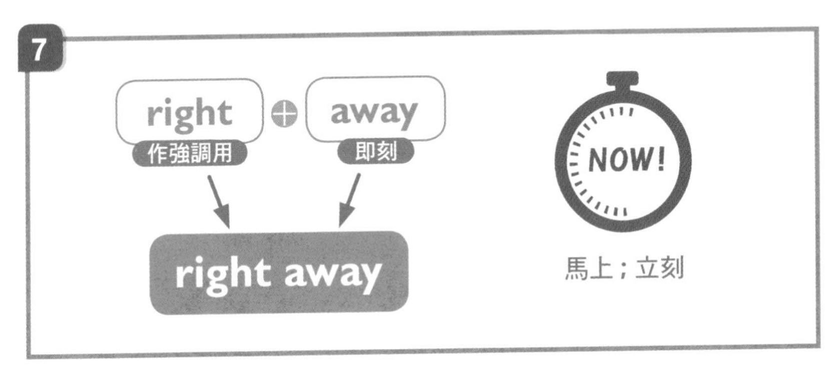

- I have to leave **right away**; otherwise, I will be late.
  我必須**馬上**離開，否則會遲到。

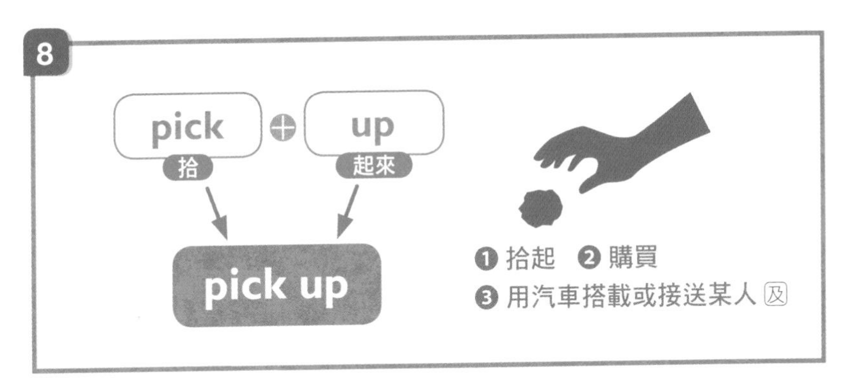

❶ Jake **picked up** the kitten and took it to its mother.
傑克**撿起**了小貓，把牠帶到媽媽的身邊。

❷ We can **pick up** some coffee and food on the way to the library.
我們可以在去圖書館的路上**買**些咖啡和食物。

❸ I have to **pick up** my sister from soccer practice and drive her home.
妹妹練完足球後我必須去**接**她，然後載她回家。

004

9

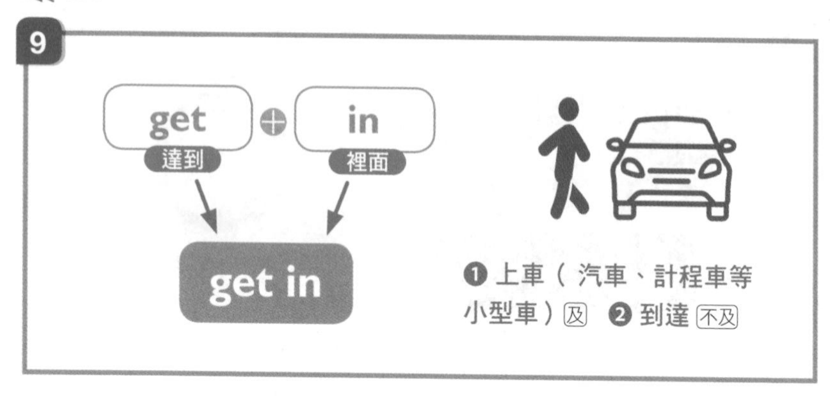

❶ **Get in** the car, and I'll give you a ride!
上車吧，我載你去！

❷ Do you know what time Mark's plane **gets in**?
你知道馬克的飛機幾點**到**嗎？

10

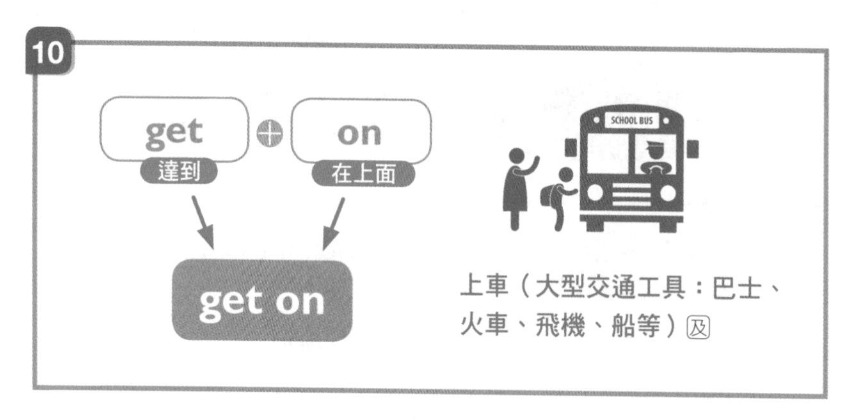

- If you don't have a ticket, you can't **get on** the train.
  如果你沒有車票，就不能**上**火車。
- The plane was almost full by the time I **got on**.
  我**上**飛機時，機上幾乎已經都坐滿人了。

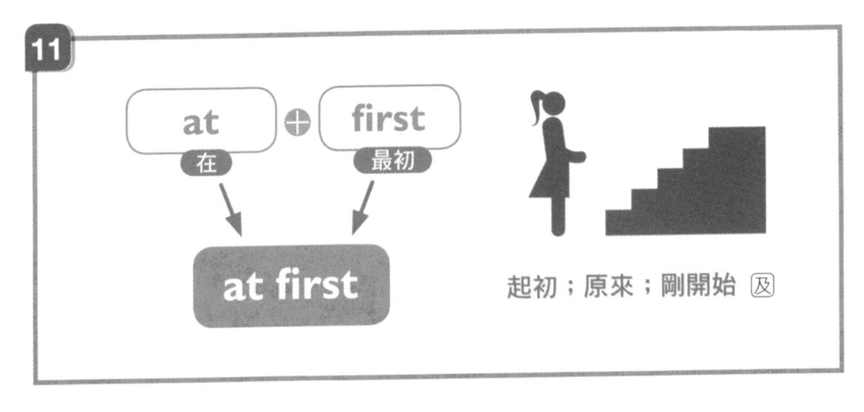

- Although English was hard **at first**, after I had studied it for a few months, it became easier.
  雖然英語**剛開始**很難，但我學了幾個月後，就變得比較容易了。
- When Joan met Lou, she didn't like him **at first**; however, ten months later, they were married. 珍和陸相遇時，她**起初**並不喜歡他，但是 10 個月後，他們結婚了。
- If **at first** you don't succeed, try and try again.
  一試不成功，就再試一次。

Shopping
逛街購物

Dylan and Natalie are talking as they walk down the city sidewalk after a long day of shopping.
在街上逛了一整天後，狄倫和娜塔莉在市區的人行道上邊走邊聊天。

005

Dylan: Did I tell you that we were invited to a party at my office next month? It'll be formal, so we'll have to **dress up**[1].

Natalie: How exciting! I guess I'd better **look for**[2] some new clothes. Hey, let's go now to my favorite shop—it's not far from here. We can **look at**[3] that dress I told you about yesterday. However, I think it's pretty expensive.

Dylan: **Never mind**[4] the price. We can pay for it in installments, **little by little**[5]. It's important that we look great and impress my boss.

Natalie: Maybe I can **find out**[6] when they're having a sale. Then we could save some money.

Dylan: That's a good idea. After we check out that shop, let's go home. We've been walking around a lot, and, **as usual**[7], all this shopping has really **tired** me **out**[8].

狄倫：　我有提過我們受邀參加公司下個月的派對嗎？派對很正式，我們必須**盛裝打扮**。

娜塔莉： 真令人興奮！我想我最好**找**些新衣服。嘿，我們現在就去我最喜歡的那家店，就離這裡不遠。我們可以去**看**我昨天跟你提過的那件洋裝。不過我覺得它很貴。

狄倫：　**別管**價格，我們可以**慢慢**用分期付款的。重要的是我們要看起來很體面，讓老闆印象深刻。

娜塔莉： 也許我能夠**查一下**何時會有折扣，這樣我們就可以省點錢了。

狄倫：　好主意。我們看完那家店就回家吧。我們已經走了好久，**就像往常一樣**，逛街真把我**累壞了**。

dress up 盛裝打扮

look for 尋找

006

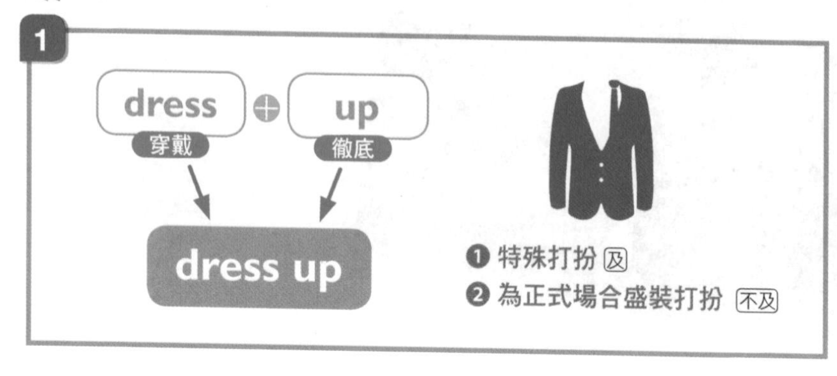

❶ He **dressed up** as a cowboy for the party.
他**打扮**成牛仔來參加派對。

❷ If you go to a wedding, it is important to **dress up**.
盛裝參加婚禮很重要。

❷ Because Lucas didn't **dress up** for his job interview, he looked unprofessional. 盧卡斯參加工作面試時沒有**穿著正式服裝**，所以看起來很不專業。

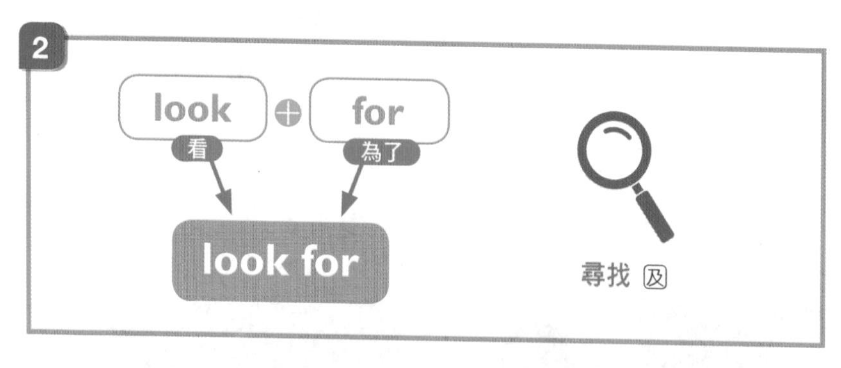

- Pablo spent the entire morning **looking for** his car keys. 帕布羅花了整個早上的時間**尋找**車鑰匙。
- The children walked all over the neighborhood **looking for** their lost dog. 孩子們走遍整個街坊**尋找**走丟的小狗。
- He spent his life **looking for** the truth.
他窮極一生都在**追尋**真理。

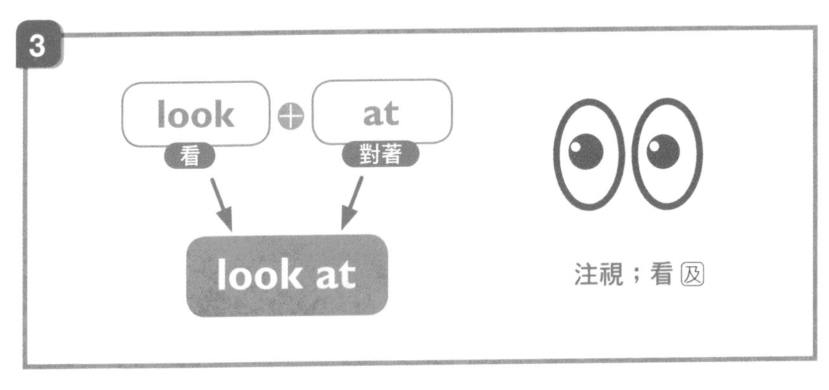

- Before his big date, Carl **looked at** himself carefully in the mirror.
  在赴重要約會前，卡羅仔細地**注視**著鏡中的自己。

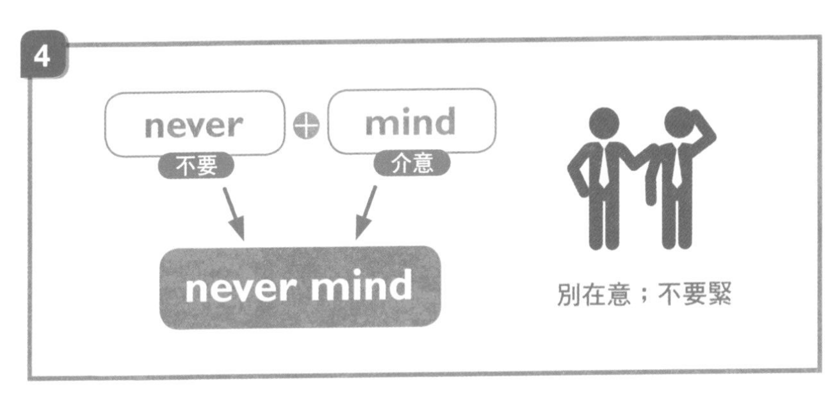

- **Never mind** your coming late; no one even noticed you weren't here.
  遲到**沒關係**，反正沒人注意到你不在這裡。
- My suggestion that you stay awake all night was a bad idea, so **never mind**.
  我提議整晚不睡是個爛主意，所以你**別放在心上**。

007

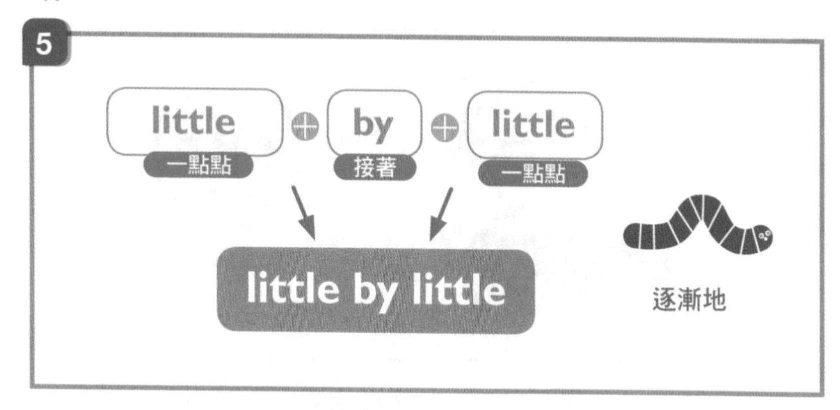

- **Little by little**, the kitten came to love and trust her new owner.
  小貓**漸漸**開始喜歡和依賴新主人了。
- At first I didn't like my math class, but **little by little**, I began to really enjoy it.
  我剛開始不喜歡數學課，但我**逐漸**得到其中真正的樂趣。

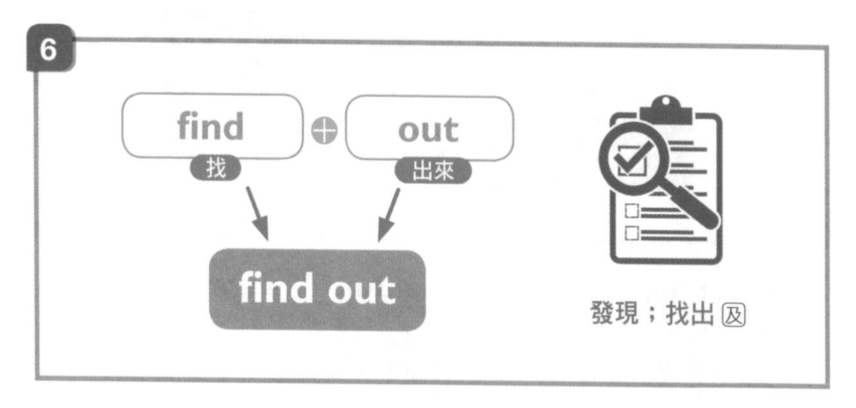

- Last Monday, Jake **found out** that he was getting a promotion. 傑克上星期一**發現**他升官了。
- I hope no one **finds out** about my embarrassing mistake! 我希望沒人**發現**這個令人難堪的錯誤！

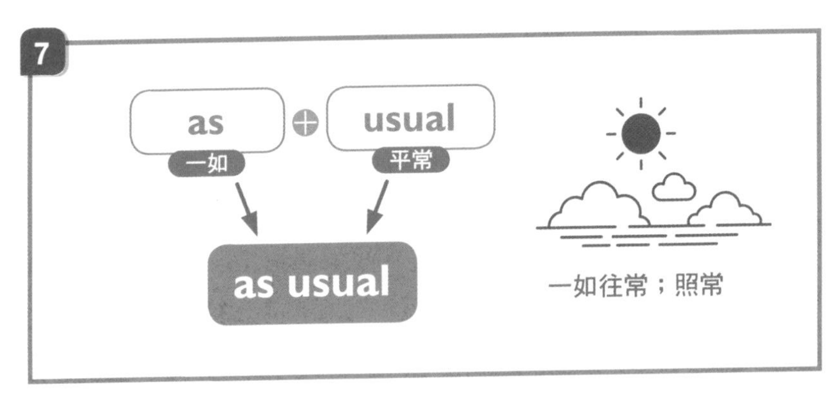

- Harry came to the meeting late, **as usual**.
  哈利**照例**開會遲到。
- **As usual**, Mom had prepared a delicious dinner for the family.
  我媽媽就**像平常一樣**為全家人準備美味的晚餐。

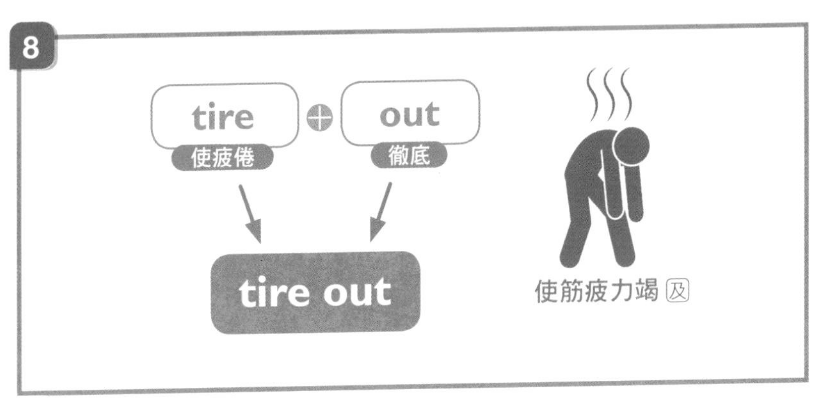

- Gabe really **tired** himself **out** by walking around New York City all day.
  在紐約走了一天，蓋比**筋疲力竭**。
- We **tired out** the dogs by playing with them in the park for a few hours.
  我們和狗狗在公園裡玩了好幾個小時，把狗狗給**累壞了**。

008

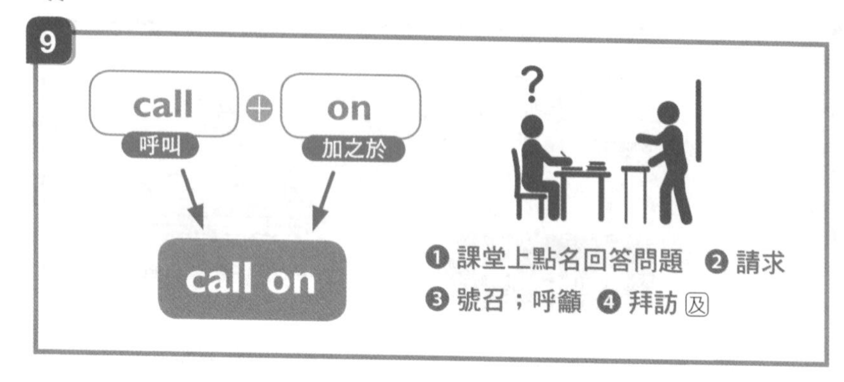

❶ I was hoping Ms. Baker wouldn't **call on** me during history class because I didn't know the answer.
希望貝克女士不要在歷史課**指名**我**回答問題**，因為我不知道答案。

❷ I now **call on** everyone to raise a glass to the happy couple. 我現在**請**每一個人舉起杯子，向這對幸福的新人致意。

❸ The university official **called on** the professors to help raise the school's reputation.
學校高層**號召**教授幫忙提升學校的聲望。

❸ Scientists **have called on / will call on** the government to end political interference in science.
科學家**呼籲**政府應該不要再對科學界做政治上的干涉。

❹ I will **call on** a friend this weekend.
我這個週末會去**拜訪**一位朋友。

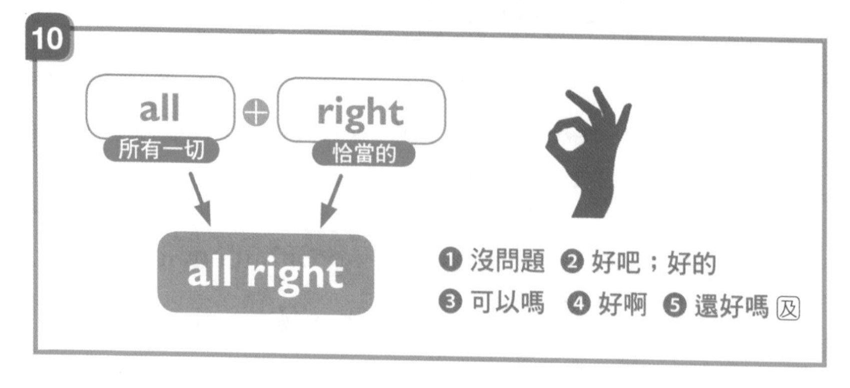

❶ This book is **all right**, but it isn't anything special.
這本書**不錯**，只是沒什麼特別之處。

❷ **All right**, so I made a mistake. **好吧**，是我的錯。

❸ Tell me if you start to feel sick, **all right**?
如果你開始覺得不舒服，就跟我說**好嗎**？

❹ **All right**! They scored! **好耶**！得分！

❺ "**All right**, Mike?" "Not bad, thanks, and you?"
「麥克**你好嗎**？」「還不錯，謝了。妳呢？」

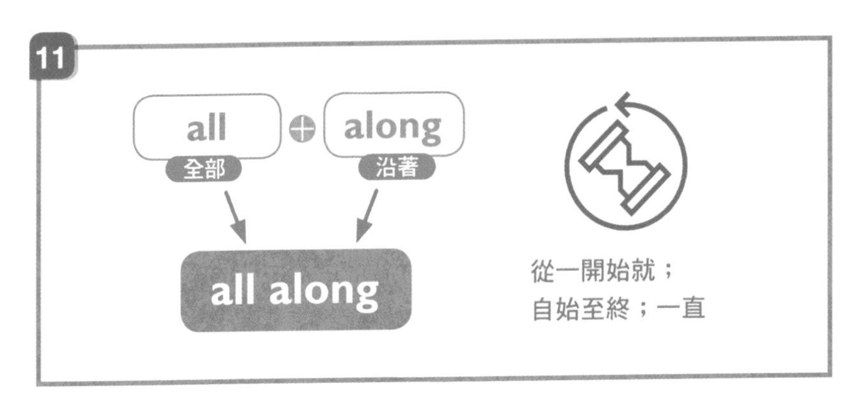

- We were shocked that Gloria had known about the late phone bill **all along** but hadn't told anyone.
  葛洛莉亞**從一開始就**知道電話帳單過期了，卻沒告訴任何人，令我們非常震驚。
- It was supposed to be a surprise party for Rudy, but actually he knew about it **all along**.
  這原本是要給魯迪的驚喜派對，但他事實上**打從一開始就**知道了。
- Do you think he's been cheating us **all along**?
  你想他是不是**從一開始就**在騙我們了？

Going to a Party
參加派對

Ron and Donna chat about a party this weekend.
朗和唐娜在聊有關這週末的派對。

009

Ron: Hey there, Donna! How are you doing?

Donna: Well, not so well. Actually, I **talked over**[1] my plan to go to your party this weekend with my parents, and they don't like the idea.

Ron: Really? I'm in no rush, so **take your time**[2] and tell me what the problem is.

Donna: Well, they are concerned that the party will be unsupervised. They also don't want me to stay out **all night long**[3].

Ron: But we won't be there **by ourselves**[4]; my parents will be there. Maybe if my dad called your mom to tell her this, it would **make a difference**[5] to her.

Donna: Yeah, maybe you're right. After all, our parents **get along with**[6] each other.

Ron: Exactly! Plus, the party won't go so late. You can be home before 11.

Donna: That will make my mom feel better.

Ron: Great! So why are you still **sitting down**[7]? **Stand up**[8], go home, and tell your mom that my dad will call later.

Donna: Okay, cool. See you soon!

朗： 嗨，唐娜！妳好嗎？

唐娜： 嗯，不怎麼好。事實上，我和我的父母**討論**過去參加你的週末派對的計畫，但他們不喜歡這個主意。

朗： 真的嗎？我不趕時間，所以**慢慢來**，告訴我問題在哪裡。

唐娜： 嗳，他們認為派對裡沒大人看著，而且他們也不希望我**徹夜**未歸。

朗： 但又不是只有我們**獨**處而已，我的父母也會在。假如我爸打電話給妳媽，告訴她這點，對她或許**有所差別**。

唐娜： 是啊，也許你說的對。畢竟我們的父母很**處得來**。

朗： 沒錯！還有，派對不會到那麼晚，妳可以在 11 點前回到家。

唐娜： 我媽會覺得那樣比較好。

朗： 太好了！所以妳為何還**坐**在這裡？快**站起來**，回家告訴妳媽，我爸晚點會打電話過去。

唐娜： 對，好極了。改天見！

010

- There's no need to make a decision now; we can **talk** it **over** tomorrow.
  不用現在就做決定；我們可以明天**再討論**。
- Kerry **talked over** her request for a raise with her boss.
  凱莉和老闆**商量**要求加薪。

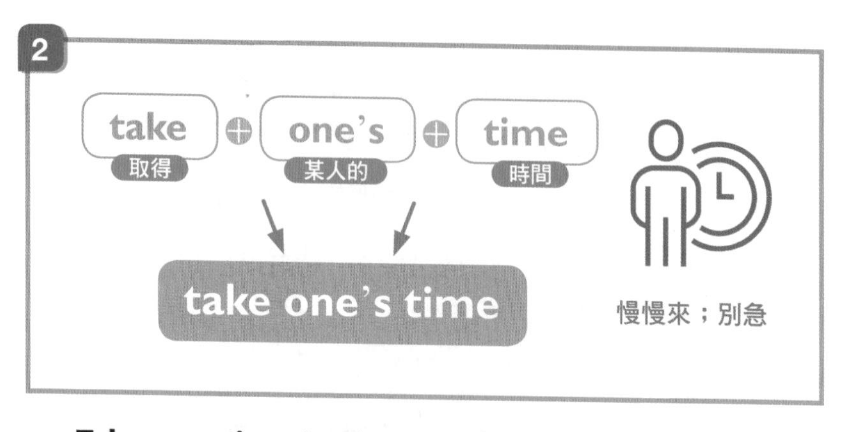

- **Take your time**; I'm in no rush. **別急**，我不趕時間。
- Bob didn't care that he was late; he continued to **take his time** eating his lunch.
  鮑伯不在乎遲到，他繼續**慢慢**吃午餐。

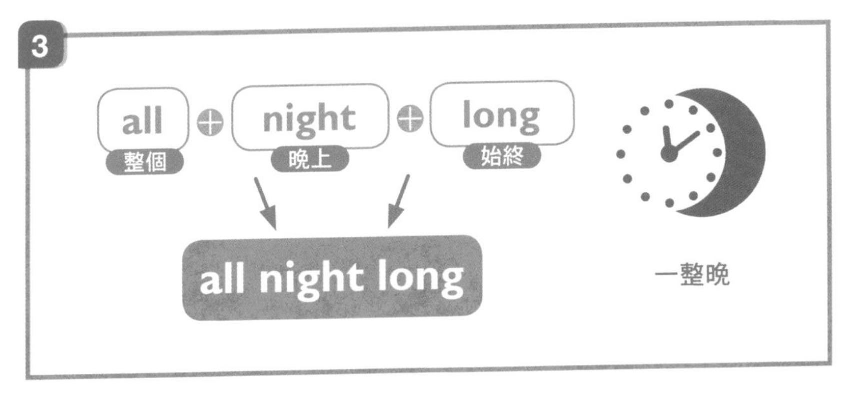

- Lou stayed up **all night long** studying.
  盧**整個晚上**都在熬夜唸書。

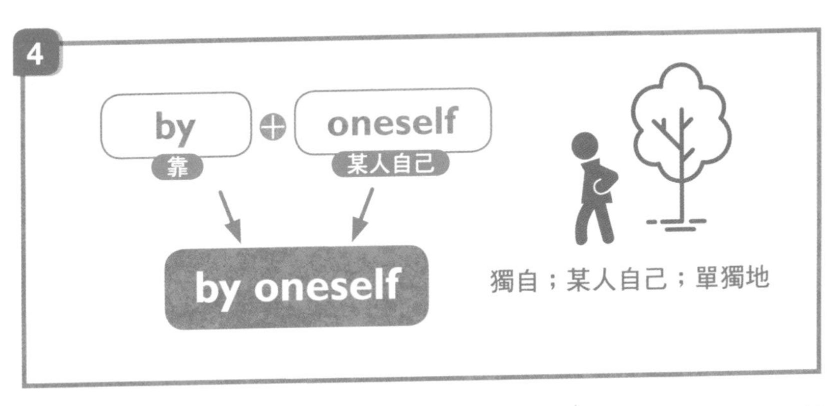

- Jenny's younger sister doesn't like to be left **by herself** for very long.
  珍妮的妹妹不喜歡長時間**一個人獨處**。
- The first day we left the puppy at home **by himself**, he made a big mess.
  我們第一次把小狗**獨自**留在家裡時，他把房子搞得一團糟。

011

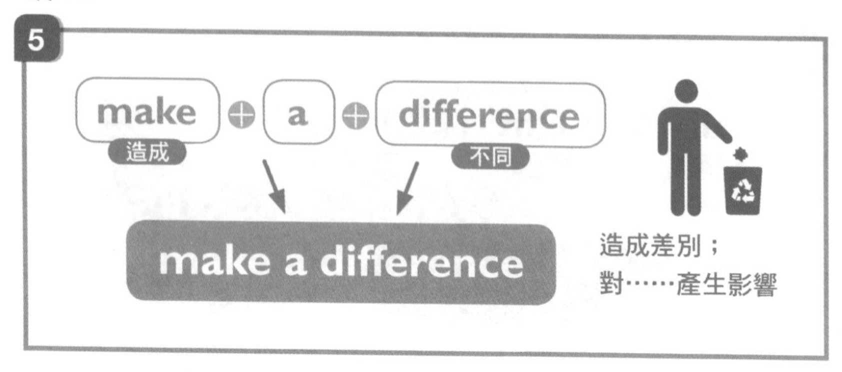

- Jill saw that cleaning her dorm **made a big difference** in how it looked.
  潔兒發現大掃除讓宿舍看起來**截然不同**。
- A healthy diet **makes a difference** in the way you feel.
  健康的飲食會對身體**產生影響**。
- Sleeping an extra ten minutes a night **makes no difference** in how I feel the next morning.
  每晚多睡 10 分鐘，對我隔天早上的感覺**不會有太大的影響**。

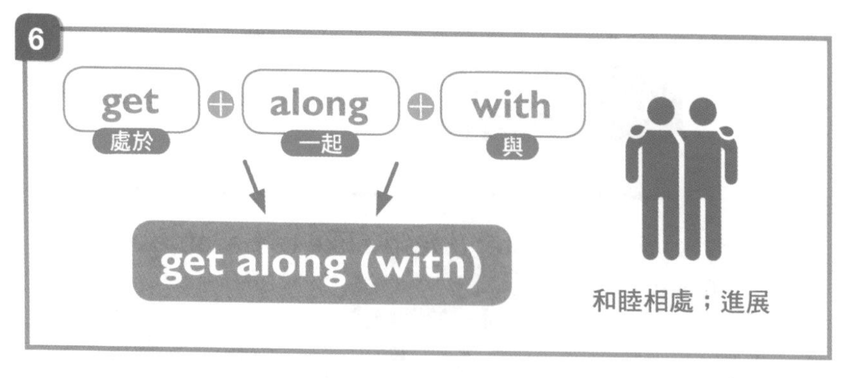

- Although Harry is a nice guy, for some reason Beth never **got along with** him.
  雖然哈利是個好人，但是基於某些原因，貝絲就是和他**處不來**。
- I wonder how Alex is **getting along** in his new job.
  不知亞力克斯的新工作**做得**如何

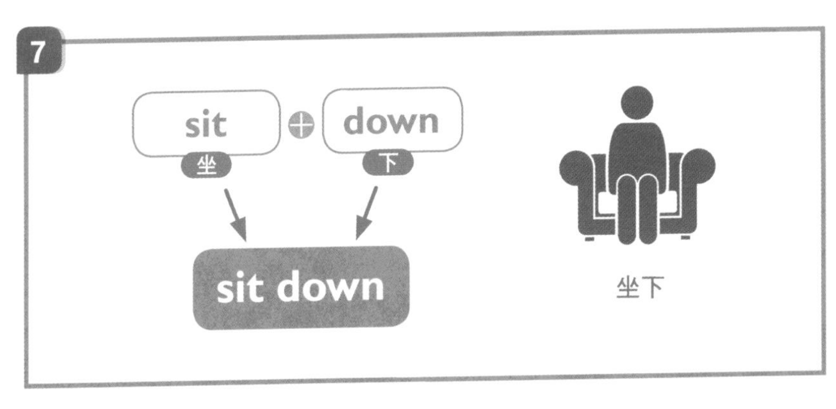

- As soon as the teacher entered the classroom, all the students **sat down** and stopped talking.
  老師一走進教室，所有學生都**坐下來**停止說話。

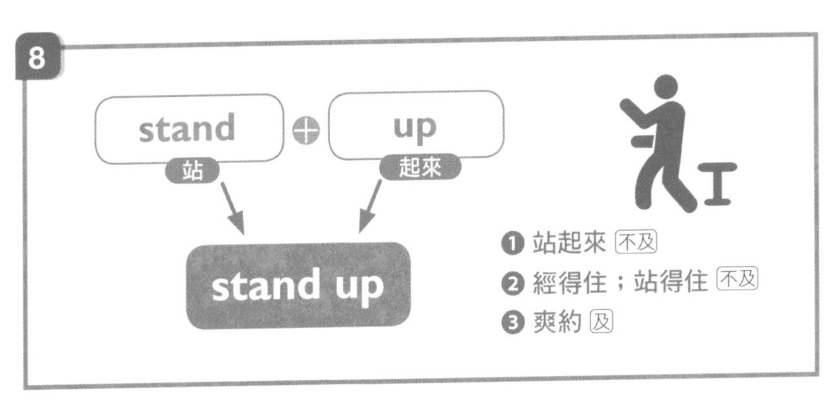

❶ After spending the entire day sitting in class, Paula said it felt good to **stand up** and walk around.
寶拉覺得上課坐了一整天後，**站起來**走一走的感覺很舒服。

❷ Their evidence will never **stand up** in court.
他們的證據在法庭上根本**站不住腳**。

❸ Xavier and I had a date for dinner, but he **stood** me **up**.
傑維爾和我約好了要一起吃晚餐，結果他**放我鴿子**。

012

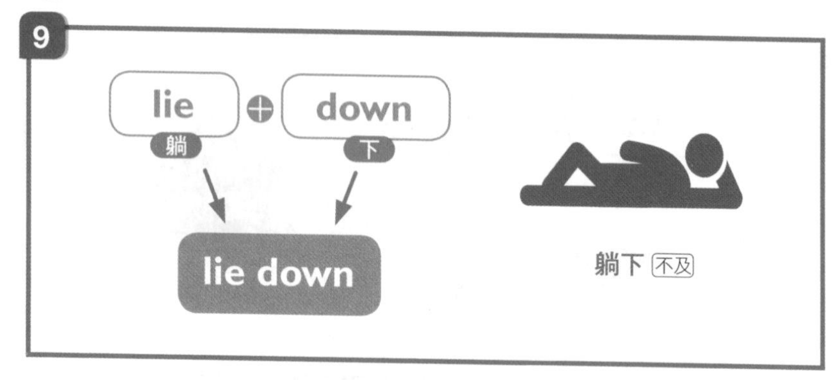

- Garth **lay down** on his bed and tried to sleep, but he couldn't. 加爾斯**躺**在床上試圖入睡，但他睡不著。
- As soon as I **lay down**, I fell asleep. 我一**躺下來**就睡著了。

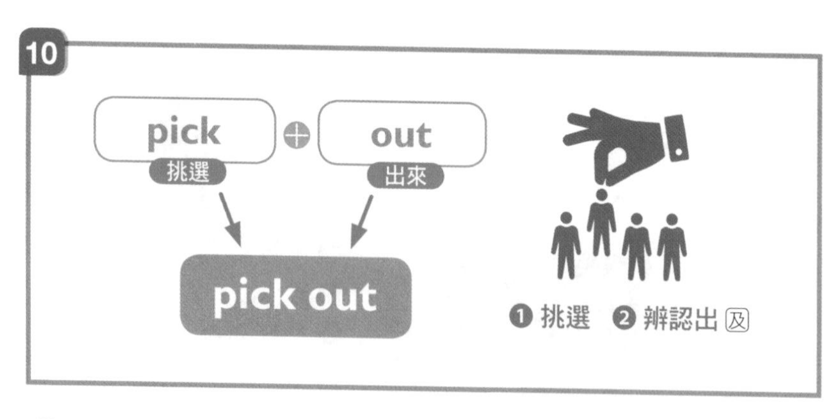

❶ When Terry arrived at the store, his father told him he could **pick out** any shirt he wanted.
泰瑞到店裡時，父親要他**挑選**任何他想要的襯衫。

❷ Kim searched the audience for her friends but had trouble **picking** them **out** of the crowd.
金在觀眾群中找尋朋友的蹤影，卻無法在人群中**找到**他們。

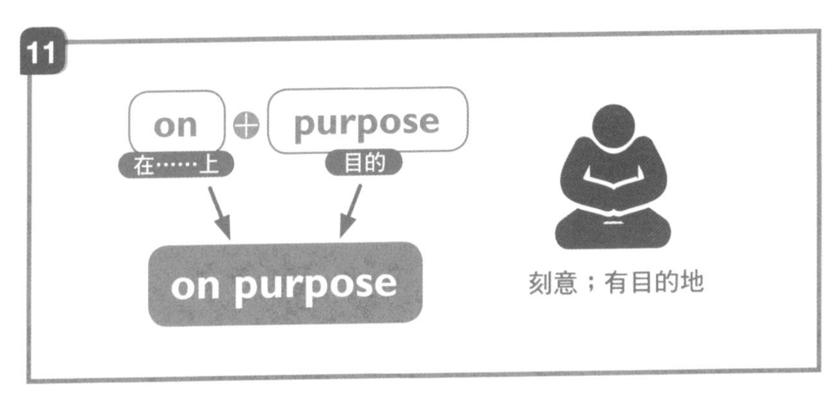

- I came late **on purpose**; it wasn't a mistake.
  我**故意**遲到，並不是誤會。
- Franz lost the card game **on purpose** because he wanted to go home.
  法蘭斯玩牌時**故意**輸掉，因為他想回家了。

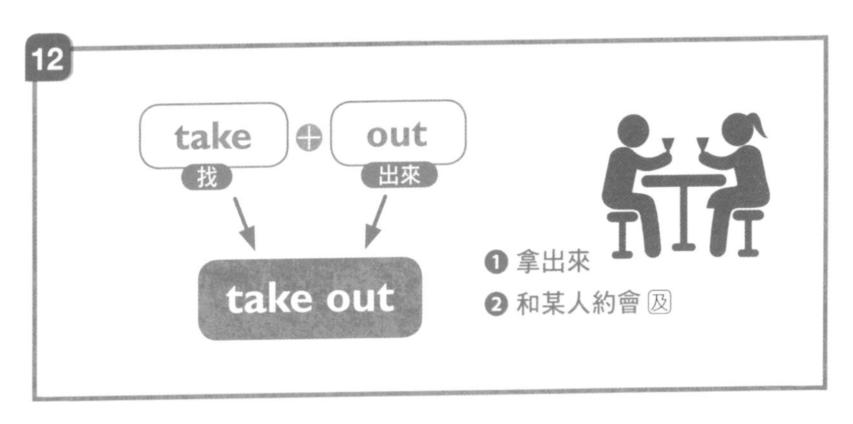

❶ Mom asked me to **take out** the trash before I left.
媽媽要我出門前把垃圾**拿出去**。

❶ The dentist **took** Jack's tooth **out**.
牙醫**拔掉**傑克的牙齒。

❷ Warren **took** Lidia **out** for the first time last Friday.
華倫和莉蒂亞上星期五第一次**約會**。

The School Play
學校戲劇表演

Mark and Cheryl have a conversation about the school play. 馬克和雪若正在談論學校的戲劇表演。

013

Mark: Did you hear about this year's school play?

Cheryl: No, tell me about it.

Mark: Well, it **takes place**[1] in London. If you're interested in learning more about it, you can **look** it **up**[2] online.

Cheryl: OK, it sounds cool. Are you **taking part in**[3] it?

Mark: Of course! In one scene, I work in a restaurant and **wait on**[4] the play's hero.

Cheryl: Wow! I'd like to be in the play, too—but I'm not a good actress **at all**[5].

Mark: Well, we are looking for **at least**[6] three more actors, so you should really consider it.

Cheryl: All right. I'll **think** it **over**[7].

Mark: OK, but don't think too much! Anyway, I'd better go and **try on**[8] my costume.

Cheryl: See you, and good luck!

馬克：妳聽說今年學校的戲劇表演了嗎？

雪若：沒有，說來聽聽。

馬克：嗯，它會在倫敦**舉行**。如果妳有興趣想知道更多訊息，可以上網**查詢**。

雪若：好，聽起來不錯。你會**參加**嗎？

馬克：當然！我在一個餐廳的場景中，負責**接待**劇中的男主角。

雪若：哇！我也想參與演出，但是我的演技**一點也**不好。

馬克：喔，我們還在找**最少**三位演員，妳真的應該考慮看看。

雪若：嗯，我會**仔細考慮**的。

馬克：好，但別想太多！總之，我最好去**試穿**我的戲服了。

雪若：再見，祝你好運！

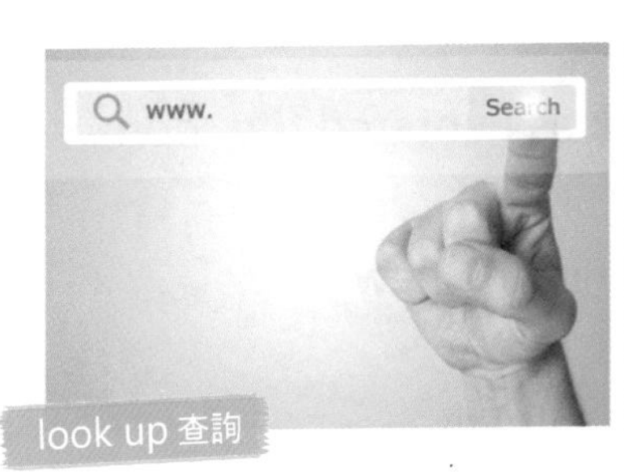

look up 查詢

wait on 接待

014

❶ The party will **take place** in two weeks.
派對會在兩個星期後**舉行**。

❷ When does the class **take place**? 那堂課何時**開始**？

❷ Not all engineering failures **take place** suddenly and dramatically. 工程問題的**發生**，不一定都是很突然很劇烈的。

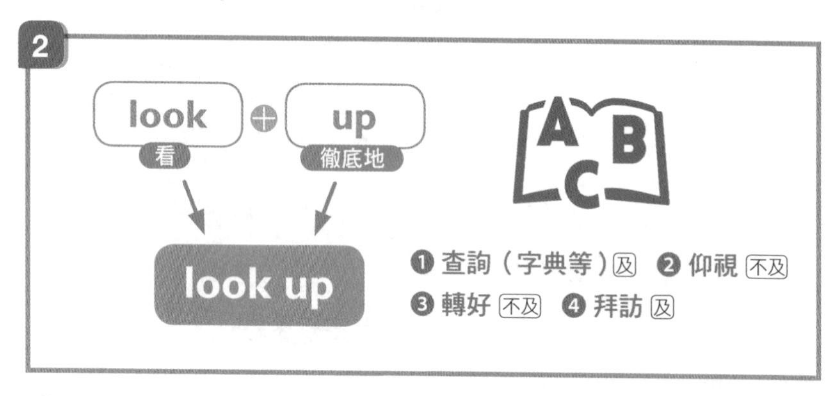

❶ If you don't know what a word means, just **look** it **up** in the dictionary. 如果不知道某個生字的意思，就**查**字典。

❷ She **looked up** from her book as I entered the room.
我進屋時，她停下看書**抬眼看**了一下。

❸ I hope things start to **look up** in the new year.
希望新的一年情況會開始**好轉**。

❹ **Look** me **up** next time you're in Paris.
下次來巴黎時要來**找**我喔。

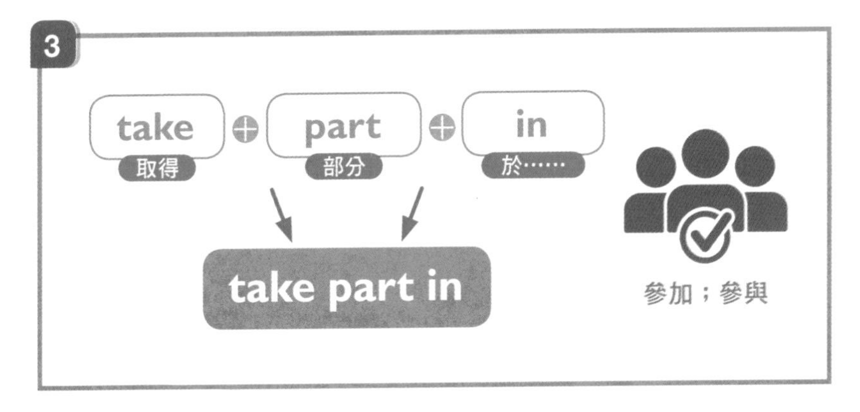

- Will you **take part in** the school musical this year?
  你會**參加**學校今年的歌舞劇嗎？
- The teacher told us that it would help our grades if we **took part in** class discussions.
  老師說我們如果**參與**課堂討論，對分數會很有幫助。

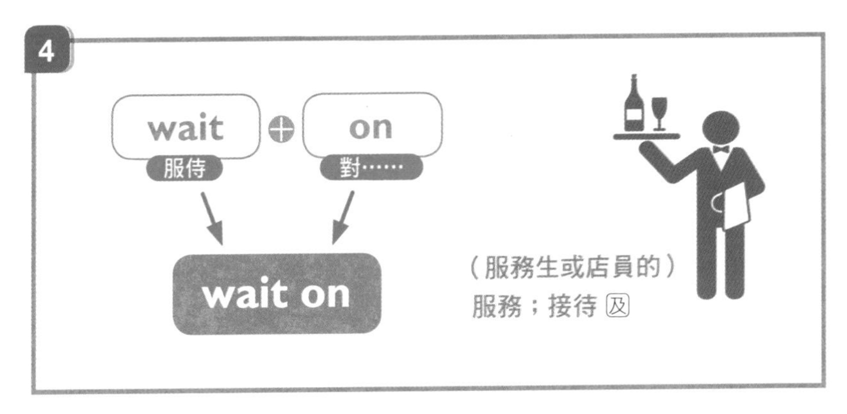

- Although the food wasn't very good, the young woman who **waited on** us at the restaurant was very nice.
  雖然這家餐廳的食物不是很好吃，但是**接待**我們的女服務生很親切。
- We sat for twenty minutes before we were **waited on**.
  我們坐了 20 分鐘才有服務生來**點餐**。

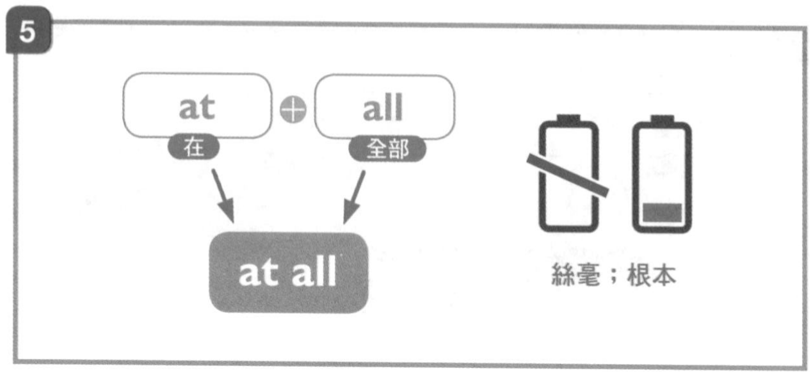

- There's nothing left in the house **at all**; everything has been moved out.
  房子裡**什麼**也沒有，所有東西都被搬光了。
- The police asked Marty why he ran away from them, but he had nothing **at all** to say.
  警察詢問馬堤為何逃跑，但他**絲毫**無話可說。

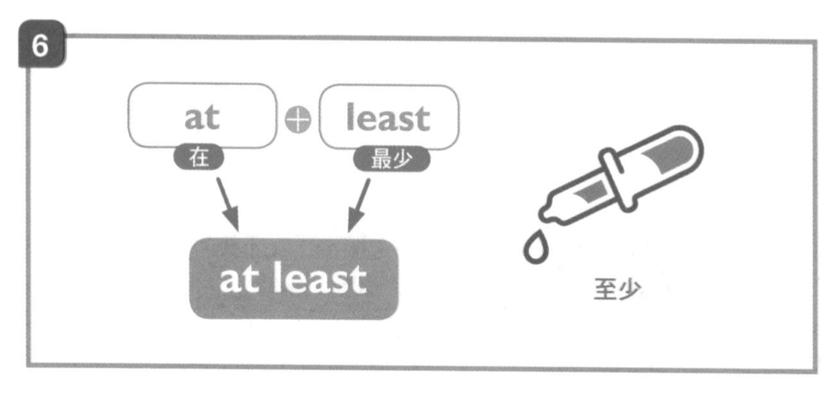

- When you are at the store, please pick up **at least** three pounds of onions.
  請你到商店買**至少**三磅的洋蔥。
- When I have a family, I want **at least** two children.
  等有了家庭後，我**最少**想要兩個小孩。

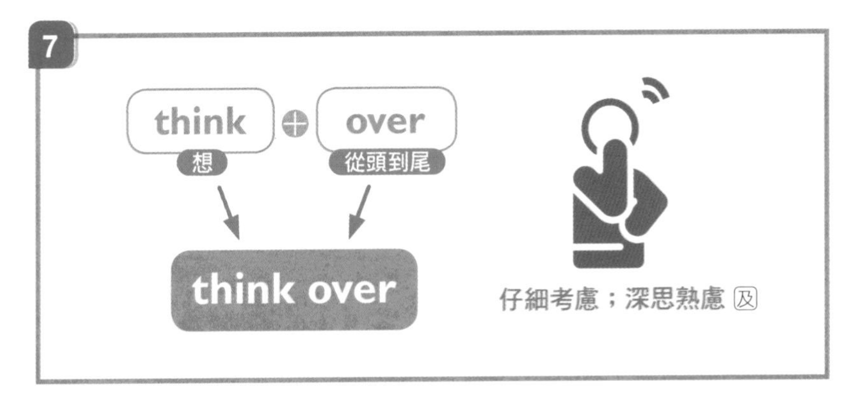

- Jan wasn't sure if it was a good idea to buy the car, so she **thought** it **over** for a few days.
  珍不確定買車是否是個好主意，所以她**仔細考慮**了好幾天。
- After **thinking over** the assignment, Marion got started with her research.
  瑪莉安在**認真思索**過這份工作後便開始進行研究。

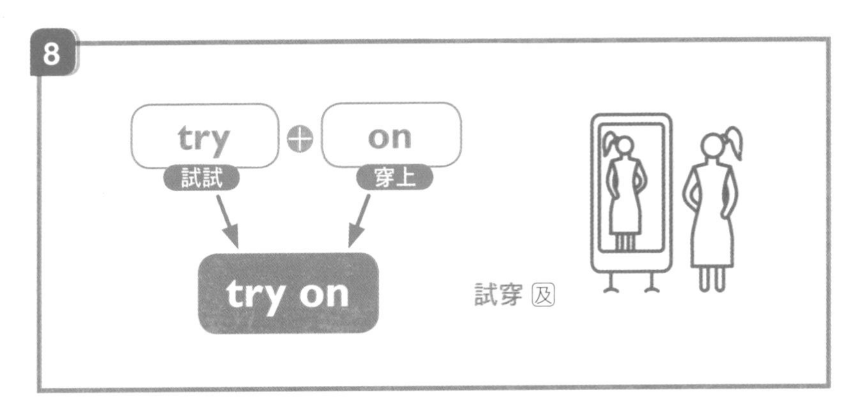

- Before you buy those jeans, **try** them **on** to make sure they fit. 買牛仔褲前，記得要**試穿**以便確定是否合身。
- If you don't have any nice shoes to wear with your suit, you can **try on** mine; if they fit, you can borrow them.
  你若是沒有好看的鞋能搭套裝，可以**試穿**我的，如果合腳你可以借去穿。

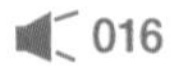

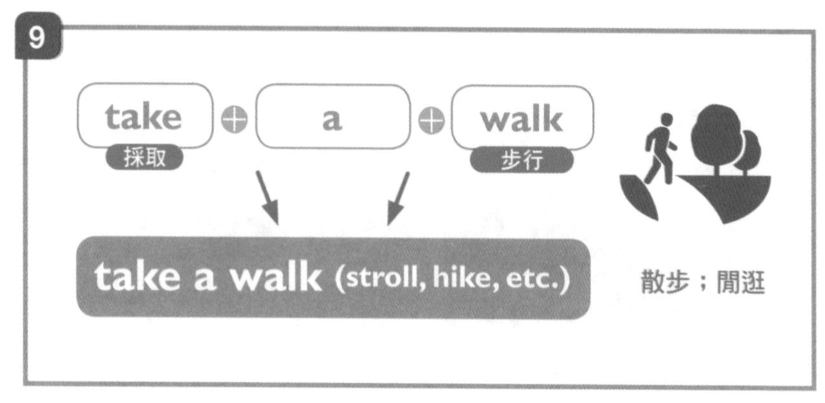

- After a large dinner, Tracy likes to **take a stroll** around the park.
  崔西喜歡在用過豐盛的晚餐後到公園裡**散步**。
- Last weekend, Franz and his family went on a picnic and then **took a hike** in the nearby hills.
  法蘭斯上星期和家人去野餐，然後在附近的山區**健行**。

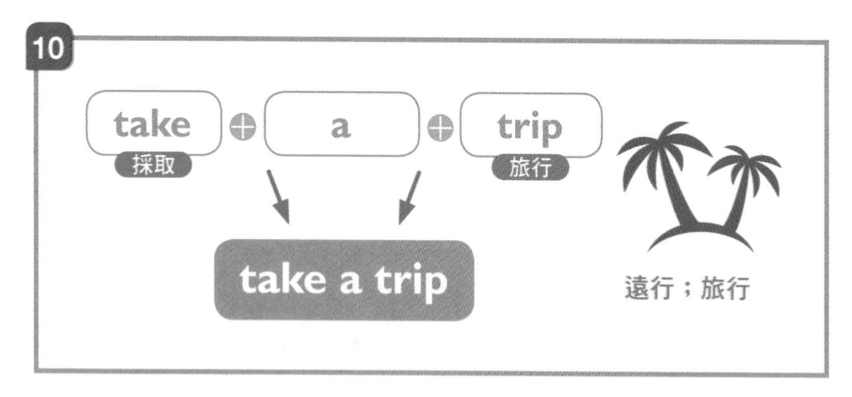

- Reg won't come in to work next week because he's **taking a trip** to Chicago for a business meeting.
  雷哲下星期不會來上班，因為他要**到**芝加哥出差開會。
- This summer, Barbara plans to **take a trip** to Mexico.
  芭芭拉計劃這個夏天到墨西哥**旅行**。

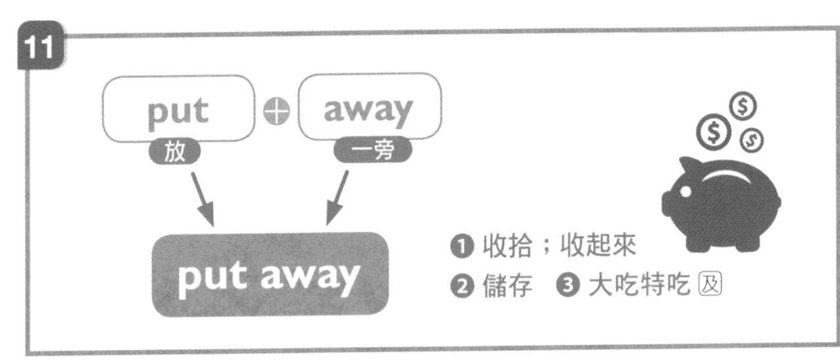

11
put
放
away
一旁
put away
❶ 收拾；收起來
❷ 儲存 ❸ 大吃特吃 ⟨及⟩

❶ James told his little sister to **put away** all her toys before their parents got home.
詹姆斯叫妹妹在父母回來前把玩具**收拾好**。

❶ The teacher told me to **put** my cell phone **away** because I was using it during class.
我上課時在用手機，老師要我把它**收起來**。

❷ I decided to **put away** a few dollars each week.
我決定每個星期都要**存下**一點錢。

❸ He **put away** a whole box of chocolates in one evening. 他一個晚上就**吃掉**了整盒巧克力。

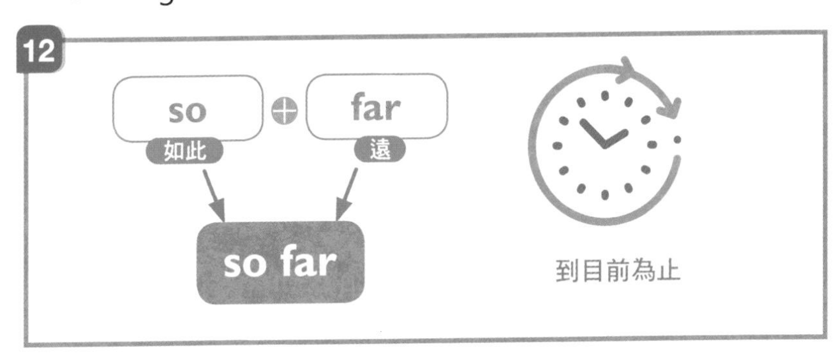

- My first semester at college is going well **so far**—though we haven't had any tests yet. 我在大學的第一個學期**到目前為止**都很順利，儘管我們還沒考過試。
- **So far** during this car ride, we've passed three gas stations without stopping. **到目前為止**，我們已經開車經過了三間加油站，但都沒有停下來。

Schoolwork
學校作業

Joe and Erin talk about schoolwork.
喬和愛琳在談論學校功課。

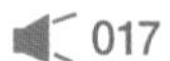

Joe: Have you finished writing your history paper yet?

Erin: No, I've been **putting** it **off**[1] until I **get over**[2] this illness.

Joe: What's wrong? Did you **catch a cold**[3]?

Erin: Yeah. I spent a weekend taking care of my sick aunt, by the time I **got back**[4] I was already feeling bad.

Joe: Well, I hope you get better soon.

Erin: Thanks. I'm taking it easy **for the time being**[5]; however, I am thinking about going to the movies tonight with my boyfriend.

Joe: I see. You know, I think you should **change your mind**[6]—otherwise, you'll never write that history paper!

Erin: You may be right, but it's too late. I've already **made up my mind**[7] to go out. There's no way I'm going to **call off**[8] my date!

Joe: Well, what can I say? Good luck!

喬： 妳的歷史報告寫完了嗎？

愛琳： 還沒，我一直**拖**到**病好了**才開始趕作業。

喬： 怎麼回事？妳**感冒**了嗎？

愛琳： 沒錯，我上週末照顧生病的阿姨，在**回**家路上就已經覺得不舒服了。

喬： 嗯，希望妳早日康復。

愛琳： 謝謝，我**現在**感覺還可以，不過我今晚想和男朋友去看場電影。

喬： 我知道了。我跟妳說，我覺得妳最好改變主意，否則妳永遠別想寫歷史報告了！

愛琳： 也許你是對的，不過太遲了，我已經**決定**要出去了，絕對不可能**取消**約會！

喬： 嗯，那我能說什麼呢？祝妳好運！

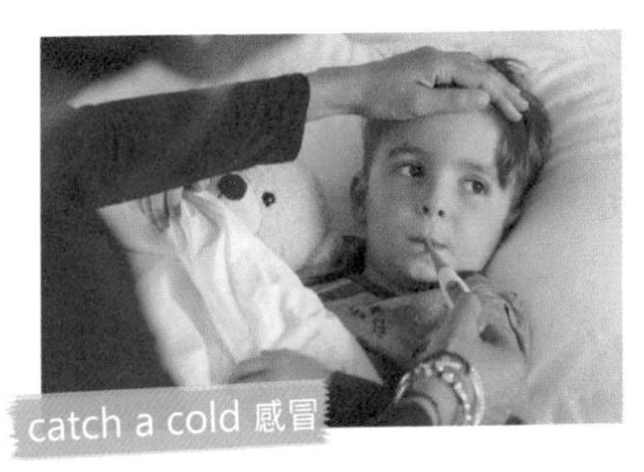

catch a cold 感冒

make up one's mind 決定

018

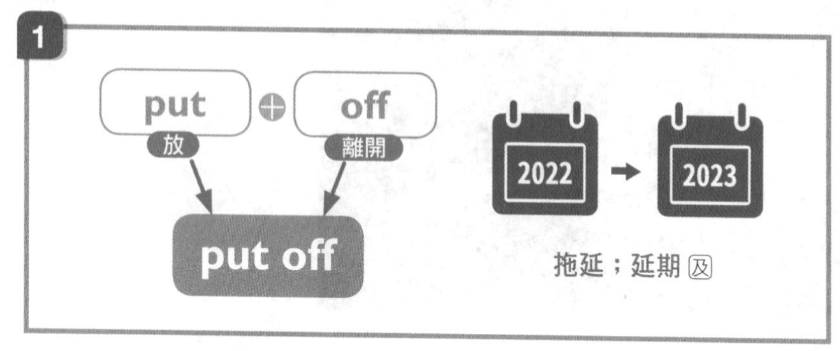

- Never **put off** till tomorrow what you can do today.
  今日事今日畢。〔俗諺〕
- If you **put off** writing this essay until the weekend, I'm sure you'll regret it.
  如果你**拖**到週末才寫報告，你一定會後悔的。
- Rudy didn't want to go to the doctor; however, when he woke up with a terrible headache, he realized he couldn't **put** it **off** any longer. 魯迪不想去看醫生，但當他頭疼欲裂地醒來時，他知道看醫生一事無法再**拖**下去了。

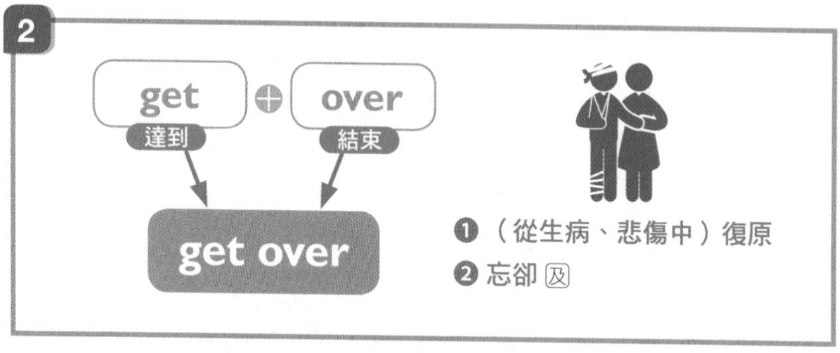

❶ It took Martin a few days to **get over** failing the final exam. 馬汀花了好幾天才**走出**期末考不及格的**陰影**。

❶ The day Wendy **got over** the infection, she returned to work. 溫蒂在病情**好轉**的那天回到工作崗位。

❷ It took him months to **get over** Nicole after she ended the relationship.
在妮可提出分手之後，他花了好幾個月的時間才把她給**忘**了。

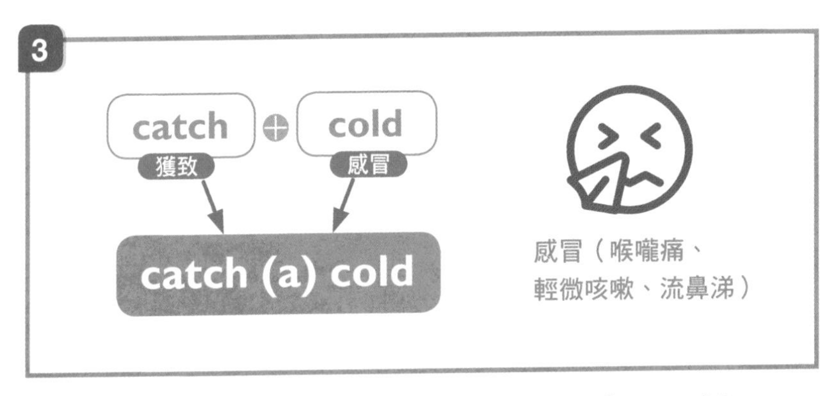

- Miranda missed class because she **caught a cold**.
  米蘭達因**感冒**而未去上課。
- Every winter, Vince **catches** at least one **cold**.
  文斯每年冬天至少會**感冒**一次。

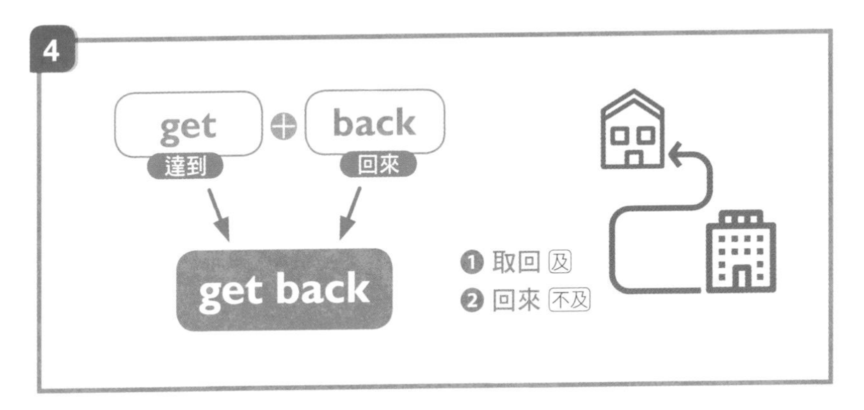

❶ Can you please **get** my MP3 player **back** from Janet?
你可以幫我向珍娜**拿回**我的 MP3 播放器嗎？

❷ Mandy **gets back** from work around 3 o'clock or so.
曼蒂約三點下班**回到家**。

019

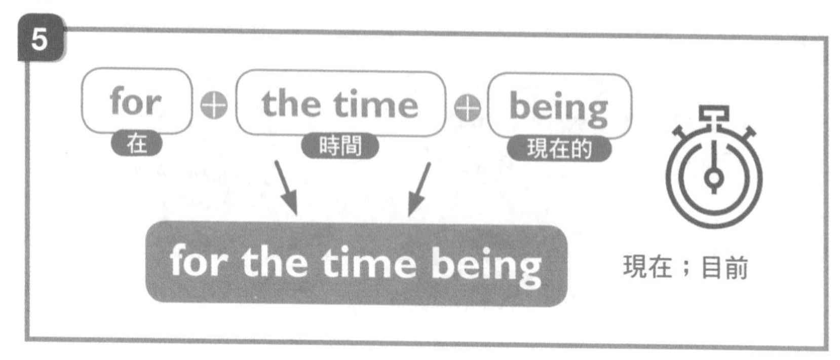

- **For the time being**, the students don't have any questions, but they may feel differently tomorrow.
學生**現在**沒有任何問題，但明天可能就不一樣了。
- I'm not hungry **for the time being**, but by noon I'll be starving. 我**現在**不餓，不過中午前就會餓了。

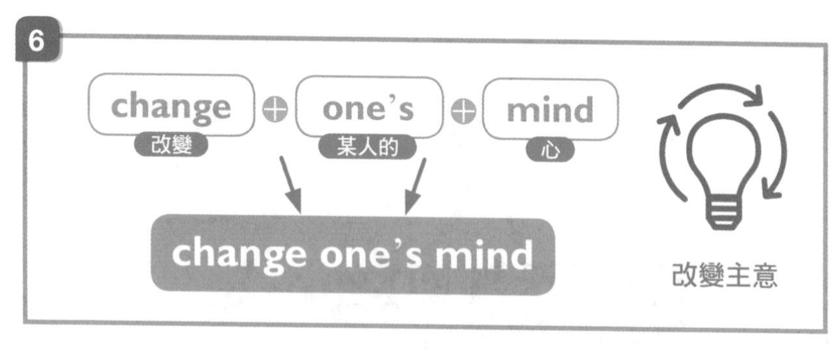

6
change
改變
one's
某人的
mind
心
change one's mind
改變主意

- My girlfriend always **changes her mind** a few times before making a big decision.
在下重大決定前，我的女朋友總會三番兩次地**改變心意**。
- You'd better be sure this is the car you want because once you agree to buy it, you can't **change your mind**.
你最好確定這台車就是你想要的，因為一旦你同意買下它，就無法**改變主意**了。
- When I first met him, I didn't like him; however, since then I've **changed my mind**. 第一次和他見面的時候，我並不喜歡他，但後來**我的看法改變了**。

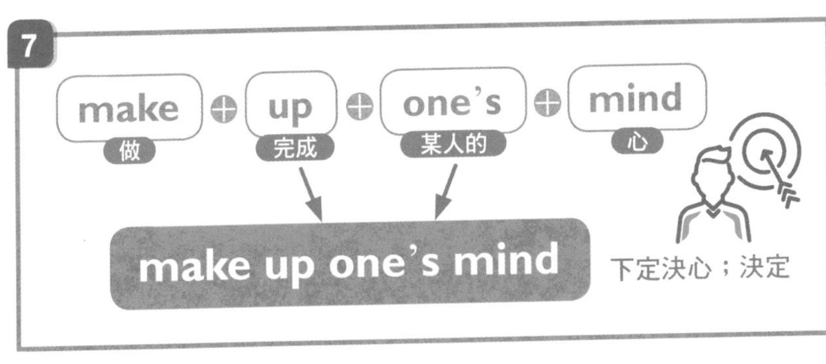

- There are so many flavors of ice cream here that it is hard to **make up my mind** and choose one.
  這裡有好多種口味的冰淇淋，我很難**決定**要選哪一種。
- Ralph couldn't **make up his mind** about going to the park or not. 瑞夫無法**決定**是否要去公園。
- Gwen can't **make up her mind** about whether to visit L.A. or Miami this summer.
  關無法**決定**今年夏天要去洛杉磯還是邁阿密。

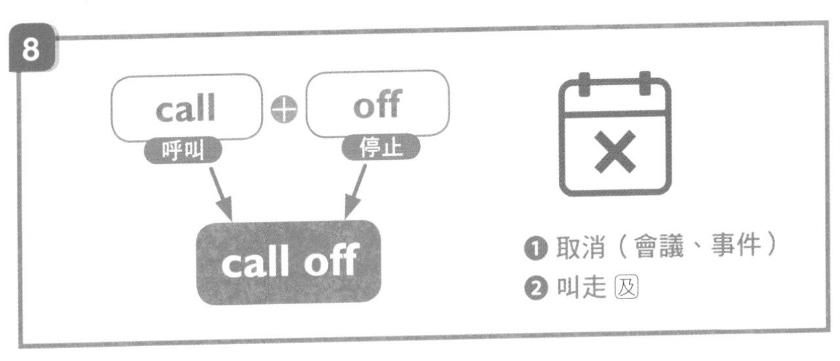

❶ Because it was raining, Diane **called off** the outdoor volleyball competition. 下雨了，黛安**取消**了戶外排球比賽。

❶ The CEO **called off** the meeting and told his employees to go home early.
執行長**取消**了會議，要員工早點回家。

❶ Tomorrow's match has been **called off** because of the weather. 由於天氣寒冷的緣故，明天的比賽已經**取消**了。

020

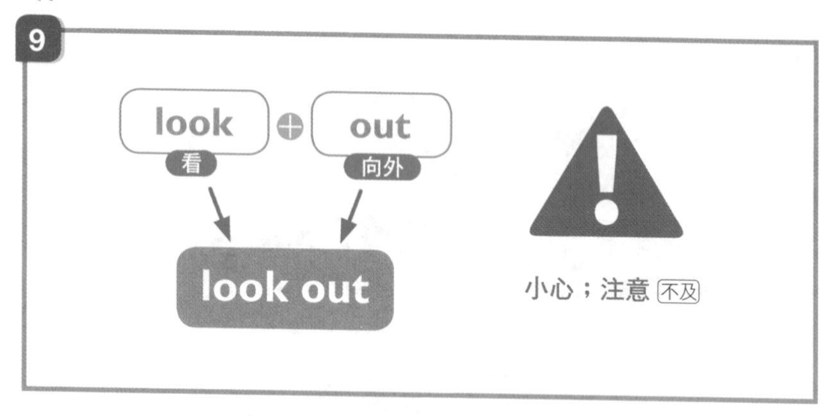

- **Look out**! The teacher is coming, and he'll see that you are skipping class.
  小心點！老師快要來了，他會發現你翹課。
- If you travel alone at night, be sure to **look out** for robbers. 晚上單獨出門，要**留意**搶匪。

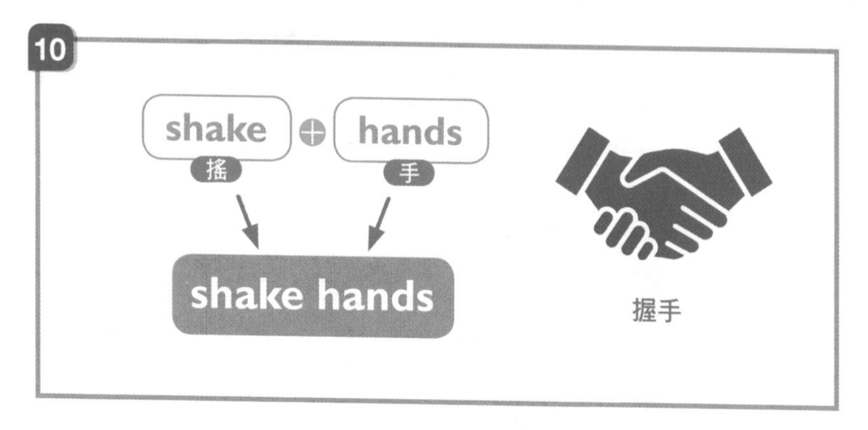

- In America, it is important to **shake hands** firmly or people will think you have a weak personality.
  在美國，**握手**時把手握緊很重要，否則別人會認為你個性軟弱。

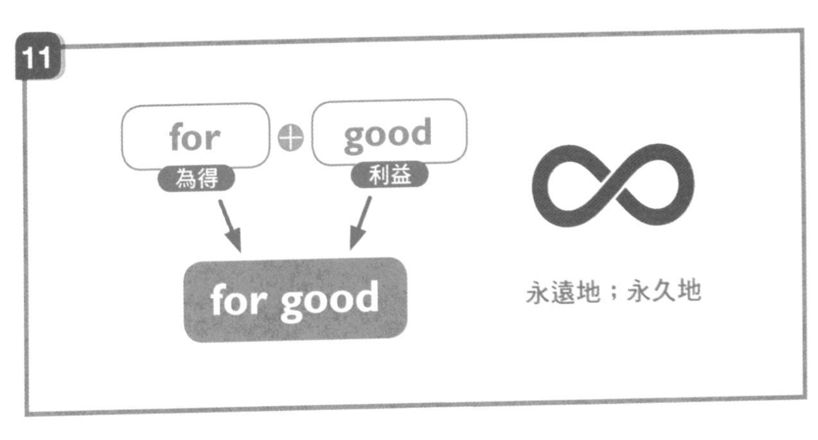

- After the graduation ceremony, Lou knew that he was done with high school **for good**.
  畢業典禮過後，盧知道他的高中生活**永遠**結束了。

Getting Sick and Stressed 生病與壓力

Didi tells her friend Jay why she is feeling sick and a bit stressed.
蒂蒂把感覺不舒服和緊張的原因告訴朋友傑。

021

Jay: What's wrong? You look a bit **under the weather**[1].

Didi: As a matter of fact, I'm not feeling so good. I just started classes in a new school, and it isn't easy **making friends**[2].

Jay: Don't worry about that! It takes time to meet people. You need to focus on feeling better.

Didi: Well, the other thing that is stressing me out is that someone keeps calling my cell, and when I answer, the person **hangs up**[3] without saying a word. I just don't know what's **going on**[4].

Jay: Oh, man! I'm sure that really **gets to**[5] you; but you know what I think? I bet somebody has a crush on you and is too scared to talk.

Didi: Really? I never thought about that before. **All of a sudden**[6], I feel a bit better. I can always **count on**[7] you to make me feel more positive.

Jay: No problem. Good people like you are **few and far between**[8]. You deserve to be happy and calm.

under the weather 生病

傑： 怎麼了？妳看起來有點像是**生病**了。

蒂蒂： 事實上，我覺得不太舒服。我剛到新學校上課，**交朋友**不太容易。

傑： 別擔心！那需要時間。妳需要集中注意力在保持好心情。

蒂蒂： 嗯，還有一件讓我很緊張的事情，就是有人一直打我的手機。當我接起來時，對方不說話就**把電話掛掉**，我不知道**發生**了什麼事情。

傑： 噢，我敢肯定妳一定很**困擾**，妳知道我的看法嗎？我打賭一定是有人愛上妳了，而且還不敢開口。

蒂蒂： 真的嗎？我從來沒想過這些。我**突然**覺得好多了，都是**靠**你幫忙，我才能往好的方面去想。

傑： 沒什麼，像妳這麼好的人已經**很少**了，妳本來就應該要快樂平靜。

make friends 交朋友

hang up 掛斷（電話）

022

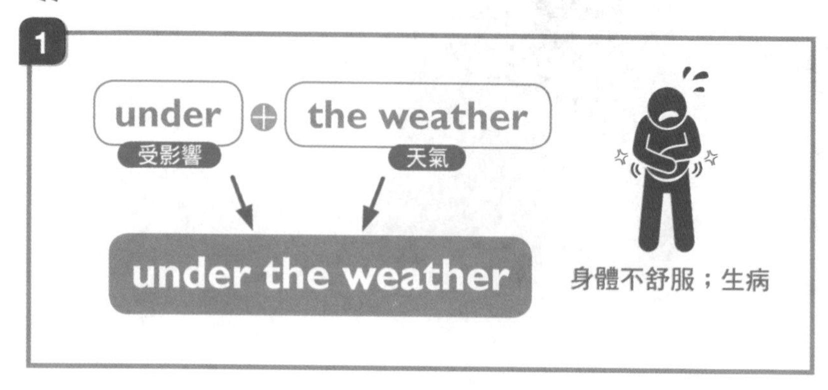

- Walt canceled the discussion group because he was feeling a bit **under the weather**.
  華特因為**身體不舒服**，取消了團體討論。
- After a long day of walking in the cold rain, Roberta felt a little **under the weather**.
  羅伯特在寒冷的雨中走了一天，感覺**身體**有點**不舒服**。

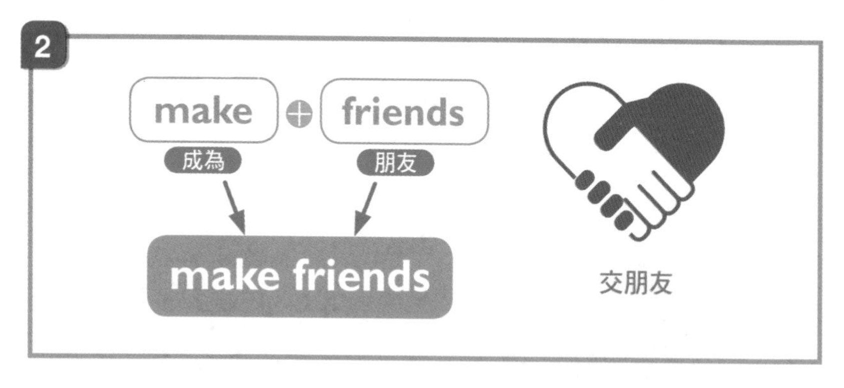

- Because Pam was new at the school, it took her a couple of weeks to **make friends**.
  潘是新生，所以她花了好幾個星期才**交到朋友**。
- Mark is a great guy, so he **makes** new **friends** easily.
  馬克是一個很棒的人，所以很容易**交到**新**朋友**。
- I've **made** a lot of **friends** at this job.
  這份工作讓我**結交**到許多**朋友**。

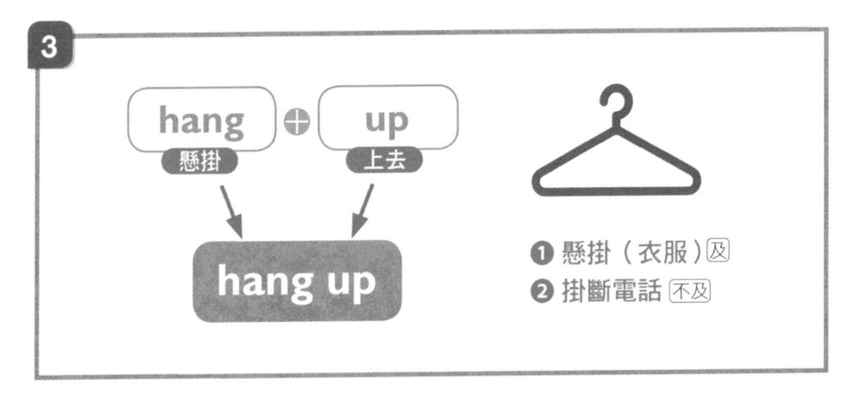

❶ Ray **hung up** all his clean shirts in the closet.
雷把所有乾淨的襯衫**掛**在衣櫥裡。

❷ Joel was so mad at his cousin that he **hung up** without saying goodbye.
喬爾很氣他的表弟沒說再見就**掛掉電話**。

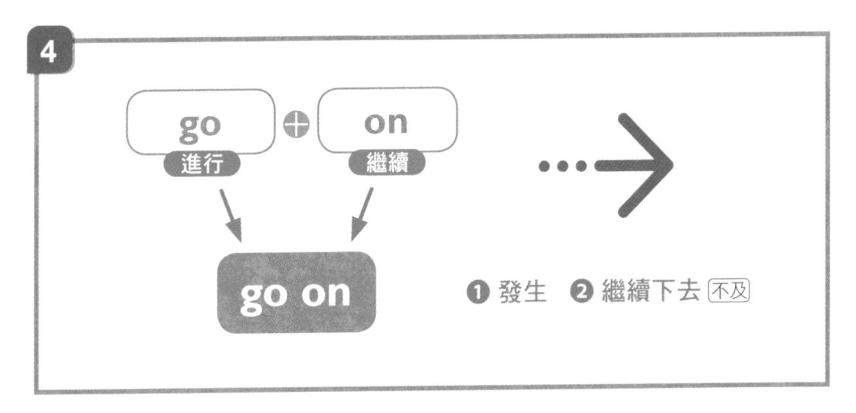

❶ Do you know what's **going on** with your son in L.A.?
你知道你的兒子在洛杉磯**發生**了什麼事情嗎？

❷ By the time Frank arrived at the meeting, it had already been **going on** for a few minutes.
法蘭克到達時，會議已經**進行**了好幾分鐘。

023

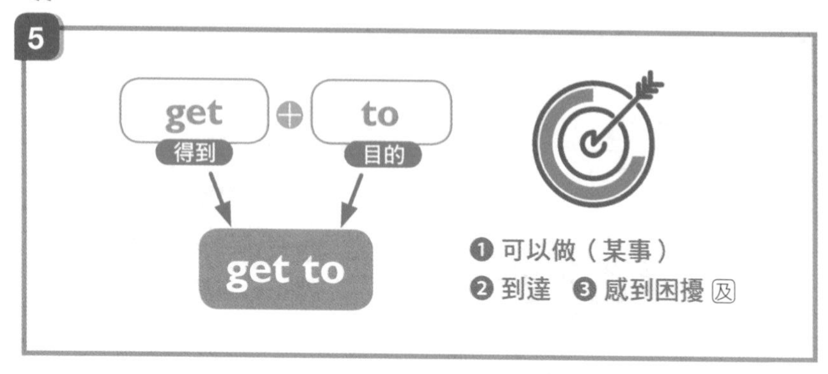

❶ If Beth gets an "A" on her history test, her mom said she'll **get to** have a party.
如果貝絲歷史考試得到「A」，媽媽說她**就可以**舉辦派對。

❷ When do you think we'll **get to** the city center?
你覺得我們什麼時候會**到達**市中心？

❸ The barking dog was really **getting to** me, so I called my neighbor and asked her to do something about it.
我**覺得**那隻狂吠的狗很**煩**，所以我打電話給鄰居要她處理一下。

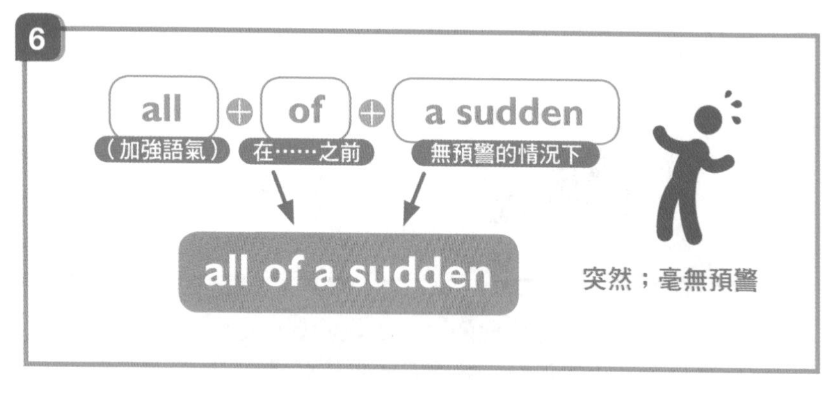

- **All of a sudden**, it started raining and we got wet.
天空**突然**開始下起雨，我們淋濕了。

- Lucy was shocked when Evan asked her **all of a sudden** to marry him. 艾文**突然**向露西求婚，令她非常震驚。

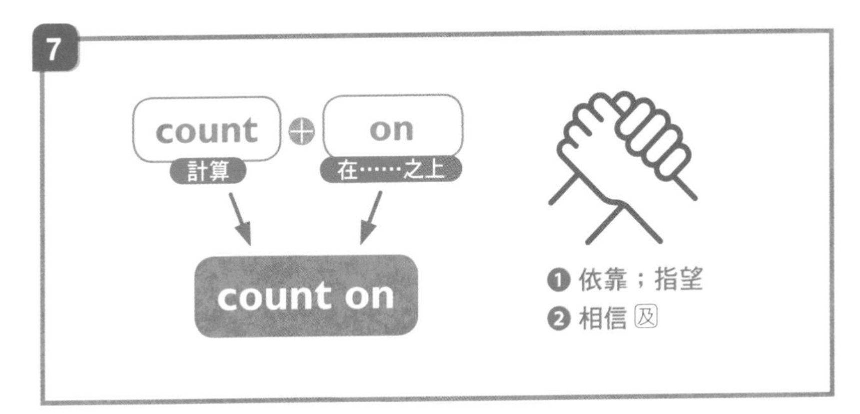

❶ If you ever need help, remember that you can **count on** me. 如果你需要幫忙，要記得你可以**依靠**我。

❷ Ryan knows that he can **count on** his uncle to meet him at the airport.
雷恩**相信**叔叔會在機場和他見面。

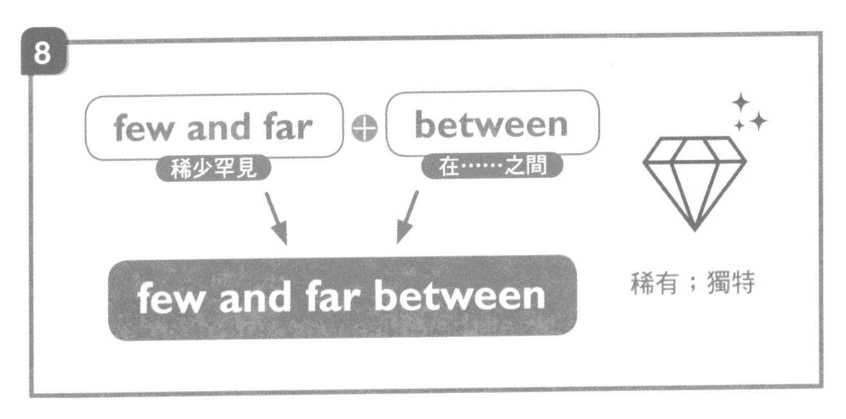

- Good Indian restaurants are **few and far between** in Austin. 奧斯汀好吃的印度餐廳**很少**。
- Apartments that are both comfortable and reasonably priced are **few and far between**.
既舒適、價錢又合理的公寓**並不多**。

024

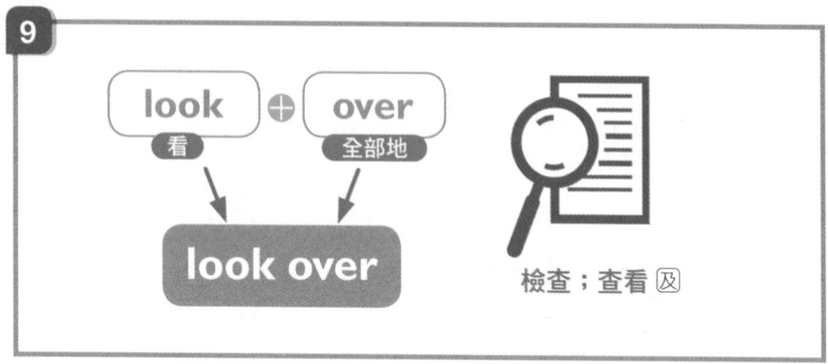

- Before buying a used car, **look** it **over** very carefully to be sure it doesn't have any problems.
  買二手車前，記得要仔細**檢查**，才能確定車子沒有任何問題。
- Ms. Perry **looked over** the students' papers before grading them. 派瑞女士在打分數前，**仔細檢查**學生的報告。

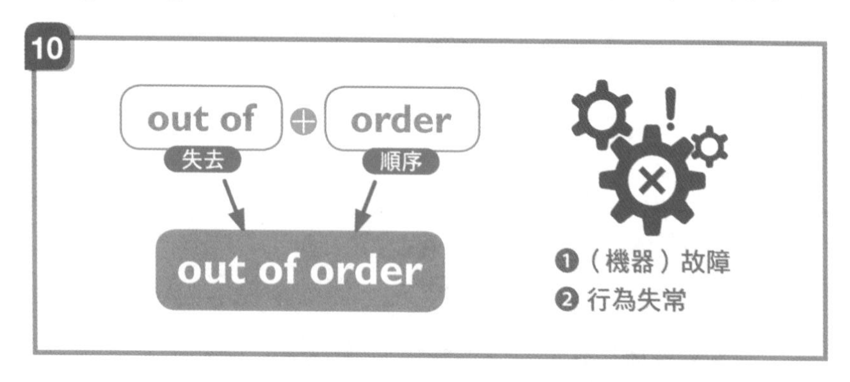

❶ The snack machine at the office was **out of order**, so we went to a restaurant for lunch.
辦公室裡的點心販賣機**故障**了，所以我們到餐廳吃午餐。

❶ The sign on the pay phone informed Tina that it was **out of order**. 緹娜由公共電話上的標示得知電話**故障**了。

❷ The remark Harry made in the workshop yesterday was totally **out of order**.
哈利昨天在研討會所做的評論完全**錯誤**。

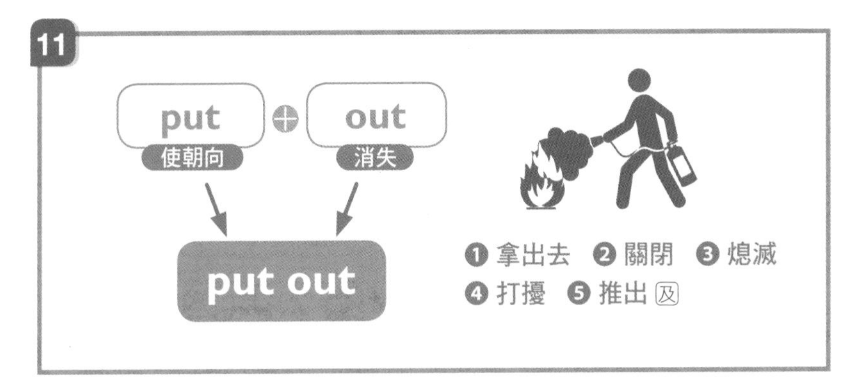

❶ Dad asked me to **put out** the trash.
爸爸要我把垃圾**拿出去**。

❷ Please **put** the lights **out** before you leave the house.
出門前請把燈**關掉**。

❸ The campers poured water on the fire to **put** it **out**.
露營的人用水把火**澆熄**。

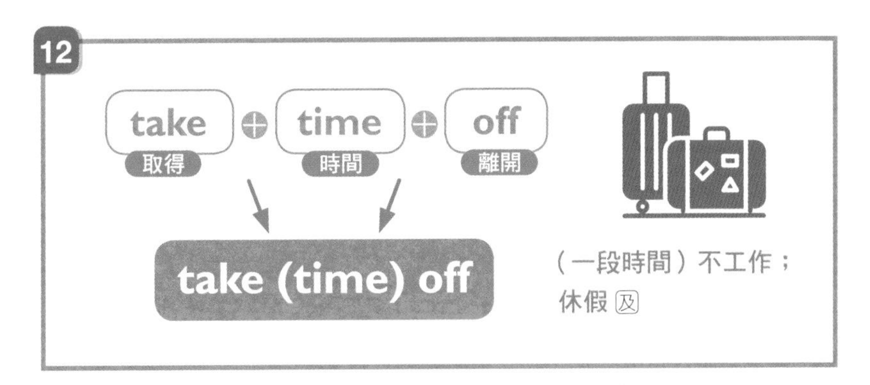

- My wife's birthday is next Monday, so if possible, I'd like to **take** that day **off** of work.
  下星期一是我老婆的生日，可以的話，那天我想要**休假**。
- The companies let the workers **take off** two weeks every year for vacation and holidays.
  這家公司的員工每年都有兩個星期可以**休假**。

Hunting for a New Job 找新工作

Steve tells Caroline why he wants a new job.
史帝夫告訴卡洛琳想要新工作的原因。

025

Caroline: You've been quiet all weekend. I can't **figure out**[1] what's bothering you.

Steve: I'm just thinking about my job. I don't like it so much. For one thing, I need to **be up**[2] at 5 a.m. if I want to get to the office **on time**[3]. And work **is**n't **over**[4] until 7 p.m.

Caroline: Oh! That sounds tough. What happens if you **get sick**[5]?

Steve: My boss always makes me come in, no matter how sick I am.

Caroline: Now I see why you're **thinking of**[6] looking for another job.

Steve: Sometimes I **would rather**[7] not work at all, but then my sister **points out**[8] that I shouldn't leave this job before I find another one.

Caroline: I think she's right.

卡洛琳： 你整個週末都好安靜，我**想**不透你在煩惱什麼。

史帝夫： 我只是在想我的工作。我不是很喜歡我的工作。首先，我若想要**準時**上班，必須早上五點**起床**，然後一直工作到晚上七點才**結束**。

卡洛琳： 噢！聽起來真難熬。生病的話怎麼辦？

史帝夫： 無論我的病情有多嚴重，老闆總是要我去上班。

卡洛琳： 我知道你為何**想**找別的工作了。

史帝夫： 我有時候**寧願**完全不工作，但我姐姐**提醒**我，在找到其他工作前，我不應該辭掉這份工作。

卡洛琳： 我想她說的對。

get sick 生病

on time 準時

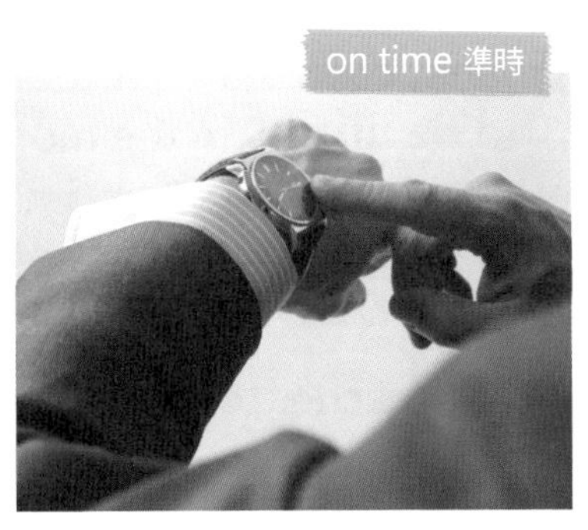

026

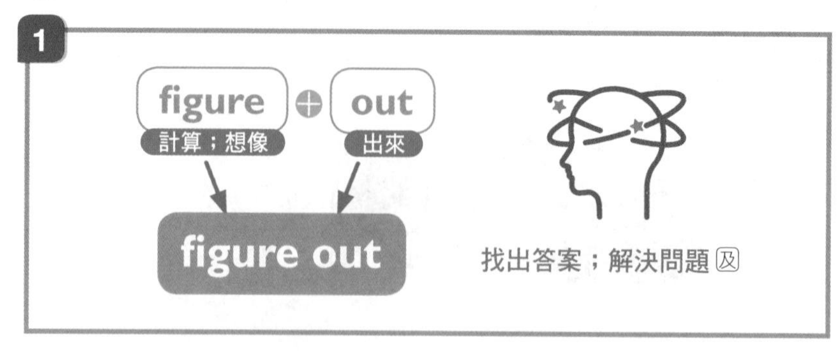

- No one could **figure out** how Darryl lost his keys.
  沒人**知道**戴倫是如何弄丟鑰匙的。
- Every student looked at the puzzles, but no one could **figure** them **out**.
  每位學生都看著文字填空的題目，但沒人**找得出答案**。
- Laura couldn't **figure out** how she spent all her money.
  蘿拉**想不透**她是如何花光所有的錢。

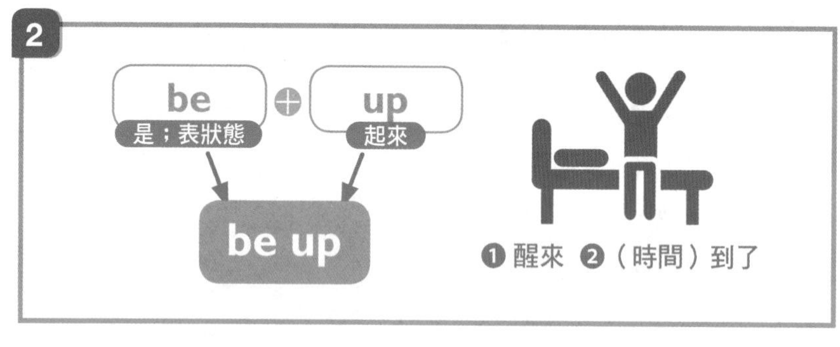

❶ Janet can't stay out too late tonight because she has to **be up** at 5 in the morning.
珍娜今晚不能在外面待到太晚，因為她必須早上五點**起床**。

❶ Although Gwen pretended to be asleep, she **was** really **up**. 雖然關假裝睡著了，但她其實是**醒著**的。

❷ The teacher told us when the time for the test **was up** and we had to put our pencils down.
老師說考試**結束**時，我們必須把鉛筆放下。

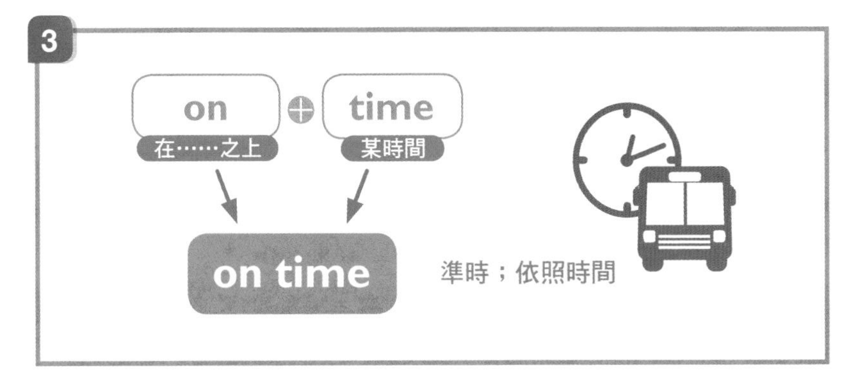

- Marianne never arrives anywhere **on time**; she's always late. 瑪莉安從來沒有**準時**抵達過，她老是遲到。
- This bus is always **on time**, so you can rely on it.
  這班公車總是很**準時**，非常靠得住。

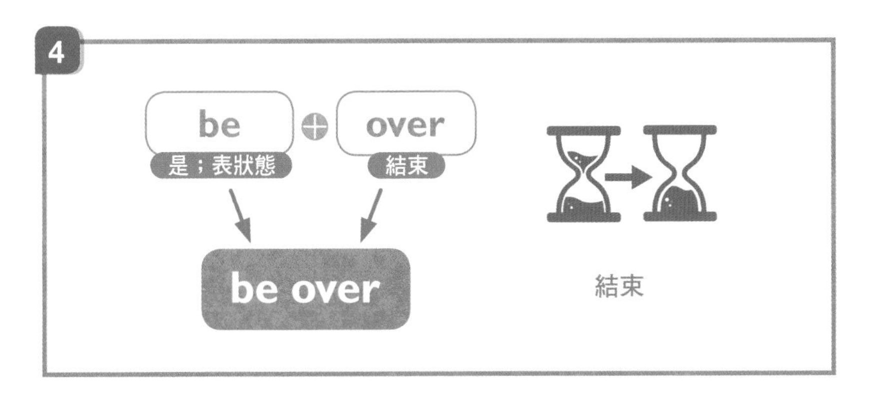

- What time **is** this show **over**?
  這場表演何時會**結束**？
- French class **is over** before lunch.
  法文課會在午餐前**結束**。

027

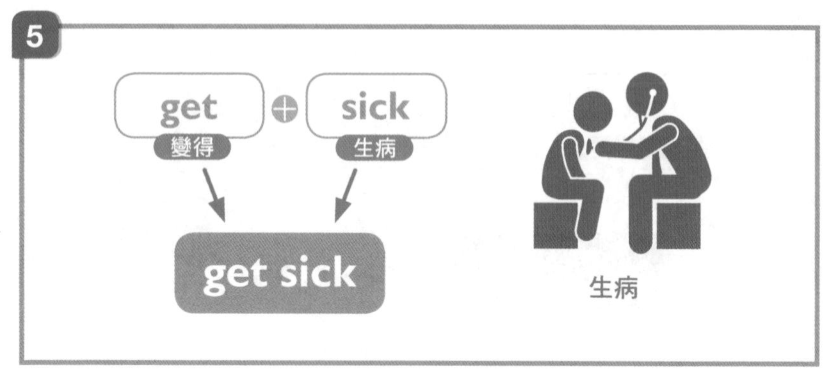

- The old man **got sick** while he was away and had to come home.
  那位老先生在外面的時候**生病**了，所以必須回家。

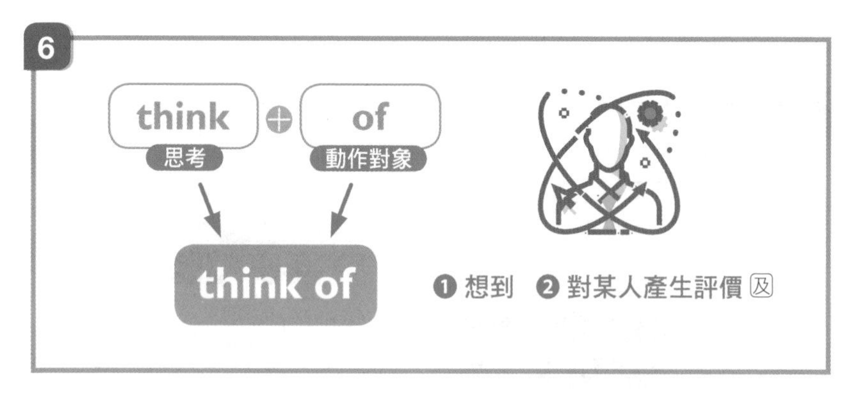

❶ Suddenly, Jon **thought of** a great idea for his new book and got to work.
強突然**想到**一個關於新書很棒的主意，並且開始進行。

❶ What do you **think of** the new mayor?
你**覺得**新上任的市長如何？

❷ Meredith was new in our class, so no one knew what to **think of** her.
瑪芮迪絲是我們班上的新生，所以沒有人**對**她**作出評論**。

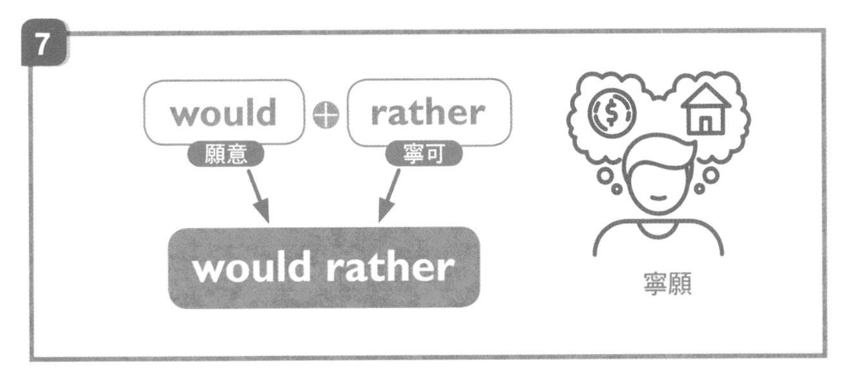

- Instead of going shopping today, I'**d** much **rather** stay home and watch TV.
  與其要我今天去逛街，我**寧願**待在家裡看電視。
- **Would** you **rather** live in Florida or Georgia?
  你**比較想**住在佛羅里達州還是喬治亞州？

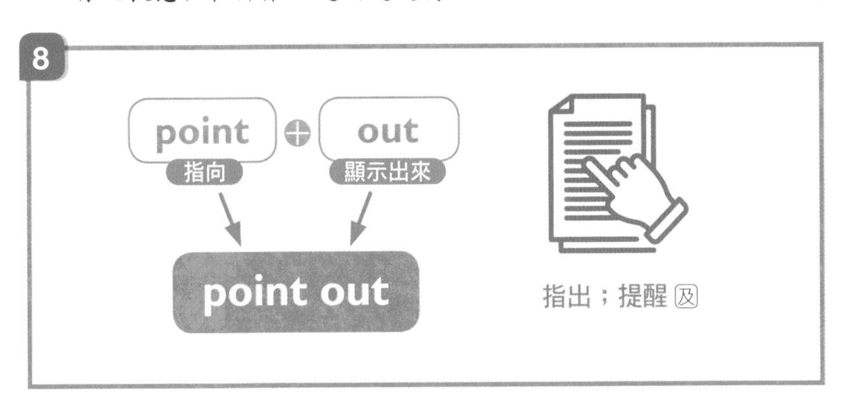

- Tory **pointed out** her sister to us.
  托莉把她的姐姐**指**給我們看。
- Before his mom **pointed out** that today is Friday, Wayne thought he had to go to school tomorrow.
  在偉恩的媽媽**指出**今天是星期五前，他一直以為隔天還要上課。
- I thought that my English was perfect, but my teacher **pointed** my mistakes **out**.
  我以為我的英文很通順，但老師**指出**了我的錯誤。

028

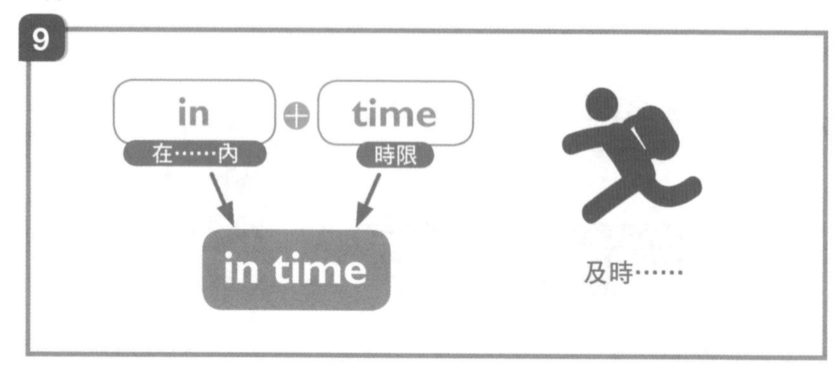

- If we don't leave now, you won't get to the airport **in time** to catch your flight.
  我們若不現在離開，你就無法**及時**趕到機場登機。
- Sean needs to be home **in time** to meet his sister.
  西恩必須**及時**趕回家，才能和他的姐姐碰面。

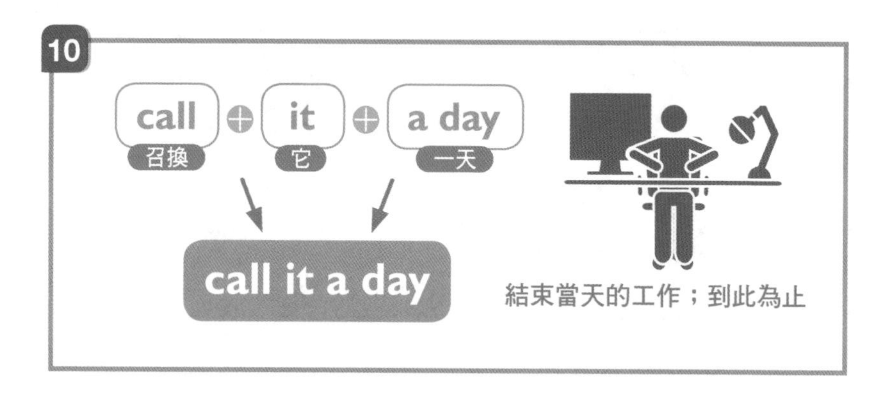

- After spending the entire morning and afternoon working on her report, Liana decided to **call it a day**.
  黎安娜整個早上和下午都在忙報告，她決定今天就**到此為止**。

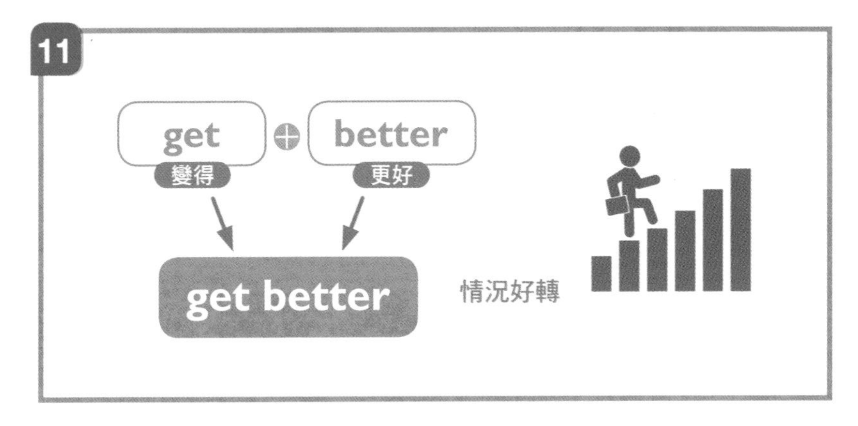

- Despite practicing every day, George never really **got better** at the piano.
  儘管喬治每天練習，但他的鋼琴技巧卻不見**進步**。

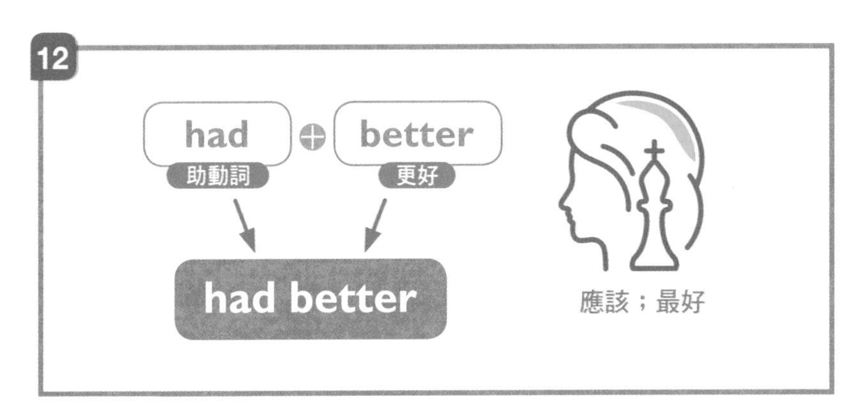

- If you want to go to Yale, you'**d better** study more.
  如果你想進入耶魯，**最好**多讀點書。
- Sam **had better** practice the flute every day if he wants to play in an orchestra.
  如果山姆想要進入管絃樂隊，**最好**每天練習吹長笛。

Planning for the Weekend 週末計畫

Douglas and Mary consider how to spend their weekend. 道格拉斯和瑪麗在考慮如何度過這個週末。

029

Mary: Let's go to the opera this weekend! It's from Italy, and it'll be a good chance for me to **brush up on**[1] my Italian.

Douglas: I know we said that we would **take turns**[2] deciding what to do on the weekends, and even though it's your turn, I was hoping we could **go out**[3] and see a baseball game.

Mary: Well, you need to **pay attention to**[4] the weather; it's supposed to rain, so going to see the game is totally **out of the question**[5].

Douglas: Who cares about a little rain?

Mary: I've told you **over and over again**[6] that I hate getting cold and wet.

Douglas: Well, I **was about to**[7] buy the tickets online—but if you're sure you don't want to go, I guess the opera won't be so bad. However, I don't think there are hot dogs at the opera.

瑪麗： 我們這週末去看歌劇吧！那是一齣義大利歌劇，對我來說，這會是一個**複習**義大利文的好機會。

道格拉斯： 我知道我們說好要**輪流**決定週末要做些什麼，不過就算這星期是輪到妳決定，我還是希望我們可以**出去**看籃球比賽。

瑪麗： 噢，你必須多**注意**天氣。那天可能會下雨，所以絕對**不可能**去看比賽的。

道格拉斯： 下毛毛雨有什麼關係？

瑪麗： 我**一再**告訴你，我討厭變冷和被淋濕。

道格拉斯： 嗳，我**正要**上網買票。但妳如果真的不想去，我想歌劇也不是個太差的主意。不過，我認為歌劇院裡不會有賣熱狗。

opera house 歌劇院

go out 外出

030

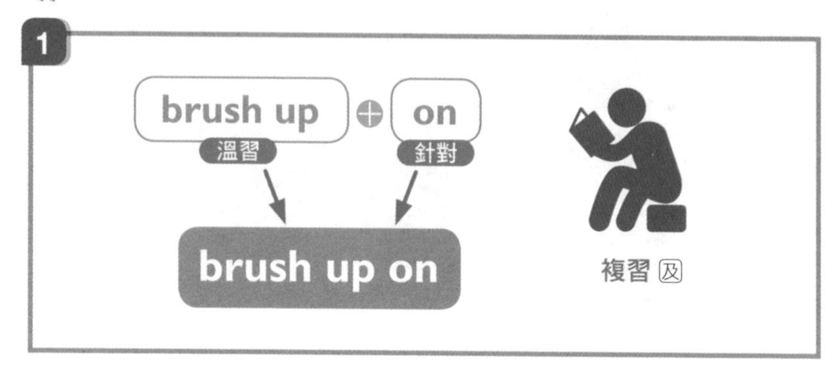

- I really need to **brush up on** my Japanese before visiting Tokyo next month.
  我真的需要在下個月去東京前，**複習**一下我的日文。
- Ivan **brushed up on** Greek history before the test.
  艾文在考試前**複習**希臘歷史。
- **Brushing up on** computer skills is important for anyone who is thinking about getting a new job.
  複習電腦技能對想換新工作的人來說很重要。

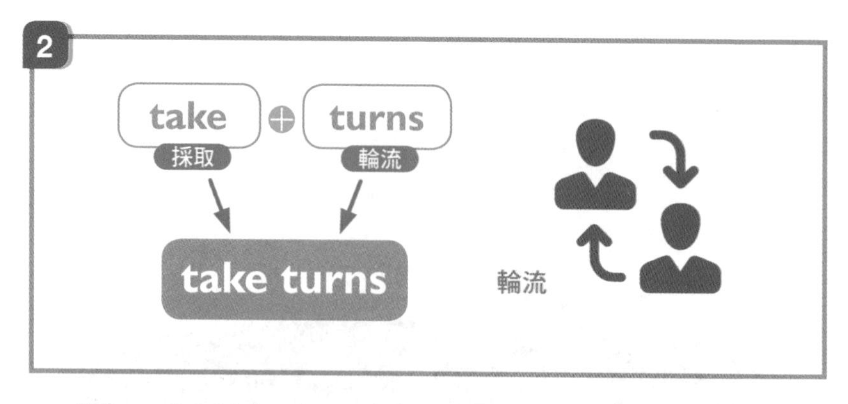

- When the kids play on the swings, we try to make sure they **take turns**.
  他們在盪鞦韆的時候，我們試著讓每個孩子**輪流**玩。
- Ariel and Mac **took turns** using the laptop.
  艾芮兒和麥可**輪流**使用筆記型電腦。

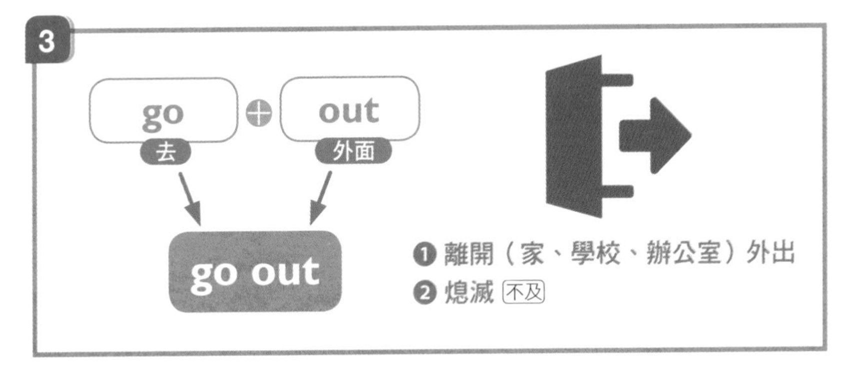

❶ We usually **go out** on the weekends and have dinner or see a movie.
我們週末通常都會**出去**吃晚餐或看電影。

❶ Do you want to **go out** after work today?
你今天下班後想要**出去**嗎？

❷ When the fire **went out**, it started to get cold.
火**熄滅**後就開始變冷了。

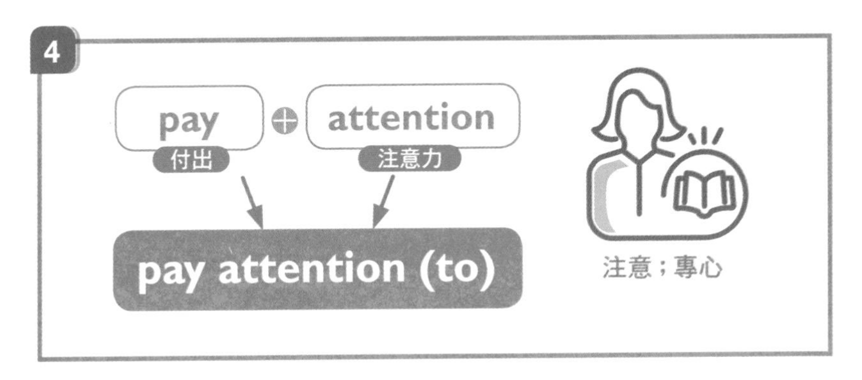

- It's no wonder you didn't pass the test; you never **pay attention** to what the professor is saying.
難怪你沒通過考試，你從不**注意**教授說的話。

- Don't **pay** any **attention** to what that woman says; she's crazy. 別去**注意**那女人說的話，她瘋了。

031

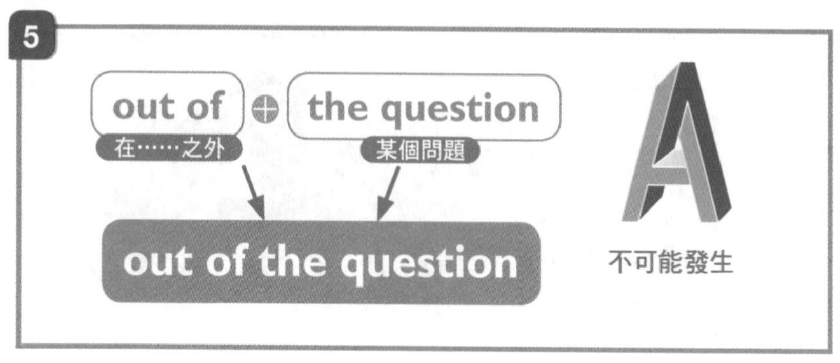

- Unless I pay for the trip myself, going to Boston is **out of the question**.
  除非我自己出錢，否則波士頓之旅是**不可能**成行的。
- Buying that huge TV is totally **out of the question** unless I win the lottery.
  除非我中樂透，否則絕對**不可能**買那台大電視。

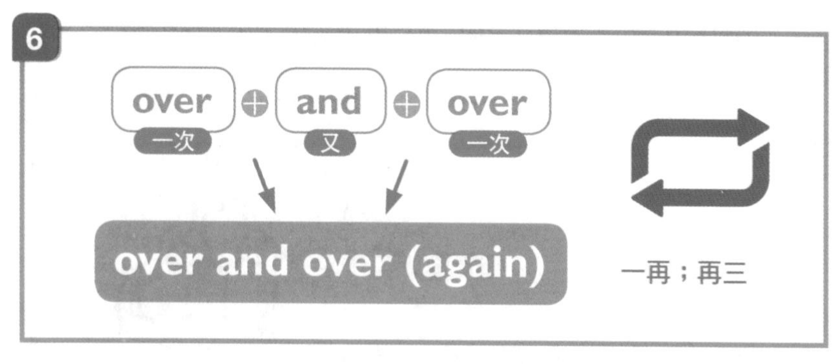

- I hate to do the same work **over and over**.
  我討厭**反覆**做同樣的工作。
- The little boy kept asking **over and over** if I'd buy him some candy. 那個小男孩**一再**問我是否會買一些糖果給他。
- Ed read the article **over and over again** until he finally understood the main idea.
  艾德把文章讀了**一遍又一遍**，直到他終於了解重點。
- I read the article **over and over** till it made sense.
  我把文章看過**一遍又一遍**，直到看懂為止。

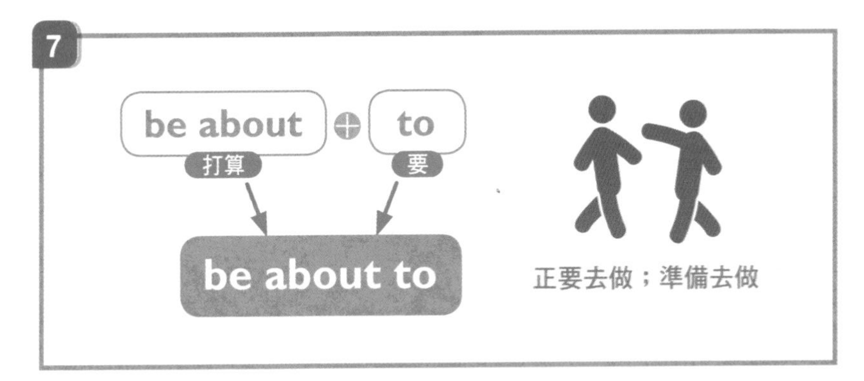

- I **was** just **about to** leave the house when the phone rang. 當我**正要**出門時，電話響了。
- What **were** you **about to** do when the Martins arrived? 馬汀一家來的時候你原本**要**做什麼？

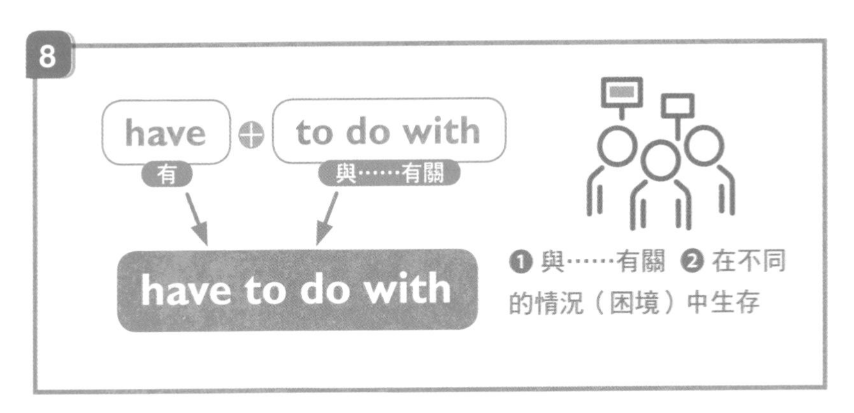

❶ This conversation doesn't **have to do with** you, so please go away. 這段談話**與**你無**關**，所以請你走開。

❷ The restaurant didn't have any cake, so Joe **had to do with** the fruit salad.
這家餐廳沒有蛋糕，所以喬**只好**吃水果沙拉。

❷ When Esther lost her job, she **had to** learn to **do with** less. 當愛絲特丟了工作，她必須學會在**困境中生存**。

032

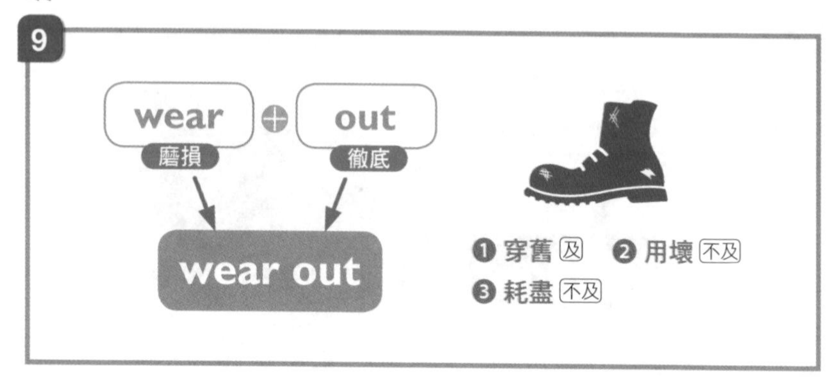

❶ I love these jeans so much, but it's only a matter of time before they **wear out**.
我很喜歡這件牛仔褲，但它遲早會被**穿舊**。

❸ If you don't turn the digital camera off when you're not using it, you'll **wear out** the batteries quickly.
不使用數位相機時若沒有關閉，電池很快會**耗盡**。

❶ Those old shirts really smell terrible; maybe you should just **throw** them **away**.
那些舊襯衫的味道真的很難聞，也許你該把它們**丟**了。

❷ You've spent four hours studying—don't **throw** it all **away**. 你已經唸了四小時了，千萬不要**白白浪費**了。

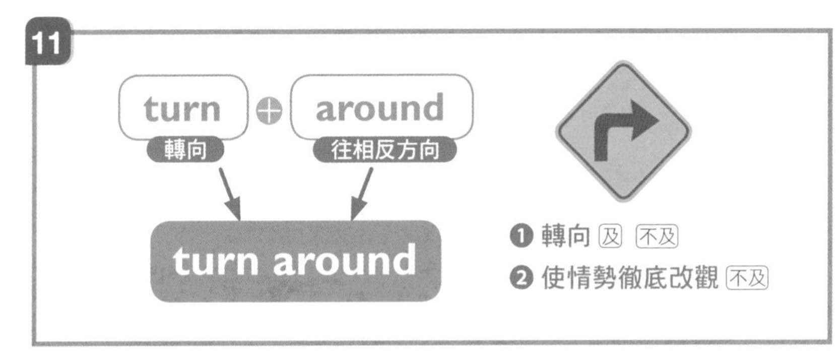

❶ When Ike **turned around**, he saw that the puppy was following him home. 艾克**轉身**發現那隻小狗在跟他回家。

❶ As soon as Rachel realized that she had forgotten her camera, she **turned** the car **around** and went back home. 芮秋一發現忘了帶相機，就**將**車**掉頭**回家。

❷ When the weather got better, the entire weekend **turned around,** and we finally had a good time at the beach. 整個週末隨著天空放晴而**改變**，我們於是在海邊度過了一段愉快的時光。

- Four weeks after **falling in love** with Maria, Jack asked her to marry him.
  傑克和瑪麗亞**墜入愛河**四星期後，他便向她求婚了。
- As soon as Verona saw Sid, she **fell in love**.
  薇諾娜一見到希德便**愛上**他了。

Writing a Children's Book 童書創作

Grace tells John about her ideas for an upcoming children's book. 葛芮絲把有關新童書的想法告訴約翰。

033

Grace: Good morning, John! Why are you so sleepy?

John: Well, when you **got in touch with**[1] me this morning to invite me out for coffee, you **woke** me **up**[2].

Grace: I'm sorry about that! Actually, I wanted to see you right away because I'd like you to help me write a children's book. I know you're a great artist, so I want you to **be in charge of**[3] the drawings in the book. Can you do that?

John: Sure. I'll have a lot of time **as soon as**[4] I finish classes next week. This sounds like a fun project. I bet I'll **have a good time**[5] working with you.

Grace: I think you will. Together, we'll have the entire book finished **in no time**[6]. Have you ever done anything like this before?

John: Well, I **used to**[7] draw cartoons for a comic book, so it shouldn't be hard to **get used to**[8] this kind of project.

Grace: Perfect!

葛芮絲：早安，約翰！為什麼你這麼沒精神？

約翰：唔，妳今天早上和我**聯絡**、約我出去喝咖啡時，把我**吵醒**了。

葛芮絲：真是抱歉！事實上，我當時急著找你，是因為我希望你能幫我寫一本童書。我知道你是一個很棒的畫家，所以想要請你**負責**書中的插畫。可以嗎？

約翰：當然。只要**一**結束下星期的課，我**就**會有許多時間。這聽起來是一個很有趣的案子。我相信和妳合作會**很愉快的**。

葛芮絲：沒錯。我們**很快**就會一起完成整本書。你曾經做過類似的工作嗎？

約翰：嗯，我**以前**畫過卡通漫畫，所以要**適應**這件案子並不難。

葛芮絲：太棒了！

get in touch with 聯絡

have a good time 很愉快

034

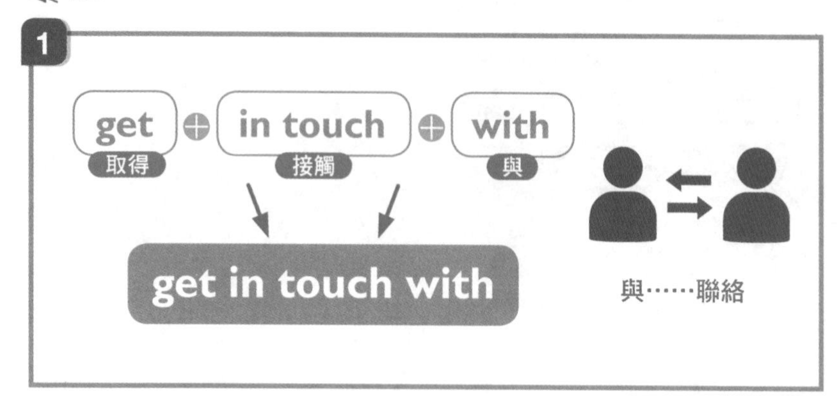

- Verona will **get in touch with** you as soon as she hears some news.
  薇諾娜一有消息就會**和**你**聯絡**。
- It's been years since he **got in touch with** my cousin.
  他已經**和**我表哥**聯絡**了好幾年。

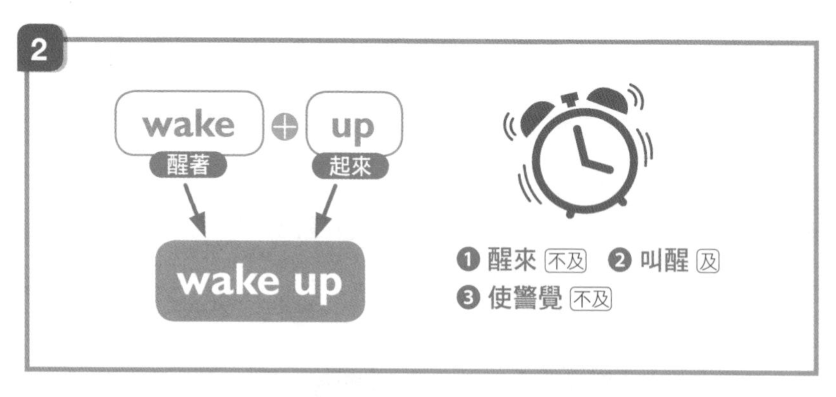

❶ What time did you **wake up** this morning?
你今天早上幾點**起床**？

❷ Companies need to **wake up** and take notice of the public's increasing concerns about the environment.
公司必須有所**警覺**，注意民眾有越來越關心環境問題的趨勢。

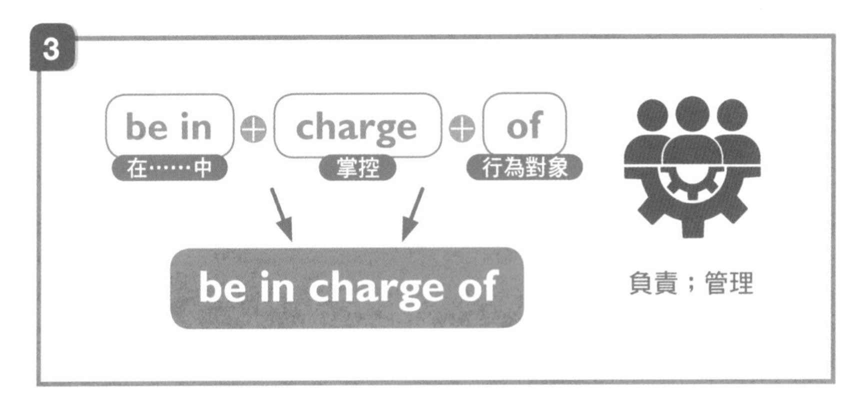

- Emily **is in charge of** the class pet this week.
  艾蜜莉這星期要**負責**照顧班上的寵物。
- Jeremy is the football team's coach, so he'**s in charge of** making sure the players perform well.
  傑諾米是足球隊的教練，所以他**負責**確保球員都能有好的表現。

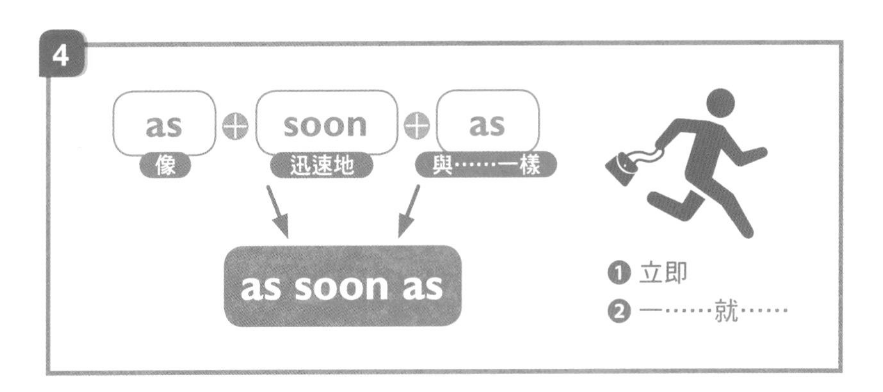

❶ I'll call you **as soon as** I can. 我會**儘快**打電話給你。

❷ **As soon as** I opened the door, I knew there was a problem. 我一開門，**就**知道有問題。

035

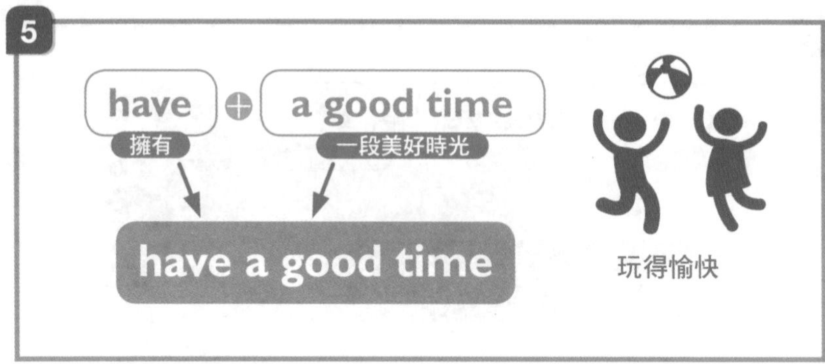

- Did you **have a good time** at the concert last weekend? 你在上週末的演唱會中**玩得愉快**嗎？
- My older sister **had a good time** at the park because the weather was perfect.
天氣很好，我姐姐在公園**玩得很愉快**。

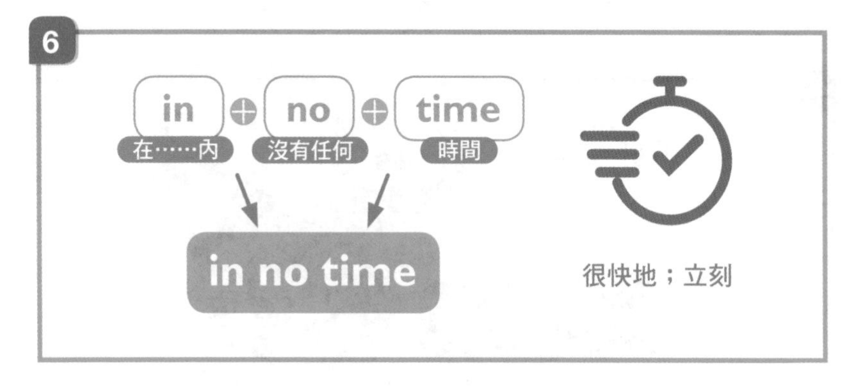

- The book was so interesting that the students finished it **in no time**. 這本書非常有趣，學生**很快**就看完了。
- Dylan had been thinking about his Greek history report for several days, so when he started working, he finished it **in no time**. 狄倫過去幾天一直在思索希臘歷史報告，所以他開始不久後，**很快**便完成了。
- I pulled my blanket around me, and **in no time**, I was fast asleep. 我蓋上毯子後**很快地**便進入夢鄉。

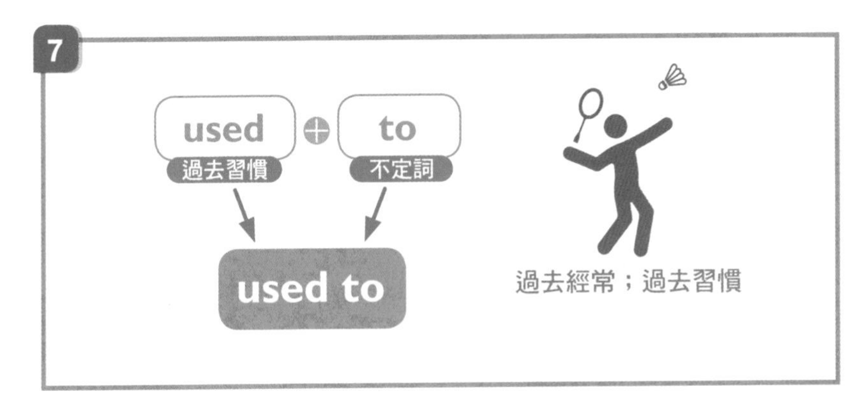

- Betty **used to** teach English, but now she has a different job.
  貝蒂**曾**是英文老師，但她現在找到了一份不同的工作。

- I **used to** go for a jog every morning, but then it got too cold outside.
  我**以前時常**每天早上去散步，但後來天氣變冷了。

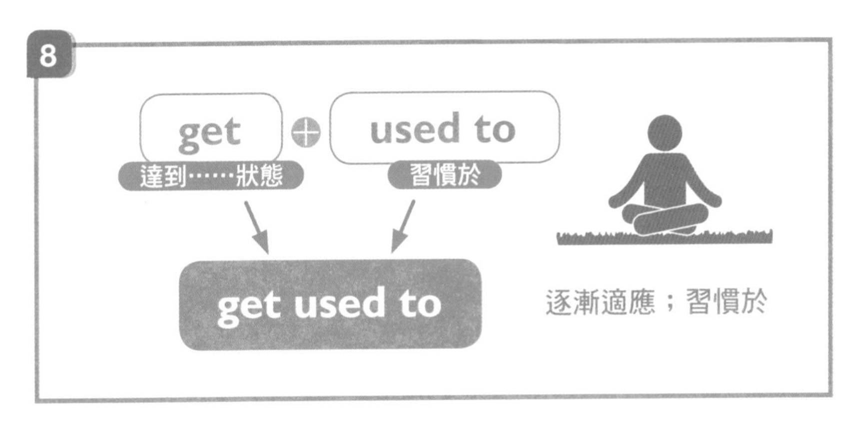

- At first, Natalie didn't like sushi; but after living in Tokyo for a few weeks, she **got used to** it.
  娜塔莉一開始不喜歡壽司，但在東京住了幾個星期後便**習慣**了。

036

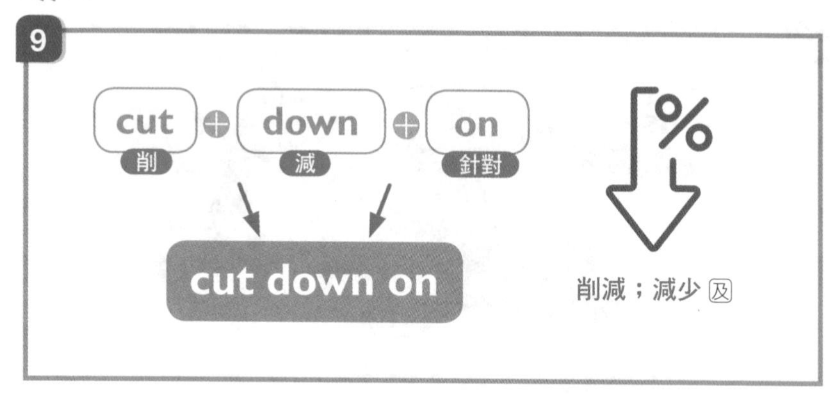

- Because Dean was trying to lose weight, he **cut down on** the number of snacks he ate.
  狄恩想要減重，所以他**減少**吃零食。
- If you want to **cut down on** the amount of money you spend at the supermarket, never shop when you're hungry.
  如果想要在超市**少**花點錢，就別在肚子餓的時候去買東西。

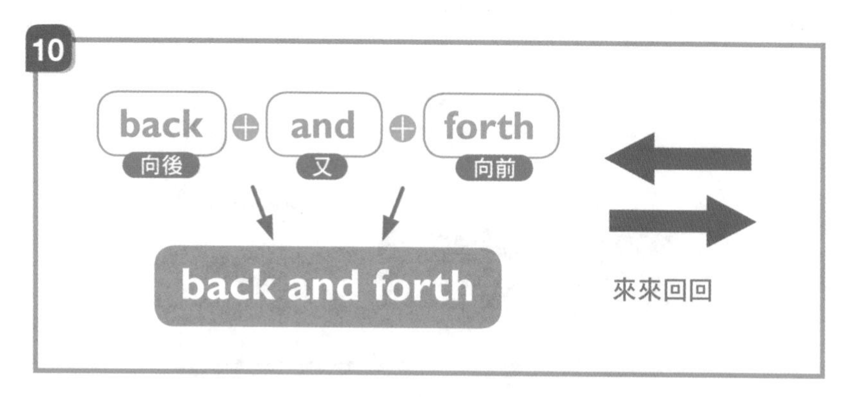

- The wind made the boat rock **back and forth** on the water. 風把船吹得在水面上**晃盪**。
- Because Rachel wanted to get in shape, she ran **back and forth** across the field every morning.
  瑞秋想要好身材，所以每天早上**來來回回地**在操場上跑步。

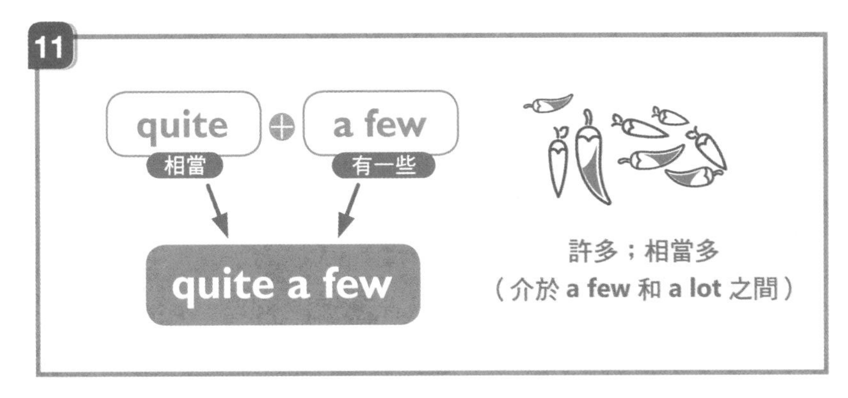

- Casey wanted to make his own apple juice, applesauce, and apple pie, so he bought **quite a few** pounds of apples at the market. 凱西想要自己做蘋果汁、蘋果醬和蘋果派，所以他到市場買了**好幾**磅的蘋果。
- There was a big sale at the bookstore, so Floyd bought **quite a few** books.
書店在大減價，所以佛洛伊德買了**許多**書。

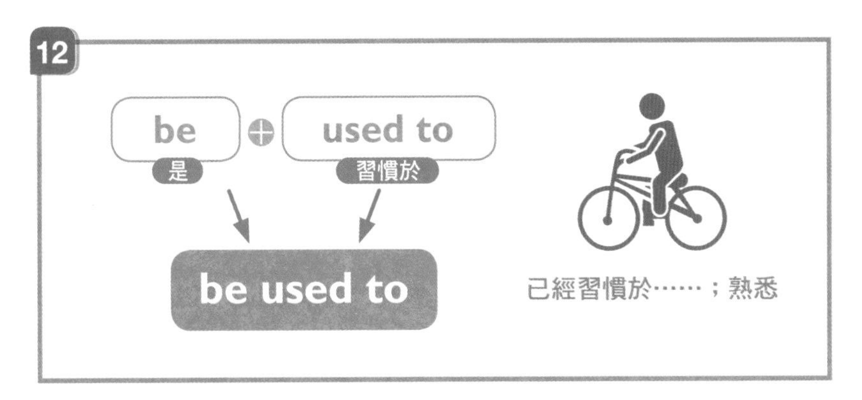

- Joan **is used to** horses, so she wasn't scared of riding one. 瓊**已經習慣**了馬兒，所以她不害怕騎馬。
- I **am used to** cooking my own dinner.
我**已經習慣**自己準備晚餐了。

Choosing a Pet
挑選寵物

Ava and Ethan are choosing a pet in a pet store.
愛娃和伊森正在寵物店挑選寵物。

037

Ethan: OK, Ava. We have to **make sure**[1] that we get a pet we'll be happy with and won't ever want to **get rid of**[2].

Ava: That's true! A pet is not something we can take care of **now and then**[3]; it's a big commitment.

Ethan: How about that white rat? His white fur will **go with**[4] your white jacket.

Ava: No way! Oh, look at those kittens playing together. Look at that one there; he's really cute.

Ethan: I agree. Let's buy him! But before we take him home, we should **see about**[5] getting some cat food and some toys for him before the stores close.

Ava: Okay, but let's go now. If we **make good time**[6], we can get back to the pet store quickly. I don't want anyone else to take our kitten!

伊森： 好了，愛娃，記得**確定**要選一隻我們滿意的寵物，而且永遠不要**丟棄**他。

愛娃： 沒錯！養寵物不是**偶爾**照顧一下而已，而是一項承諾。

伊森： 這隻白老鼠如何？他身上的白毛和你的白色夾克很**配**。

愛娃： 不要！噢，看那些玩在一起的小貓。你看那邊那隻，好可愛噢。

伊森： 我也這麼認為。我們就買他吧！但是帶他回家之前，我們應該**考慮**在商店打烊前去買一些貓食和玩具給他。

愛娃： 好，不過我們現在就走吧。我們如果**走快**一點，就能夠趕快回到寵物店。我不希望有人買走我們的小貓！

038

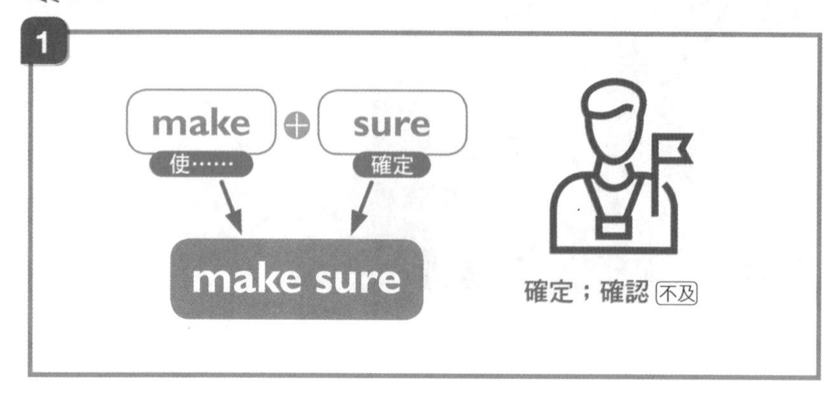

- Before you leave the house, **make sure** that you turn all the lights off. 出門前，要**確認**所有的燈都關了。
- I need to **make sure** that I call my parents if I'm going to be late. 若是要晚歸，我一定要**確定**先打電話給爸媽。

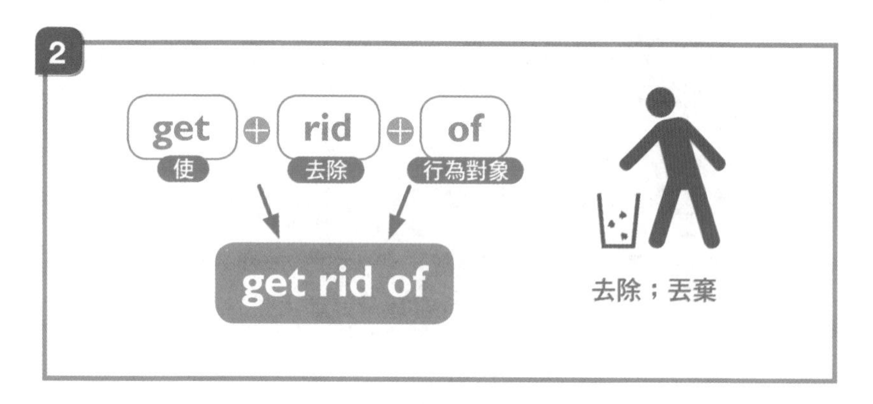

- How do I **get rid of** all these ants in my house? 我該如何**消除**屋內所有的螞蟻？
- Drinking herbal tea will help you **get rid of** your sore throat. 飲用花草茶能幫助你**消除**喉嚨痛。

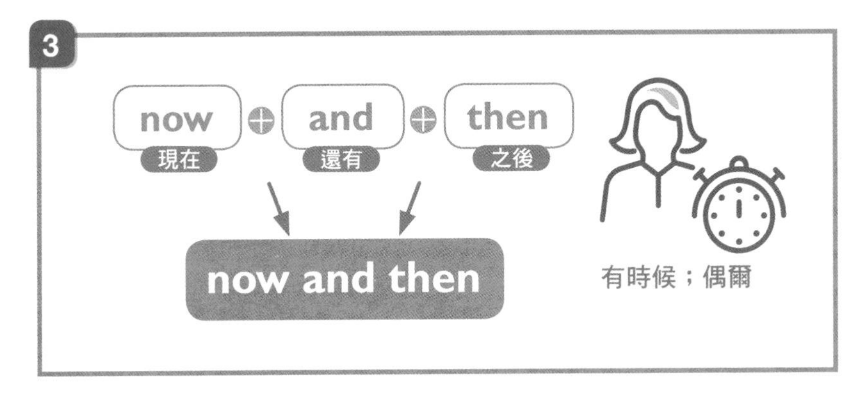

- We meet up **now and then**, maybe once every few months. 我們**偶爾**會見面，大概幾個月見一次面。
- Call your parents **now and then** and let them know you care. **偶爾**打電話給你的父母，讓他們知道你很關心他們。
- Every **now and then** I'll take the kids to the playground. 我**有時候**會帶孩子們去遊樂場玩。

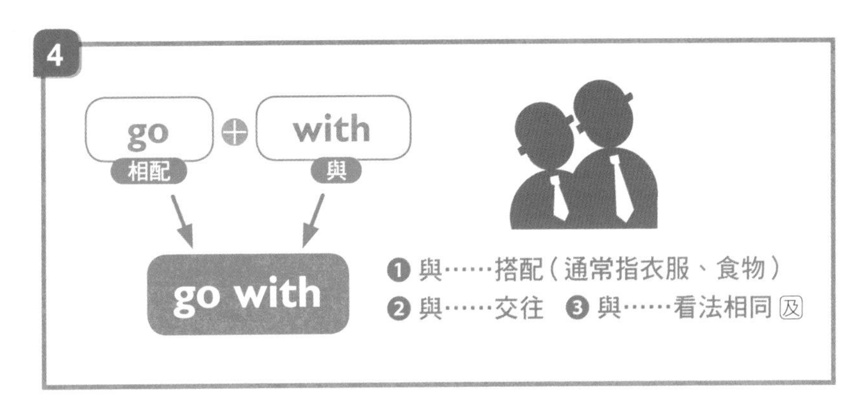

❶ That orange tie definitely does not **go with** that pink shirt! 那條橘色領帶顯然和粉紅色襯衫不太**相配**！

❶ Do you think red or white wine **goes with** this lasagna? 你覺得這道千層麵要**配**紅酒或白酒呢？

039

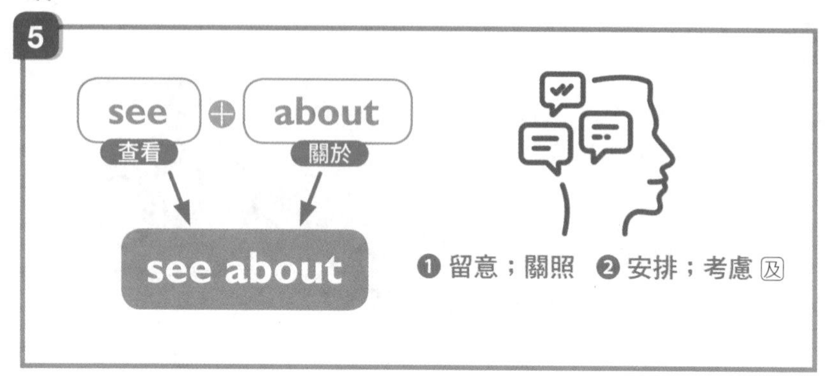

❷ I'm not sure if Carla is coming to the party; I'd better **see about** sending her an invitation.
我不確定卡拉是否會來參加派對，我**打算**寄邀請卡給她。

❷ My dad said he was going to **see about** buying me a motorcycle. 我老爸說他**打算**買一台摩托車給我

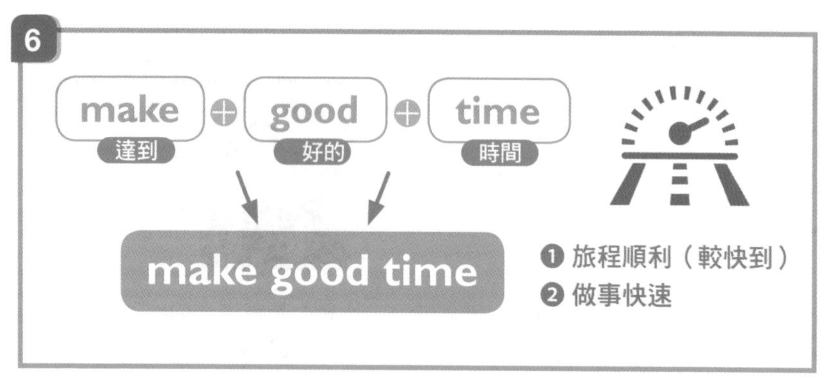

❶ We **made good time** driving to Taipei because the traffic was light. 由於路況順暢，我們**很快**就開車到達台北。

❷ Although we left later than planned, we **made good time** and arrived before the show started.
雖然我們比計畫中還要晚離開，但我們**速度很快**，所以到達時並不會太晚。

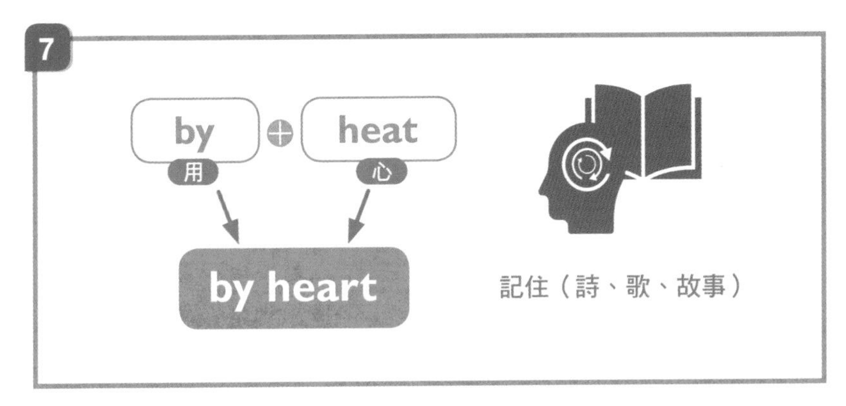

- Annabelle loves *Hamlet*; she knows most of the famous lines **by heart**.
  安娜貝爾最愛《哈姆雷特》，她**記住**了大部分有名的詩詞。
- Jack studied his lines in the play until he was sure he knew them **by heart**.
  傑克一直在背他在劇中的臺詞，直到他確定都**記住**了。

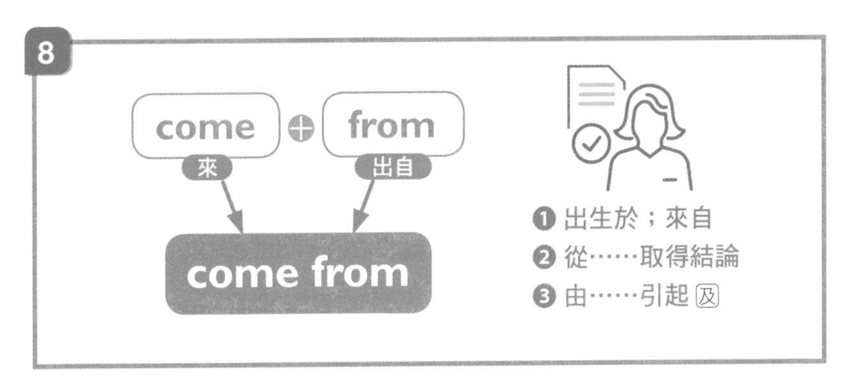

8
come
來
from
出自
come from
❶ 出生於；來自
❷ 從……取得結論
❸ 由……引起 及

❶ My best friend Bill **comes from** Chicago.
我最好的朋友比爾**來自**芝加哥。

❶ Where did all these hats **come from**?
這些帽子是**哪裡**來的？

❶ If you ask me, the best cherries **come from** Washington.
如果你問我，我會說最好吃的櫻桃**來自**華盛頓。

040

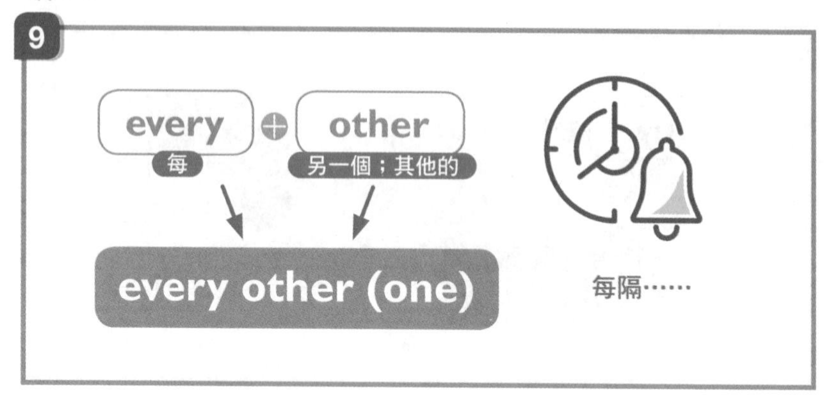

- Terrance visits his uncle and aunt **every other** week.
  泰倫斯**每隔**週都會去拜訪叔叔和阿姨。

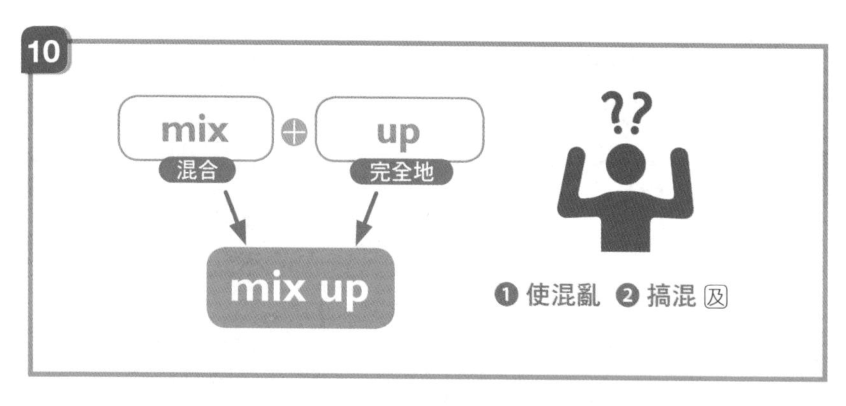

❷ It's easy to **mix up** Richie and Lou because they're twins.
瑞奇和盧是雙胞胎，所以很容易把他們**搞混**。

❷ I always **mix** your birthday **up** with Seth's.
我老是把你和塞斯的生日**搞混**。

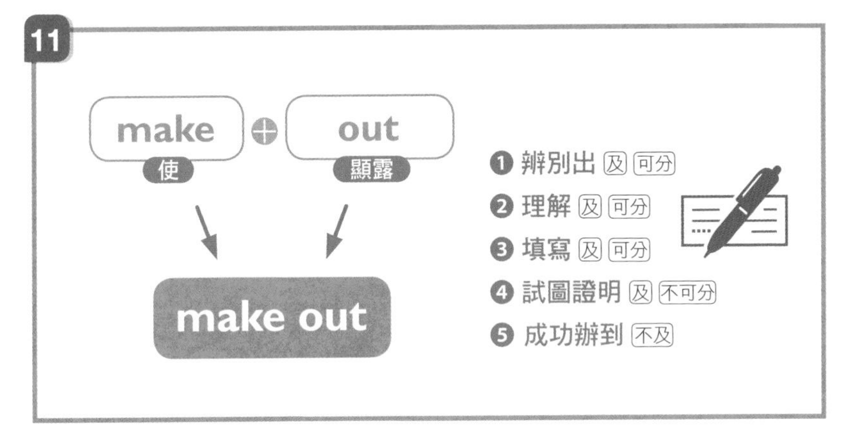

❶ The TV volume was so low that it was hard to **make out** what the actors were saying.
電視的音量很小，實在很難**聽出**演員在說什麼。

Waiting for a Friend
等朋友

Jaime is waiting for Marc under an apple tree. Finally, he arrives—15 minutes late. 潔咪在蘋果樹下等馬克，終於，他出現了，在遲到了 15 分鐘後。

041

Jaime: Hey, Marc! Why are you late?
What have you **been up to**[1]?

Marc: Sorry! I had a hard day at school. Can we talk about it for a minute? This morning, my professor seemed to **find fault with**[2] everything I said during class. He wanted me to totally **do** my report **over**[3]. Really, he seemed to **be carried away**[4] with new ideas, and his thoughts were hard to **keep track of**[5].

Jaime: Don't worry! You'll **get through**[6] it; it's only a paper!

Marc: I guess you're right. But **from now on**[7], I think I'd better try being a better student. Hey, did you bring any food in that bag? I'm hungry.

Jaime: **Keep away from**[8] my bag! There's a surprise in there for you—but you have to wait. I don't want you to see it yet.

潔咪： 嘿，馬克，你為什麼遲到？你**都在做**什麼呢？

馬克： 對不起，我今天在學校過得很不愉快。我們可以聊一下嗎？今天早上教授對我在課堂上的發言好像很**有意見**，他要我**重寫**報告。真的，他似乎**被**新的思想**影響**，很難**猜測**他在想什麼。

潔咪： 別擔心！你**寫**得**完**的，不過是報告而已！

馬克： 妳說得對，但是我想我**今後**最好試著當個好學生。嘿，那個袋子裡頭有吃的嗎？我餓昏了。

潔咪： **別靠近**我的袋子！裡面是要給你的驚喜，但是你必須等等，我還不想給你看。

find fault with 挑毛病

keep away 遠離

042

❶ What **are** you **up to** this weekend? 你這週末**要做**什麼？

❷ I don't know if we'll play video games tonight; it'**s up to** you. 我不知道今晚是否要打電動，**由**你**決定**。

❸ I'm sure Walt **is up to** something; he's been acting so strangely lately. 我確定華特一定**在做**什麼**見不得人的事情**，他最近的行為很奇怪。

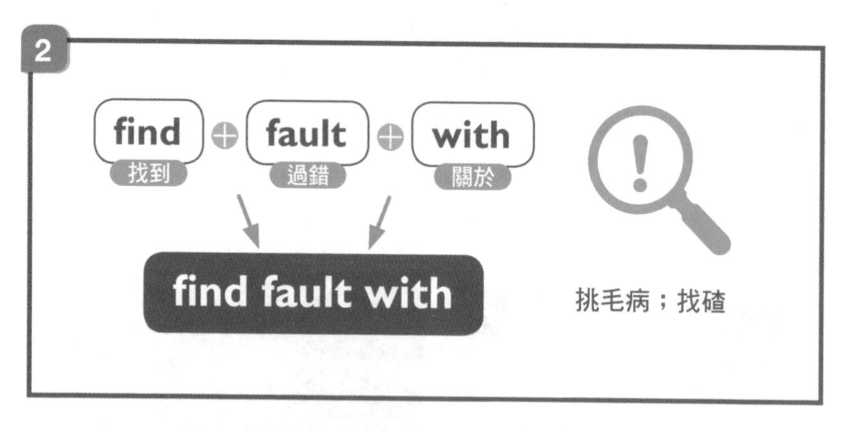

- George is so critical; no matter how good things are, he always **finds fault with** something.
喬治很吹毛求疵；就算東西再好，他也能夠**挑出毛病**。

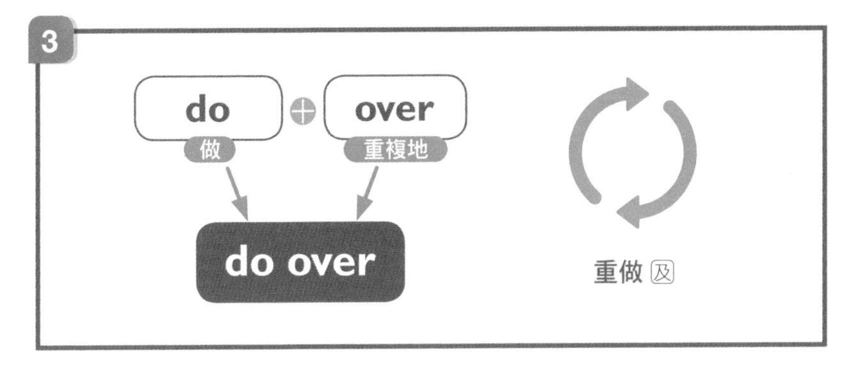

- My math teacher said I could **do** the last quiz **over** because I did so poorly on it.
  因為我考得很差，所以數學老師說我可以**重考**上次的小考。

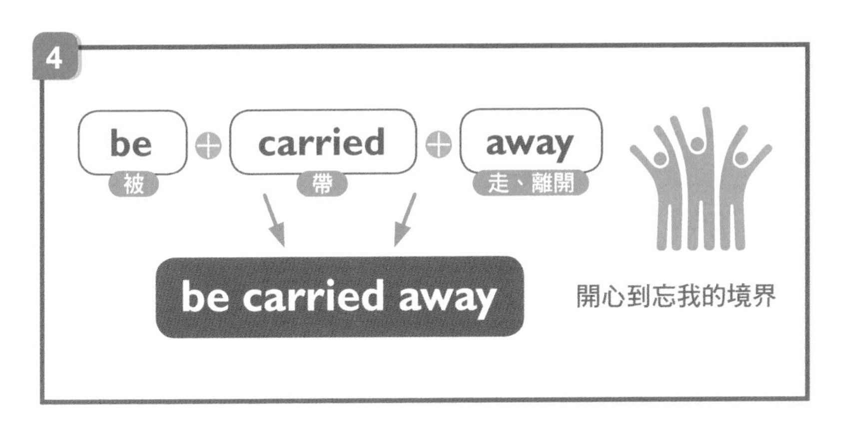

- Tina likes baking so much that she **was carried away** and made hundreds of cookies.
  堤娜熱愛烘焙**到忘我的境界**，她不小心做了一堆餅乾。

- Harry **was** so **carried away** by the good news that he couldn’t calm down.
  哈利**沉醉**在好消息中，無法冷靜下來。

- People in the crowd **were carried away** by Clinton’s passionate speech.
  觀眾因柯林頓滿腔熱血的演講而**興奮不已**。

043

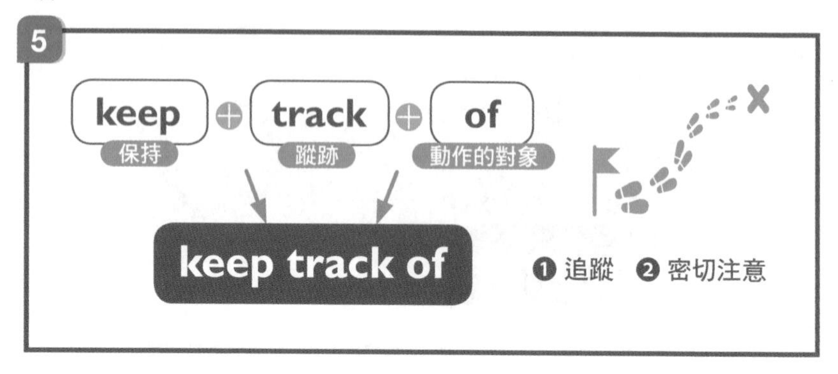

❶ Agatha is always traveling, and I can never **keep track of** where she is.
雅嘉薩老是在旅行，所以我永遠無法**掌握**她的**行蹤**。

❷ The babysitter is supposed to **keep track of** my little sister. 保姆應該要**隨時注意**我的妹妹。

❶ Please leave Jimmy alone; he won't **get through** his work if you keep chatting with him.
請不要煩吉米，你一直和他聊天，他無法**完成**工作。

❷ Jimmy **got through** his exams without too much trouble.
吉米輕輕鬆鬆地**通過**了考試。

❸ I tried to phone her, but I couldn't **get through**.
我試著打電話給她，但是**聯絡**不**上**。

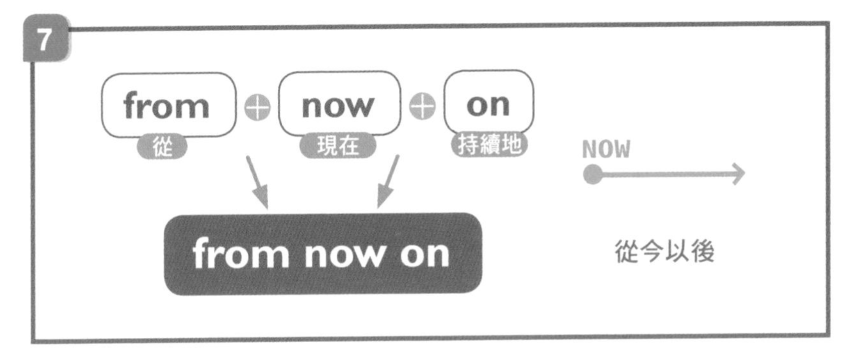

- **From now on**, you must be home before midnight.
  從今以後，你必須在午夜前回家。
- Because I overslept again, I have to work the late shift **from now on**.
  由於我又睡過頭，**從現在開始**我必須上晚班。
- **From now on**, the gates will be locked at midnight.
  從現在開始，大門半夜都會上鎖。

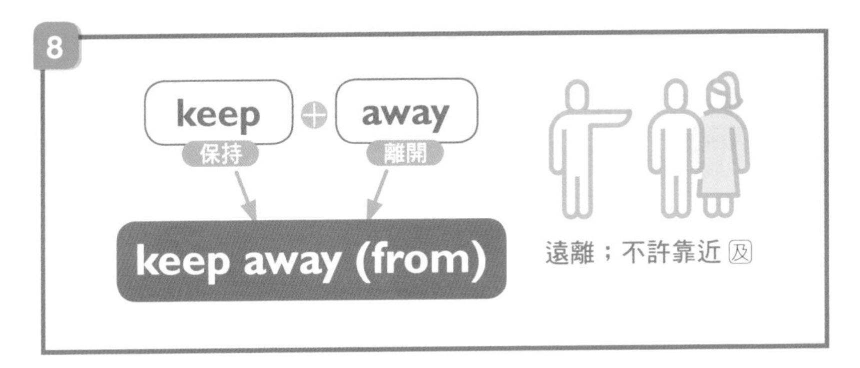

- Danielle is just a child, so be sure to **keep** her **away from** the road.
  丹妮葉拉還是個小孩，所以千萬**別**讓她**靠近**馬路。
- I suggest you **keep away from** Jane; she has a cold.
  我建議你**別靠近**珍，她感冒了。
- **Keep away from** the edge of the cliff. **別太靠近**懸崖。

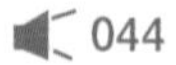
044

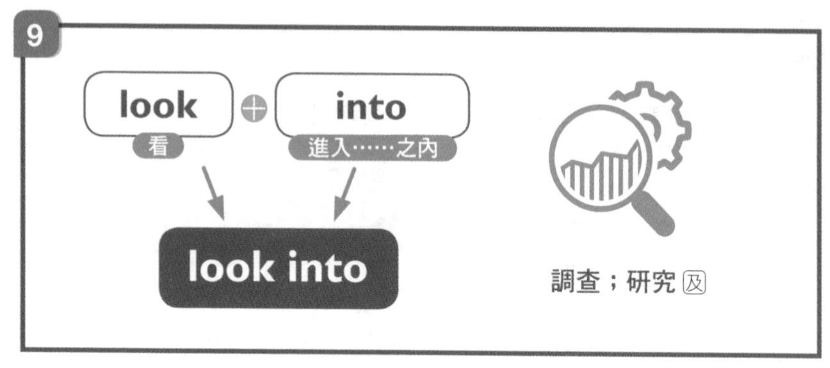

- Vince was **looking into** the possibility of working in Canada. 文斯正在**研究**到加拿大工作的可能性。
- I'm not sure if that's a good price for that car; let me **look into** it. 我不確定那是那台車最好的價錢，我**研究**一下。
- They're **looking into** the possibility of merging the two departments. 他們正在**研究**合併兩個部門的可能性。

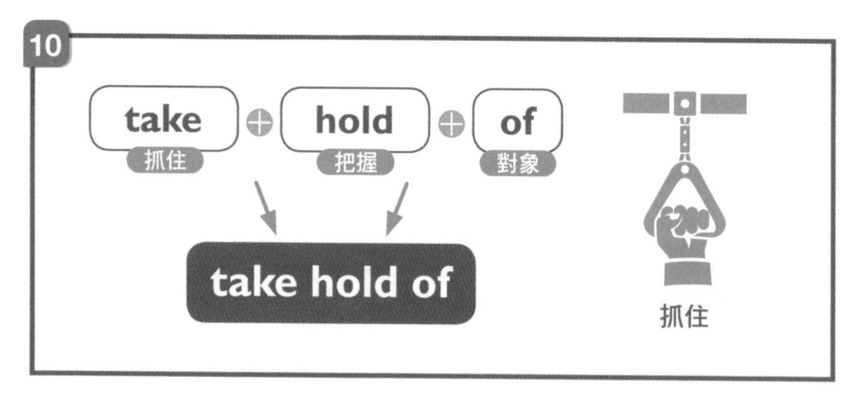

- The boy **took hold of** his mother's hand before they crossed the street. 男孩在過馬路前**抓住**媽媽的手。
- When they got to the city center, Patty **took hold of** her camera and didn't let go because she was afraid it would get stolen.
他們進入市中心後，派蒂怕相機被偷，所以**緊抓著**不放。

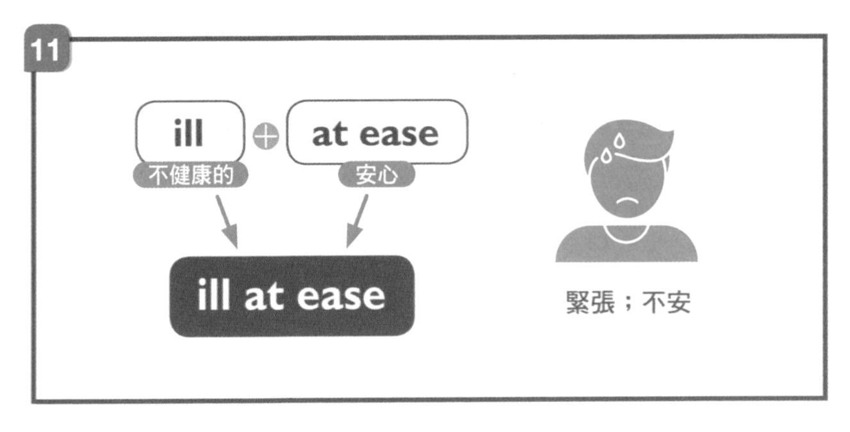

• As he was waiting for the test results, Carl felt **ill at ease**.
卡爾在等待考試成績時感到**緊張**。

❶ I want some privacy now, so please **keep out** of my room. 我現在想要有一點隱私，所以請**不要進入**我的房間。

❷ If you see two people arguing, it's best to **keep out** of it. 如果你看到兩個人在爭吵，最好**別被牽扯進去**。

The New Mobile Phone 新手機

Josh tells Abby about his new mobile phone. 喬許把新手機的事情告訴艾比。

045

Abby: Wow! Is that your new cell phone?

Josh: You bet. Cool, isn't it? My old one was really **out-of-date**[1].

Abby: Well, this one sure is **up-to-date**[2]. But I thought your old phone worked fine.

Josh: Actually, I really needed this one. Last weekend, the old charger **caught fire**[3] when I plugged it in. Good thing it happened when I was around; otherwise, I might have **burned down**[4] the apartment building!

Abby: Okay, so it **stands to reason**[5] that you needed a new phone—but what made you choose this model?

Josh: I think it looks cool! **As for**[6] the old phone, I gave it to my friend.

艾比： 哇，那是你的新手機嗎？

喬許： 沒錯，很棒吧？我的舊手機真的**過時**了。

艾比： 嗯，這支確實**很新**。但我以為你的舊手機還可以用。

喬許： 事實上，我真的需要換支新的了。我上週末使用舊的充電器時，竟然**著火**了。好險我當時就在旁邊，否則整棟公寓可能會**燒掉**！

艾比： 嗯，那你**理所當然**需要新手機。但你為何會選擇這個款式呢？

喬許： 我覺得它很好看！**至於**舊手機，我送給朋友了。

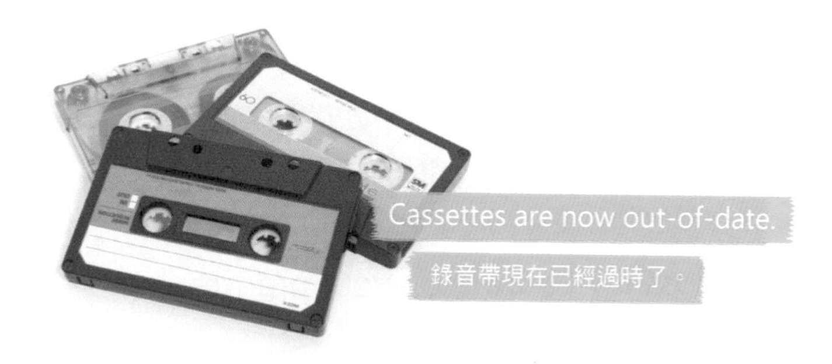

Cassettes are now out-of-date.

錄音帶現在已經過時了。

046

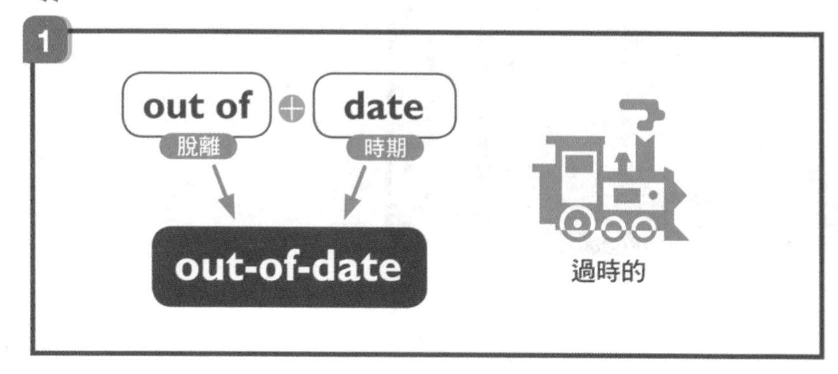

- This computer is so **out-of-date** that it can't even connect to the Internet.
  這台電腦很**老舊**了，就連網路也無法連接。

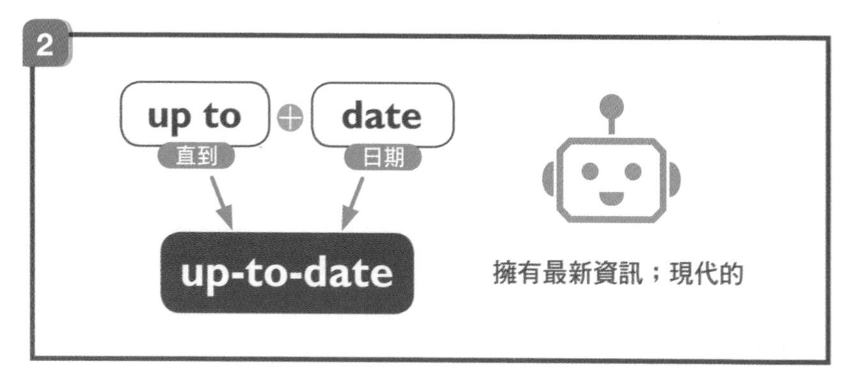

- If you want to work as a reporter, you really must keep yourself **up-to-date** on current events.
  如果你想成為記者，就必須隨時掌握**最新**消息。
- A good fashion designer stays **up-to-date** on the newest styles and trends.
  優秀的服裝設計師總是能夠掌握**最新**的流行款式和趨勢。
- This new laptop player is really **up-to-date**—it's a new model. 這台新的筆記型電腦確實是**最新的**，它是全新的機種。
- Keep your boss **up-to-date** on your progress.
  隨時向你的老闆報告**最新**進度。

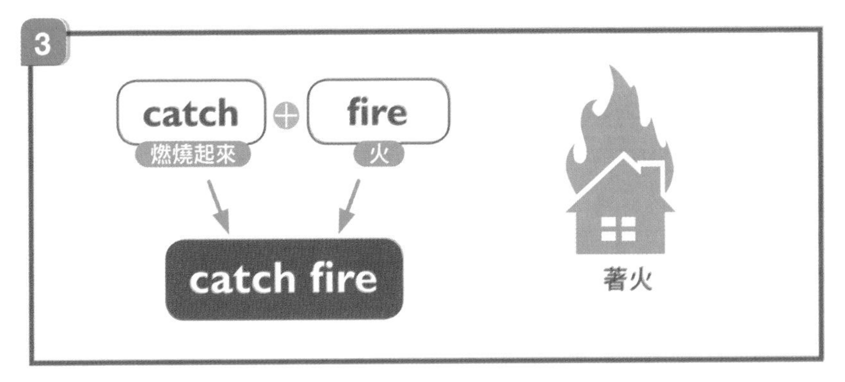

- Despite being wet, the wood that they put on the stove finally **caught fire**.
  儘管他們放在火爐上的木頭是濕的，最後還是**燃燒**了起來。
- If you don't move that candle away from the curtains, they may **catch fire**.
  如果你不把蠟燭從窗簾移走，窗簾可能會**著火**。

❶ Don't ever light matches in my house. I'm afraid you'll accidentally **burn** it **down.**
不要在我家點火柴，我很怕你不小心會把房子**燒掉**。

❷ Fortunately, the Stern family had fire insurance, so when their house **burned down**, they were able to buy a new one. 幸好史坦家有保火災險，所以他們的房子**燒掉**後，有能力買新房子。

047

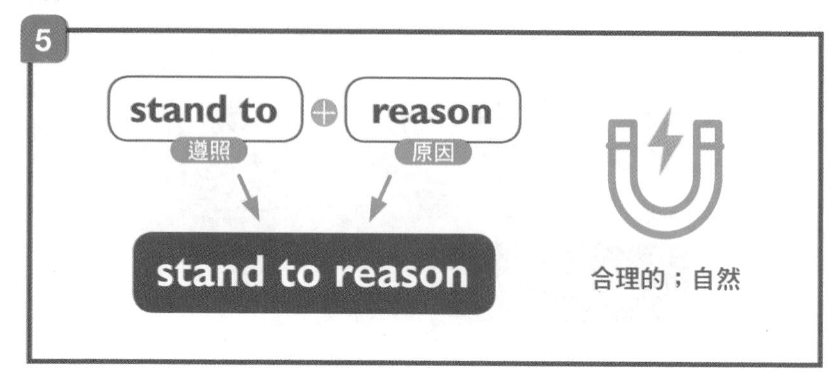

- If you never brush your teeth, it **stands to reason** that you'll spend a lot of money at the dentist's office.
  如果你從不刷牙，花很多錢看牙醫是很**合理**的。
- It **stands to reason** that students who study the hardest get the best grades.
  用功的學生成績較好，這是**理所當然**的。

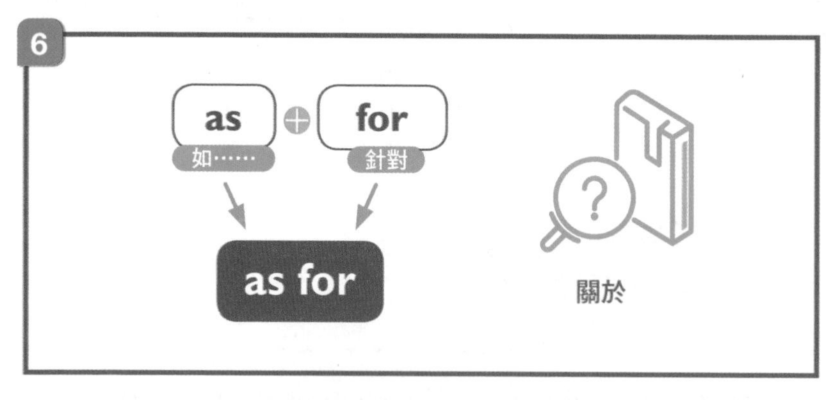

- **As for** Bill, he ended up writing a book and becoming famous.
  至於比爾，他最後因寫了一本書而變得很有名。
- Today is a beautiful day; **as for** tomorrow, however, we can expect rain.
  今天天氣晴朗。**至於**明天，可能會下雨。

❶ The photographs in Ray's bedroom were **burned up** in the fire. 雷房間的那場大火，**燒光**了他的照片。

❷ The bad news really **burned** him **up**.
那個壞消息真的令他很**生氣**。

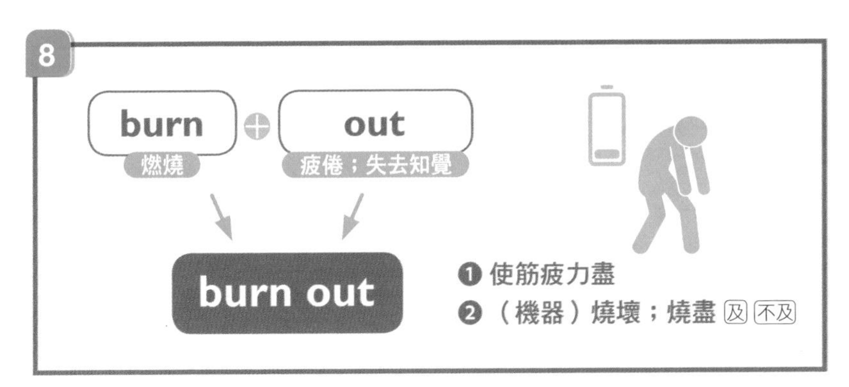

❶ In his last year of high school, Louis **burned out** and got terrible grades.
路易在高中的最後一年**累壞**了，所以成績很糟糕。

❶ The writer **burned** himself **out** as he finished his first book. 作者完成了第一本書後便**累壞**了。

❷ After she used the old laptop for six hours straight, it **burned out** and wouldn't turn on anymore. 那台舊筆記型電腦在她使用了整整六個鐘頭後便**燒壞**，再也無法開機了。

048

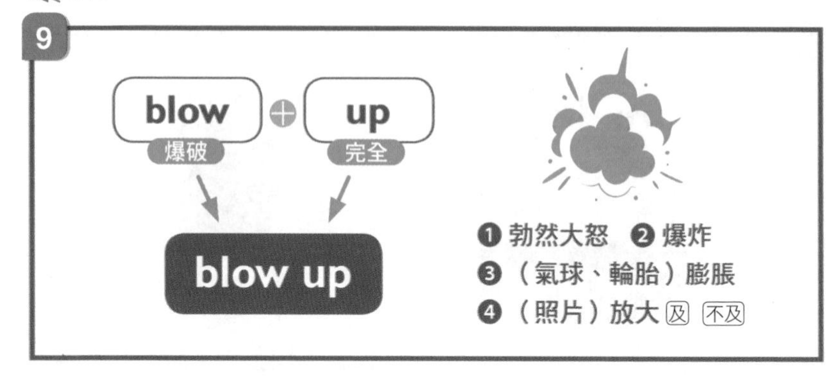

❶ My dad **blew up** when he saw the phone bill.
我爸爸看到電話帳單後氣**炸了**。

❷ The best part of the action movie was when the gas tank **blew up** and started a huge fire.
這部動作片最精采的部分，就是油箱**爆炸**而引發大火了。

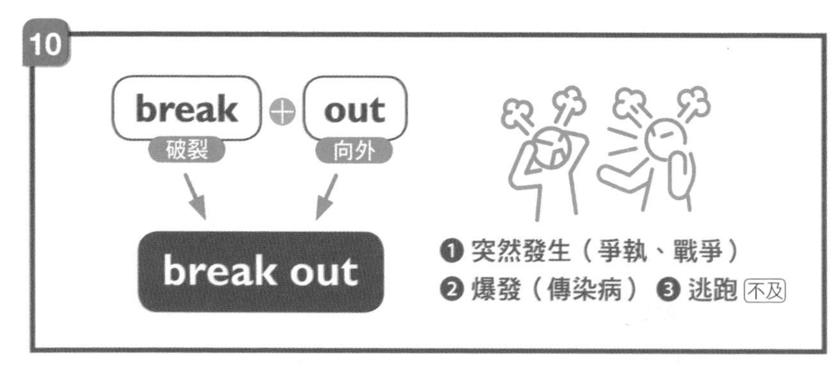

❶ Irma and Gina got more and more angry with each other, and it wasn't long before an argument **broke out** between them. 由於娥瑪和吉娜越來越生對方的氣，於是他們之間的爭吵**爆發**了。

❷ When Damian returned from school, his mother saw that he had **broken out** with chicken pox.
當戴明恩從學校返家後，媽媽發現他突然**長**了水痘。

❸ In the news today I saw that three thieves **broke out** of jail! 我在今天的新聞上看到有三位小偷**逃**獄了！

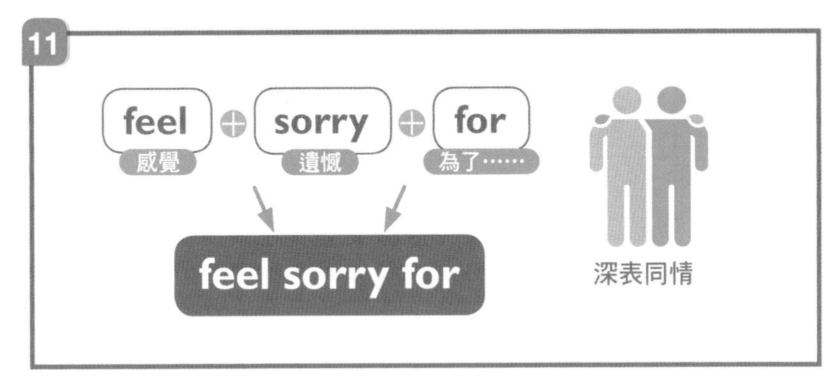

- I **felt sorry for** Matilda when I heard she was kicked out of her apartment.
  當我聽到瑪蒂蓮達被趕出公寓時，我對她**深表同情**。

- Seeing that poor bird in the little cage really made me **feel sorry for** it.
  我**很同情**那隻被關在小籠子裡可憐的鳥兒。

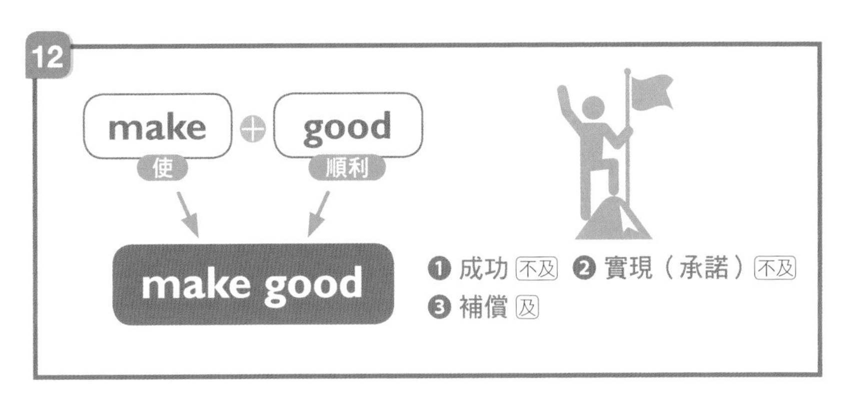

❶ She was described as the local girl who **made** it **good** in Hollywood. 她代表了在好萊塢**大放光彩**的鄉村女孩。

❷ Brad **made good** on his promise to study more and get better grades. 布萊德**說他會用功進步，他說到做到了**。

❷ Linda **made good** on her decision to study economics. 琳達**實現**了決定讀經濟學**的承諾**。

Walking Along the Beach 海邊散步

Jolene and Charlie are talking while taking a walk along the beach.
裘琳和查理在海邊一邊聊天一邊散步。

049

Charlie: You know, it's **once in a blue moon**[1] that we have this kind of weather in the spring. It's perfect for taking a walk on the beach! It's something we shouldn't **take for granted**[2].

Jolene: You're right, Charlie, especially if we **take into account**[3] that usually it's raining this time of year. Things really **turned out**[4] well.

Charlie: Hmm, maybe it'll rain after all. Let's go back. Taking a walk on the beach this time of year really **calls for**[5] umbrellas.

Jolene: You **give up**[6] too easily! A little rain never hurt anyone.

Once in a blue moon, a woman gives birth to triplets.
很少有女人能生出三胞胎。

查理： 唉，我們**很少**能在春天有這樣的天氣，到海邊散步正好！我們不應該**認為這是稀鬆平常的**。

裘琳： 你說的沒錯，查理。尤其是**考慮到**現在已經是春天了，每年這個時節通常都在下雨，天氣能**變成**這樣真好。

查理： 嗯，可能快要下雨了。我們回去吧。每年此時到海邊散步真**需要**帶把傘。

裘琳： 你太容易**放棄**了！這種毛毛雨不會有影響的。

take into account 考慮

give up 放棄

050

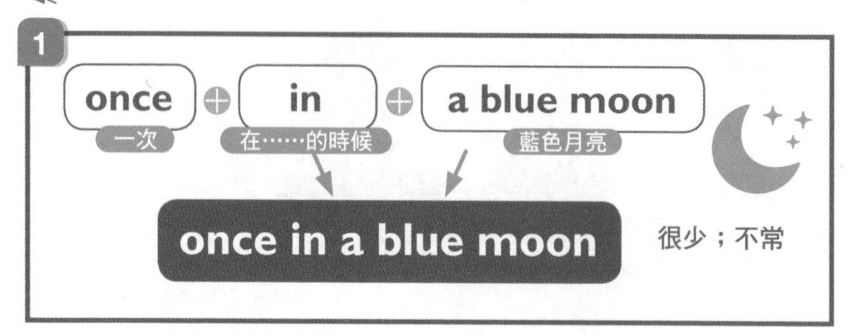

- Amy's brother is always traveling, so they see each other only **once in a blue moon**.
  艾咪的哥哥一直都在旅行，所以他們**很少**見面。
- **Once in a blue moon,** a woman gives birth to triplets.
  很少有女人能生出三胞胎。
- My cousin lives in Philadelphia, so I get to see him only **once in a blue moon**. 我表弟住在費城，所以我**不常**和他見面。

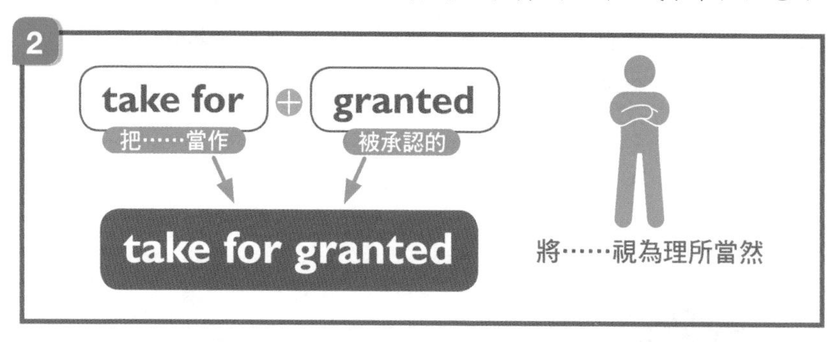

- Sheila helps her brother a lot, but sometimes she feels **taken for granted**.
  席拉幫了她哥哥很多忙，但她有時感覺**不被重視**。
- Only after her computer broke did she realize how much she **took** having a laptop **for granted**.
  她在電腦壞掉後，才知道她**忽視**了電腦的重要性。
- Many people **take** it **for granted** that the future will be better. 許多人都**認為**未來**理所當然**會更美好。
- So many of us **take** clean water **for granted**.
  許多人都**把**乾淨的水**視為理所當然**。

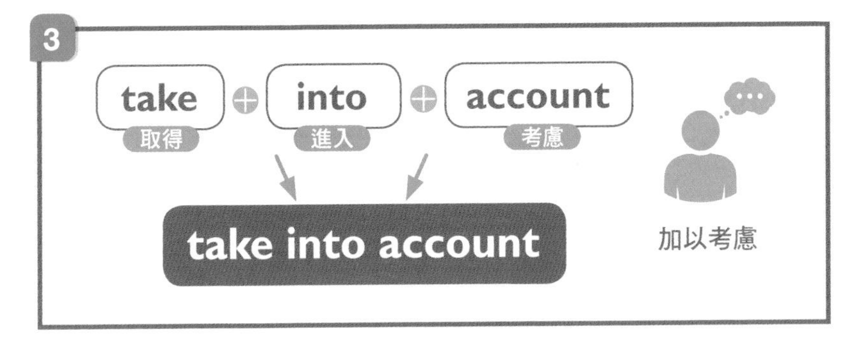

- Even if you don't do well on this test, the teacher is sure to **take** your good attitude and hard work **into account** when she gives you your final grade.
  就算你這次考不好，老師在打總成績前，會把你良好的學習態度和努力**列入考慮**的。
- Beth had planned to write her research paper over the weekend, but she forgot to **take into account** the fact that the library would be closed then. 貝絲計劃在週末寫研究報告，但她沒有**考慮**到週末圖書館不開放。

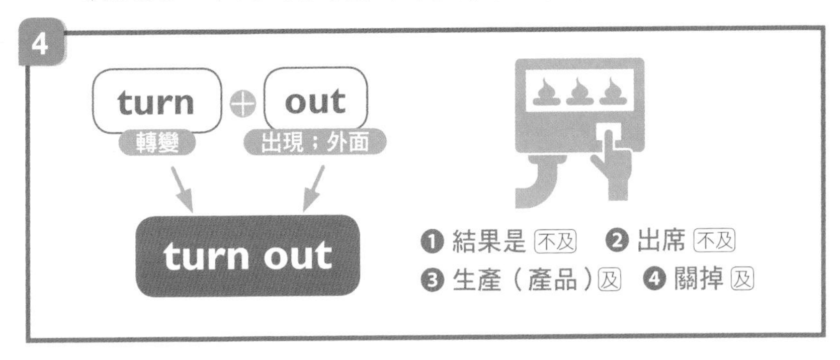

❶ As things **turned out**, it was a good idea to go on vacation last month. 事情**證明**了上個月去度假是個好主意。

❷ When the president gave a speech in Central Park, thousands of people **turned out**.
總統在中央公園發表演說，有上千名民眾前往**參加**。

❸ They **turn out** thousands of shoes every week.
他們每個星期**生產**好幾千雙鞋子。

051

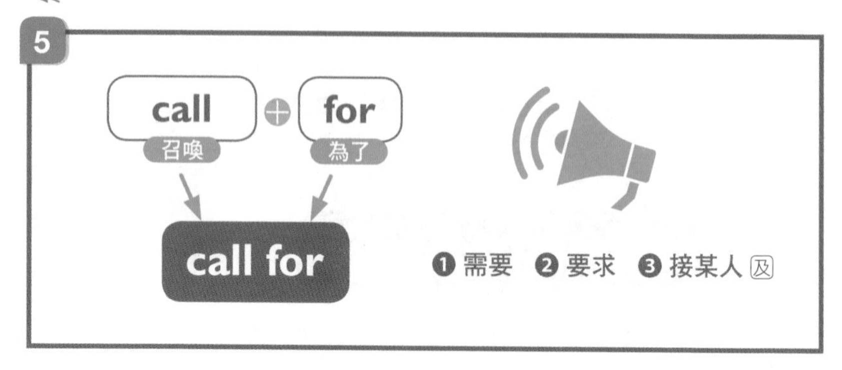

❶ Wow, a toothache like that definitely **calls for** a dentist.
哇，牙齒痛成那樣絕對**需要**看牙醫。

❷ When Tommy couldn't finish the project on his own, he **called for** help.
當湯米無法自己完成這項企畫，他**要求**支援。

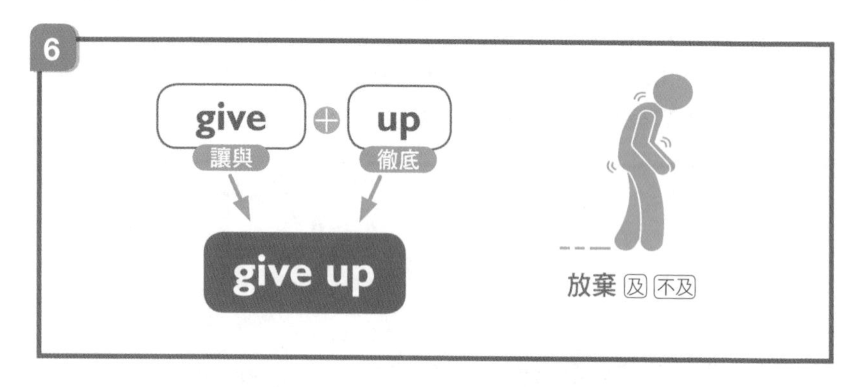

- Don't ever **give up**; just keep trying.
  永遠不要**放棄**，要不斷嘗試。
- I know things look difficult now, but don't **give up** on your dreams; if you work hard enough, things may get better. 我知道事情現在看起來很難，但別**放棄**你的夢想。只要你夠努力，情況就會好轉。
- Starting next week, Felix plans to **give up** smoking.
  菲力斯計劃從下星期開始**戒**菸。

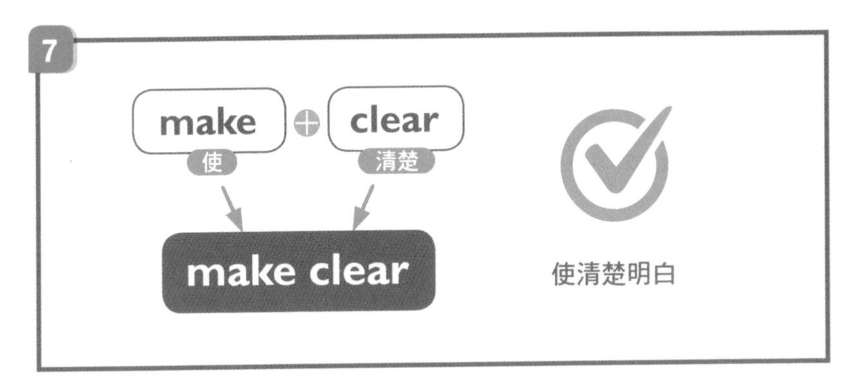

- Ronald really didn't **make clear** what time we were supposed to show up.
  羅納多並沒有**清楚說明**我們應該何時出席。

- Dr. McCormack **made** it perfectly **clear** that you were supposed to come to work early today.
  麥科馬克醫師**清楚交代**過，你今天應該要提早來上班。

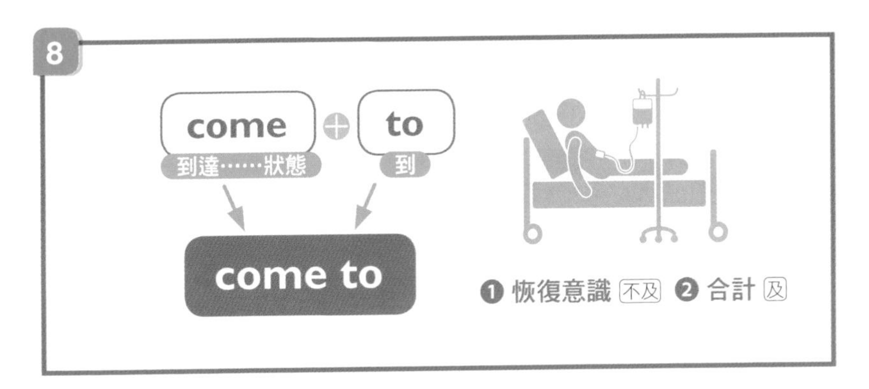

❶ It took Amy a few hours to **come to** after the operation.
艾咪在手術過後幾個小時才**恢復意識**。

❶ Has she **come to** yet? 她**恢復意識**了嗎？

❷ With tax, your bill **comes to** $450.24.
加上稅金後，您的帳單**總共**是 450.24 元。

052

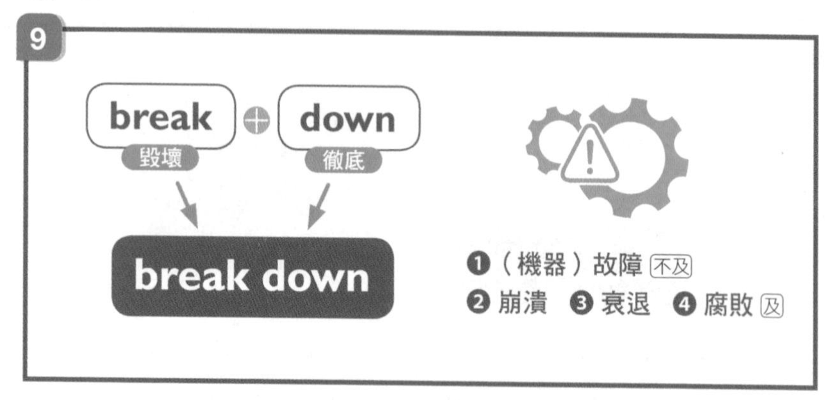

- Just as we were driving away from the house, our car **broke down**.
  我們正要開車離家時，車子**壞**了。

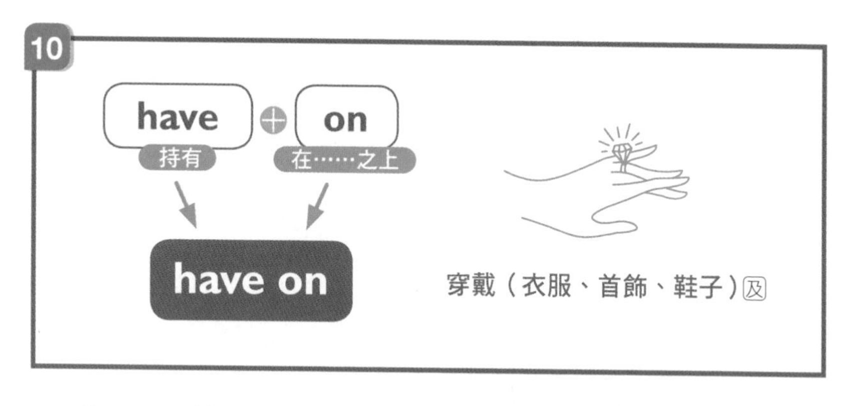

- Gary's wife was angry with him when she saw that he didn't **have** his wedding ring **on**.
  蓋瑞的太太發現蓋瑞沒**戴**婚戒時，她很生氣。
- Carol didn't want to answer the door because she **had on** only a bathrobe.
  卡蘿不想開門，因為她身上只**穿著**浴袍。

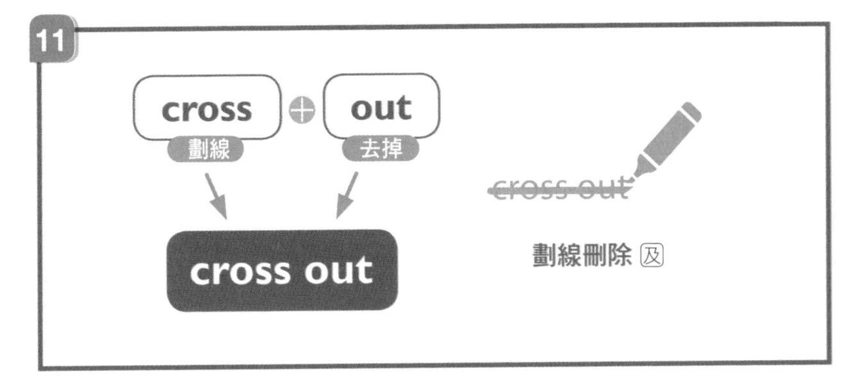

- The teacher **crossed out** a lot of my text and told me to write those parts over.
  老師把許多我寫的字**劃掉**了，還要我把那些部分重寫。
- It was hard to see who the letter was from because someone had **crossed out** the return address.
  有人把回信地址**劃掉**了，所以很難看出信是誰寄的。

Babysitting
照顧小孩

Sam and Nancy have a chat.
山姆和南西在聊天。

053

Sam: What are you doing tonight?

Nancy: I have to **look after**[1] my little cousin Billy while his parents are **eating out**[2].

Sam: You have a cousin named Billy? I've never **heard of**[3] him.

Nancy: That's because his family lives in Ontario, Canada. They're visiting my mom for a few weeks.

Sam: Are you **looking forward to**[4] spending time with your cousin?

Nancy: **As a matter of fact**[5], it won't be fun at all. Billy always **has his way**[6], so he is really poorly behaved.

Sam: Oh, sorry to hear that. Do you have to do this? Maybe your uncle and aunt can find someone else to take care of him.

Nancy: I have no choice; it's **cut-and-dried**[7]. But I'll **hear from**[8] my aunt as soon as they're on their way home. If you **feel like**[9] it, we can see a movie afterward.

Sam: Good idea!

山姆： 妳今晚要做什麼呢？

南西： 我必須**照顧**我的表弟比利，他的父母今晚要**在外面吃飯**。

山姆： 妳有個表弟叫做比利？我怎麼從來沒**聽說**過他。

南西： 因為他們家住在加拿大安大略省。他們這幾個禮拜是來探望我媽媽。

山姆： 妳**期待**和你的表弟一起玩嗎？

南西： **其實**，那一點也不好玩。比利總是**為所欲為**，他是一個不聽話的孩子。

山姆： 噢，真遺憾。妳一定要照顧他嗎？也許你的叔叔和阿姨可以找其他人幫忙照顧他？

南西： 我別無選擇，這是**事先安排**好的事情。但在他們回來的路上，我阿姨會**通知**我。如果你**想要**的話，我們之後可以去看場電影。

山姆： 好主意！

054

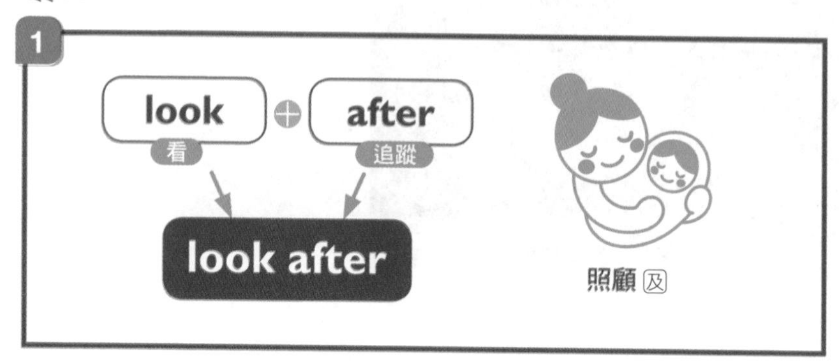

- When my folks are at work, I **look after** my little sister.
  父母去上班時，我要**照顧**我妹妹。
- Who **looks after** your dog when you are in class?
  你去上課的時候，誰來**照顧**你的狗？
- I **look after** the neighbors' cat while they're away.
  鄰居不在的時候，我替他們**照顧**貓咪。

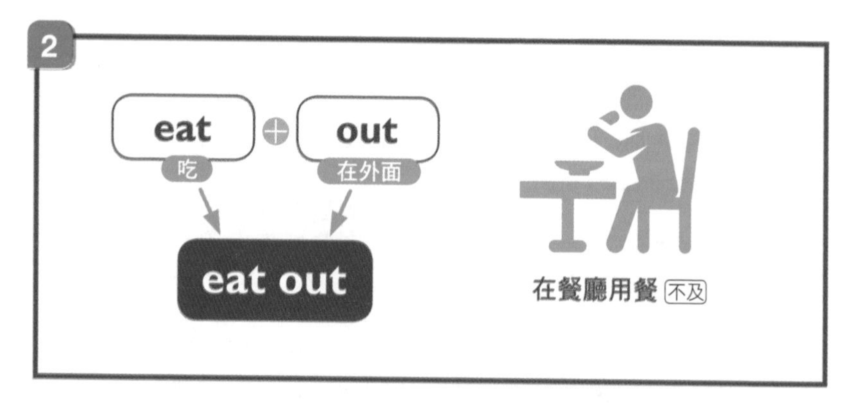

- There's nothing good to eat at home, so let's **eat out** for dinner.
  家裡沒有什麼好吃的東西，所以我們**到外面吃飯**。
- When I lived in Seattle, I used to **eat out** all the time.
  我住在西雅圖的時候，都**在外面吃飯**。

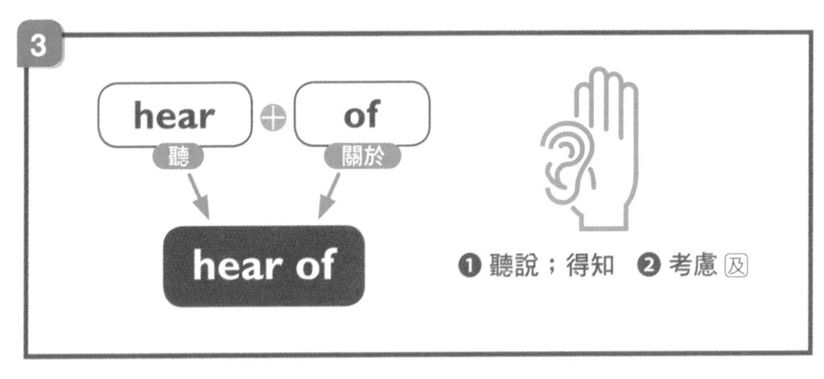

❶ Before my trip to Africa, I had never **heard of** Madagascar. 到非洲旅遊前，我從沒**聽說**過馬達加斯加島。

❶ There are many classical musicians whom I've never **heard of**. 有許多古典音樂家我都沒有**聽**過。

❷ Damien wanted to go out with his friends Wednesday night, but his mother wouldn't **hear of** it because he had school the next day. 戴明恩星期三晚上想要和朋友出去，但他媽媽因為隔天要上課所以不**同意**。

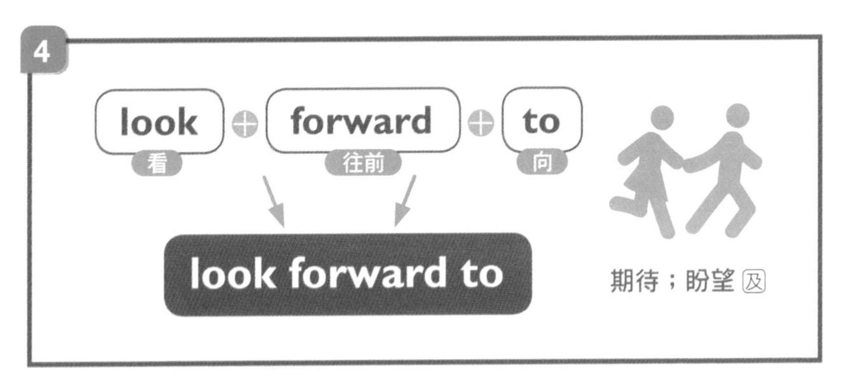

- I always **look forward to** three-day weekends because I am able to do some traveling.
我總是**盼望**著一連三天的週末到來，那樣我就可以出外旅遊。

- My little brother is **looking forward to** his birthday party. 我的小弟**期待**著生日派對的到來。

055

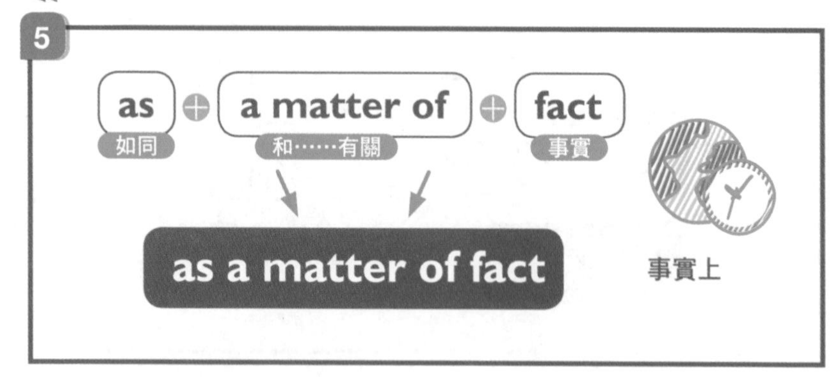

- **As a matter of fact**, Martin recently graduated from college. **事實上**，馬汀最近大學畢業了。
- Cindy just got a new TV, **as a matter of fact**.
事實上，辛蒂才剛買了一台新的電視。

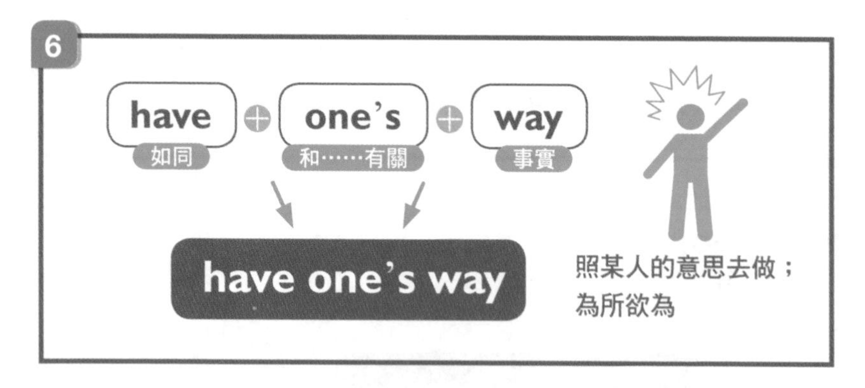

- Sometimes it feels like I never **have my way**.
我有時覺得天不**從人願**。
- Because Carol is the youngest child, she always **has her way**. 卡蘿是家中的么女，所以她好像老是**為所欲為**。

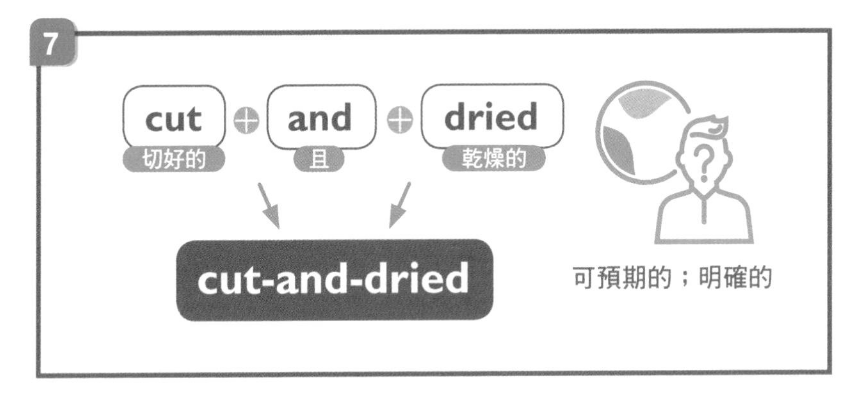

- After the discussion, the CEO reached a **cut-and-dried** decision. 討論結束後，執行長得到了一個**預料中**的結論。
- The choices we make in life are rarely as **cut-and-dried** as we would like.
  我們在人生中所做的選擇，通常是無法**預期的**。

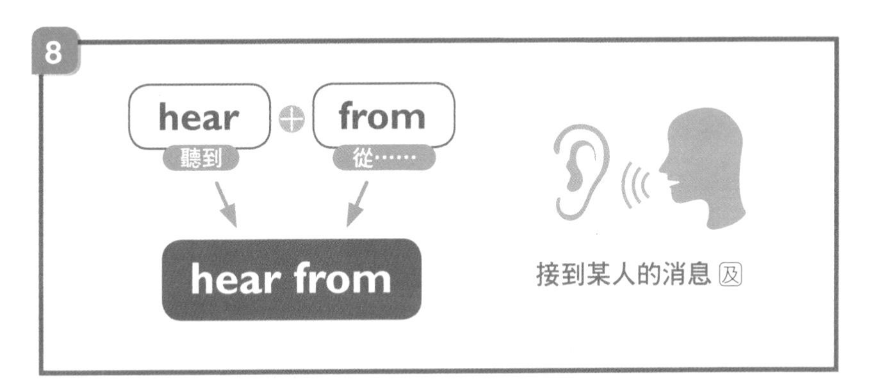

- I hope Ray is okay. I haven't **heard from** him since he arrived in the United Kingdom.
  我希望雷沒事。自從他去了英國，我就沒**聽到**他的**消息**。
- Teresa expects to **hear from** Samuel next week.
  泰瑞莎盼望下星期能**接到**山姆爾**的消息**。

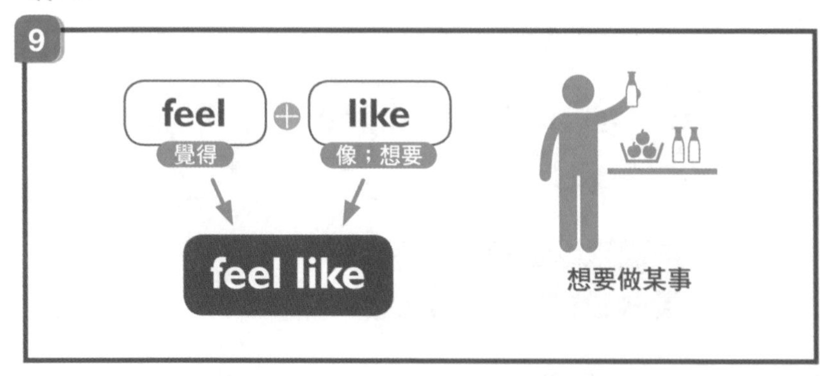

- Do you **feel like** going to the movies tonight?
  你今晚**想要**看電影嗎？
- I don't **feel like** going out for Chinese food; my stomach hurts.
  我今晚不**想**出去吃中國菜，我胃痛。

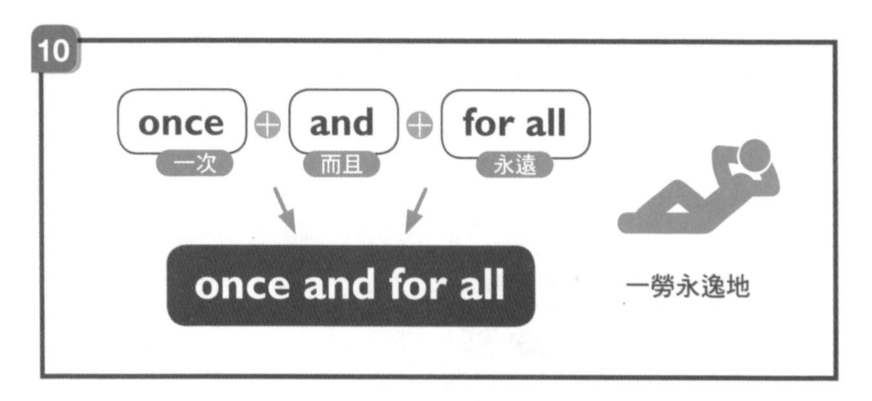

- As soon as Jared stapled the pages of his report together, he knew he was done with it **once and for all**. 傑瑞德把報告裝訂好後，便了解到他終於把它完成了。

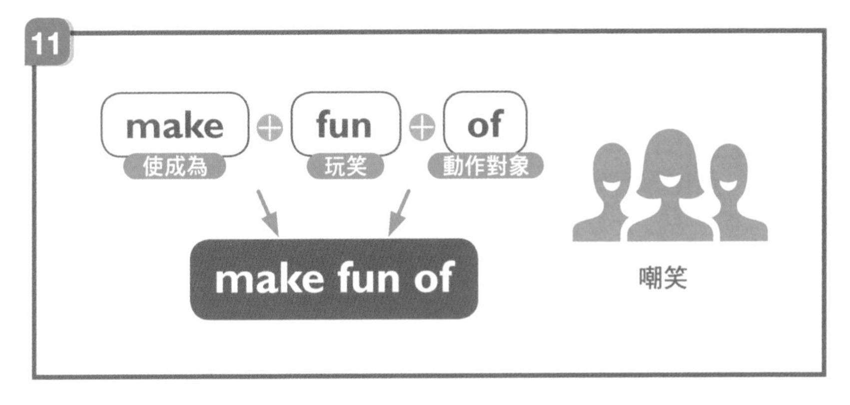

- Diane's new suit was so unusual that it was hard not to **make fun of** her.
  黛安新買的套裝很奇怪，令人很難不去**取笑**她。

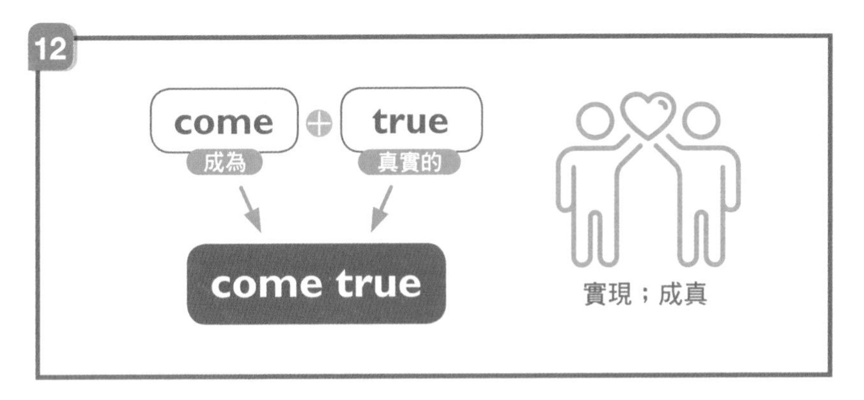

- Although Warren always dreamed of buying a Ferrari, he never thought the dream would **come true**.
  雖然華倫常常幻想能買一輛法拉利，但他從沒想過會**實現**。
- The party was everything I had hoped for; it was as if all my wishes **had come true**.
  這個派對就是我想要的，假如我的願望都能**成真**的話。
- The good things we've been hoping for are actually **coming true**. 我們一直期望的好事真的**實現**了。

School Life
學校生活

Raul and Emily gossip about school life.
勞爾和艾蜜莉在討論學校生活的八卦。

057

Emily: Did you hear what happened with the teacher who is **filling in**[1] for Ms. Santos today?

Raul: No. What happened?

Emily: She arrived for her first day of teaching with her shirt **inside out**[2]!

Raul: Ha, ha, ha! That's funny! Is she a good teacher at least?

Emily: Yeah, she's ok. First she made us **fill out**[3] some forms, and while we were doing that, she left for a few minutes. Some people started making jokes and talking. When she came back, she was mad.

Raul: What did she say?

Emily: She said that she is **in touch**[4] with Ms. Santos, and if we don't behave, she'll **take** this problem **up with**[5] her personally.

Raul: It may be tempting for the students to **take advantage of**[6] the situation now, but **in the long run**[7], it isn't a good idea. Ms. Santos isn't a forgiving person!

艾蜜莉： 你聽說今天**代替**山托斯女士的那位老師所發生的事情了嗎？

勞爾： 沒有，怎麼了？

艾蜜莉： 她第一天代課就把襯衫**穿反**了！

勞爾： 哈哈哈！真好笑！至少她是個好老師吧？

艾蜜莉： 是啊，她還不錯。她一開始要我們**填寫**一些表格，我們在填的時候，她離開了一下子。有些人便開始講話和開玩笑，所以她回來後就生氣了。

勞爾： 那她說了些什麼？

艾蜜莉： 她說如果我們表現不好，她會**和**山托斯女士**聯絡**，然後當面**和**她**商量**。

勞爾： 現在這種情形其實**對**學生很**有利**，但這**終究**不是一個好主意。山托斯女士並不是一個性情溫和的人！

058

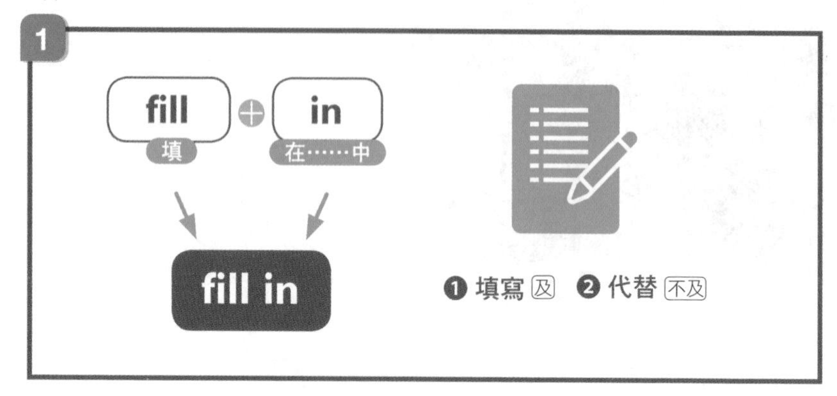

❶ The directions on the test were to **fill in** the spaces with the correct answers.
作答方式為在試卷上的空格**填入**正確答案。

❷ I'm not his regular secretary—I'm just **filling in**.
我並不是他固定的秘書，我只是來**代班**的。

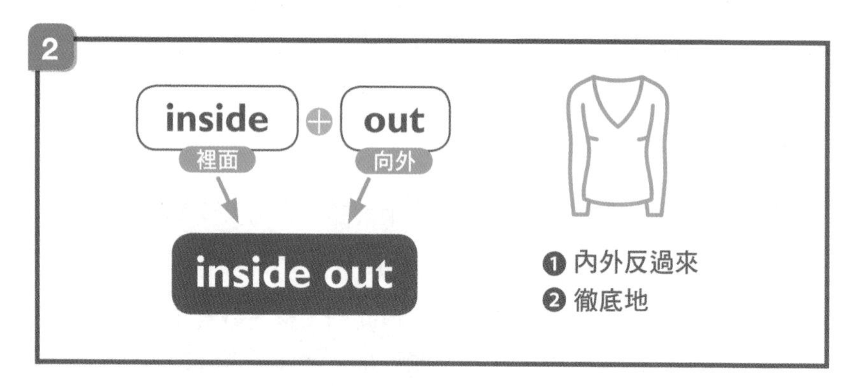

❶ How embarrassing it was to arrive at school with my pants **inside out**.
我到學校才發現把褲子穿**反**了，真糗。

❶ She had her sweater on **inside out**.
她把毛衣穿**反**了。

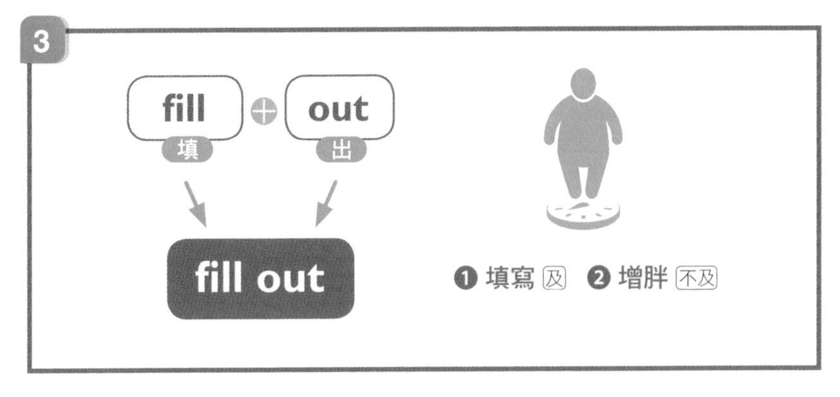

❶ If you want to apply for a passport, you have to **fill out** many forms. 如果你想申請護照，必須要**填寫**許多表格。

❶ All students must **fill** this document **out** before taking the SAT. 所有參加 SAT 考試的學生都必須先**填寫**這份文件。

❷ Her figure began to **fill out** once she started college. 她上大學後便開始**增胖**了。

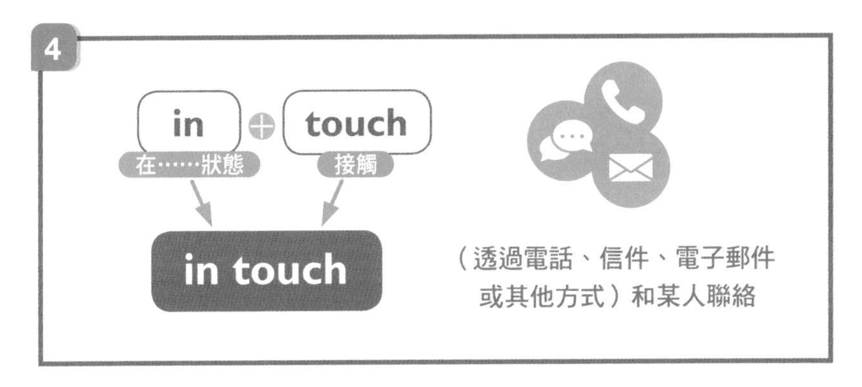

- Katherine and I have been **in touch** since high school. 我和凱瑟琳從高中到現在一直都有**聯絡**。
- I want to keep **in touch** with you even after I move away. 我就算搬家也想和你**聯絡**。

059

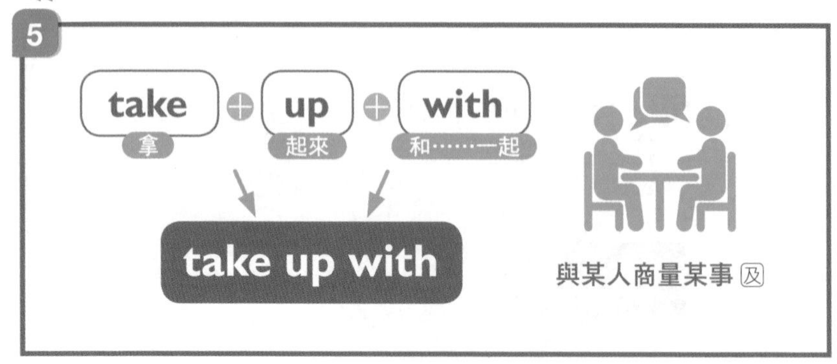

- I think it's time to **take up** the issue of a raise **with** my boss. 我想我該和老闆**商量**加薪的事情了。
- If you don't like the policy, **take** it **up with** the manager. 如果你不喜歡這項政策，就和經理**商量**。

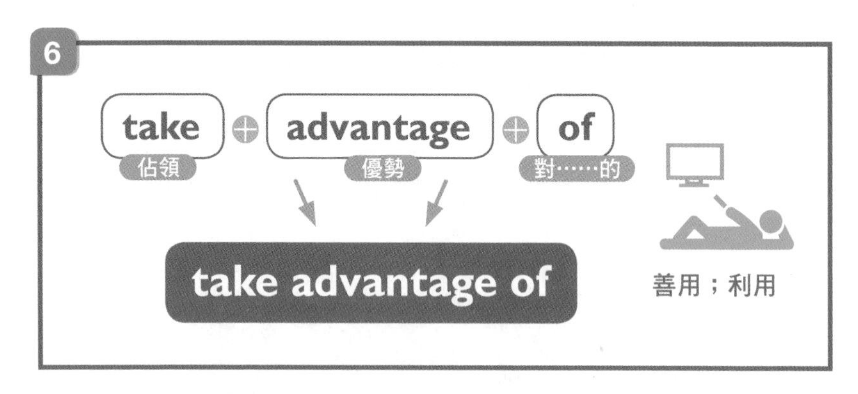

- Suzanna **took advantage of** the gym on campus and worked out every day.
  蘇珊娜**善用**學校的健身房，她每天都去健身。
- I think he **takes advantage of** her good nature.
  我覺得他在**利用**她善良的本性。
- I thought Francesca was nice until I saw how she **took advantage of** Dale and made him do all her work.
  在我發現法蘭西絲卡**利用**戴爾替她完成所有的工作前，我一直以為她是個好人。

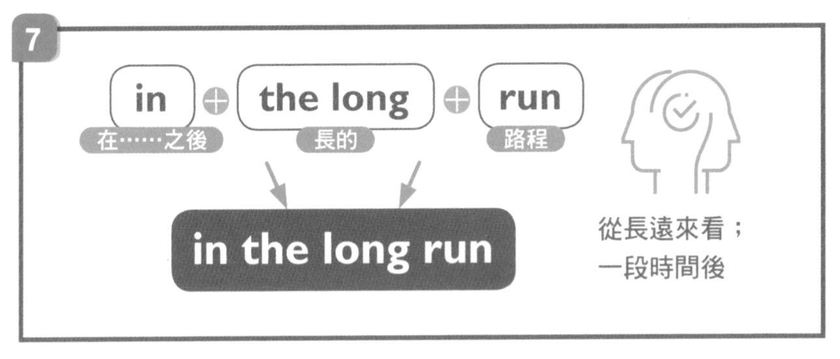

7
in
在……之後
the long
長的
run
路程
in the long run
從長遠來看；
一段時間後

- You may not like the idea of getting braces, but **in the long run**, it is the right thing to do.
  你也許不喜歡戴矯正器，但**久了以後**你會發現這麼做是正確的。
- Buying these baby kittens may seem like a good idea now, but **in the long run**, it may be a mistake. 買小貓現在看來是一個好主意，但**一段時間後**你可能會覺得這是個錯誤。

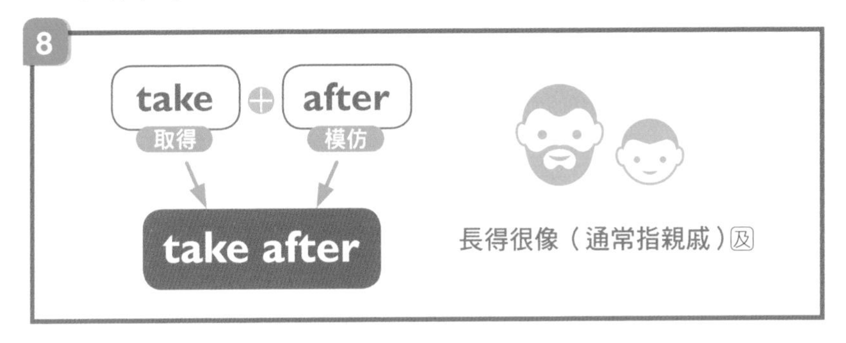

- Everyone tells me I **take after** my father because we are both tall and have red hair. 每個人都說我和父親**長得很像**，因為我們都很高，也都有一頭紅髮。
- Francine really **takes after** her older brother; they have such similar interests.
  法蘭欣和她哥哥真的**長得很像**，他們的興趣也很相近。
- Most of my children **take after** my wife, both in appearance and character.
  我孩子的外貌和個性都和我太太**很像**。
- Tina **takes after** her mother's side of the family.
  緹娜和她媽媽那邊的親戚**長得很像**。

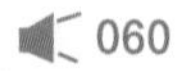

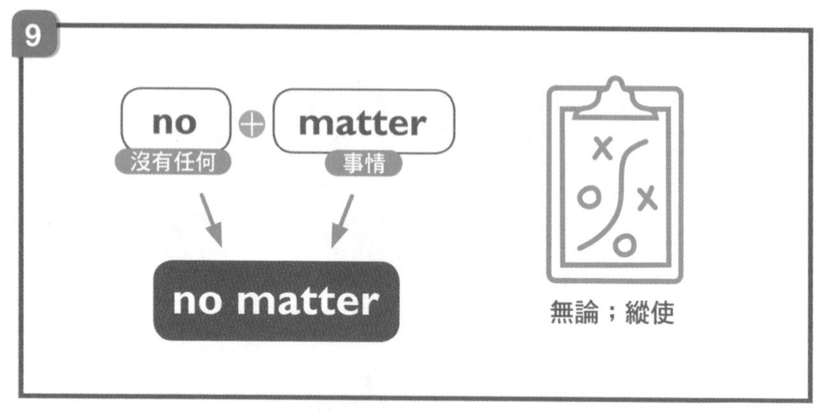

- I don't want to take any calls, **no matter** who it is.
  我不想接任何電話，**不管**誰打來都一樣。
- We'll definitely play basketball this weekend, **no matter** what the weather; we'll play even if it is raining!
  無論天氣如何，我們這週末一定會去打籃球，就算下雨也會去打球！

My Note

The New Neighbor
新鄰居

Tommy and Adrian talk about a new neighbor.
湯米和雅德恩娜在討論新鄰居。

061

Tommy: How are you getting along with your new neighbor, Mr. Dasey, these days?

Adrian: Well, to be honest, things aren't as bad as before. Although we don't always **see eye to eye**[1], we've been **making the best of**[2] things.

Tommy: That's good. **For once**[3], there doesn't seem to be any serious problem between you two.

Adrian: I **keep in mind**[4] that Mr. Dasey is an old man and that he's **hard of hearing**[5], so sometimes he doesn't understand everything I say. The only problem now is that he keeps the TV on very loud because of his hearing problems.

Tommy: I bet you'd like it if his TV suddenly **went off**[6] and never came back on.

Adrian: I'm not that mean!

湯米： 妳這幾天和妳的新鄰居戴西先生相處得如何？

雅德恩： 嗯，老實告訴你，比以前好多了。雖然我們的**看法**常常不**相同**，不過我們都**盡力**了。

湯米： 那很好啊。**至少這次**你們兩個之間沒什麼嚴重的問題。

雅德恩： 我會**記住**戴西先生是一個老人家，而且有**重聽**，所以有時會聽不懂我說的話。現在唯一的問題就是，由於他聽力很差，他老是把電視開得很大聲。

湯米： 我相信妳一定想要他的電視會突然**壞掉**，而且修不好。

雅德恩： 我沒那麼壞心！

see eye to eye 看法相同

hard of hearing 重聽

062

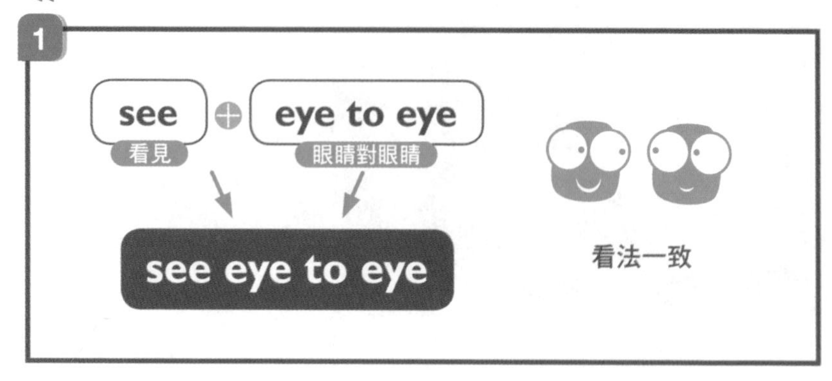

- Although Beth and I don't get along, we definitely **see eye to eye** on a lot of political issues.
  雖然我和貝絲處不來，但我們的政治理念許多都是**一致**的。

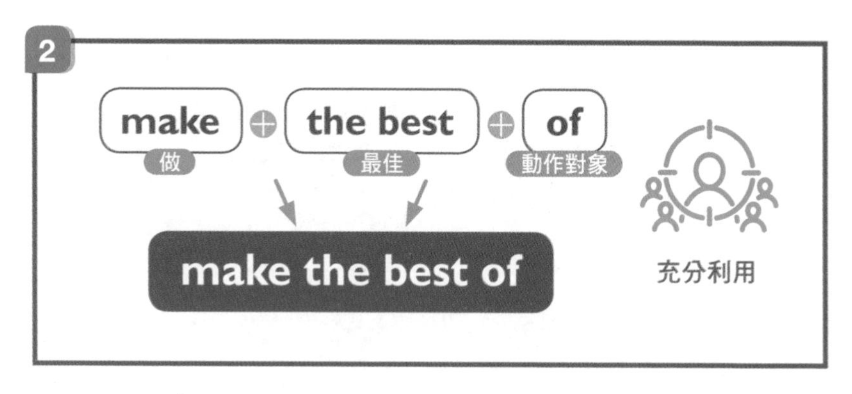

- Although it rained the entire time, we decided to **make the best of** our camping trip and went fishing and hiking. 這次露營雖然一直在下雨，我們還是決定**把握機會**去釣魚和健行。

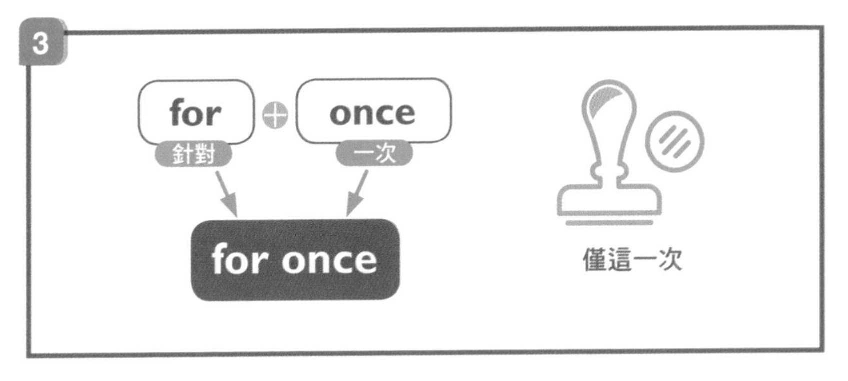

- **For once**, Darren arrived to class on time.
  戴倫就**這麼一次**準時到學校上課。

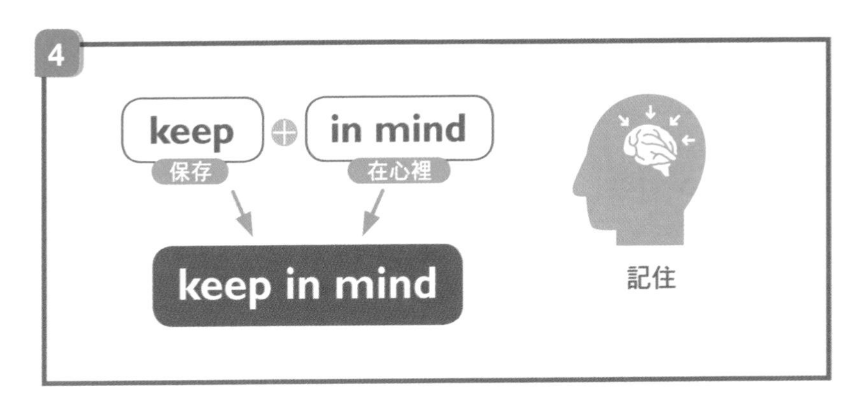

- Before you go out to the party this weekend, **keep in mind** that there is an exam on Monday .
  在你週末去參加派對前，**記住**星期一要考試。
- When you are making dinner, you must **keep in mind** that Anne's brother doesn't eat meat.
  你在準備晚餐時，要**記住**安的哥哥不吃肉。

063

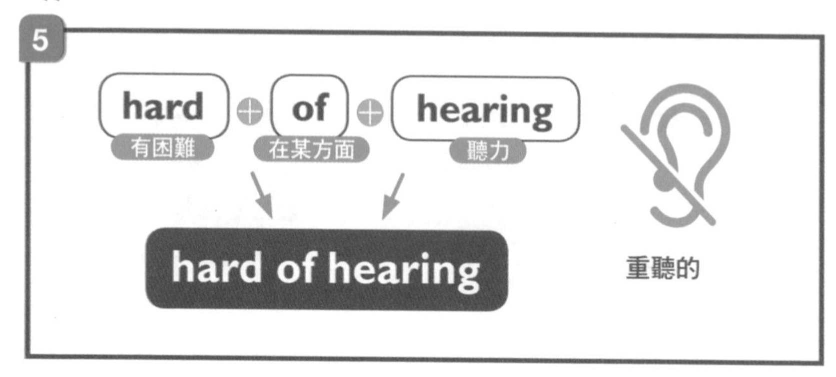

- When Erin's grandmother watches TV, she has to turn the volume way up because she is **hard of hearing**.
因為艾琳的奶奶**重聽**，所以她看電視時必須把音量轉很大聲。

- My father is quite old now, and he's increasingly **hard of hearing**. 我的父親年紀大了，**重聽**也越來越嚴重了。

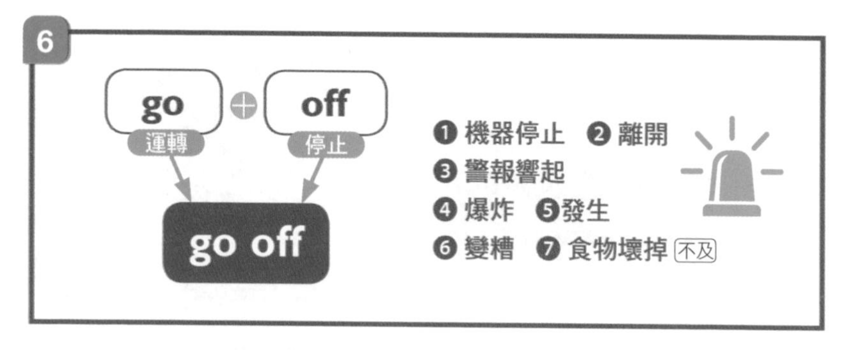

❶ During the thunderstorm, all the lights in the house suddenly **went off**.
暴風雨來臨時，屋內所有的照明突然都**斷**電了。

❷ I think Janet **went off** to the market a few minutes ago.
我想珍娜幾分鐘前才剛**離開**到市場去了。

❸ The alarm on Dean's wristwatch **goes off** every day at lunch. 狄恩手錶上的鬧鐘每天午餐時間都會**響**。

❹ The bomb **went off** at midnight. 炸彈在半夜的時候**爆炸**。

❺ The protest march **went off** peacefully with only two arrests. 示威遊行在和平中**進行**，只有兩個人被逮捕。

❻ That paper has really **gone off** since they got that new editor. 那家報社聘請了那位新編輯之後，品質就**變得很糟糕**。

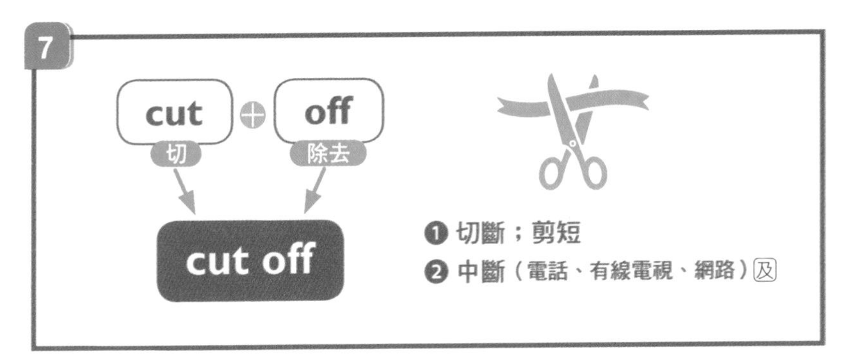

❶ Nina **cut off** the top of the carrots before cooking them. 妮娜在煮紅蘿蔔前先**去頭**。

❷ When Todd stopped paying his bills, the company **cut off** his Internet connection so he couldn't go online anymore. 陶德停付帳單後，電信公司便**中斷**了他的網路，所以他再也不能上網了。

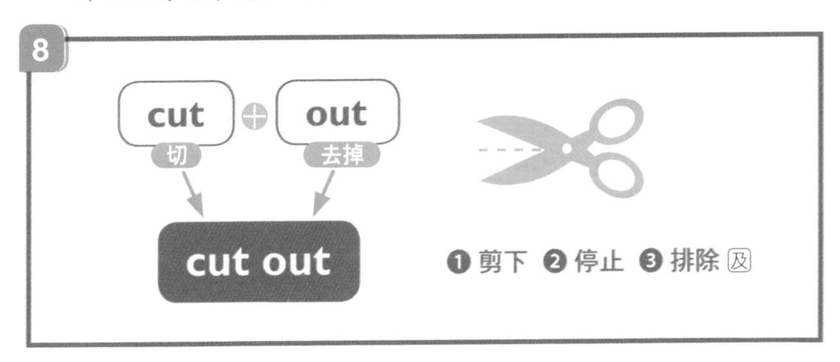

❶ Nelly **cut** her ex-boyfriend **out** of all the photos she had of them. 奈莉把所有前男友的照片都**剪掉**。

❷ Phillip, will you **cut** that **out**! I can't study if you're making noise. 菲力普，你能**停止**嗎！你這麼吵我沒辦法唸書。

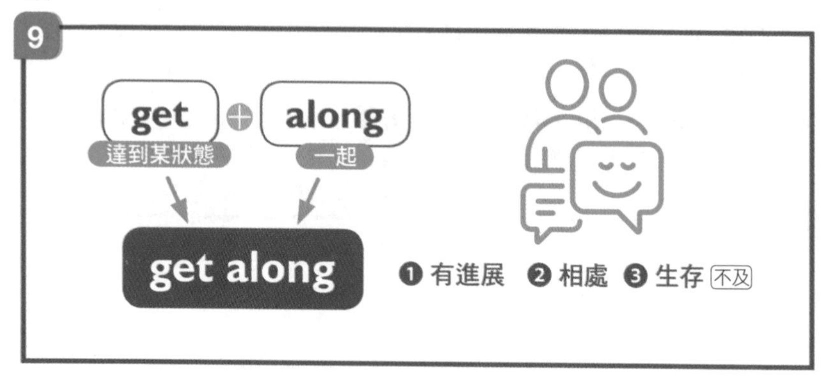

❸ It's hard **getting along** in a new city.
在陌生的城市中很難**生存**。

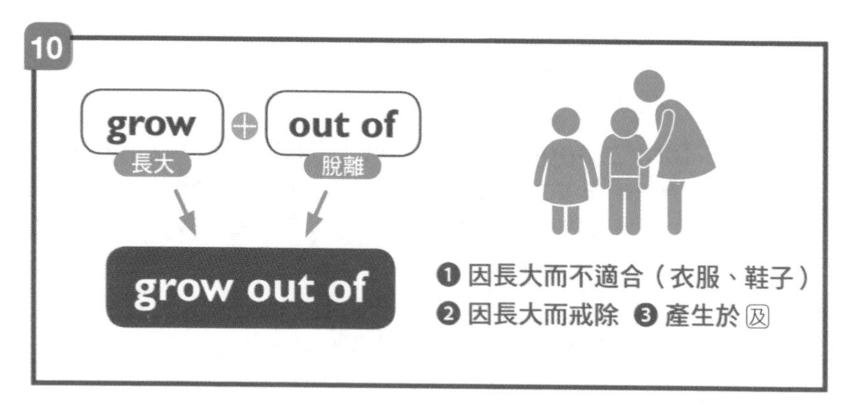

10
grow
長大
out of
脫離
grow out of
❶ 因長大而不適合（衣服、鞋子）
❷ 因長大而戒除 ❸ 產生於 及

❶ The new mother didn't want to spend too much money on shoes for her baby because she knew he'd **grow out of** them quickly.
新手媽媽不想要花太多錢買寶寶的鞋子，因為她知道他**長大後**很快就會**穿不下**。

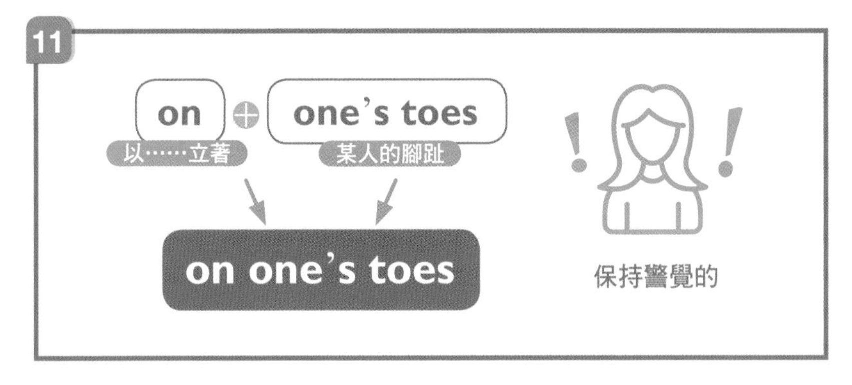

- Having twins really keeps my mom **on her toes**.
  有雙胞胎小孩真的讓我媽變得**非常小心**。

The Surprise Party
驚喜派對

Rob and Gale discuss a surprise party.
羅伯和格兒在討論一場驚喜派對。

065

Gale: It's funny to think that just two days ago, I was convinced that celebrating my birthday was a **lost cause**[1].

Rob: What do you mean?

Gale: Well, I had invited my friends over, but they all **turned** me **down**[2].

Rob: That's terrible!

Gale: It was! Then, as my dad and I were **shutting up**[3] his shop last night, I heard some strange noises.

Rob: Oh! Was someone **breaking in**[4]?

Gale: No, it was a surprise party! My dad and my friends were there with a cake, so I made a wish and **blew out**[5] the candles.

Rob: That sounds like a big shock; **above all**[6], it sounds like you had a great time!

格兒： 現在回想起來很好笑，但兩天前，我還覺得要好好慶祝我的生日是**不可能**的事情呢。

羅伯： 什麼意思？

格兒： 唔，我那時邀請我的朋友，但他們全都**拒絕**了我。

羅伯： 真糟糕！

格兒： 本來很糟！然而，昨晚我和我老爸在**關**店時，我聽到一些奇怪的聲音。

羅伯： 噢！有人**闖進去**了嗎？

格兒： 不，是個驚喜派對！我爸和我朋友都在那裡，還有一個蛋糕，所以我許了願望，然後把蠟燭**吹熄**。

羅伯： 聽起來像是個超級大驚喜。**最重要的是**，妳似乎度過了一段很愉快的時光！

turn down 拒絕

break in 闖入

066

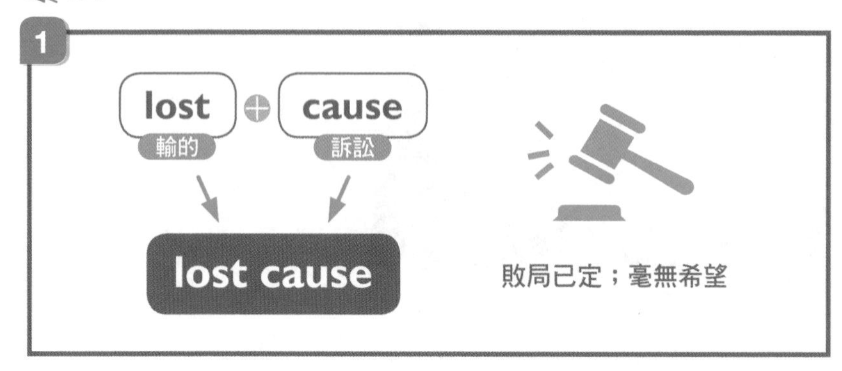

- I tutored Jane every day for a few months, but when I realized it was a **lost cause**, I gave up. 我每天教珍功課已經好幾個月了，但當我發現**毫無幫助**時便放棄了。
- Arnold practiced the trumpet every day for three months, but finally he decided it was a **lost cause** and sold it. 阿諾三個月來每天練習吹喇叭，但最後他認為**沒有希望**便把它賣掉了。
- Gina has already made up her mind, and it's a **lost cause** to try to change it.
吉娜已經下定決心了，想要使她改變心意是**不可能的**。

❶ When Mike asked Barbra to the dance, she **turned** him **down**. 當麥可邀請芭芭拉跳舞時，她**拒絕**了他。

❶ Ryan **turned down** the job because it involved too much traveling. 萊恩因為這份工作需要常出差，所以**拒絕**了。

❷ Please **turn down** the volume on the computer; I can't concentrate when you are playing video games.
請把電腦的音量**轉小**，你打電動會讓我無法專心。

❶ Before leaving for the night, the manager **shut up** the shop. 經理晚上離開前把店門**關上**。（英式用法）

❷ Please **shut up**! I'm trying to study.
請**閉嘴**！我在試著唸書呢。

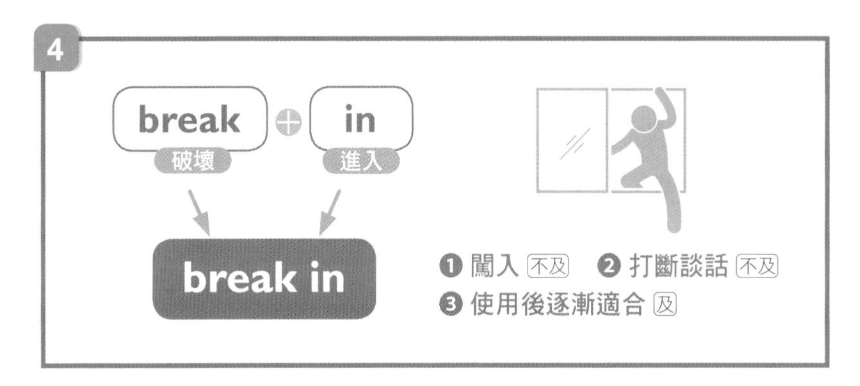

❶ Ralph was shocked to find that someone had **broken in** and stolen his laptop.
瑞夫發現有人**闖入**，並且偷走他的筆記型電腦時，他很震驚。

❷ Fran **broke in** on the conversation and asked my name. 法蘭**打斷**了談話並問了我的名字。

067

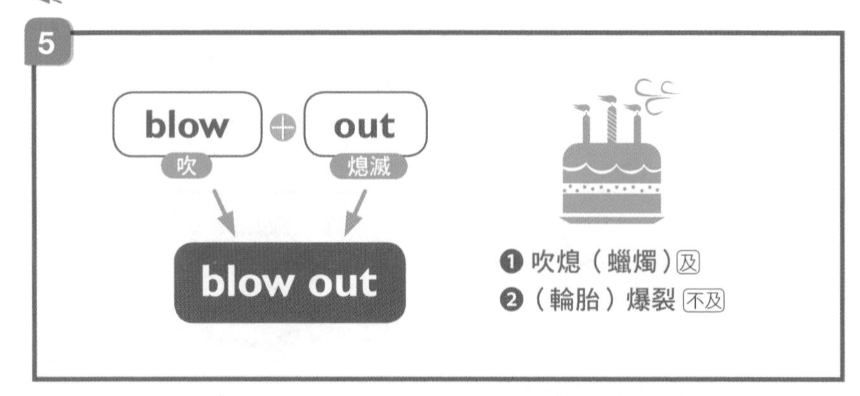

❶ Steve took a deep breath and **blew out** all the candles on his birthday cake. 史帝夫做了一個深呼吸，然後把生日蛋糕上所有的蠟燭都**吹熄**了。

❶ Richie lit a cigarette and quickly **blew** the match **out**. 瑞奇點燃香菸後，立刻把火柴**吹熄**。

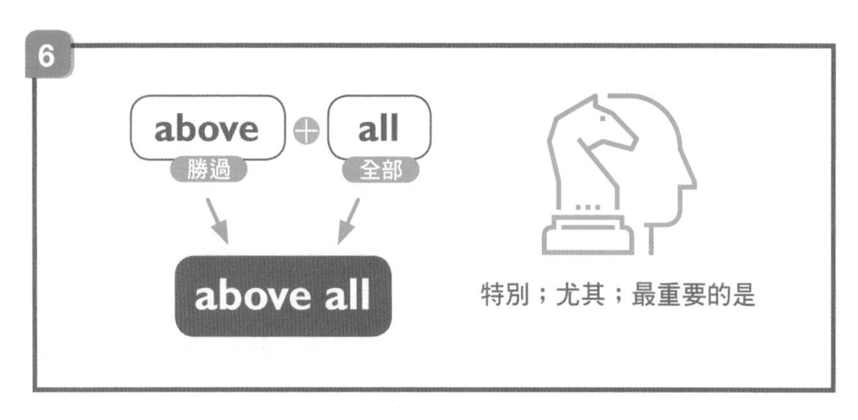

- Mindy is a nice girl—she's hard-working, clever, and **above all**, honest. 敏蒂是個好女孩，她做事認真、聰明，**最重要的是**，她很誠實。
- She loved swimming and jogging; but **above all**, she loved her family. 她熱愛游泳和慢跑，但**最重要的是**，她愛她的家人。

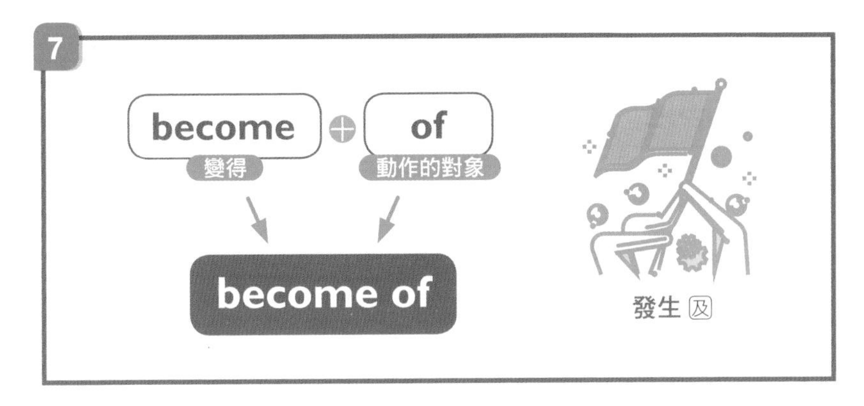

- After she moved to Egypt, Aunt Sarah stopped sending letters, and no one knew what **became of** her.
  莎拉阿姨自從搬到埃及後便不再來信，所以沒人知道她**發生**了什麼事。
- I'm not sure that we'll ever know what **became of** my cat after it ran away.
  我的貓不見後，我不確定我們是否能知道牠**發生**了什麼事。

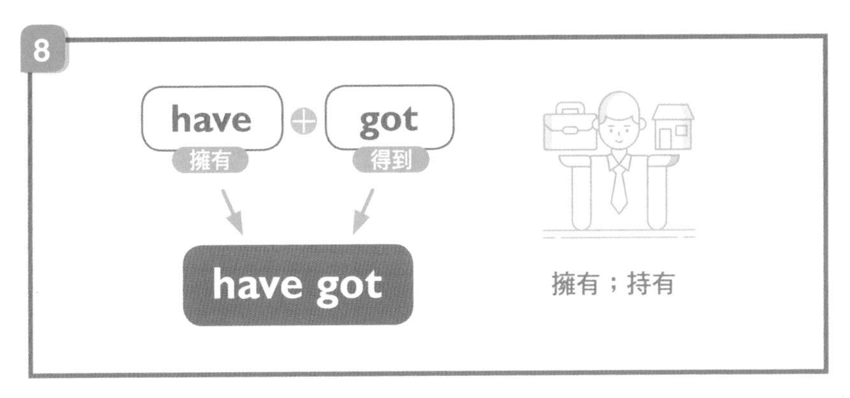

- I **have gotten** a new bicycle, and I am riding it every day.
  我**得到**一台新腳踏車，而且我每天都會騎它。
- What **have** you **got** in your bag? 你的包包裡**有**什麼？

068

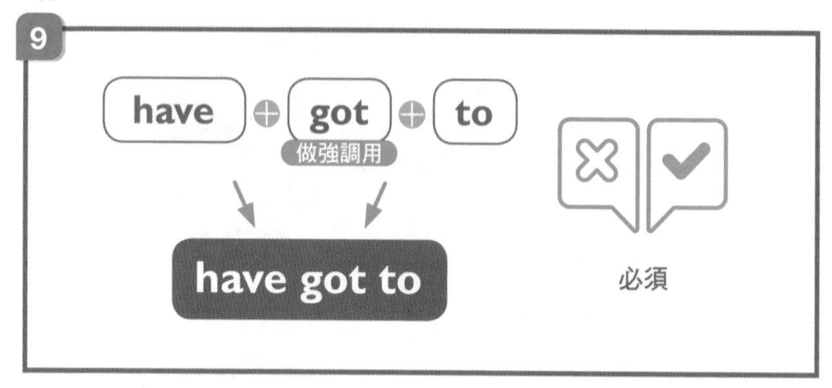

- I **have got to** get to class now, or I'll be in trouble.
  我現在**必須**去上課，不然會有麻煩。
- Frank **has got to** leave the party before 8, or he'll miss his bus home.
  法蘭克**必須**在八點前離開派對，否則他會錯過回家的公車。

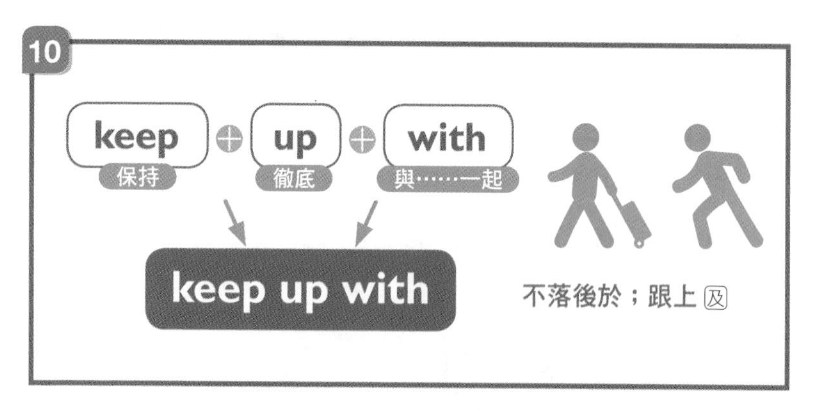

- Terrance walks so fast, it's hard to **keep up with** him sometimes.
  泰倫斯走路很快，有時候要**跟上**他的腳步很難。

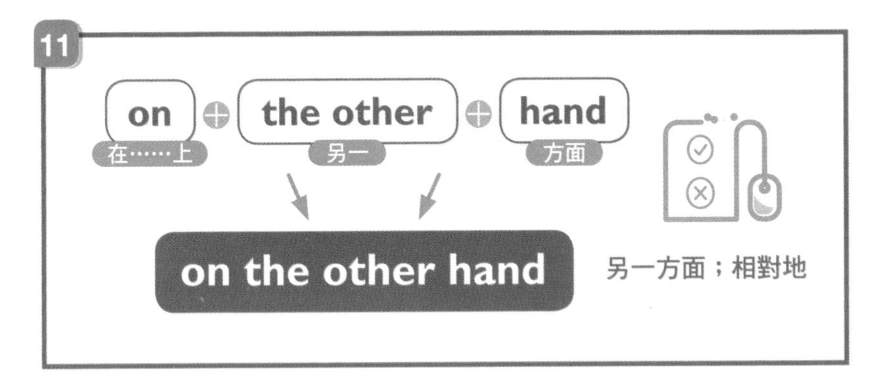

- That car looks so cool, but **on the other hand**, it is very expensive. 那台車看起來真酷，但**另一方面**，它也很貴。
- I was happy we bought a new flat screen TV, but **on the other hand**, it was so big I didn't know where we would put it.
  我很高興我們買了一台平面電視，但**另一方面**，因為它很大台，所以我不知道要把它擺在哪裡。

Unit 18

Finding a Lost Dog
尋狗啟示

Sally and Mohammed talk about a lost dog.
莎莉和穆罕默德在談論走丟的狗狗。

069

Sally: Have you seen my dog, Rex? I've been looking for him all day.

Mohammed: No, but **according to**[1] my neighbor, there was a dog digging in our garden earlier.

Sally: That **is bound to**[2] be Rex!

Mohammed: How did he get away, anyway?

Sally: Well, when we **ran out of**[3] dog food, my mom sent me to the store to buy some more. I opened the door and **was about to**[4] go out when Rex just ran away.

Mohammed: Oh man! Let's go to my house and see if he's around there.

Sally: I hope so. It'll feel nice to **tear up**[5] all these "Lost Dog" signs once I get Rex back.

莎莉： 你有看到我的狗狗雷克斯嗎？我已經找他找了一整天了。

穆罕默德： 沒有，但**根據**鄰居的說法，之前有隻狗在我家院子裡挖洞。

莎莉： 那**肯定**是雷克斯！

穆罕默德： 話說他是怎麼不見的？

莎莉： 就是我們家的狗飼料**沒**了，我媽要我去商店買。我**正好**打開門要出去，雷克斯就跑了出去。

穆罕默德： 噢，天啊！那我們去我家那看他是否還在那裡吧。

莎莉： 希望他還在。只要找到了雷克斯，就可以開開心心地把這些尋狗啟示給**撕掉**了。

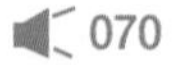

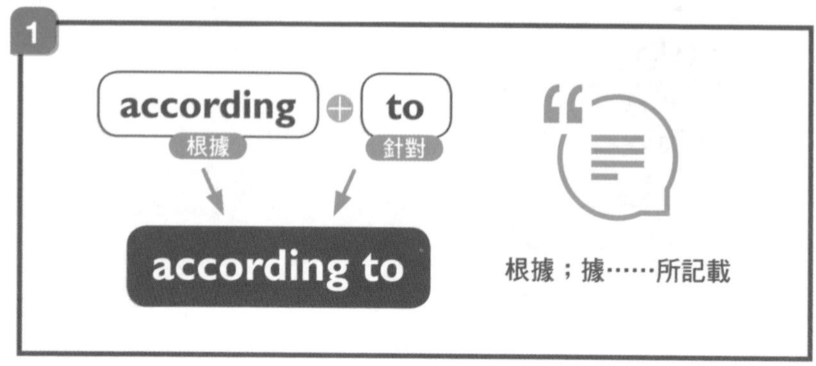

- **According to** many scientists, it will be possible to live on Mars one day.
  根據多位科學家的說法，人類也許有一天能夠居住在火星上。
- You've spelled the word incorrectly **according to** the dictionary. **根據**字典上所寫，你拼錯字了

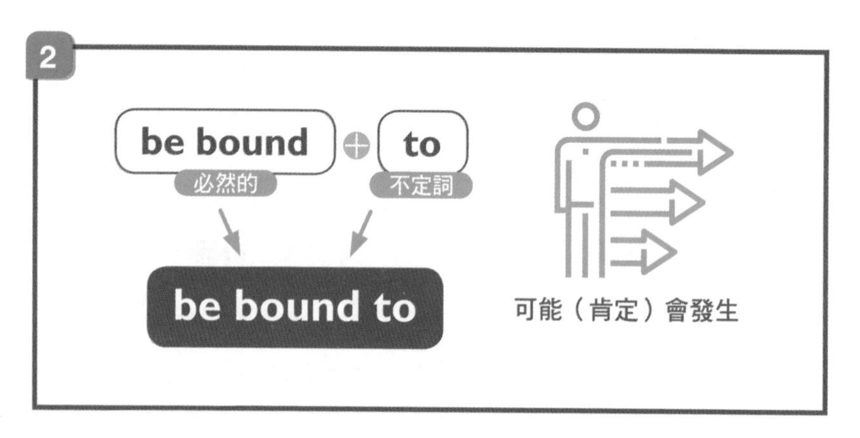

- With all the traffic tonight, Craig **is bound to** arrive late.
  今晚大塞車，克雷格**鐵定**會遲到。

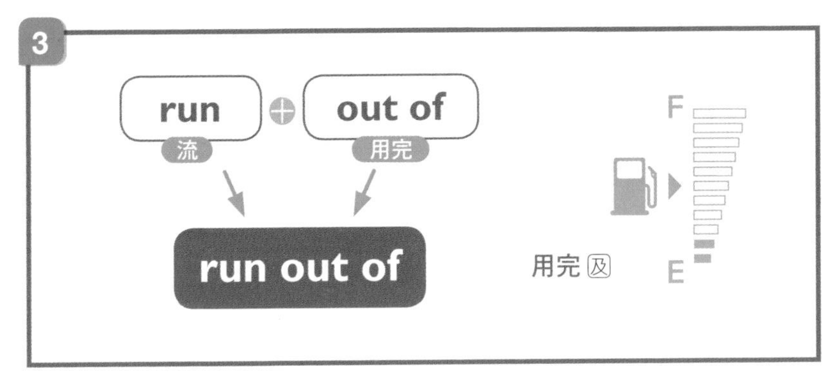

- So many people came to our restaurant yesterday that we **ran out of** eggs.
  昨晚餐廳的生意很好，所以我們的雞蛋都**用完**了。

- When Gina's grandpa **ran out of** coffee, he sent her to the store to buy more.
  吉娜的爺爺**喝完**咖啡後，便要吉娜到商店再多買一些。

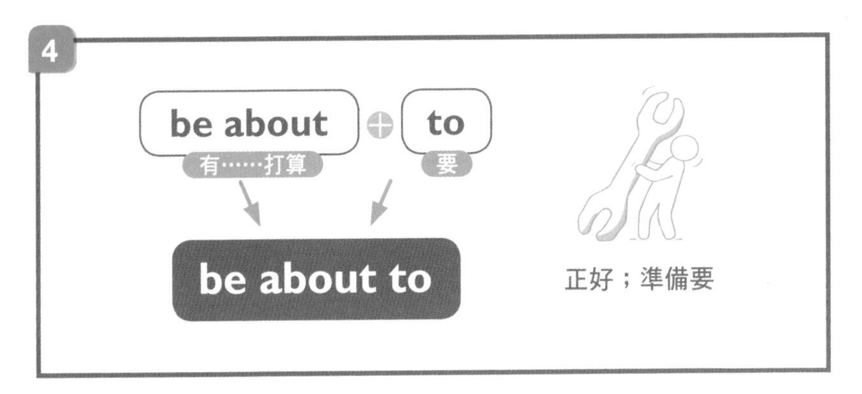

- I **was about to** call my girlfriend when she knocked on my door.
  我女朋友敲我的房門時，我**正好要**打電話給她。

- Diane **is about to** have her first baby.
  黛安**就快要**生第一胎了。

071

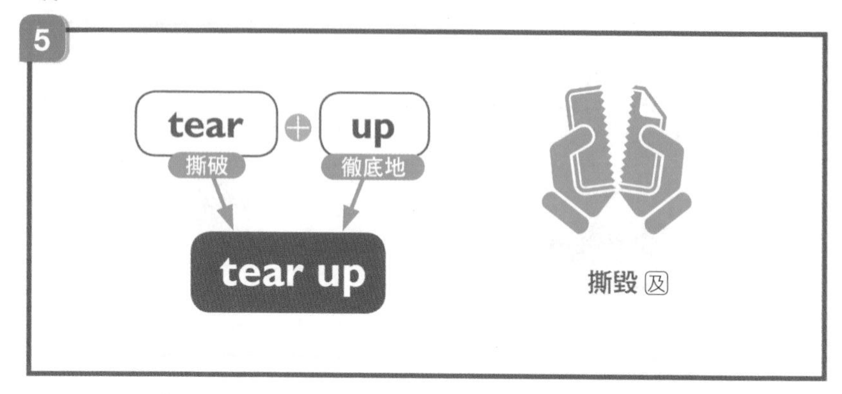

- When Florence got an "F" on her essay, she **tore** it **up** before her mom could see it.
  佛羅倫絲的作文得到了「F」，所以她在媽媽看到前就先**撕掉**了。
- After Eric broke up with his girlfriend, he **tore up** all the love letters she had sent him.
  艾瑞克和女朋友分手後，他把所有她寄的情書都**撕掉**了。

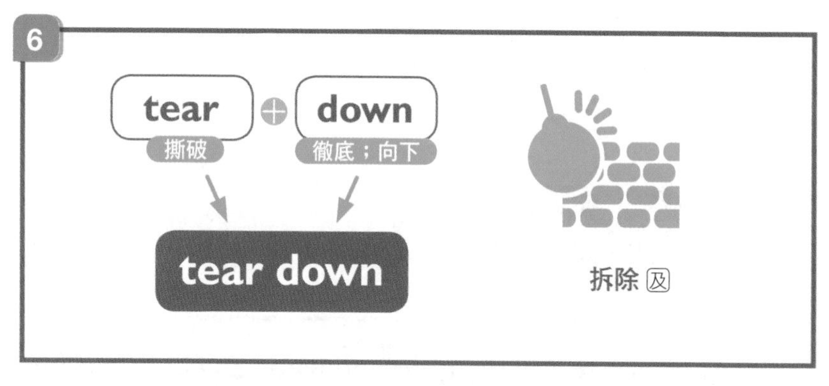

- The family **tore down** some of the old walls before adding a new room to the house.
  這戶人家在蓋新房間前，把一些舊的牆**拆掉**。
- Because the tree house seemed unsafe for the children, Mr. Grey **tore** it **down**.
  對孩子來說，樹屋好像很不安全，所以蓋瑞先生把它**拆掉**了。

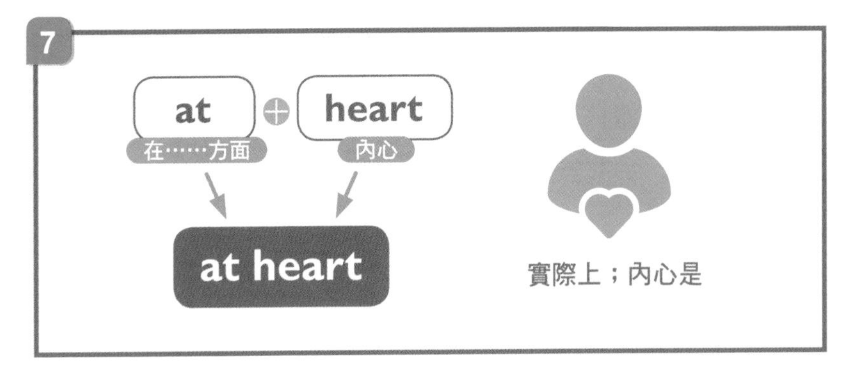

- Although Mr. Williams may act grumpy, he's a good guy **at heart**.
  雖然威廉斯先生性情乖戾，然而他**實際上**是個好人。

- No matter how much bad news I read, I still believe that most people are good **at heart**. 無論看了多少不好的新聞，我還是相信大部分人的**內心**都是善良的。

- Jessica will win the race **for sure**; she's a fast runner.
  潔西卡**肯定**會贏得比賽，她跑得很快。

- We're coming to visit you **for sure** this weekend.
  我們這星期**肯定**會去拜訪你的。

072

❶ Mr. Belvedere's first class was long and boring, so it didn't **go over** very well.
貝維德雷先生的第一堂課既漫長又無趣，因此不太**被接受**。

❸ Let's **go over** the article one more time before the test.
我們在考試前再把文章**複習**一遍吧。

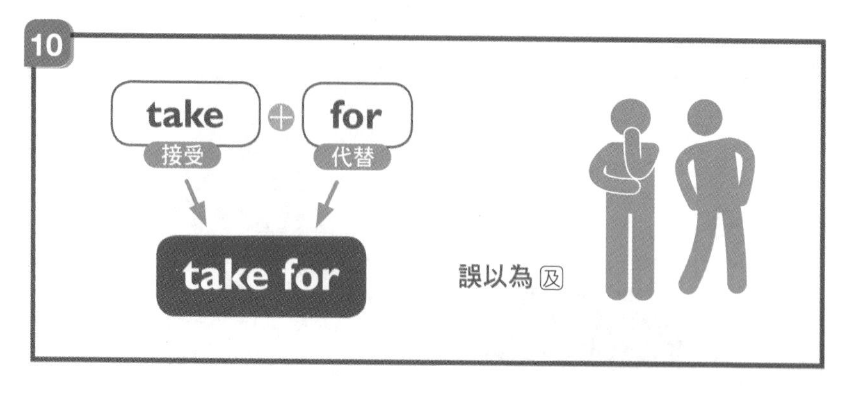

- After Roxanne made a big mistake, some teachers **took** her **for** a fool; however, she's very clever. 在羅姍妮犯下大錯後，有些老師把她**當**傻瓜，但其實她非常聰明。
- Do you **take** me **for** a fool? 你**以為**我是傻瓜嗎？
- I **took** her **for** Mrs. White. 我把她**誤認為**懷特太太。

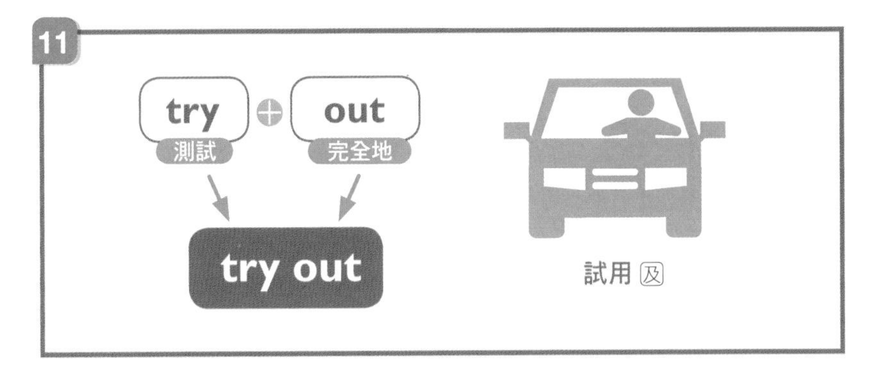

- Before you buy a new scooter, you should **try** it **out** to make sure you like it.
  買新摩托車前最好要先**試騎**，以便確定你是真的喜歡。
- Do you want to **try out** my new digital camera?
  你想要**試用看看**我新買的數位相機嗎？
- Don't forget to **try out** the equipment before setting up the experiment. 開始實驗前別忘了先**測試**一下儀器。

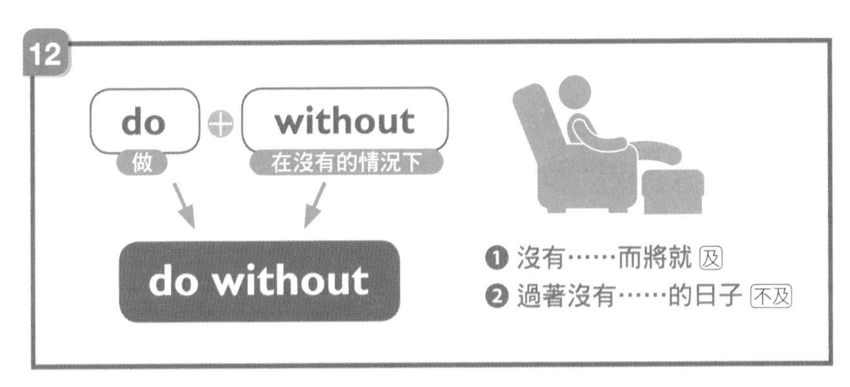

❶ When Brenda lost her job, the family had to learn to **do without** many luxuries.
布蘭達丟了工作後，她的家人必須要學會**放棄**許多奢侈品。

❷ While spending the summer in China, Bill had to **do without** some of his favorite foods.
比爾在中國度過夏天時，必須要**放棄**他最愛的食物。

Unit

19 Applying to a University 申請大學

Leo and Catherine talk about applying to a university. 里歐和凱瑟琳在討論申請大學的事情。

073

Leo: So, did you get any university acceptance letters yet?

Catherine: No, I didn't. I'm afraid **putting up with**[1] all the boring applications that the guidance counselor **passed out**[2] and comparing all the different programs was **in vain**[3].

Leo: You haven't received any replies yet? Oh man! I bet that is all you think about **day in and day out**[4].

Catherine: You better believe it! I've applied to so many colleges, I can't **tell** their names **apart**[5].

Leo: Maybe you should have focused on just two or three schools and put more effort into the applications.

Catherine: I suppose so. **All in all**[6], I should have thought about this more carefully.

里歐：　妳接到任何一所大學的入學許可了嗎？

凱瑟琳：　沒有。我**受不了**指導老師**發**的無聊申請書，還有**白費力氣**比較所有不同的課程。

里歐：　妳還沒收到回覆嗎？ 噢，老天！我敢肯定妳**每天**都在想這件事情吧。

凱瑟琳：　沒錯！我申請了好幾間大學，但**分**不**清楚**它們的名字。

里歐：　也許妳應該專心申請兩、三家學校就好，然後多做點努力。

凱瑟琳：　我想也是。**總之**，我應該再仔細想一想。

pass out 分發

tell the twins apart 辨別雙胞胎

074

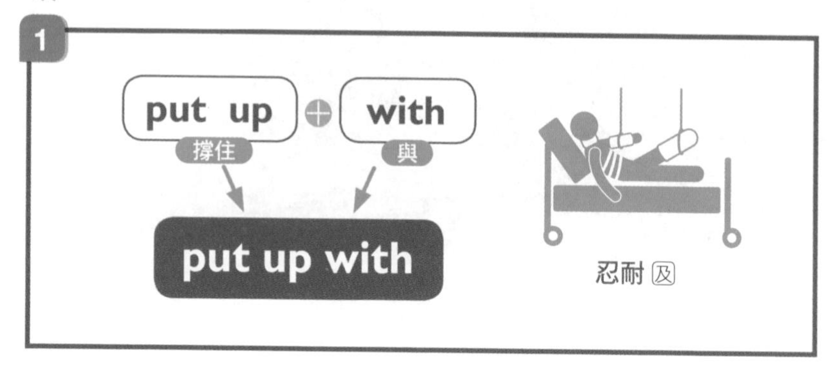

- When Rich moved near the highway, he had a hard time **putting up with** the noise.
瑞奇搬到公路附近後，他無法**忍受**噪音。

- After a long, tough day at school, it is sometimes hard to **put up with** my little sister.
在學校過了漫長又艱難的一天後，我有時會無法**忍受**我妹妹。

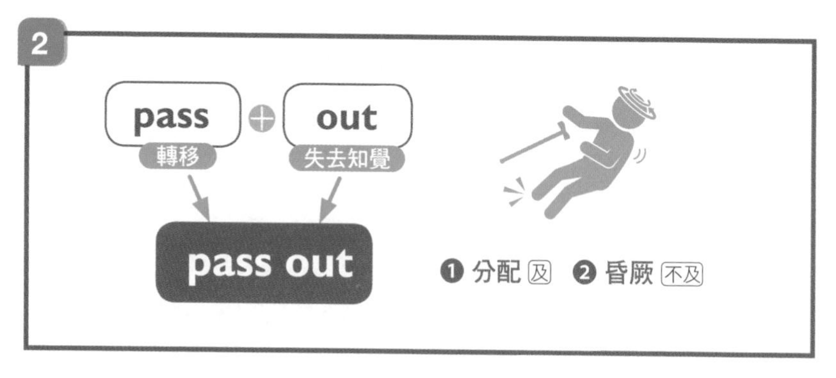

❶ Please **pass out** these forms to everyone who comes to the meeting. 請把這些表格**發**給所有出席這次會議的人。

❶ The professor asked Mindy to **pass out** a test to each student. 教授要敏蒂把考卷**發**給每一位學生。

❷ When a baseball hit Martha in the head during the game, she **passed out** for a few minutes.
馬莎在比賽中被棒球打到，**昏**過去好幾分鐘了。

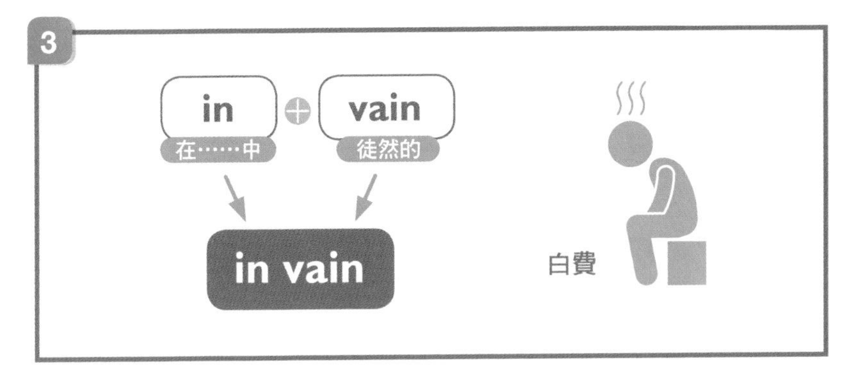

- Two weeks of constant studying were **in vain** as Mabel got a "D" on her chemistry exam.
  美貝的化學考試得到「D」，她連續唸了兩個禮拜的書都**白費**了。

- Francis tried **in vain** to arrive on time to her first class of the semester.
  法蘭西絲為準時上這學期第一堂課所做的努力都**白費**了。

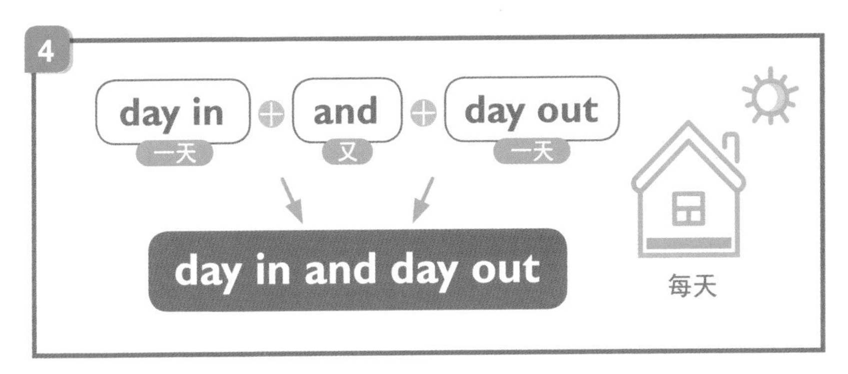

- The traffic to New York City is terrible **day in and day out**. 往紐約市區的交通**每天**都很亂。

075

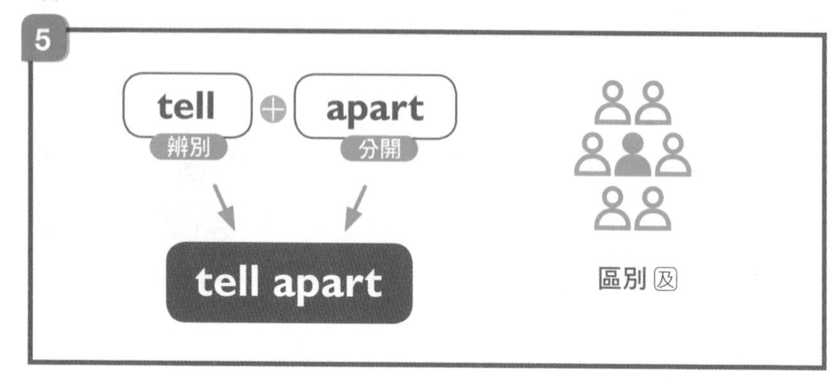

- The teacher had a hard time **telling** the twins **apart**.
  老師不太能夠**辨別**雙胞胎。
- Can you **tell** these two kittens **apart**?
  你可以**分辨**出這兩隻小貓嗎？

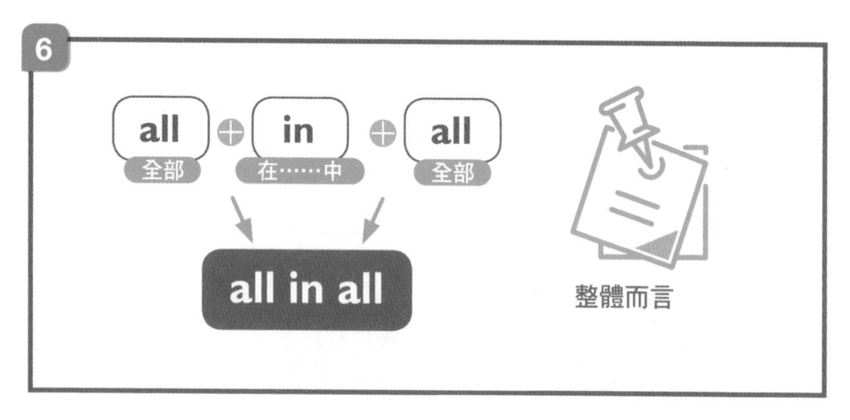

- Despite the fact that the car broke down, **all in all** it was a fun day.
  儘管車子壞了，**整體而言**，今天依然是愉快的一天。
- **All in all**, this is a very interesting class.
  大致說來，這堂課非常有趣。

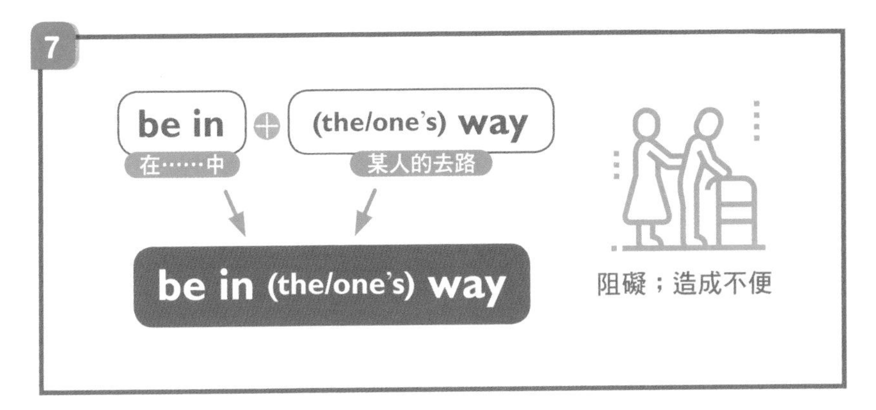

- The only annoying thing about having a puppy is that he **is** always **in the way**.
  養狗最擾人的就是**不方便**。
- You'**re in the way**; please give me some space!
  你**妨礙**到我了，請給我一些空間！

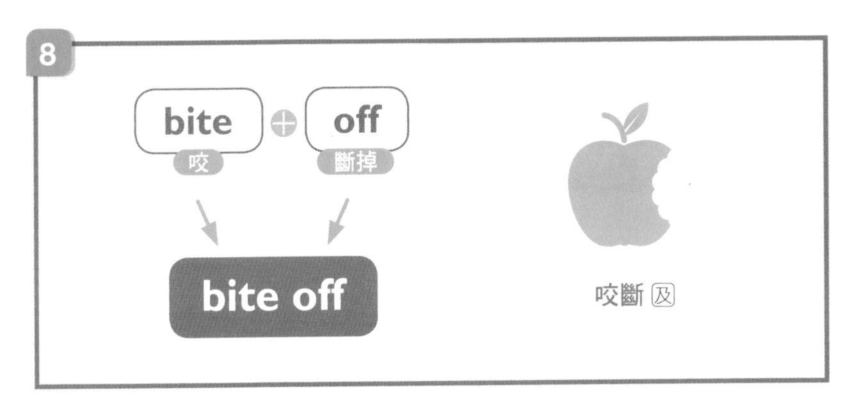

- Your dog **bit off** a piece of my Christmas decoration.
  你的狗**咬掉**了我的耶誕裝飾。
- Felix **bit off** a piece of the chocolate bar and threw the rest away because it tasted terrible.
  因為巧克力棒很難吃，菲力斯**咬**了一塊後便把剩下的都丟掉。

076

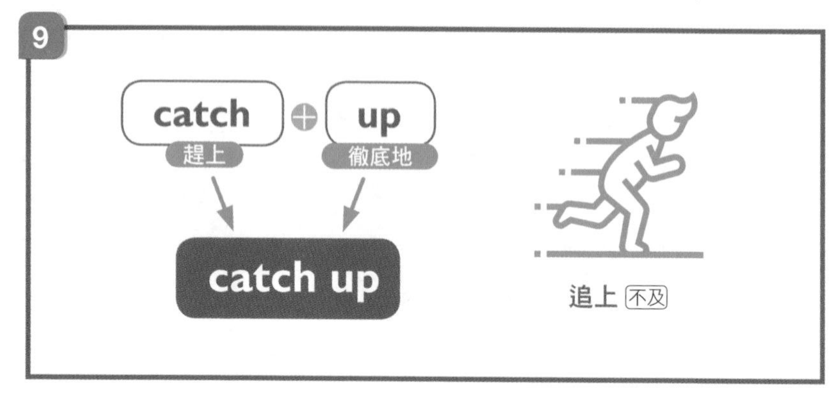

- He was out of school for a while and is finding it hard to **catch up**. 他一陣子沒去學校上課，所以很難**趕上進度**。

❶ Let's **go around** the lake on our walk; it looks so peaceful.
我們今天就在這座湖的**四周逛逛**吧，這裡看起來一片祥和。

❸ At the picnic, there were hardly enough sandwiches to **go around**.
三明治根本不夠**分**給野餐的每個人。

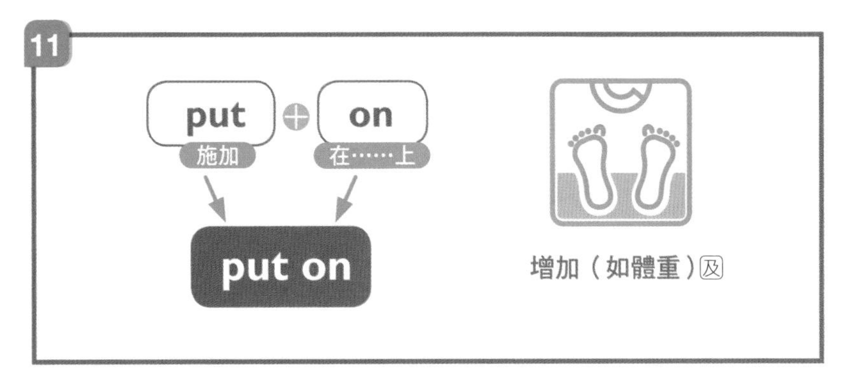

- When Clarence returned from visiting his family for the summer, he had **put on** a few pounds.
  克萊倫斯自從夏天探望家人回來後，他的體重便**增加**了好幾磅。

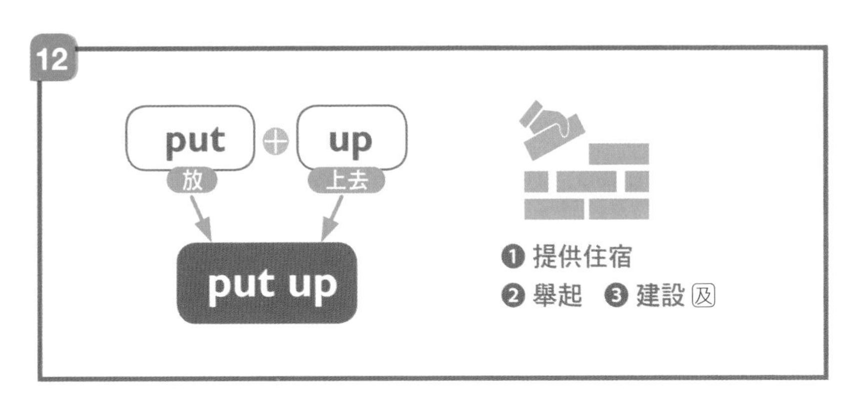

❶ When Carl visited Chicago, I **put** him **up** in my apartment. 卡爾來芝加哥玩時，我**安排**他住在我的公寓。

❷ Vicky **put** the painting **up** above the fireplace.
薇琪把畫**舉**起來，掛在火爐上方。

❸ Did you know that they're **putting up** a new cafe next to the supermarket?
你知道他們要在超市旁邊**蓋**一家咖啡廳嗎？

Finding a Lost Cat
尋貓啟示

Ivy and Andy talk about a funny incident with a cat. 艾薇和安迪在討論一個有關貓咪的有趣意外。

077

Ivy: What's **the matter**[1]? You look exhausted.

Andy: I took the cat in for his first visit to the vet, and he just couldn't **hold still**[2]. It was annoying!

Ivy: What happened? Did he run away?

Andy: Yes, he did! The vet said this was the craziest cat he's ever seen, **by far**[3].

Ivy: Well, **no wonder**[4]! It sounds like your dear cat was pretty mad! I hope he hasn't **gotten lost**[5].

Andy: Don't worry, I'll find him; I **know** him **by sight**[6].

Ivy: Get going! I'll **see** you **off**[7] right now. And remember to look everywhere; don't **rule out**[8] any possible hiding places.

艾薇： **怎麼了**？你看起來累壞了。

安迪： 我第一次帶我的貓去看獸醫，可是他就是不能**不動**。很討厭！

艾薇： 發生了什麼事情？他跑走了嗎？

安迪： 沒錯，他跑了！獸醫說他**顯然**是他所看過最難馴服的貓。

艾薇： 嗯，也**難怪了**！聽起來你的貓不太聽話！希望他別**迷路**才好。

安迪： 別擔心，我會找到他的，我**認得**他。

艾薇： 快點開始找吧！我現在就**送**你**離開**。記得每個地方都要找，別**漏掉**任何地方。

hold still 不動

run away
離家出走；逃跑

078

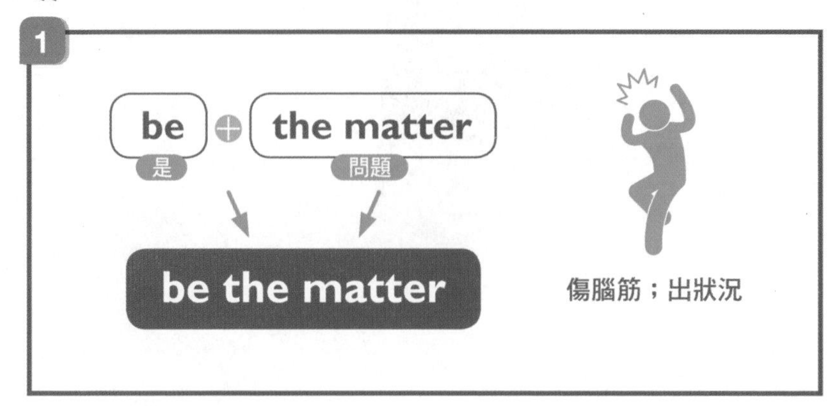

- Are you okay, or **is** something **the matter**?
  你沒事吧？還是哪裡**不舒服**嗎？

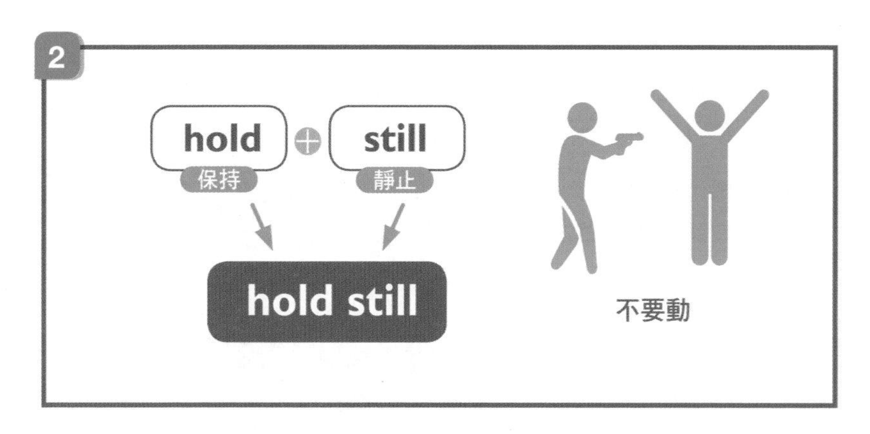

- Amy is only three years old, so it is hard for her to **hold still** when she visits the dentist.
  艾咪才三歲，所以看牙醫時很難要她**不要動**。
- **Hold still**; this won't hurt. **不要亂動**，不會痛的。

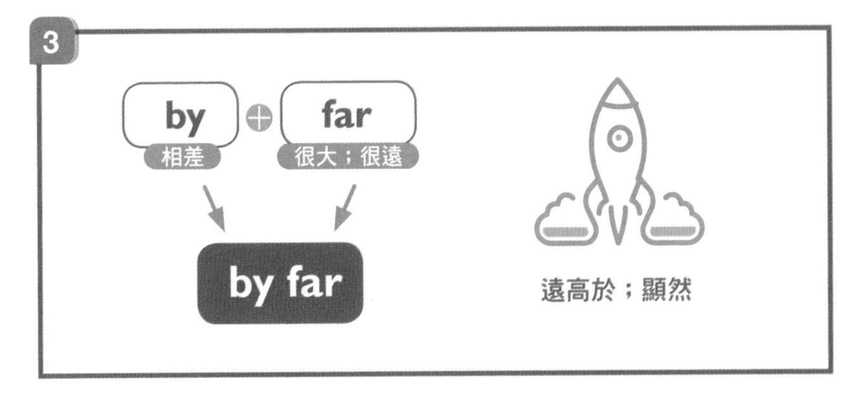

- This weekend in Venice was one of the best weekends of my life, **by far**.
  這次在威尼斯度週末**顯然**是我這輩子最棒的週末之一。
- This lesson is, **by far**, one of the most boring I've ever seen. 這堂課**顯然**是我上過最無聊的課之一。

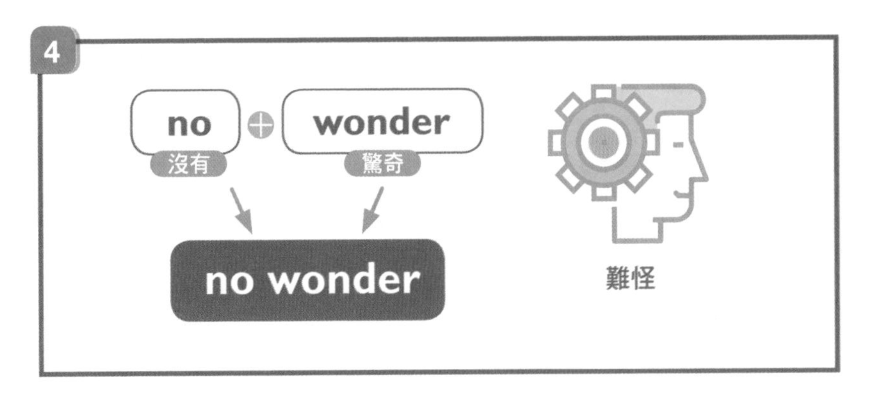

- **No wonder** you're tired; you were up till 3 a.m. last night! **難怪**你累了，你昨晚熬夜到凌晨三點！
- **No wonder** I couldn't find my keys! They were in the car all along. **難怪**我找不到鑰匙！原來一直都在車上。

079

- It was Dan's first time visiting San Francisco, so it's no surprise that he **got lost**.
  這是丹第一次到舊金山，所以他會**迷路**一點也不令人意外。

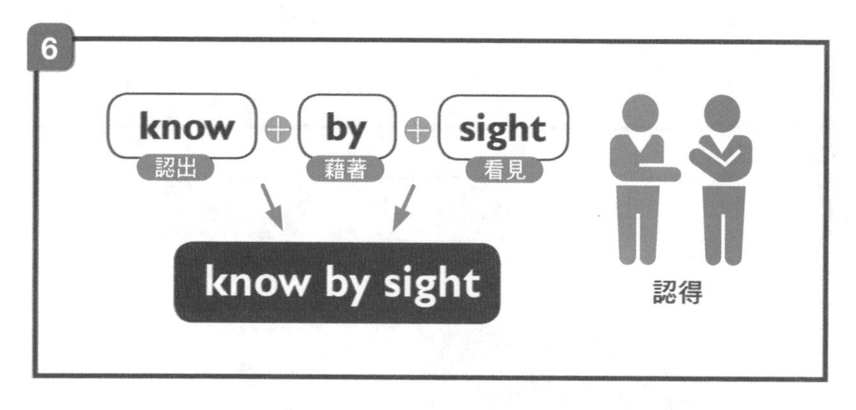

- I'm not sure of Gina's address, but I **know** the house **by sight**.
  我不確定吉娜家的地址，但我**認得**她的房子。
- Although Carla has never spoken with Will, she **knows** him **by sight**.
  雖然卡拉從未和威爾說過話，但她**認得**他。

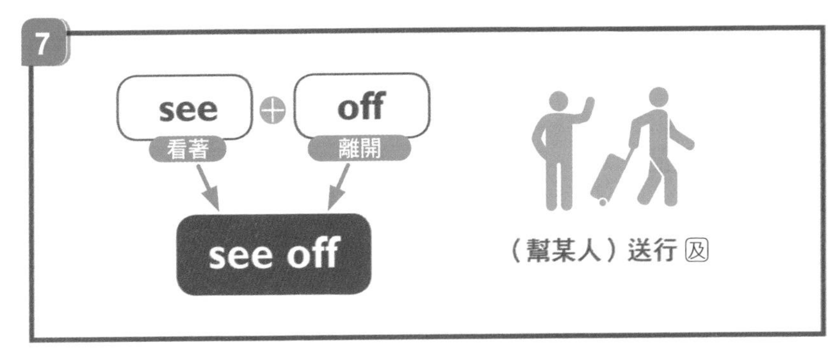

- When my uncle Chip was leaving, the whole family went with him to the airport to **see** him **off**.
  我叔叔奇普要離開時，我們全家人陪他到機場**為**他**送行**。
- I'd like to go to lunch with you tomorrow, but I have to **see off** my friend who is traveling to Bermuda.
  我明天想和你吃中餐，但我必須**為**要去百慕達的朋友**送行**。
- My parents **saw** me **off** at the airport. 父母到機場**為**我**送行**。
- Families gathered at the dock to **see** the sailors **off** to war. 家人聚集在碼頭邊**為**征戰的船員們**送行**。

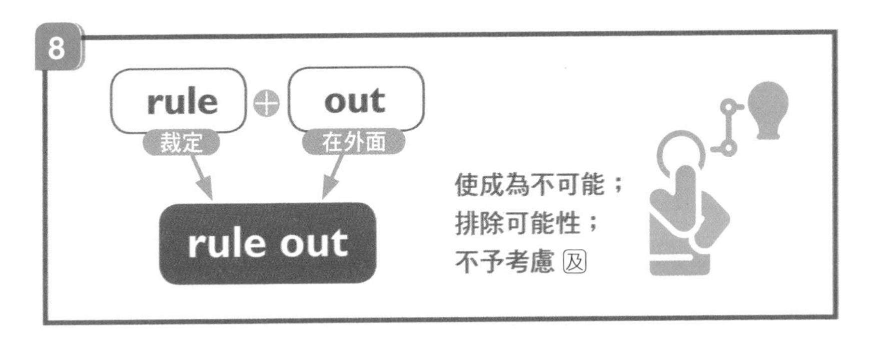

8
rule
裁定
out
在外面
rule out
使成為不可能；
排除可能性；
不予考慮 及

- The constant rain **ruled out** Sophia's plans to go sunbathing. 外頭一直下雨，蘇菲亞做日光浴的計畫**泡湯**了。
- Because mom **ruled out** my plans to get a pet snake, I decided to ask her for a pet spider.
  既然媽媽**不考慮**讓我養寵物蛇，我決定要求她讓我養寵物蜘蛛。

080

❶ After dinner, we **saw** Ben **out** the front door.
晚餐後，我們**送**班**到**前門口。

❶ It is polite to **see** your guests **out** after they visit.
送來訪的客人**到門口**是一種禮貌。

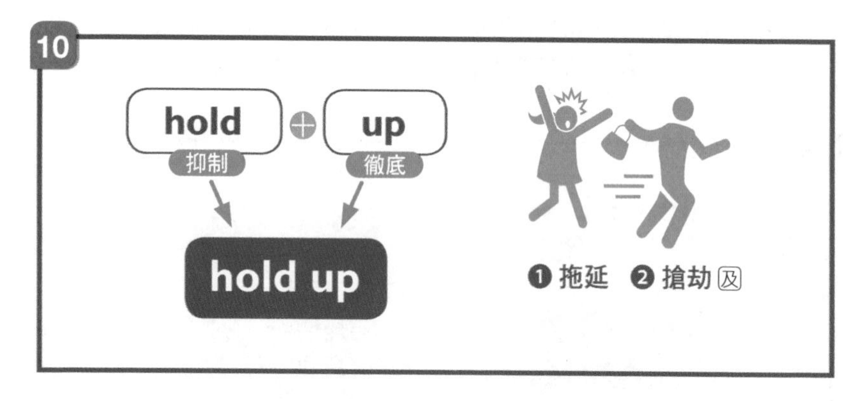

❶ Because my mother was stuck in traffic, the family meeting was **held up**.
我媽媽遇上塞車，因此家庭聚會**延後**了。

❶ Derek's delayed flight **held** the workshop **up**.
由於戴瑞克的班機延誤，所以研討會**延後**了。

- Last week my dog **ran away**, and I haven't seen him since. 自從上星期我的狗**跑掉**後，我就沒再見過他。
- When the children heard the loud bang of the fireworks, they got scared and **ran away**.
  小朋友聽到巨大的煙火聲後，都被嚇**跑**了。

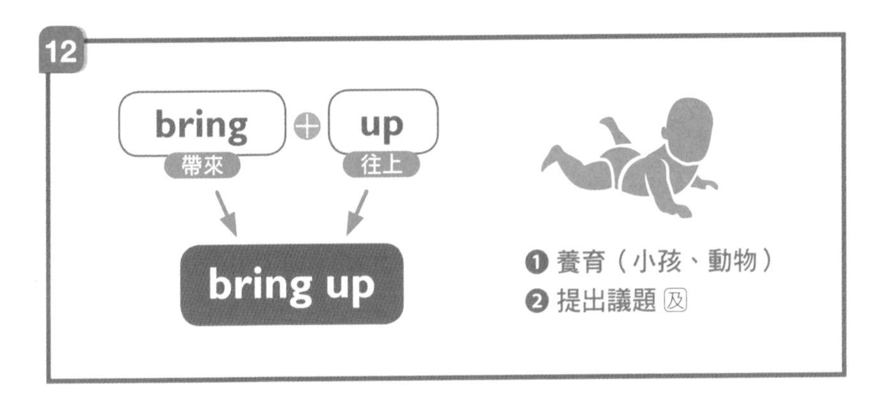

❶ Gary **brought up** his five children by himself.
蓋瑞獨自**扶養**五個小孩。

❶ They **brought** him **up** as a Christian.
他們將他**養育**成為基督教徒。

❷ Some of the students **brought** questions **up** with the teacher after class. 下課後，有些學生向老師**提出**問題。

Handing in a Paper
交報告

Francine and Albert talk about the deadline for their papers.
法蘭欣和艾伯特在談論有關報告的截止日期。

081

Francine: Did you finish your research paper? You know you have to **hand** it **in**[1] today.

Albert: I was up all night checking it over **in case**[2] I made some mistakes. I don't want to be **taken by surprise**[3] with a bad grade.

Francine: Good job! I'm nearly done too. However, as soon as class starts, I'm going to **go up to**[4] the professor and ask him a few questions.

Albert: It may be a bit late for that. You'd better try to finish now. Trust me, you'll **be better off**[5] that way.

Francine: You know, Albert, that's a good idea. You're smart! I bet you're **named after**[6] Albert Einstein!

法蘭欣： 你的研究報告寫完了嗎？你知道今天一定要**交**吧。

艾伯特： **以防**錯誤，我昨晚整夜沒睡仔細檢查了一遍。我可不想看到成績時**嚇一跳**。

法蘭欣： 做得好！ 我也快要寫完了，只要一開始上課，我就要**過去**問教授一些問題。

艾伯特： 那可能有點太遲了吧。妳最好現在就完成。相信我，我覺得那樣會**比較好**。

法蘭欣： 艾伯特，這主意不錯。你真聰明！我想你的名字是以艾柏特．愛因斯坦來**命名**的吧！

hand in 繳交

be taken by surprise 嚇一跳

082

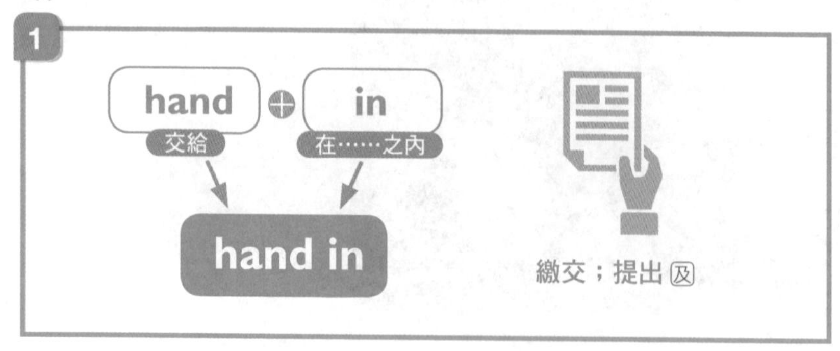

- Ms. Applebee told us we had to **hand in** our reports by next week. 艾波比女士說我們下星期前一定要**交**報告。
- Did you **hand** your essay **in** yet? 你**交**論文了嗎？
- I've decided to **hand in** my resignation. 我已經決定要**遞出**辭職信了。
- The teacher told the children to **hand in** their exercise books. 老師要孩子們**繳交**練習簿。

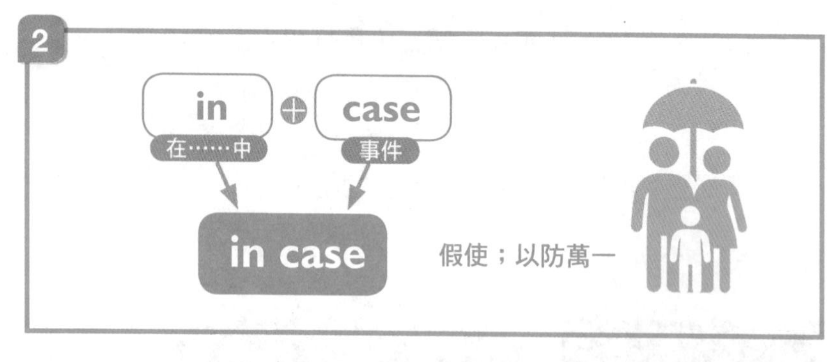

- You should take your umbrella to work today **in case** it rains. 你今天最好帶把傘去上班，**以防**下雨。
- **In case** of emergency, remember that you can always call my cell phone. 有任何緊急狀況，記得都可以打手機給我。
- I don't think I'll need any money, but I'll bring some just **in case**. 我不認為我會需要用到錢，但我會帶著**以防萬一**。
- Bring a map **in case** you get lost. 把地圖帶著，**免得**迷路。

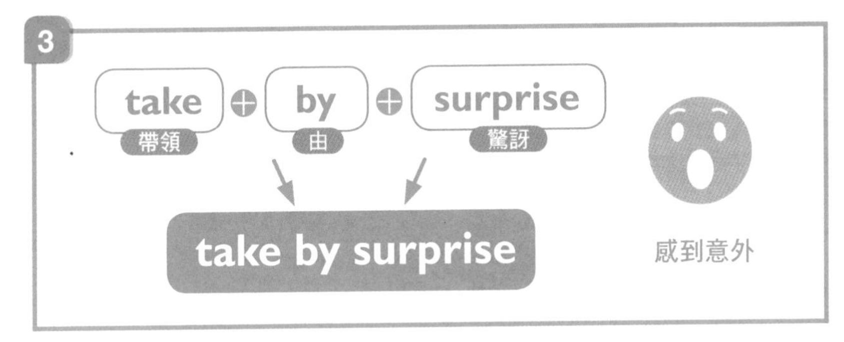

- Mohammed's new haircut really **took** me **by surprise**; I hardly recognized him!
  穆罕默德的新髮型**讓**我**很意外**，我幾乎認不出他來了！
- I was **taken by surprise** with your mobile's new ringtone—it is very original!
  我對你的手機鈴聲**感到很意外**，真有創意！
- Lisa's resignation **took** us completely **by surprise**.
  莉莎的辭呈**令**所有人感到相當地**意外**。

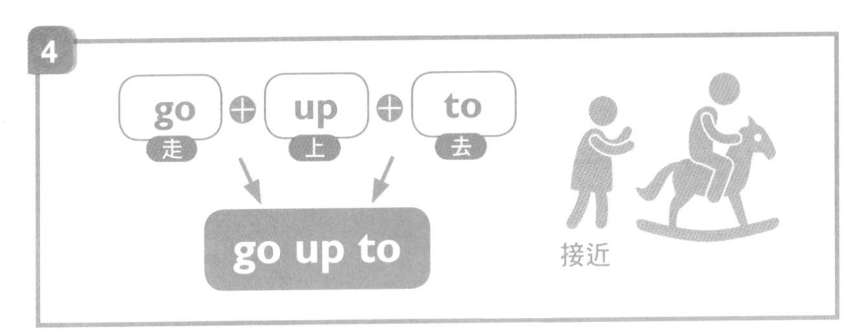

- Bill told his little sister never to **go up to** strangers.
  比爾告訴妹妹不要**接近**陌生人。
- Irene **went up to** the next person she passed on the street and asked for directions.
  艾琳**走向**街上迎面而來的路人問路。
- Let's **go up to** the second floor of the restaurant to eat because there are more tables there.
  我們**上**這家餐廳的二樓吃東西吧，樓上的座位比較多。

083

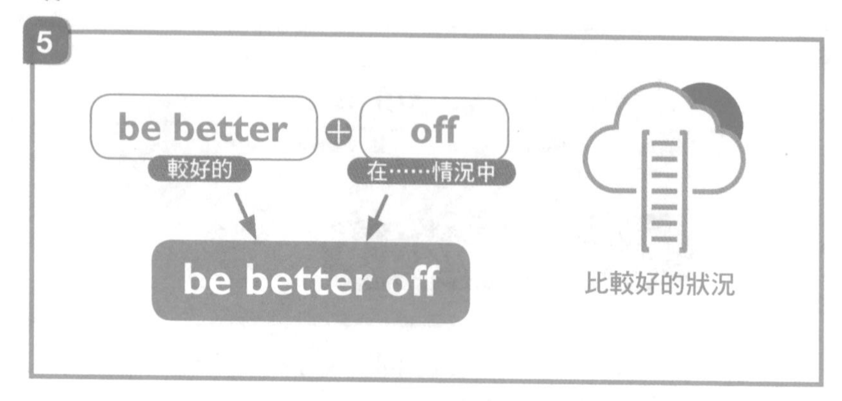

- After a few months in driving school, Victoria **was better off** on the roads.
  維多莉亞到駕訓班上了幾個月的課後，她的開車技術**好多了**。
- We **were better off** once we got off the plane and got some fresh air.
  我們在下了飛機、呼吸到新鮮的空氣後，便**感覺好多了**。
- He'd **be better off** working for a bigger company.
  他在大公司工作的話大概會**比較有錢**。

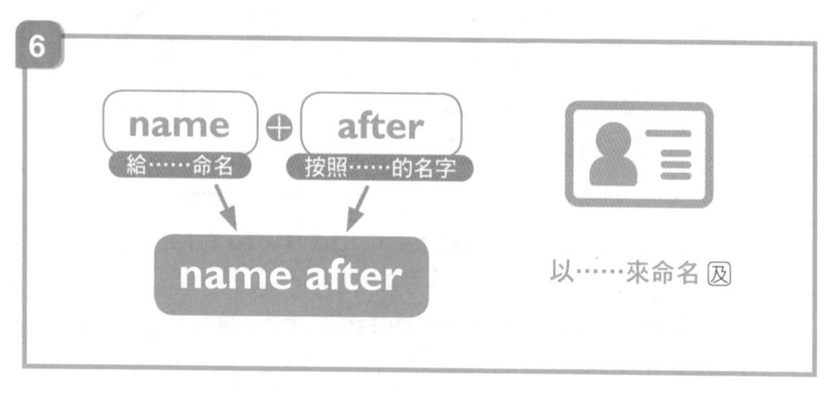

- Harriet is **named after** her grandmother.
  哈莉特是**以其祖母的名字來命名**。

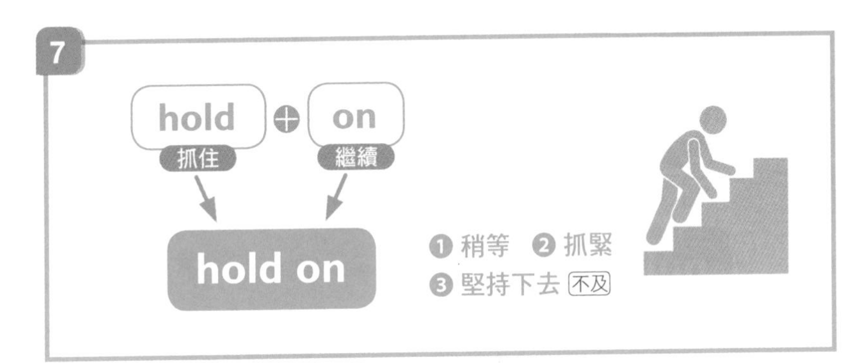

❶ **Hold on**, I'll be with you in a minute.
請您**稍等一下**，我馬上就回來。

❶ The receptionist asked us to **hold on** for a while because there were many visitors in the office.
由於辦公室有許多訪客，所以接待員請我們**稍等**一下。

❷ **Hold on** to your hat when the wind is blowing, or it will blow away! 起風時要**抓緊**你的帽子，否則會被吹走！

❸ If you can **hold on**, I'll go and get some help.
如果你能夠**撐**下去，我會去找人幫忙的。

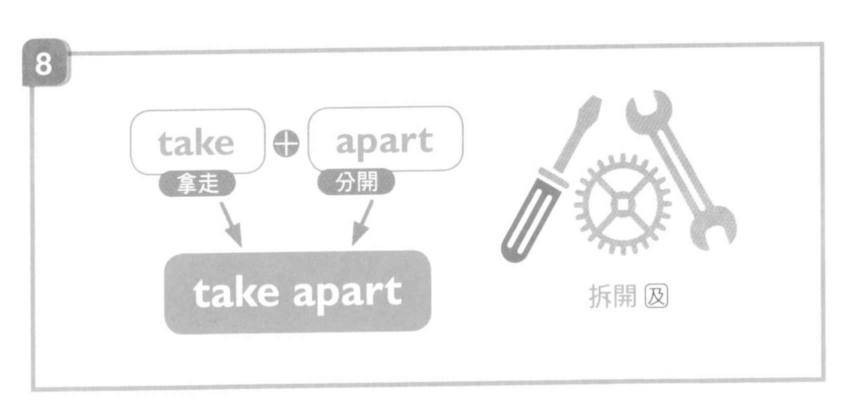

- If you **take** the computer **apart**, you may end up breaking it.
如果你把電腦**拆開**，最後可能會把它弄壞。

084

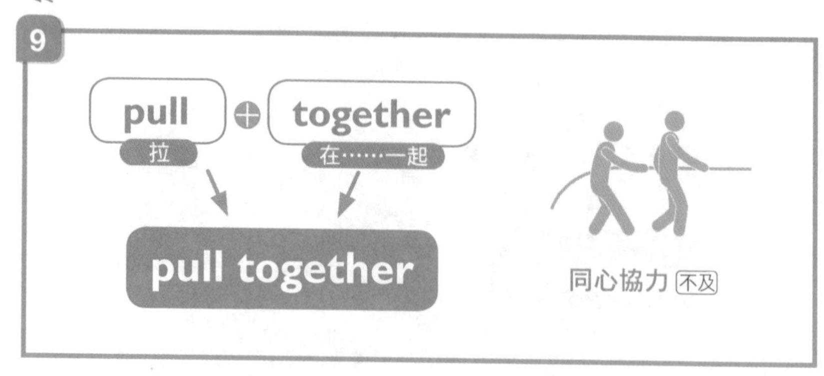

- Everyone in the office **pulled together** to finish the project. 這份企畫案是由公司上上下下每個人**共同合力**完成的。
- If we want to meet the deadline, everyone has to **pull together** and work all night.
  如果我們想要趕上截止日期，就必須**同心協力**，熬夜趕工。
- Everyone on our street really **pulled together** after the fire. 火災發生後，街上的人全都**團結**在一起。

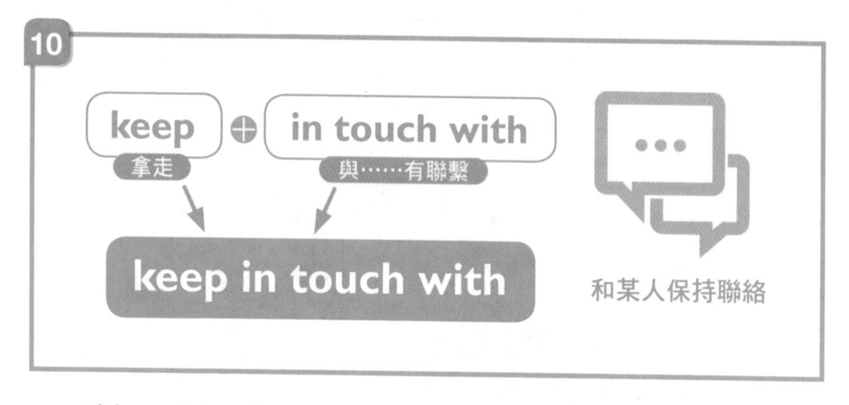

- Although Rachel moved away from home, she **keeps in touch with** her family by calling every week.
  雖然瑞秋離家了，但她依然每個禮拜打電話**和**家人**保持聯絡**。
- Karin bought a new cell phone so she could **keep in touch with** her friends more easily.
  卡琳買了一支新手機，好更方便她**和**朋友**保持聯絡**。

My Note

The New Teacher
新老師

Molly and Philip have a chat about their new teacher. 茉莉和菲利普在聊他們新來的老師。

085

Molly: How do you like our new history teacher?

Philip: Well, after hearing that he studied at Harvard, I really **look up to**[1] him; but the fact is, he seems to **look down on**[2] his students.

Molly: Yeah, he may be a smart guy, but he's not so friendly. Yesterday I **came across**[3] him in a café, and though I **took pains**[4] to be nice, he was pretty cold.

Philip: I know what you mean. I **stopped by**[5] his office a little while ago with some questions, and he wasn't very helpful.

Molly: Nope. The last teacher was better; he even told us to **drop** him **a line**[6] by email if we had any questions about the assignments.

Philip: Exactly. Plus, this class seems harder—
I don't think I **stand a chance**[7] of getting an "A."

茉莉： 你喜歡新來的歷史老師嗎？

菲利普： 唔，自從知道他是哈佛畢業的，我就很**尊敬**他。但事實上，他似乎有點**瞧不起**學生。

茉莉： 是啊，他博學多聞，但不是很友善。我昨天在咖啡店**巧遇**他，雖然我**努力**釋出善意，但他看來很冷漠。

菲利普： 我懂你的意思。我前一陣子**到**辦公室請教他一些問題，但他不是很樂意幫忙。

茉莉： 沒錯，之前的老師比較好。他甚至說如果我們有課業方面的問題，隨時可以**用電郵寫信**給他。

菲利普： 是啊，加上課程越來越難了，我不認為我**有希望**得到「A」。

drop a line 寫信

look down on 瞧不起

086

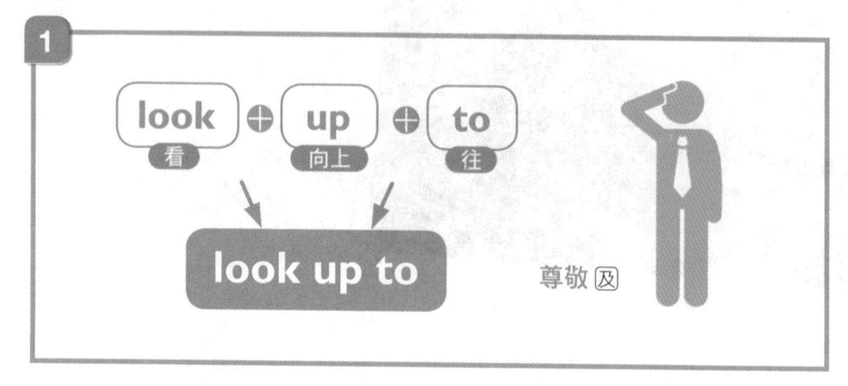

- Ariel **looks up to** her older sister. 艾芮兒很**尊敬**她姐姐。
- Whom do you **look up to** most? 你最**尊敬**的人是誰？
- Judy was older and more experienced, and I **looked up to** her. 裘蒂年紀較長，經驗較豐富，我很**尊敬**她。

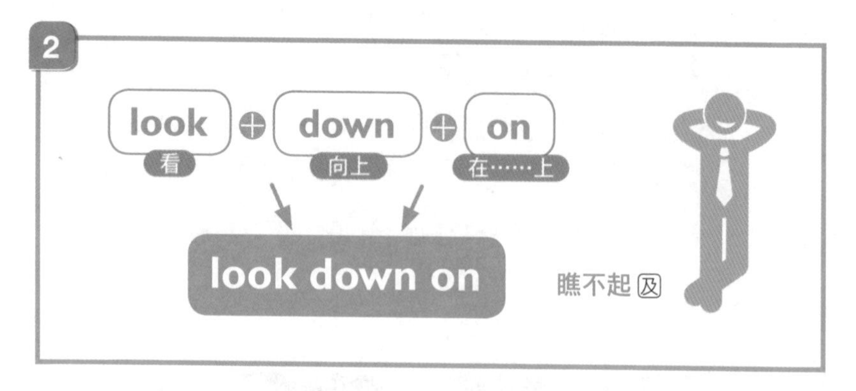

- A good boss doesn't **look down on** his employees.
  好老闆不會**看不起**員工。
- Sometimes I feel as if my professor is **looking down on** me because I got a "D-" on the exam.
  自從考試得到「D-」後，我有時覺得教授**看不起**我。

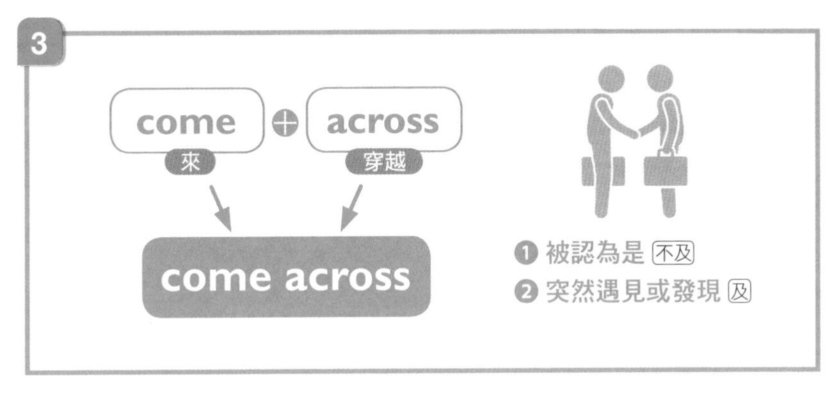

❶ Mariah **comes across** really well on television.
瑪莉亞在銀光幕前的形象很好。

❶ Although Melinda is a nice girl, she can **come across** as a bit mean sometimes.
記住，就算瑪琳達是個好女孩，她有時也是很難相處的。

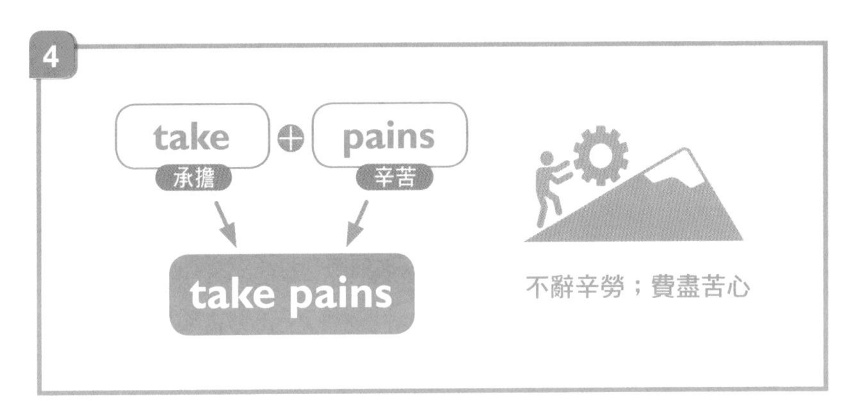

- Adriana **took pains** to walk quietly so as not to awaken the baby. 艾卓恩娜**努力**走路不發出聲音，以免吵醒小寶寶。
- Dan **took** great **pains** to eat right so he would lose weight. 丹為了減輕體重，很**努力**養成正確的飲食習慣。

087

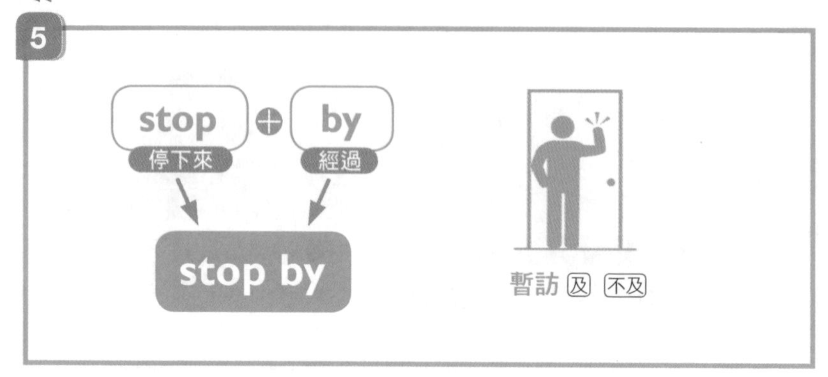

- If you have time tomorrow, **stop by** in the afternoon.
  明天如果有空，就下午**過來**吧。
- **Stop by** on your way home, and I'll give you that DVD.
  回家路上**順便到**我這裡來一下，我要拿那片 DVD 給你。

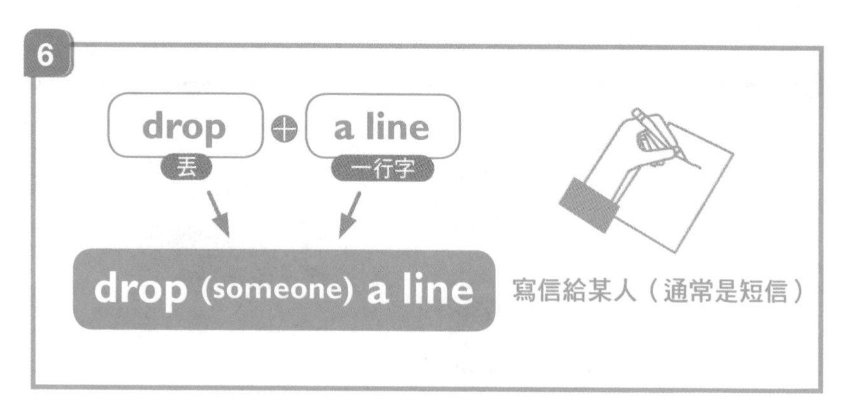

- This weekend, I'll **drop** my friend Jerry **a line** if I have time. 如果有時間，我這週末會**寫信**給我的朋友傑瑞。
- I would have **dropped** you **a line** earlier, but I lost your address. 我之前本來要**寫信**給你，但我弄丟了你的地址。
- I really do like hearing from you, so **drop** me **a line** and let me know how you are.
  我真的很想知道你的消息，**寫封信**給我，讓我知道你的近況。

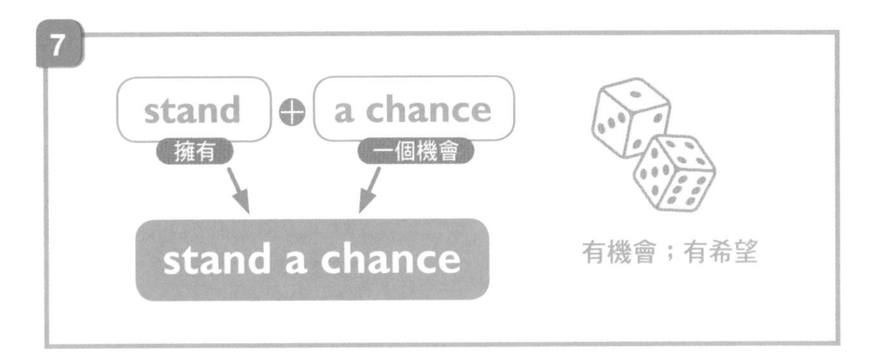

- Matilda isn't a very good swimmer; she doesn't **stand a chance** of winning the gold medal.
  瑪蒂蓮達游得不快，她沒什麼**希望**贏得金牌。
- Rory's mom is mad at her, so she doesn't **stand a chance** of going to the movies with us this weekend.
  蘿芮的媽媽在生蘿芮的氣，所以她這週末不**可能**和我們去看電影。

❶ Don't use foul language with me; I won't **stand for** that kind of talk.
和我講話別用粗話，我無法**忍受**那種說話方式。

❸ The stars on the U.S. flag **stand for** states.
美國國旗上的星星**代表**各州。

088

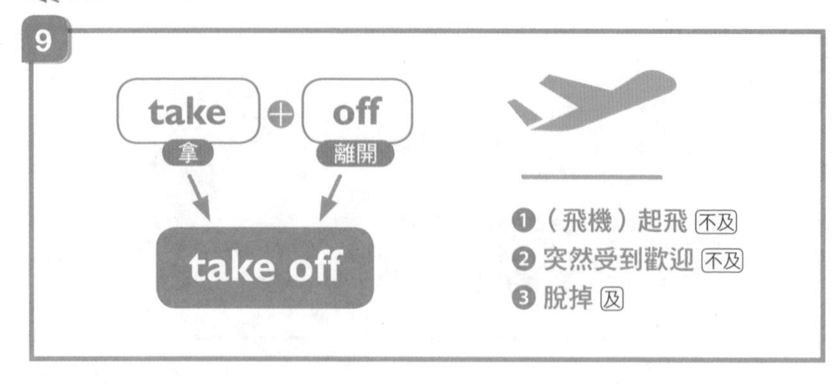

❶ Because of the snowstorm, no planes **were taking off** or landing at the airport.
由於暴風雪的因素，機場所有的飛機都無法**起**降。

❷ Her singing career had just begun to **take off**.
她的歌唱事業才剛**爆紅**。

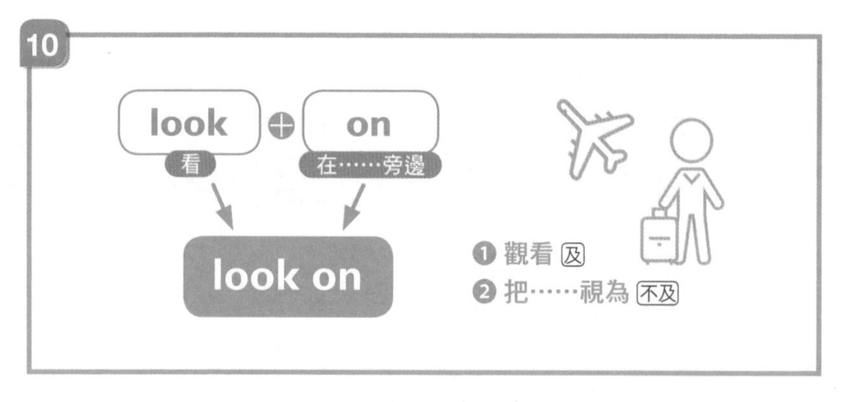

❶ Because Toby arrived at the airport late, he could only **look on** as the plane left without him.
陶比太晚到機場，所以他別無選擇只能**眼看**著飛機離開。

❶ Janet had a broken leg, so she could only **look on** as the other students played soccer.
珍娜自從腿骨折後，就只能**看**著其他學生踢足球。

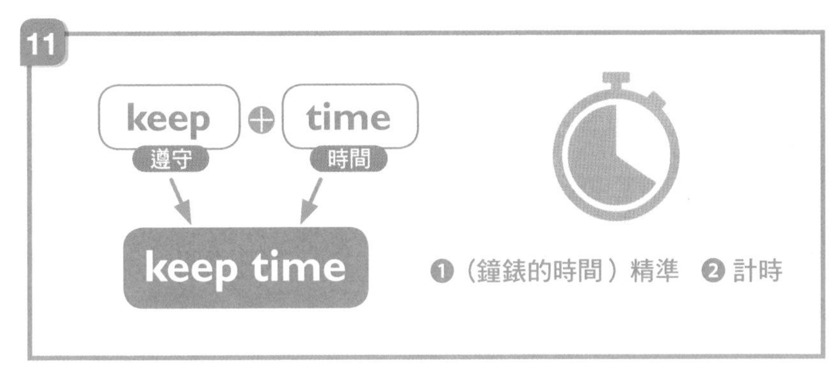

❶ This old clock doesn't **keep** good **time**.
這個老舊的時鐘不**準**。

❶ Does your cell phone **keep time**? 你手機的時鐘**準**嗎？

❷ When I go running, I like to **keep time** on my watch.
慢跑時，我喜歡用手錶來**計時**。

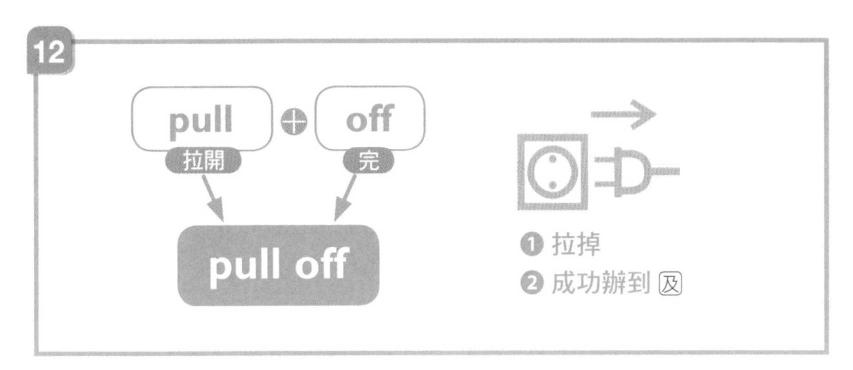

❶ I **pulled off** my wet clothes as soon as I got home.
我一到家就趕緊**脫掉**濕衣服。

❷ It was a hard exam, but in the end I **pulled** it **off** and got an "A." 考試很難，但我還是**成功地得到**「A」。

❷ Although no one thought he could do it, Corey **pulled off** the best business deal in company history.
雖然沒有人認為柯瑞能夠成功，但他**談成**了公司有史以來最好的一筆交易。

The Weekend Party
週末派對

Zack and Ursula talk about Ursula's party.
查克和娥蘇拉在討論娥蘇拉的派對。

089

Zack: How did your party go last weekend?

Ursula: Bad. I worked so hard to make it nice. I **cleaned out**[1] all the shelves and cabinets and washed all the dishes; I really did my best to **make do**[2] with my small apartment.

Zack: Did your roommates **go in for**[3] the idea of a party?

Ursula: At first, my roommates **got on my nerves**[4] when they **put down**[5] the idea of a party. However, when I told them that their friends could come too, they almost **took over**[6] the party planning.

Zack: So what went wrong? It sounds good so far.

Ursula: I **stayed up**[7] the entire night before to make sure all the details were right. The next day, I **stayed in**[8] waiting for the guests. I didn't go to work; I didn't study. I just waited.

Zack: And?

Ursula: No one **showed up**[9]!

查克： 上週末的派對辦得如何？

娥蘇拉： 糟透了。我非常努力想讓一切看起來都很棒，我把床鋪下面都**清理乾淨**了，也把所有的盤子都洗乾淨了。我真的**盡力**把公寓整理乾淨了。

查克： 妳的室友們**喜歡**辦派對這點子嗎？

娥蘇拉： 他們剛開始**批評**這個想法時**讓**我**很緊張**，但我說他們的朋友也可以來參加後，他們幾乎**接手**計畫了整個派對。

查克： 那是哪裡出了錯？到目前為止聽起來都很好啊。

娥蘇拉： 我為了確認所有細節都沒錯，前一天晚上**熬夜**沒睡。隔天我**在家**等候客人的光臨，沒去上班，也沒唸書，我只是等待。

查克： 然後呢？

娥蘇拉： 都沒有人**來**！

clean out 清理乾淨

stay up 熬夜

090

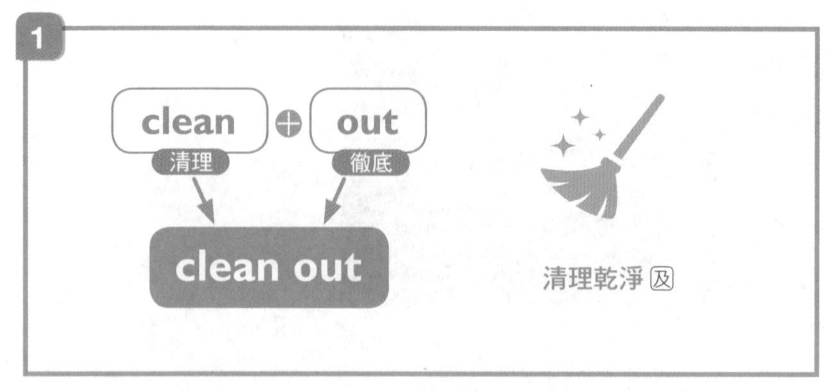

- The fridge smelled terrible, so Damian **cleaned out** all the old food.
  冰箱的味道很臭，所以戴明恩把過期食物都**清理乾淨**。

- Someone better **clean out** the garage soon; it is filling up with junk.
  車庫推滿了垃圾，最好盡快把它**清理乾淨**。

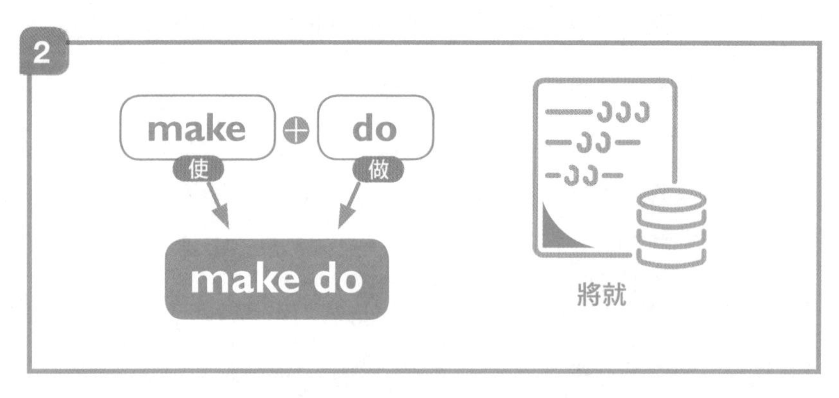

- After Mindy quit her job, she had to **make do** with less.
  敏蒂辭職後，必須依存較少的物資**得過且過**。

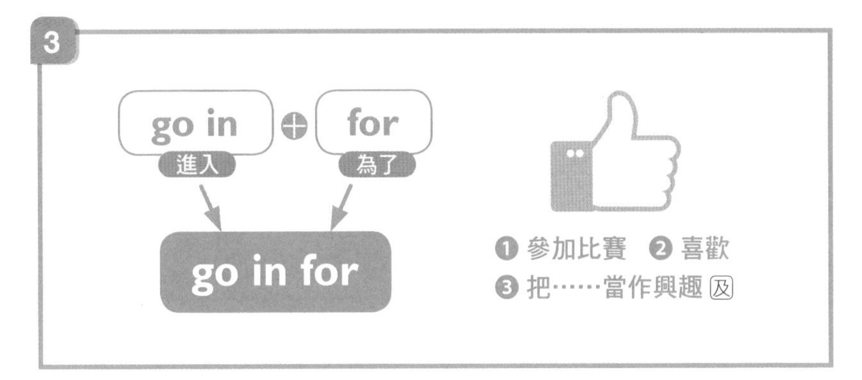

❶ All Scott's coworkers **went in for** the idea of having a surprise party for his retirement.
史考特所有的同事都**參與**了為他舉辦退休驚喜派對的計畫。

❷ Abe doesn't **go in for** baseball, but he sometimes watches his friends play.
艾比不**喜歡**棒球，但他有時會去看朋友打球。

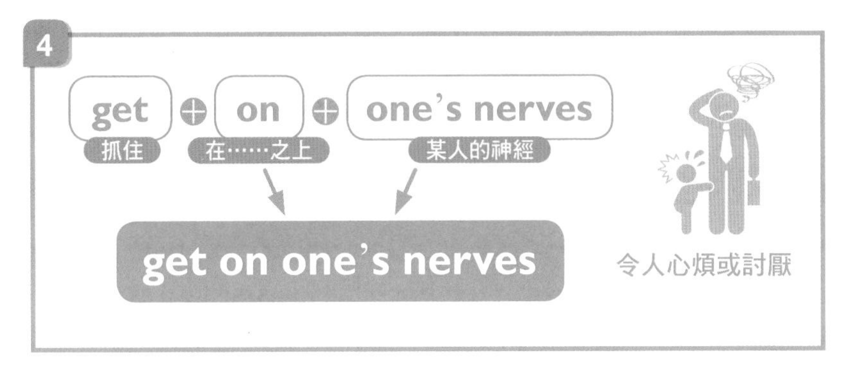

- My neighbor's dog really **gets on my nerves** when he barks all night.
鄰居的狗叫了整晚，**令我心浮氣躁**。

- After spending so much time together on the cruise, Jan and Gary **got on each other's nerves**.
珍和蓋瑞自從一起參加郵輪之旅後便很**討厭**對方。

091

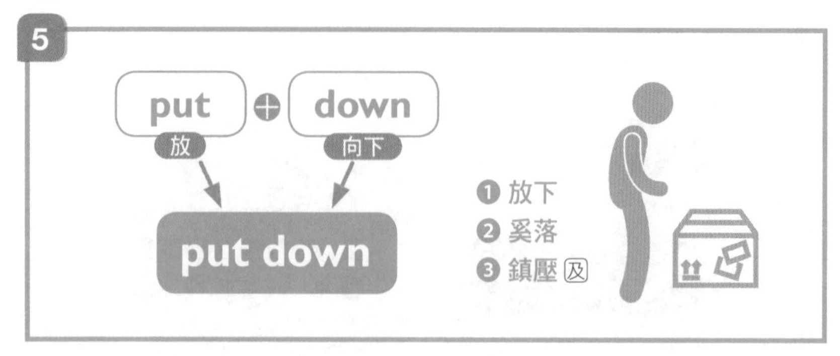

❷ It was very embarrassing when my brother **put** me **down** in front of all my friends.
我的哥哥在所有朋友面前**奚落**我，令我很難堪。

❸ The dictator used the army to **put down** the democratic rebellion. 獨裁者用武力**鎮壓**民主反抗團體。

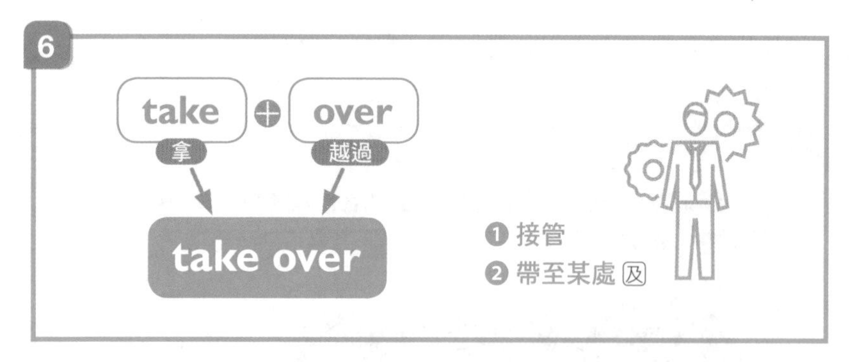

❶ When the CEO was in the hospital, his assistant **took over** the company for a few weeks.
執行長住院時，他的助理**接管**了公司好幾個星期。

❶ After the rebellion, a new leader **took** the country **over**.
叛亂結束後，新的領導者**接管**了整個國家。

❶ Richard has **taken over** responsibility for this project.
理查已經**接手**負責整個企劃。

❷ The delivery boy **took** the package **over** to my aunt.
送貨員把包裹**交**給我阿姨。

- The children get to **stay up** all night on New Year's Eve.
  孩子們除夕夜可以整晚**不睡覺**。
- How late did you **stay up** last night? You look very tired.
  你昨晚**熬夜**到幾點？你看起來很累。

- Although Ralph planned to go to a club, he ended up **staying in** and watching a movie on TV.
  瑞夫雖然計劃要去俱樂部，但他最後**待在家裡**看電影。
- Instead of going to a restaurant, let's **stay in** and make dinner here.
  我們**待在家裡**自己做晚餐，別上館子了。

092

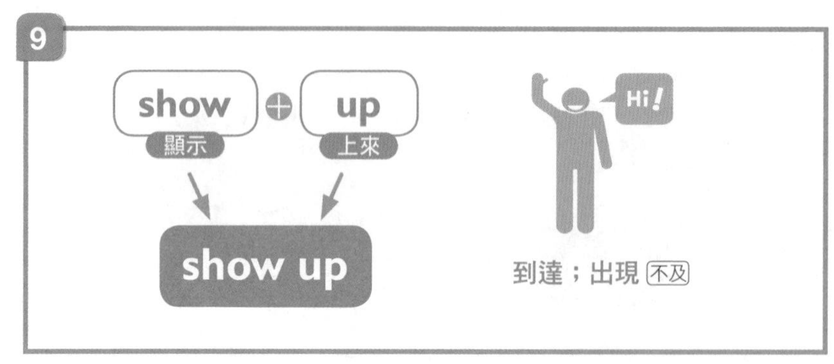

- Unfortunately, we **showed up** at the movie a few minutes late, so we missed the beginning.
  可惜我們電影開演了幾分鐘才**進場**，所以錯過了開頭。
- I invited her for eight o'clock, but she didn't **show up** until eight-thirty.
  我約她八點見面，但她一直到八點半才**出現**。

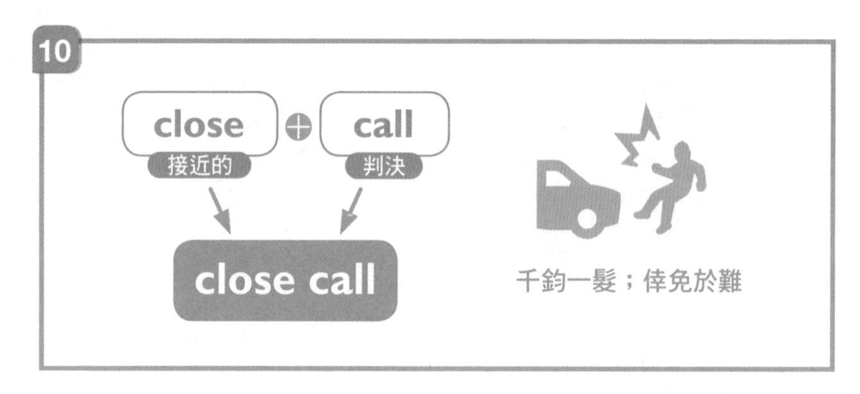

- I almost didn't get into the university; my test scores were barely high enough, so it was a **close call**.
  我差一點就上不了大學，我的考試成績勉強夠高，真是**千鈞一髮**。
- I really had a **close call** today on the way home from school—I almost drove off the icy road!
  我今天放學回家真的**差點就發生意外**，我的車子在結冰的路上打滑，差點就駛出車道。

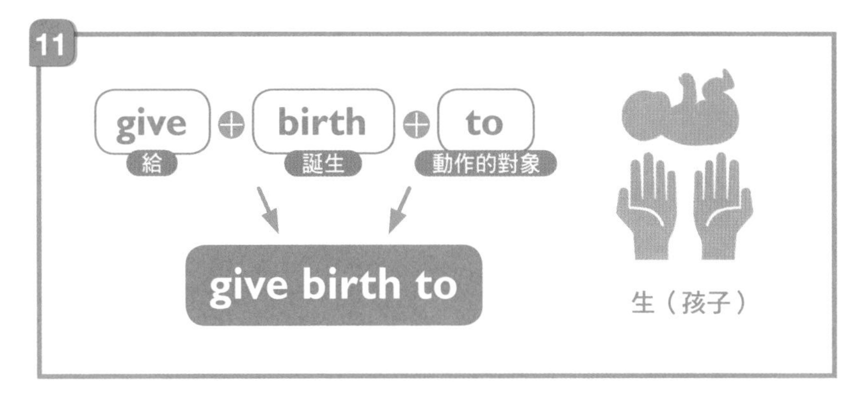

- Our rabbit **gave birth to** seven baby bunnies last weekend! 我們養的兔子上週末**生**了七隻小兔子！

Unit 24

Schoolwork Problems 課業問題

Walt is telling Debby about some problems in his class.
華特告訴黛比他上課遇到的一些問題。

093

Debby: Is everything ok? You look like you need to **cheer up**[1].

Walt: Well, I **ran into**[2] some problems with my schoolwork in philosophy.

Debby: What happened? Are you having trouble doing what you **set out to**[3] do in that class?

Walt: Bingo. I just can't finish this report. I'm even thinking about **dropping out of**[4] this philosophy class.

Debby: That's so extreme that it doesn't even really **make sense**[5]. If I were you, I'd **draw up**[6] a list of goals you need to **carry out**[7] and then complete them one by one.

Walt: But I set out to finish this report by next week!

Debby: Relax, I **believe in**[8] you. Just don't give up, and everything will be okay, I'm sure.

黛比：一切還好嗎？看來你需要**振作**一下。

華特：唉，我在寫哲學作業時**遇到**一些問題。

黛比：怎麼了？你在**準備**做那堂課的作業時遇到困難了嗎？

華特：沒錯。這份報告我就是寫不完。我甚至考慮**退掉**這門哲學課。

黛比：太誇張了，那樣做一點**意義**也沒有。如果我是你，我會**擬訂**一張要**達成**目標的清單，然後一項一項去完成。

華特：但我打算下星期前要完成這份報告耶！

黛比：放輕鬆，我**相信**你。只要別放棄，我確定一切都會很順利的。

cheer up 振作

draw up a list 擬定清單

094

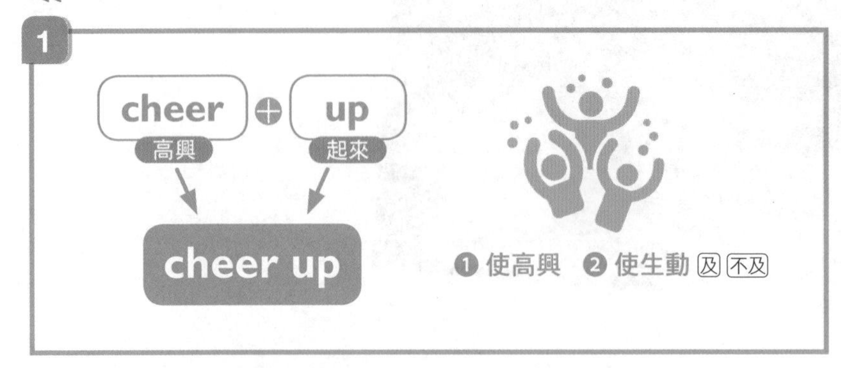

❶ When Gary was sick in bed for a month, his friend visited him dressed in a funny costume to try and **cheer** him **up**. 蓋瑞在病床上躺了一個月，為了**讓**他**開心**，朋友去探望他時穿了很滑稽的服裝。

❷ A coat of paint and new curtains would really **cheer** the kitchen **up**. 油漆和新的窗簾**讓**廚房完全**明亮**了起來。

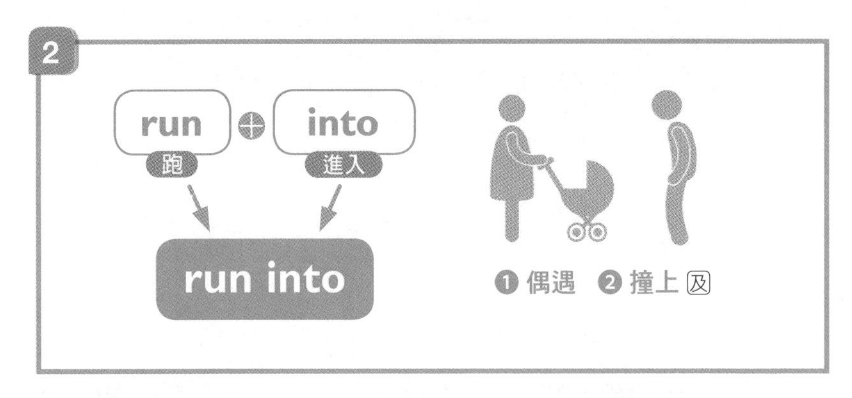

❶ We **ran into** a lot of traffic on the way to the airport.
我們在前往機場的路上**遇上**塞車。

❶ Jack **ran into** Betty at the supermarket; it was the first time he had seen her in years.
傑克在超市**偶遇**貝蒂，這是他多年來第一次看到她。

- Although we **set out to** buy some milk and eggs, we ended up buying a new laptop. 雖然我們**計劃**要買一些牛奶和雞蛋，但最後我們卻買了一台新的筆記型電腦。
- What will you **set out to** do after graduation? 你大學畢業後**計劃**做什麼？
- Ryan **set out to** write the perfect college application letter. 雷恩**打算**寫一份最理想的大學推薦信。

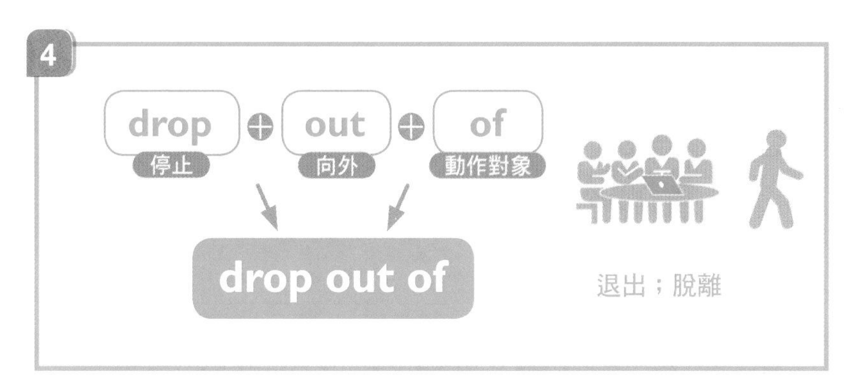

- After breaking his leg, Will **dropped out of** the race. 威爾腿骨折後便**退出**了比賽。
- When the judges discovered that Tracy had copied her artwork from another painting, they made her **drop out of** the competition. 當評審發現崔西的作品是模仿別幅畫時，便要她**退出**比賽。

095

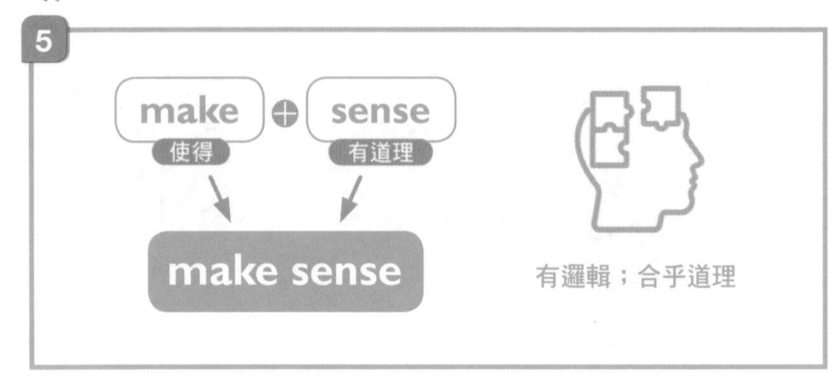

- If you didn't do the homework, the teacher's lecture will not **make sense**.
  你如果不做功課，會聽不懂老師教的。

- This assignment is hard; I don't think it **makes** any **sense**. 這份作業很困難，我不認為這是**合理**的。

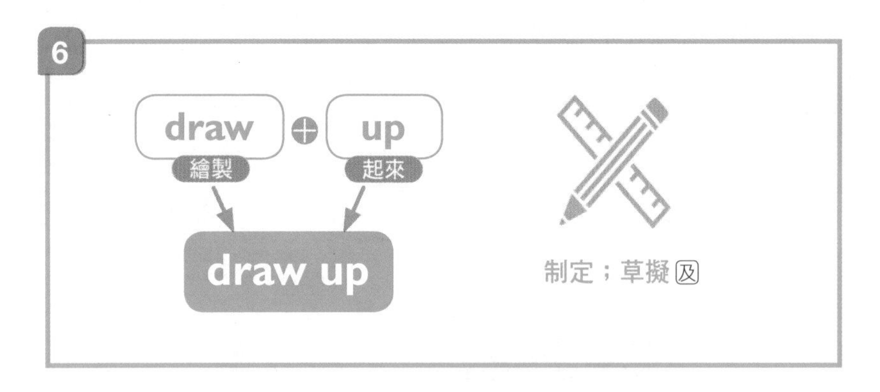

- The lawyer **drew up** a document putting Calvin in charge of his elderly mother's affairs.
  律師**擬定**了一份文件，指定凱文負責照顧年邁母親的生活起居。

- Felix **drew** a list **up** so that he could plan his week better. 菲力斯**擬定**了一張週計畫表以便做規畫。

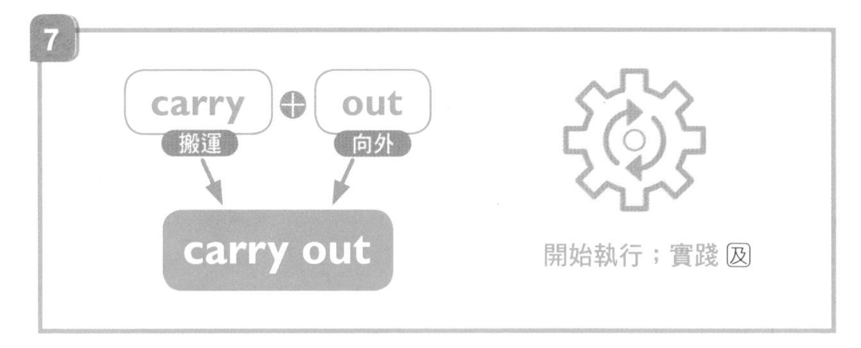

- The students were told to **carry out** every task their teacher expected of them.
  老師期望學生能**完成**所有的任務。
- I know you have a plan, but I hope you have time this weekend to **carry** it **out**.
  我知道你有計畫，但我希望你有時間在這週末**開始執行**。

❶ Although Rachel failed a few classes this semester, I **believe in** her; I think she'll be successful.
雖然瑞秋這學期有幾門課被當掉，但我還是**相信**她。我認為她會成功的。

❷ Patty doesn't **believe in** ghosts.
派蒂不**相信**幽靈的存在。

096

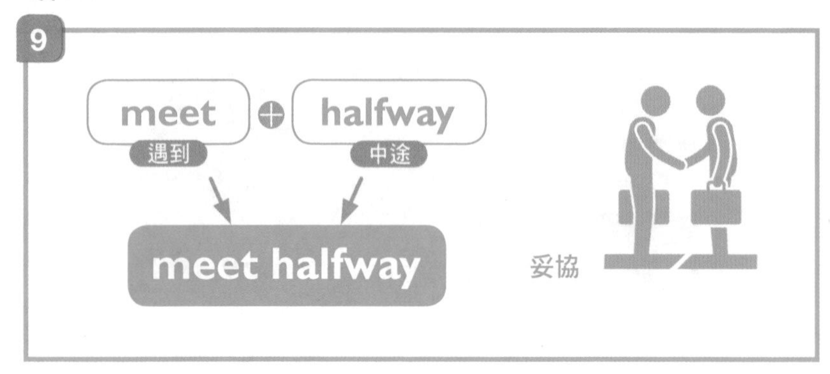

- Diane wanted to be paid $500 for her translation, and I wanted to pay her only $250. In the end, we **met** each other **halfway** and agreed on $375.
  黛安想要我付她 500 元的翻譯費用，而我只想付她 250 元，我們最後以 375 元**妥協**。
- Just when it seemed that the negotiations would never end, Jane found a way to **meet halfway** and lowered the price of the minivan.
  眼見協商沒完沒了，珍發現降低小卡車的售價是一種**妥協**的方法。

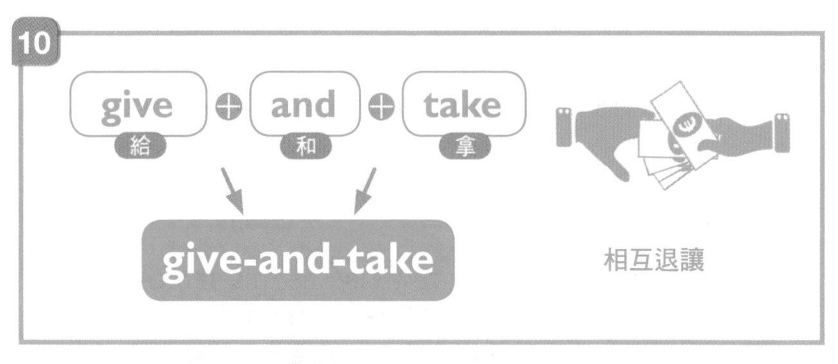

- Good business practices require a level of **give-and-take**. 想要完成一筆愉快的交易，包括一定程度的**相互妥協**。
- Happy family relations require **give-and-take**, I think.
  我認為家庭的和諧需要**相互讓步**。

- They reached an agreement after many hours of bargaining and **give-and-take**.
  經過了好幾個小時的協商和**退讓**後，他們終於達成了協議。
- In every friendship, there has to be some **give-and-take**. 每一段友情中都會需要**相互退讓**。

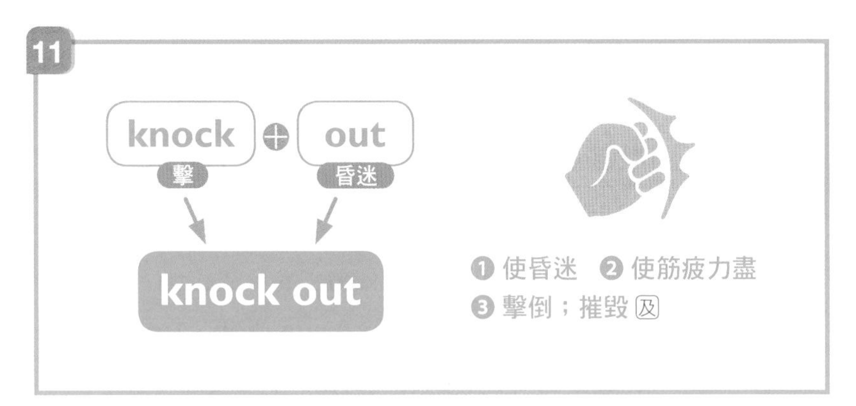

❶ Phil fell off his bike and **knocked** himself **out**.
菲爾從腳踏車上摔下來後**昏倒**了。

❶ The sleeping tablets **knocked** me **out** for 18 hours.
安眠藥讓我**昏睡**了 18 個小時。

❷ The doctor warned me that this painkiller might **knock** me **out**. 醫生警告我，服用這種止痛藥可能會**感到疲倦**。

Cheating on a Test
考試作弊

Diane and Pete have a chat about a recent test.
黛安和彼得在聊最近的考試。

097

Diane: I can't believe you **got away with**[1] cheating on the test.

Pete: Well, it was tough. I think the girl next to me knew what I was doing, but she didn't **let on**[2]. If she did, I'm sure things would have **gone wrong**[3].

Diane: Lucky for you that you don't **stand out**[4] as the kind of person who would cheat.

Pete: Right. It's a good thing that the teacher never **checked up on**[5] me too carefully.

Diane: Well, if you ask me, getting caught would **serve** you **right**[6].

Pete: Hey! How else can I **keep up with**[7] this class?

Diane: Try studying like the rest of us!

黛安： 我不敢相信你考試作弊竟然還能**逃過一劫**。

彼得： 是啊，這件事實在很棘手。我想隔壁的女生知道我在做什麼，但她沒有**洩漏**出去。如果她說了，我想事情一定會**變得很嚴重**。

黛安： 幸好你不像那些會作弊的人那麼**引人注目**。

彼得： 是啊，老師從來不會仔細**檢查**我，真好。

黛安： 唔，我認為啊，你**活該**被抓。

彼得： 嘿！不這麼做，我怎麼**趕上**班上的程度呢？

黛安： 就和我們其他人一樣讀書啊！

let to 洩漏（祕密）

098

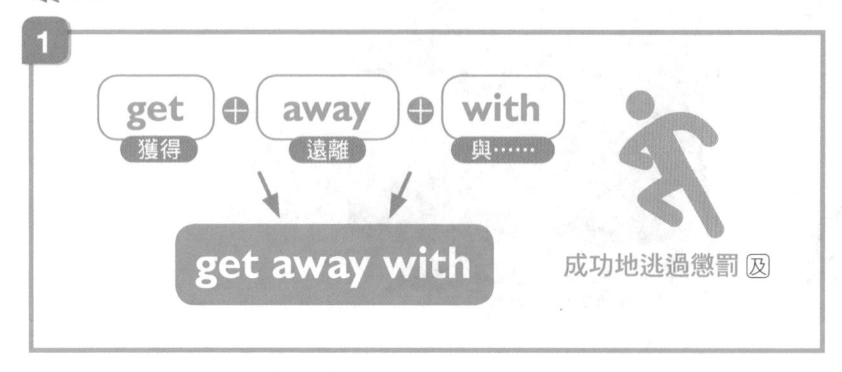

- Mindy **got away with** stealing strawberries from her neighbor's garden; nobody ever caught her. 敏蒂在鄰居家的院子裡偷摘草莓卻**逃過一劫**，至今還沒有人抓到她。
- Nobody **gets away with** cheating in this class.
  這個班上從來沒有人能夠作弊而**不受到懲罰**。

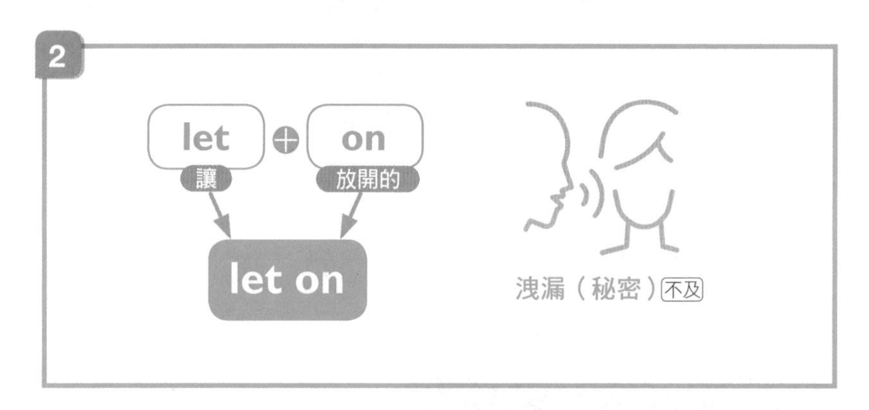

- I suspect Sally knows more about this than she's **letting on**.
  我懷疑莎莉知道的比她所**透露**的還要多。
- I tried not to **let on** that I knew the answer.
  我試著不**透露**其實我已經知道答案。

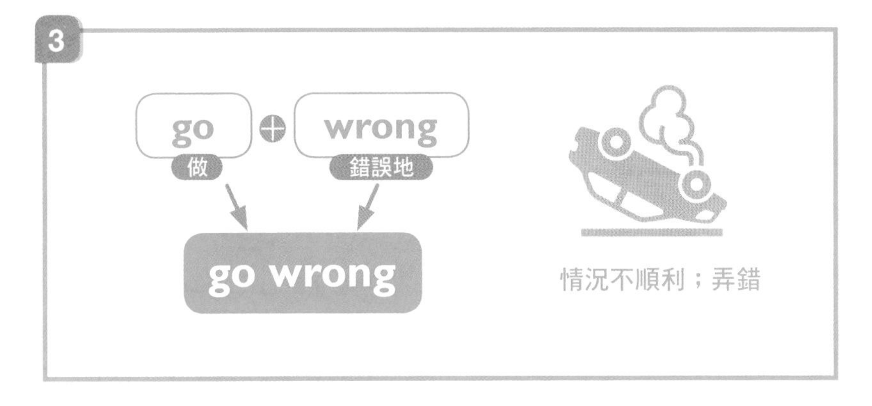

- Every detail about the trip to the seaside had been carefully planned, so we believed nothing could **go wrong**. And then it poured.
  海邊之旅的所有細節都經過詳細的規畫，因此我們相信事情是不會**出錯**的，不過後來卻下了傾盆大雨。
- After studying for a week, Amanda was confident about the test; she was sure nothing would **go wrong**.
  亞曼達唸了一整個星期的書，所以對考試很有信心，她確信一切不會**有問題**的。
- I thought I had done this correctly; I can't understand where I **went wrong**.
  我以為這件事情我做對了，我不知道究竟是哪裡**出了錯**。

 099

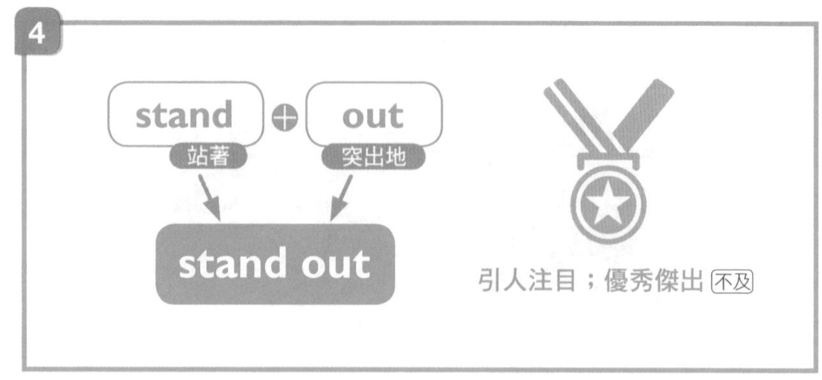

- Donald never dressed conservatively like his colleagues, and the bright colors he wore really made him **stand out** in a crowd.
  唐諾的穿著從不像同事那麼保守，因此穿著鮮豔的他在人群中非常**引人注目**。
- It **stands out** as an excellent school among many very good schools. 在許多好學校中，它顯然是一所聲譽極佳的學校。
- We had lots of good applicants for the job, but one **stood out** from the rest.
  這個職位有許多條件不錯的人選，但其中一位應徵者在所有人當中**脫穎而出**。
- His bright red hair helps him **stand out** at comedy clubs. 他那亮紅色的頭髮是他在喜劇俱樂部**引人注目**的原因。

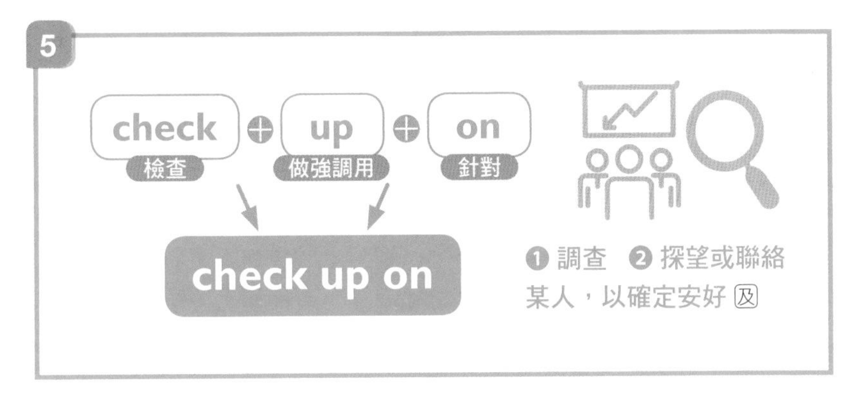

5
check
檢查
up
做強調用
on
針對
check up on
❶ 調查 ❷ 探望或聯絡某人，以確定安好 及

❷ Derek's mother called him at summer camp to **check up on** him.
戴瑞克的母親打電話到夏令營找戴瑞克，**以確定**他**安然無恙**。

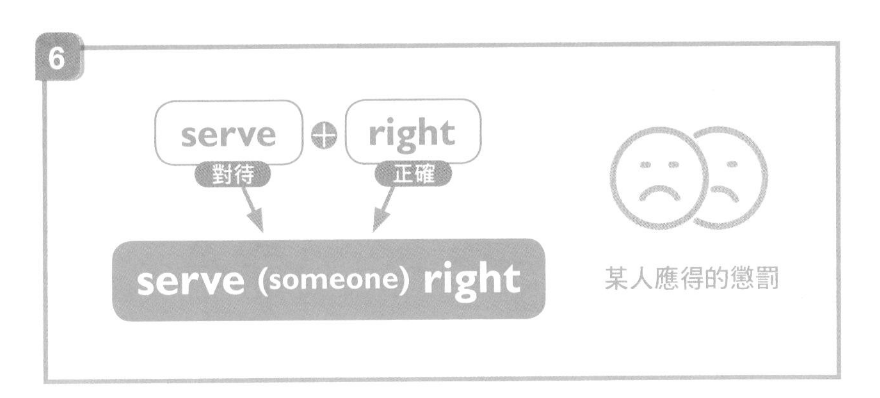

- Because Lucas delayed the flight by coming late, everyone onboard thought that losing his first-class seat **served** him **right**.
  由於盧卡斯遲到使得班機延誤，機上所有人都認為他**活該**喪失頭等艙的位子。
- It **serves** Marla **right** that she got an "F" in class because she never studied.
  因為瑪拉從不唸書，所以她**本該**得到「F」。

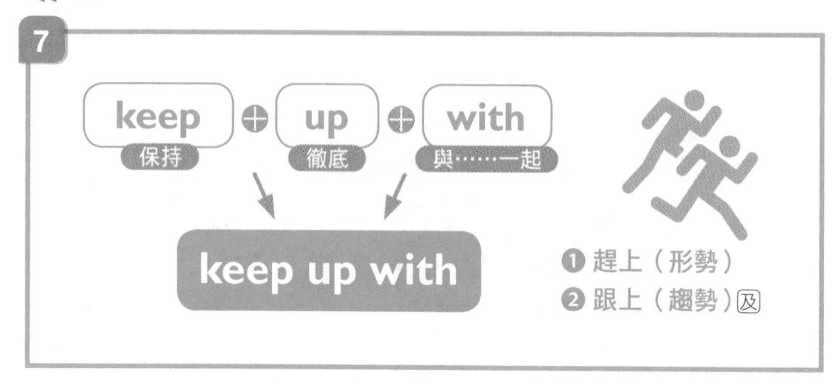

❶ Because Alfred missed a few weeks of class, he had a hard time **keeping up with** his classmates. 亞佛烈德好幾個星期沒去上課，他為了**趕上**同學的**進度**所以很辛苦。

❷ My grandmother doesn't **keep up with** new product. 我外婆不太能**跟上**流行產品。

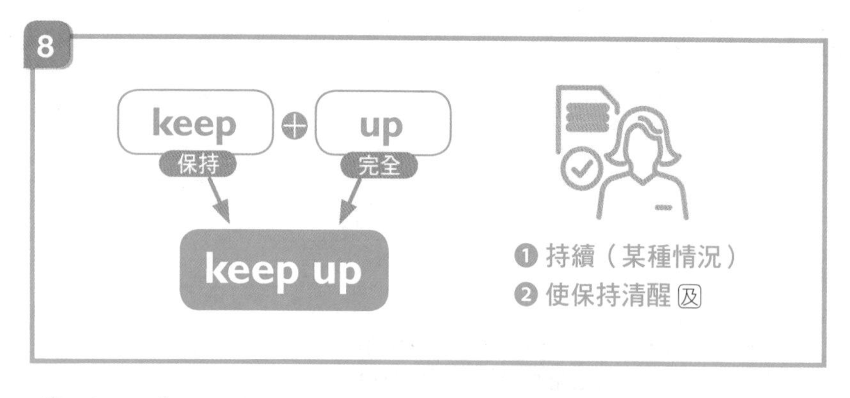

❶ If you **keep up** the good work, there's no question that you'll get an "A" in this class.
你如果**繼續**努力，這堂課肯定能得到「A」。

❶ Wow, you're doing great work; be sure to **keep** it **up**!
哇，你做得很好，一定要**繼續保持**！

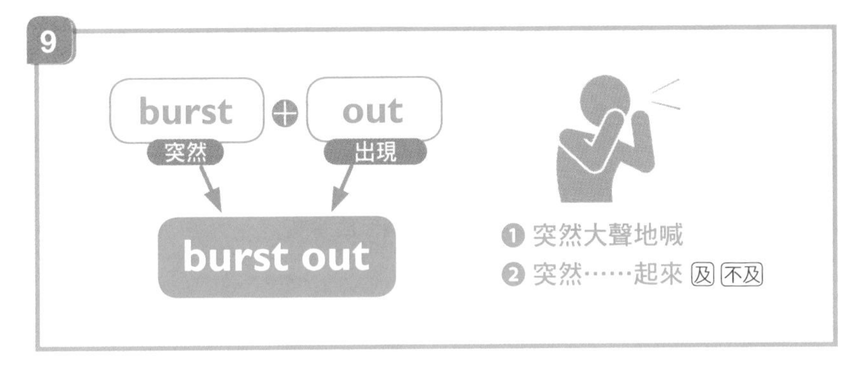

❶ "Come back!" Marc **burst out** as his girlfriend walked away.
馬克的女朋友離去時，他**大聲地喊**：「回來！」

❶ Some large rocks were **sticking up** out of the water.
有一些巨大的石頭**伸出**在水面上。

❶ When Betsy wakes up in the morning, her hair is always **sticking up**. 貝西早上起床時，頭髮總是**翹起來**。

❷ The robbers **stuck up** the bank and stole all the money. 搶匪**持槍搶劫**銀行，並且拿走了所有的現金。

The New Coworker
新同事

Amy tells Carl about a new coworker.
艾咪把新同事的事情告訴卡爾。

101

Amy: The new employee we hired is really **living up to**[1] my expectations.

Carl: Is that so? I'm glad to hear it, but I thought you didn't want to hire anyone new at your company.

Amy: Well, this one guy does the work of four people; so, in a way, hiring him has helped us **cut corners**[2].

Carl: You think he'll help **bring about**[3] some positive change, too?

Amy: Definitely. His former boss really **built up**[4] his reputation when we spoke on the phone, and I can see that he deserves it.

Carl: How so?

Amy: For example, when he starts a project, he **sticks to**[5] it until he is totally done. He also knows how to **stand up for**[6] his ideas, even if the boss disagrees.

Carl: Wow! He sounds like the perfect coworker.

艾咪： 新來的員工真的很**符合**我的期望。

卡爾： 真的嗎？真替妳高興，但我以為你們公司不想聘人。

艾咪： 嗯，這個人做了四人份的工作，所以就一定的程度來說，僱用他能幫公司**節省**成本。

卡爾： 你認為他還會**帶來**一些正面的改變嗎？

艾咪： 當然，我和他之前的老闆通過電話，他可是對他讚譽**有加**，我看得出來他說的沒錯。

卡爾： 怎麼說？

艾咪： 舉例來說，當他開始進行一項企畫後，便會**堅持**到完成。就算與老闆意見不合，他也知道要如何**支持**自己的想法。

卡爾： 哇！聽起來他是一位很理想的工作伙伴。

stick to 堅持

stand up for 維護權利；支持

102

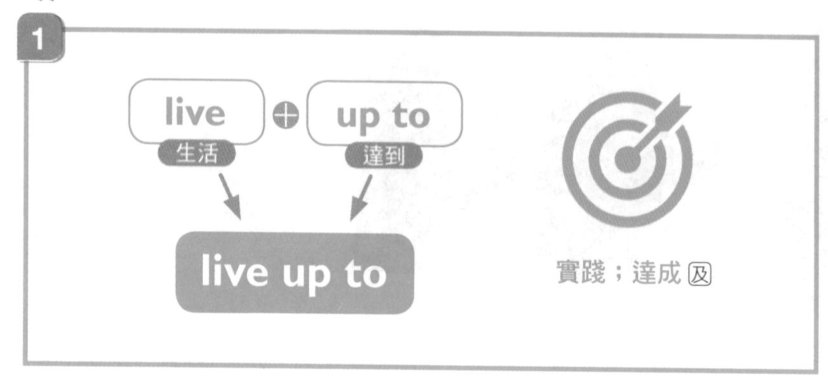

- Linda's parents were both world-famous surgeons, so she had a hard time **living up to** their expectations.
  由於琳達的雙親是世界有名的外科醫生，所以她很努力地想要**達成**父母的期望。

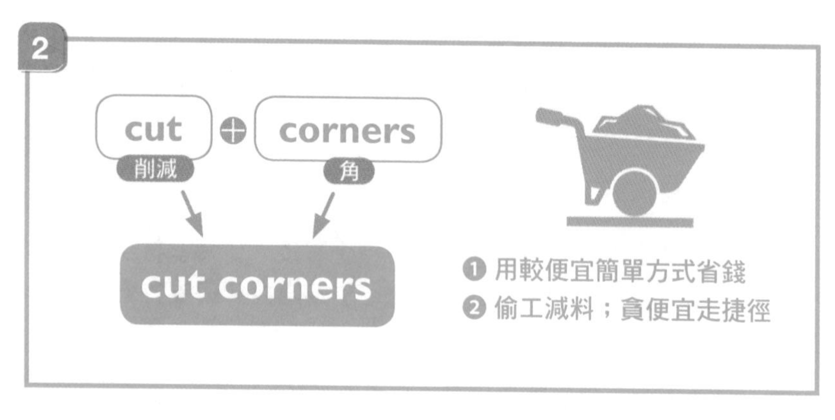

❶ The trick to saving money is knowing when to **cut corners**. 存錢的竅門就是要知道何時該**節省開銷**。

❶ If we **cut corners** this year, maybe we can afford to go on vacation next summer.
如果我們今年**省一點**，也許明年夏天就有足夠的錢能夠去度假。

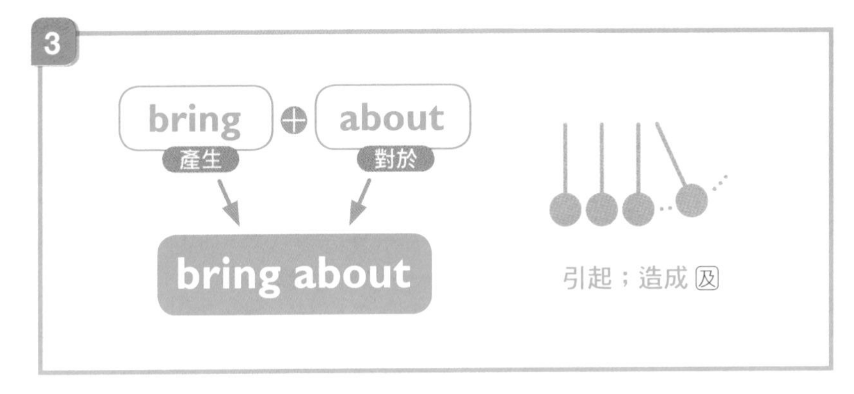

- Mike **brought about** his company's collapse with his reckless spending. 麥可無盡的揮霍是**造成**公司倒閉的原因。
- Eleanor is the kind of woman who can **bring about** results; that's why my company hired her.
  伊莉諾是個能**帶來**成效的女人，這就是我們公司僱用她的原因。

❶ Aaron is a great visionary; he **built up** a new business from nothing.
亞倫是個極有遠見的人，他白手起家，**開創**了新的事業。

❸ Natalie **built** her Spanish vocabulary **up** in preparation for her trip to Mexico.
娜塔莉**學**了許多西班牙文單字，為墨西哥之旅作準備。

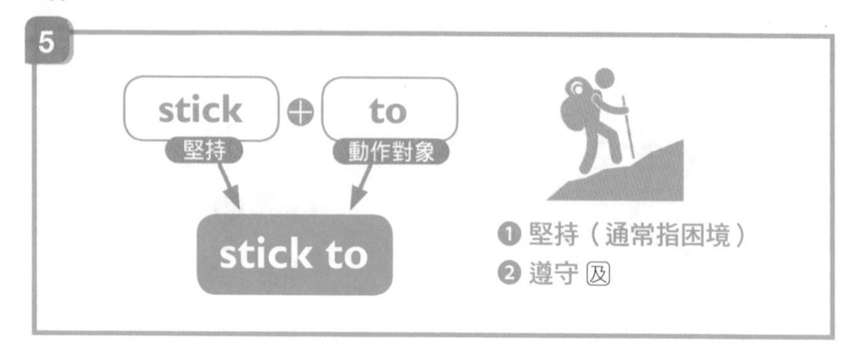

❶ I understand that you're having a hard time in this class, but just **stick to** the schedule and do the best you can. 我知道這堂課你上得很辛苦，但你只要**堅持**下去、全力以赴就行了。

❶ It is hard to understand the class because the teacher never **sticks to** his point—he always changes the topic and never finishes any ideas. 這門課很難理解，因為老師從不**堅守**立場。他總是任意變換主題，而不下結論。

❷ It won't be easy to **stick to** my academic schedule because I have classes every morning at 8:30.
我每天早上 8 點 30 分都有課，所以要我**遵守**課表很難。

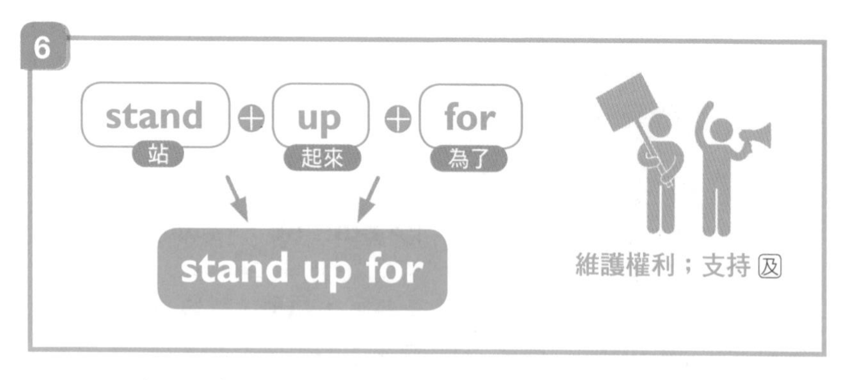

- Martin Luther King, Jr., **stood up for** the rights of his fellow African Americans.
馬丁路德金恩**捍衛**了非裔美國人的權利。

- I **stood up for** my math teacher when all my friends were complaining about him.
  當我所有的朋友都在抱怨數學老師時，我卻為他**挺身而出**。

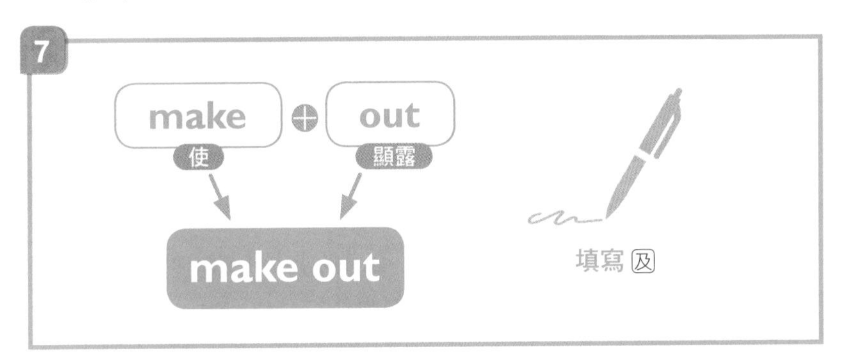

- Elaine **made out** a legal will that leaves everything to her daughter. 伊蓮在遺囑上**註明**會將所有財產留給她女兒。
- Jared **made** a check **out** for $50 to cover the expenses.
  傑瑞德**開了**一張 50 元的支票把費用付清。

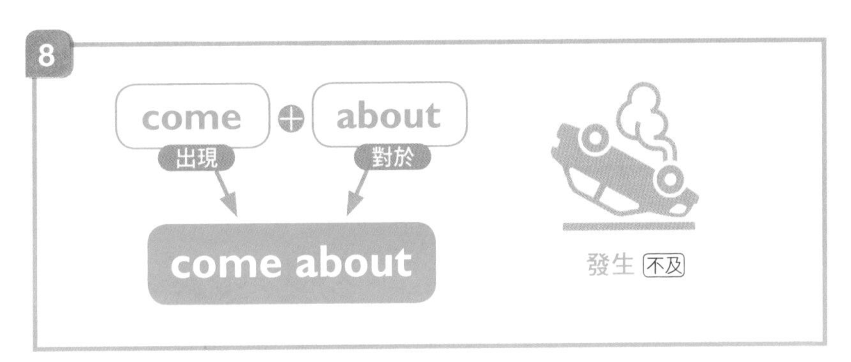

- How did this terrible situation **come about**?
  怎麼會**發生**這麼嚴重的事情？
- Do you know how the tradition of decorating a Christmas tree **came about**?
  你知道裝飾聖誕樹的傳統是如何**出現**的嗎？
- How did the problem **come about** in the first place?
  問題是怎麼**發生**的呢？

104

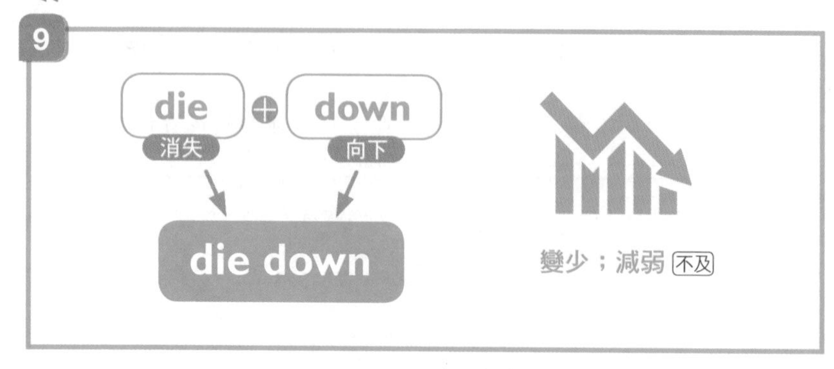

- As the party was ending, the noise level began to **die down**. 喧鬧聲在派對結束後**逐漸消失**。
- Pam's anger over her son's decision to leave school took a few weeks to **die down**.
  潘很生氣兒子決定休學，她花了好幾個星期才**逐漸氣消**。
- By morning, the storm had **died down**.
  暴風雨在早晨的時候**逐漸平息**下來。
- It was several minutes before the applause **died down**.
  掌聲持續了好幾分鐘才**減弱**下來。

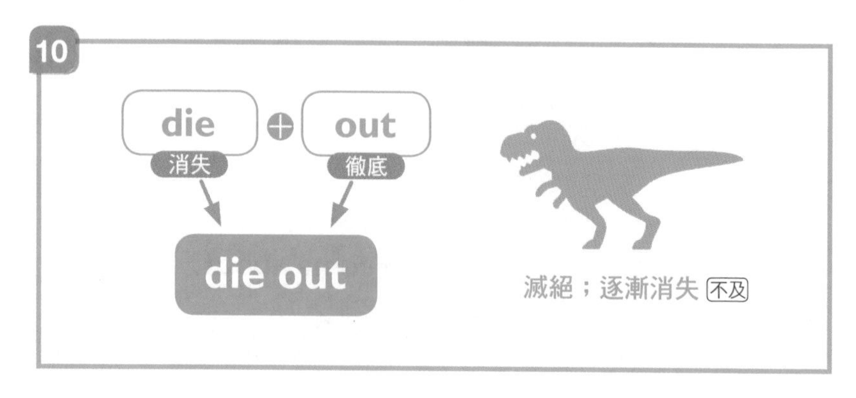

- No one knows for sure why the dinosaurs **died out**.
  沒人知道恐龍為何會**滅絕**。

- The traditional customs of the native people **died out** after a few years. 幾年後，原住民的傳統習俗**漸漸消失**。
- It's a custom that is beginning to **die out**.
  這項習俗正在**慢慢消失**。

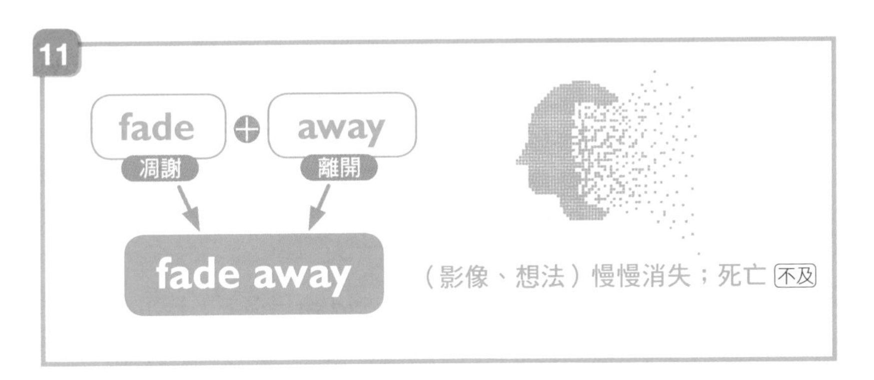

11
fade
凋謝
away
離開
fade away
（影像、想法）慢慢消失；死亡 不及

- As the harbor filled with fog, the boats **faded away**.
  船隻因為濃霧籠罩著港口而**漸漸消失**。
- As time went by, my childhood memories began to **fade away**. 我的童年記憶隨著時間過去而**逐漸消失**。
- As the years passed, the memories **faded away**.
  記憶隨著時間的過去而**逐漸消失**。

Unit 27

Falling Behind in Class
課業落後

Ricardo is telling Pauline about some troubles at school. 里卡多把在學校遇到的困難告訴寶琳。

105

Ricardo: Sometimes I think Ms. Conway really **has it in for**[1] me.

Pauline: Why do you say that?

Ricardo: For one thing, she seems mad at me for **falling behind**[2] in class.

Pauline: I didn't know you were behind. I guess your plans to catch up last weekend **fell through**[3].

Ricardo: Unfortunately, they did. And now both my parents and Ms. Conway want to **have it out with**[4] me.

Pauline: Did you at least prepare for tomorrow's test? Ms. Conway **gave out**[5] a handout to help us review.

Ricardo: Actually, I'm going to **hold off**[6] on studying; I'm spending all my free time trying to beat this new video game I got.

Pauline: Well, if you ask me, you should either forget about the game or **give in**[7] and accept an "F" in the class . . .

Ricardo: No way! I can pass this test without studying.

Pauline: Really? I doubt it. It seems like you **took on**[8] more classes than you can handle.

里卡多： 有時候我覺得康威女士常常**和我過不去**。

寶琳： 怎麼說？

里卡多： 首先，我**跟不上**學習進度，她似乎很生氣。

寶琳： 我都不曉得你跟不上進度。我想你上週末準備趕進度的計畫**泡湯了**。

里卡多： 是不幸取消了，而現在我父母和康威女士都想要**找我算帳**。

寶琳： 至少你會準備明天的考試吧？康威女士**發**了一張幫助我們複習的講義。

里卡多： 事實上，我的讀書計畫要**延後**了。我現在一有空，就在玩新買的電動玩具。

寶琳： 唔，我認為你應該忘掉電動，或是**默默接受**得到「F」的事實……。

里卡多： 不可能！我不用唸書就可以考及格了。

寶琳： 是嗎？我很懷疑。看來你**修**的課數超出你的負荷。

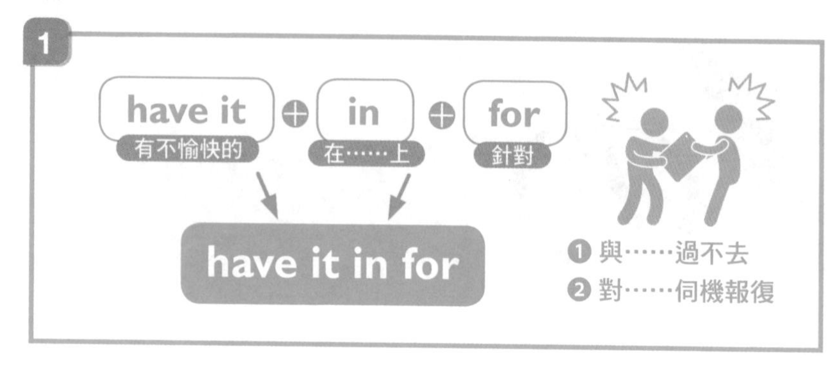

❶ Sometimes I think my tutor really **has it in for** me; no matter how hard I work, she always complains. 有時我覺得助教常常**和我過不去**。無論我多用功，她老是有話要說。

❶ My boss must really **have it in for** me; that was the third lecture this week!
我老闆一定是在**和我過不去**，那已經是這星期第三次訓話了！

❶ After three weeks' vacationing in the United Kingdom, Nick realized he was **falling behind** on his research project.
尼克在英國度假三個禮拜後，才發現他的研究報告**進度落後**了。

❶ Frank **fell behind** on his schoolwork and couldn't graduate with his friends.
法蘭克**跟不上**課業，所以無法和同學一起畢業。

❷ You're **falling behind** with the rent. 你**遲交**房租了。

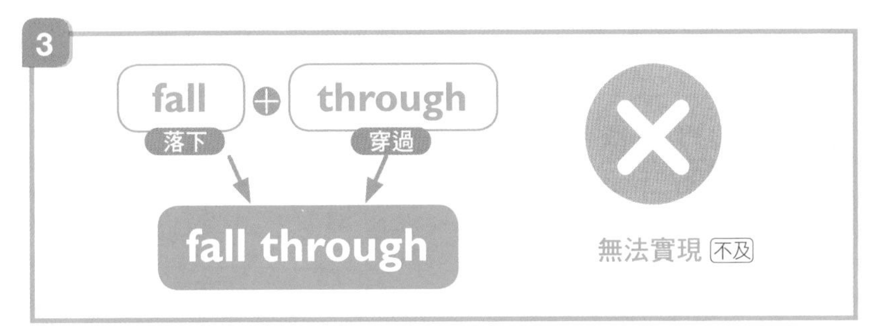

- Corey's plan to buy a car **fell through** when he lost his job. 柯瑞買車的計畫在工作丟了後便**告吹**了。
- Wade's plan to be the coolest kid in school **fell through** when he got an embarrassing haircut.
  偉德的頭髮剪壞了，他**無法**成為全校最酷的小孩了。
- We found a buyer for our house, but then the sale **fell through**. 我們找到了房子的買主，但這場交易後來**告吹**了。

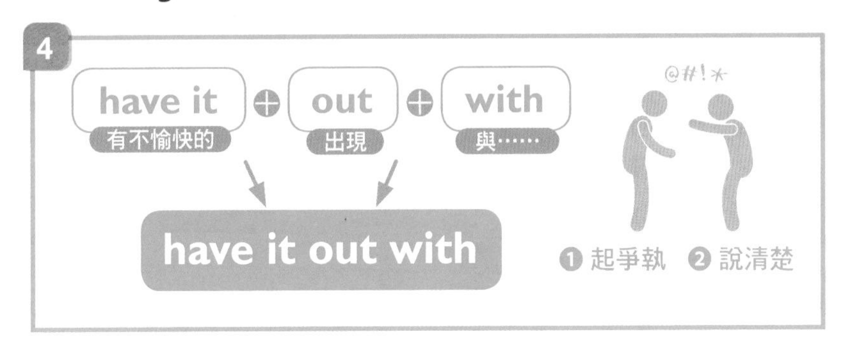

❶ I really **had it out with** Archie when I found out he was the one who stole my bike.
當我發現就是阿奇偷了我的腳踏車後，便和他**起了口角**。

❶ Taylor and Lydia disagree about how best to do the project; I think they'll **have it out with** each other soon. 泰勒和莉蒂雅對執行這項企畫的最佳方式意見不一，我認為他們很快就會**吵起來**。

❷ Judy was late for work every morning this week, and I thought I'd better **have it out with** her.
茱蒂這星期每天早上上班都遲到，我認為我最好和她**說清楚**。

107

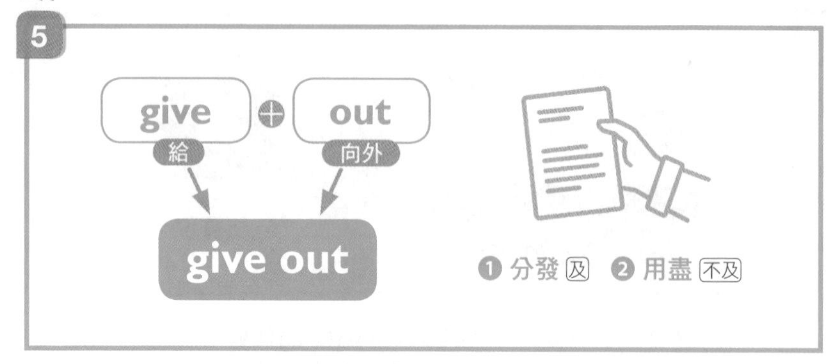

❶ To promote its new flavor of gum, the company hired some people to **give out** samples to passersby.
公司為了宣傳新口味的口香糖，請了一些人把試吃包**發**給路人。

❶ The teacher **gave** a study guide **out** to everyone who asked for one. 老師把學習導引手冊**發**給需要的人。

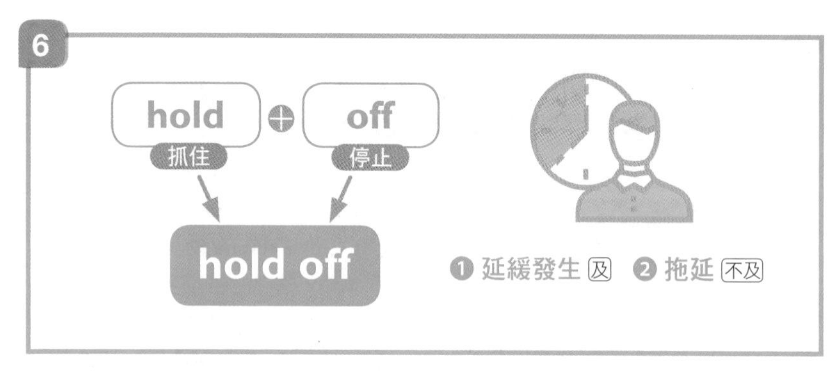

❶ They **held off** buying a new digital camera until the price went down.
他們一直**拖**到數位相機降價才買了一台新的。

❶ I think we should **hold off** going downtown until we find the bus schedule.
找出公車時間表前，我們應該**暫緩**去市中心的計畫。

❷ **Hold off** on calling a taxi; maybe my aunt can give us a ride. **先別**叫計程車，也許我阿姨可以載我們一程。

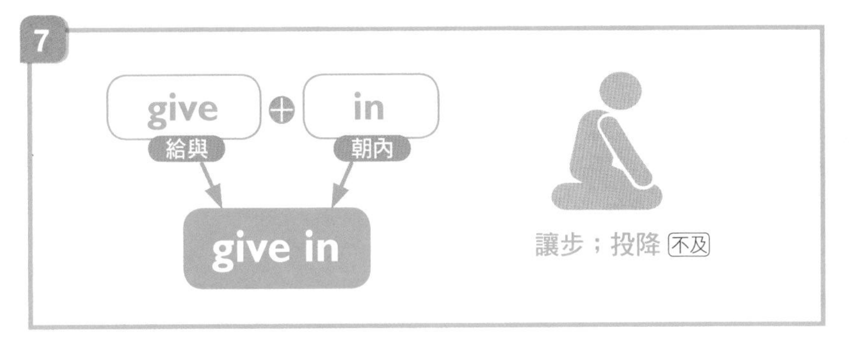

- I know you're not the best football player, but you shouldn't **give in** and quit the team without trying a little harder. 我知道你並非最棒的足球員，但你不應該沒再多試幾個星期，就**輕易放棄**和退出球隊。
- After a few months of trying to live without a TV, I finally **gave in** and bought one.
過了幾個月沒有電視的日子後，我終於**放棄**且買了一台新的。
- I finally **gave in** and let him stay up to watch TV.
我終於**讓步**，讓他熬夜看電視。

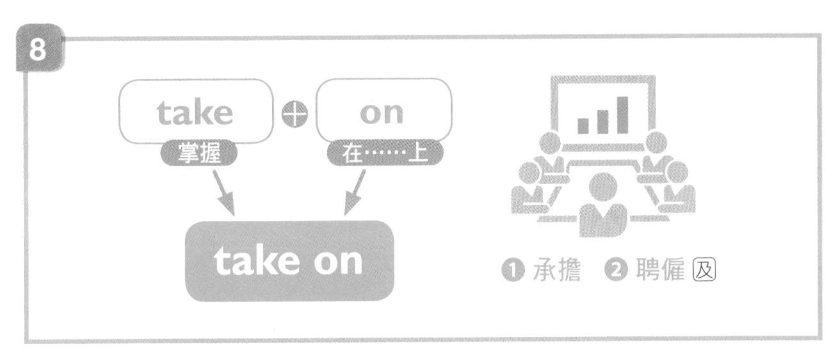

❶ I'm not sure if I can **take on** any more classes; my schedule is already full.
我不確定我是否能應付多**修**幾門課，我的課表很滿了。

❷ My company **took on** three new employees last week.
我們公司上星期**聘用**了三位新員工。

108

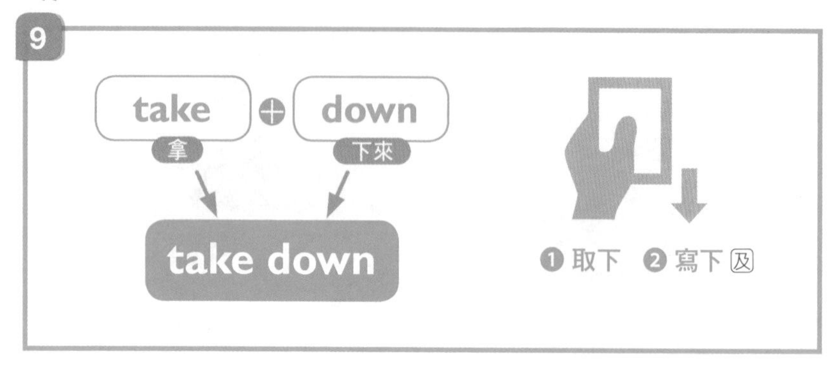

❶ After Florence's art exhibit, the workers **took down** all of the paintings that hadn't sold. 佛羅倫斯的藝術展覽結束後，工作人員把所有沒賣出的畫**拿了下來**。

❶ Jim's mom made him **take** the rock 'n' roll posters **down** from his wall.
吉姆的媽媽要他把牆上的搖滾樂團海報**拿下來**。

❷ Did you **take down** any notes during physics class?
你有**抄**物理課的筆記嗎？

❶ Don't buy the first car you find; **hold out** until you see the perfect model.
別買你第一輛看到的車，要**堅持**到你看到最理想的車款才下手。

❷ The waiter **held out** a tray of drinks and offered them to everyone at the party.
服務生把飲料放在托盤上，給所有參加派對的人喝。

My Note

Breaking Up[1]
分手

Gavin calls Judy on the phone.
蓋文打電話給裘蒂。

109

Gavin: Hello, Judy! It's me, Gavin.

Judy: Gavin? Please **leave** me **alone**[2]! I told you never to call me again!

Gavin: Judy, please don't **break off**[3] our relationship. I know that things have been very **touch and go**[4] between us lately, but I miss you! I must see you again.

Judy: I don't think so. Your attitude really **wears** me **down**[5]. You can drop by one more time, but only so you can **bring back**[6] those CDs I lent you.

Gavin: And that's it? After that, I must **let** you **alone**[7]?

Judy: Yes. Although we had some good times, **on the whole**[8] our romance was pretty boring. I'm sorry, but it's over!

蓋文： 哈囉，裘蒂！我是蓋文。

裘蒂： 蓋文？請不要**煩**我！我說過別再打電話給我！

蓋文： 裘蒂，拜託不要**結束**我們的關係。我知道最近我們的關係變得**岌岌可危**，但我很想念妳！我一定要見妳。

裘蒂： 我不覺得。你的態度真的令我很**累**。唔，我們再見一面吧，只有這樣你才可以把我借給你的 CD **還**給我。

蓋文： 就這樣？之後我便**不再打擾**妳？

裘蒂： 是的。雖然我們在一起很快樂，但這段感情**大致來說**非常無趣。很抱歉，我們之間結束了！

wear down 使疲累

leave sb. alone 讓某人獨處

110

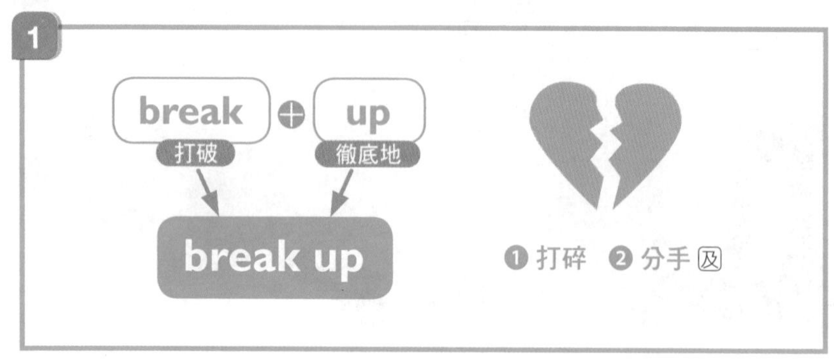

❶ The company has been **broken up** and sold off.
這家公司已經**解散**，並且廉價售出了。

❷ I've just **broken up** with my boyfriend.
我才剛和男朋友**分手**。

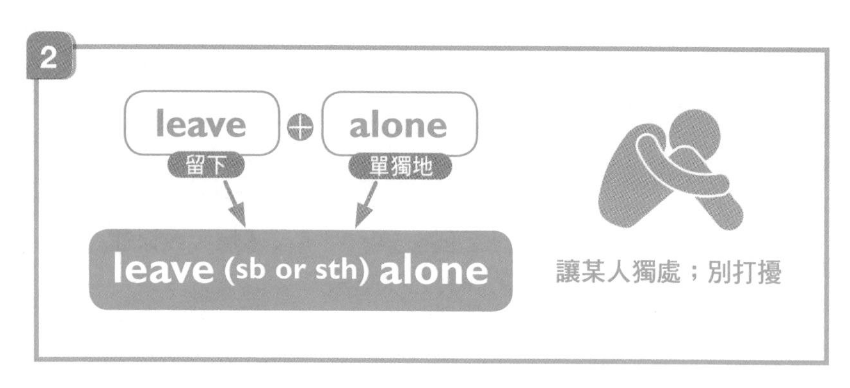

- **Leave** Rick **alone**. He's making a very important phone call.
  別打擾瑞克，他在講一通很重要的電話。

❶ Corey **broke off** a piece of the cookie and gave it to his younger brother.
柯瑞把餅乾**分**成一小塊給弟弟。

❶ Can you **break** me **off** a piece of that chocolate?
可以**分**一塊巧克力給我嗎？

❷ When the phone rang, Mrs. Williams **broke off** the conversation and ran to answer it.
電話聲響起時，威廉斯太太**停止**了談話，然後跑向電話。

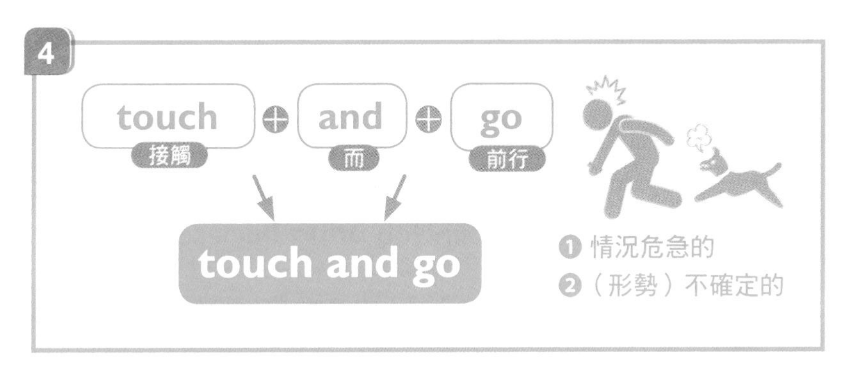

❶ The dental work was going well at first, but then it was **touch and go** for a while.
牙醫的工作剛開始很正常，但後來有一段時間**不是很順利**。

❷ Marc wasn't sure if he had passed his exams; it was really **touch and go**.
馬克不確定他考試是否及格，**不到最後關頭真的無法論定**。

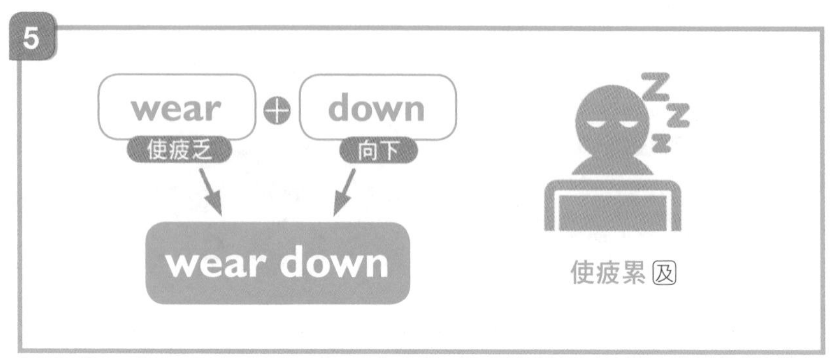

- This boring class really **wears** me **down**; I'm always nearly asleep before it's even half over!
這堂無聊的課**把**我**累壞**了，通常課還不到一半我就快要睡著！

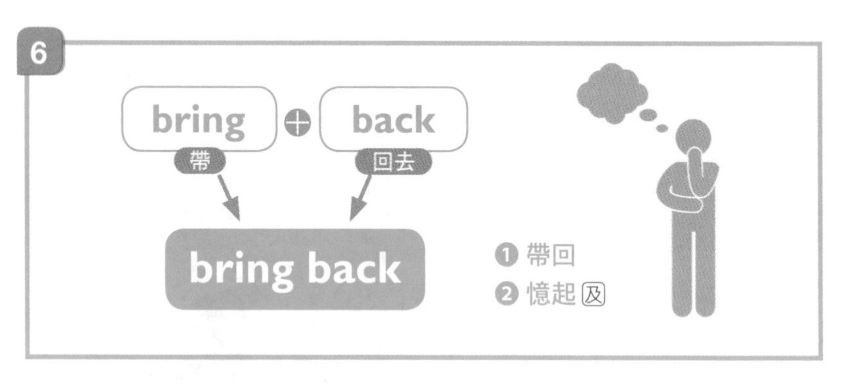

❶ If you go to the store, can you **bring back** some ice cream?
如果你要去商店，可以**帶**些冰淇淋**回來**嗎？

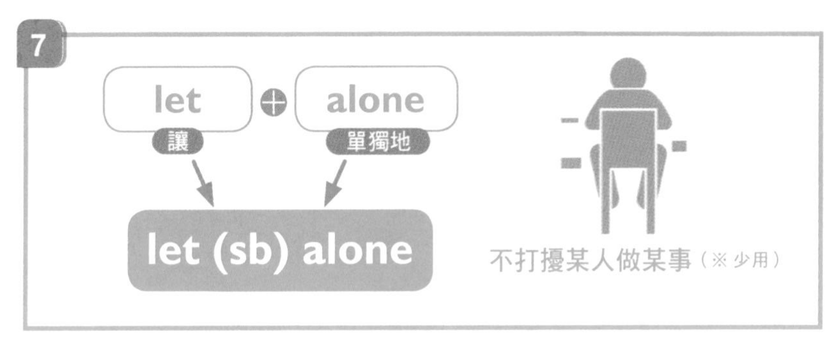

- **Let** Seth **alone**. He's trying to finish his report.
  別煩塞斯，他正試著要完成報告。
- I wish she would **let** me **alone** so I could get some sleep.
  我希望她**不要來打擾**我，這樣我才可以睡點覺。

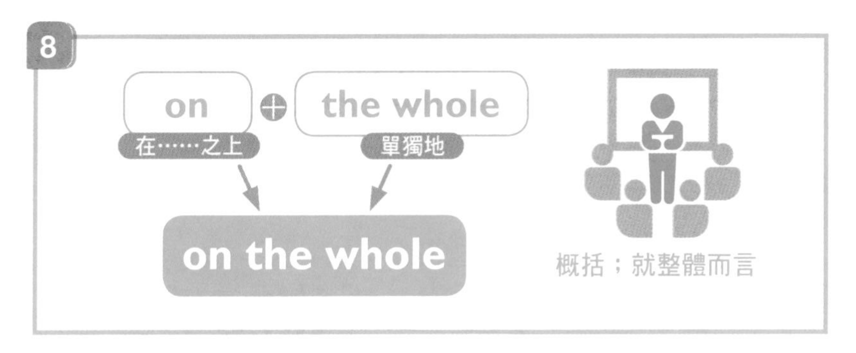

- **On the whole**, my vacation was excellent, though there were a few problems.
  雖然遇到了一些困難，但**整體而言**，我的假期還是很棒的。
- It was a fun party **on the whole**, but I wish the music had been better.
  整體而言，這個派對很好玩，但我希望音樂能有所改善。
- **On the whole**, I think my dinner party was a success.
  整體而言，我認為這次的晚餐聚會辦得很成功。
- We have had some bad times, but **on the whole** we're fairly happy.
  我們遇到了一些不開心的事情，但**整體來說**還是過得很快樂。

112

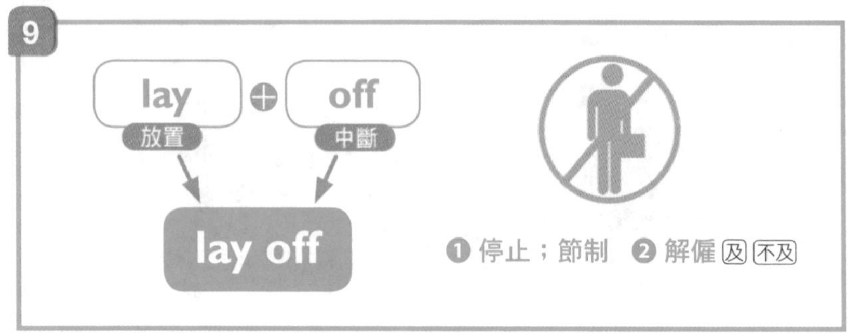

❶ My coworkers didn't **lay off** our boss for the entire dinner; they were very critical of her.
用餐時，我的同事**毫不客氣地批評**老闆，他們對她非常不滿。

❶ I usually run several miles every day but **lay off** in the hot weather. 我每天通常會跑好幾英里，但大熱天就**不**跑了。

❷ He was **laid off** along with many others when the company moved to New York City.
公司搬遷至紐約市時，他和許多員工都被**解僱**了。

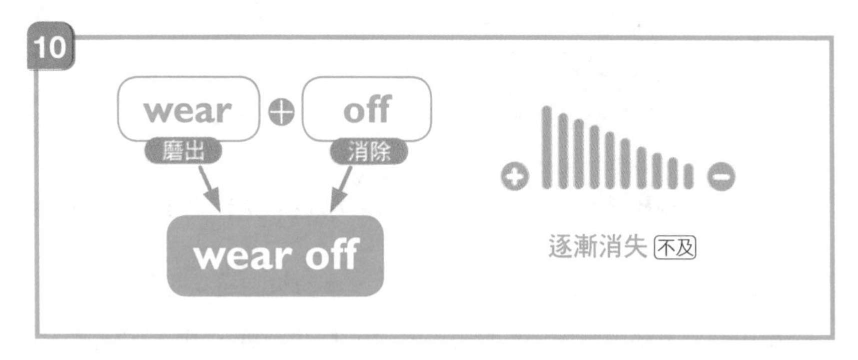

- As soon as the coffee began to **wear off**, Jill felt tired.
  隨著咖啡的效用**逐漸消失**，吉爾感覺很累。
- When the aspirin **wore off**, Lou's headache returned.
  當阿斯匹靈**逐漸失去**效用時，盧的頭又痛了起來。
- The effect of the injection will gradually **wear off**.
  打針後的藥效會**逐漸消失**。

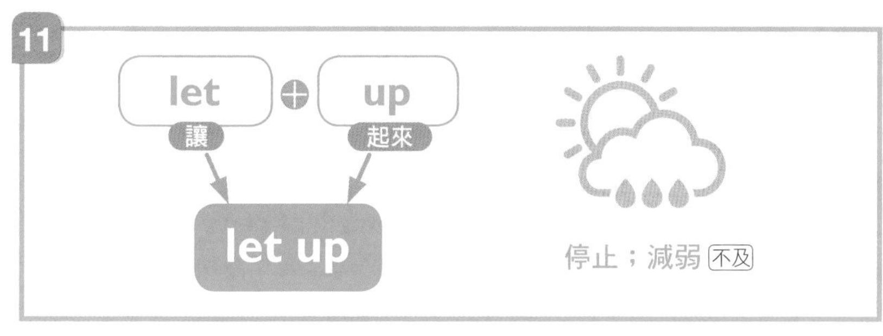

- If the snow ever **lets up**, we'll drive to the store.
  如果**停止**下雪，我們就會開車去商店。
- When the rain **lets up,** we'll go for a walk.
  我們雨**停**後就去散步。
- The rain shows no sign of **letting up**.
  雨一點也沒有要**停**的樣子。

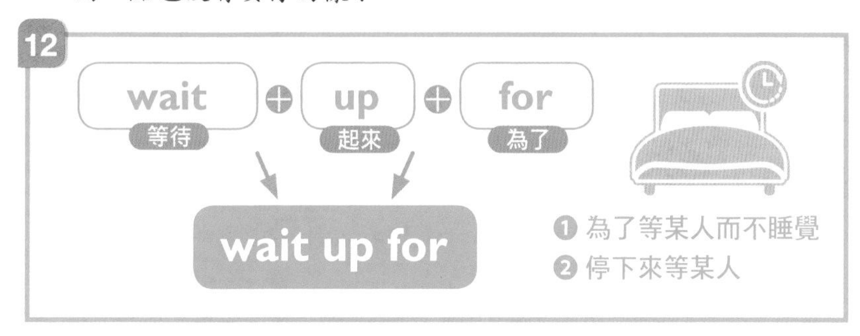

❶ Mom was **waiting up for** me when I walked in the door, and she was not happy!
當我回到家時，媽媽**還沒睡在等**我，而且不太高興！

❶ If you're planning on returning home before midnight, I'll try to **wait up for** you.
如果你打算在午夜前回家，我會**等**你的。

❶ I'll probably be out very late tonight, so don't **wait up for** me. 我今天晚上會很晚才回來，所以不要**為我等門**了。

❶ Let's **wait up for** Sherry to see how her date went.
我們**等**雪莉回來吧，了解一下她的約會是否進展順利。

❷ We're so far ahead of our friends; let's **wait up for** them here. 我們超前了朋友許多，我們**停**在這裡**等**他們吧。

Being a Designer
成為設計師

Amanda has some excellent news to share with Joy. 亞曼達有天大的好消息要和喬伊分享。

113

Amanda: I've got great news! You know that I **have my heart set on**[1] becoming a designer and have worked a lot lately on making my own clothes.

Joy: So what's the news? Did your style **catch on**[2]?

Amanda: It sure did! It seems I'm really **cut out for**[3] fashion design.

Joy: Why? What happened, exactly?

Amanda: Well, I was showing a few samples to a local store, and they loved the style so much that they **bought up**[4] everything. The next day, they called to tell me that everything had already **sold out**[5].

Joy: Fantastic! Did you make a lot of money?

Amanda: Yup! It **works out**[6] to about a 200% profit for me.

Joy: Congratulations!

亞曼達：好消息！因為我**已經下定決心**要成為一名設計師，所以我最近都在設計衣服。

喬伊：所以妳要告訴我的消息是什麼？是妳設計的衣服**廣受歡迎**嗎？

亞曼達：沒錯！看來我真的很**適合**成為一位服裝設計師。

喬伊：怎麼說？究竟怎麼回事？

亞曼達：嗯，我拿了一些樣本到這附近的一家店，他們非常喜歡我的設計，而且全數**買下**。隔天，他們還打電話跟我說衣服全**賣完**了。

喬伊：真了不起！妳賺了不少吧？

亞曼達：是啊！我**一共**約賺了兩倍的利潤。

喬伊：恭喜妳！

buy up 全部買下

sell out 銷售一空

114

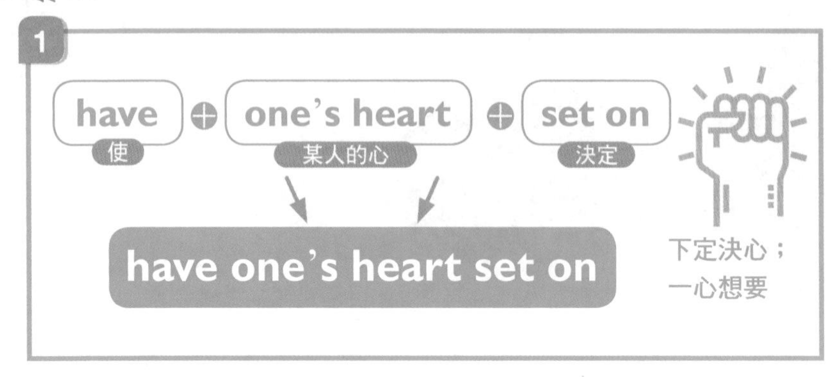

- I **had my heart set on** becoming a doctor.
  我已經**下定決心**要成為一名醫生了。
- Sarah **has her heart set on** going to Bermuda next year. 莎拉**下定決心**明年要去百慕達。

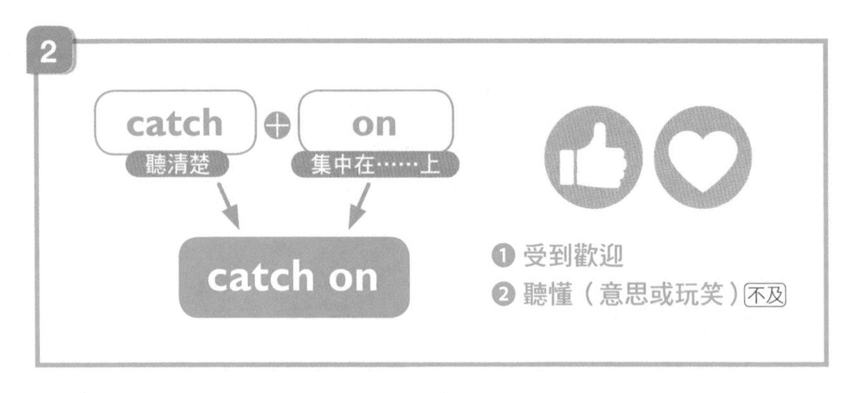

❶ The new clothing brand has really **caught on** among college students.
這個新牌子的衣服很**受到**大學生的**歡迎**。

❷ Raul didn't **catch on** that we were making fun of him.
勞爾**聽**不**懂**我們在開他玩笑。

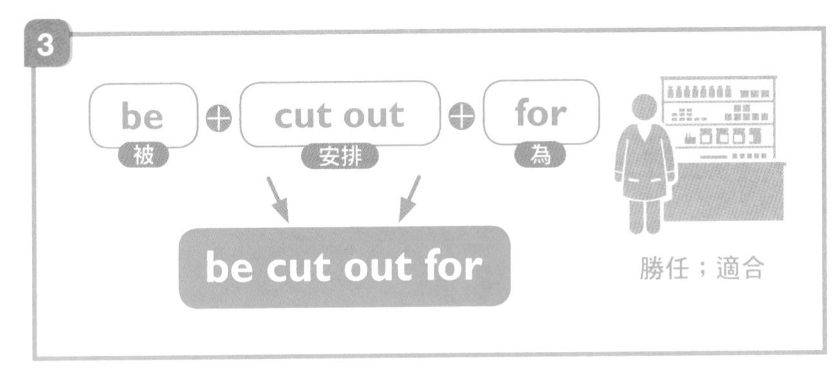

- Darren **is** not **cut out for** a job in a big company.
  戴倫不**適合**在大公司工作。
- Francesca **is cut out for** environmental work with her master's degree in natural science.
  法蘭契斯卡擁有自然科學碩士學位，她很**適合**環保工作。

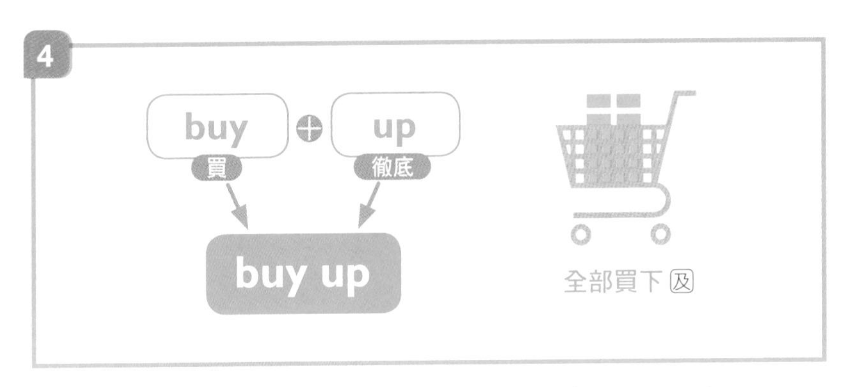

- Tabitha **bought** all the chocolate **up** because she was crazy for it.
  由於泰貝莎超愛吃巧克力，所以她**買下**了所有的巧克力。
- Flynn **bought up** all the batteries in the store because he needed them for his stereo.
  佛林為了音響而**買下**了這家店所有的電池。
- Chris **bought up** all the land in the surrounding area.
  克里斯**買下**了附近所有的土地。

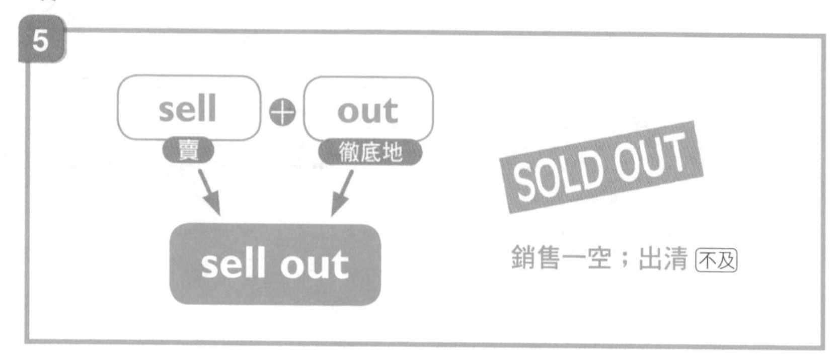

- The new edition of his book **sold out** in just a few hours!
  他的書出了新版本，幾個小時內便**銷售一空**了！
- The store **sells out** of ice cream whenever it is hot.
  每當天氣很熱時，店裡的冰淇淋便會**銷售一空**。

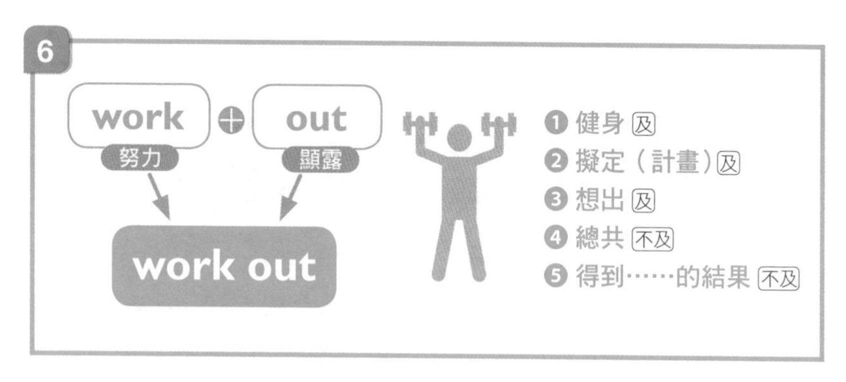

❶ Emmy wants to be healthier, so she **works out** three times a week.
艾咪想要健康的身體，所以每星期會**做**三次**運動**。

❸ Byron **worked out** a way to save a lot of money over the summer.
拜倫**想出**了一個夏天的省錢大計。

❹ The total cost **worked out** to around $400.
一共約 400 元。

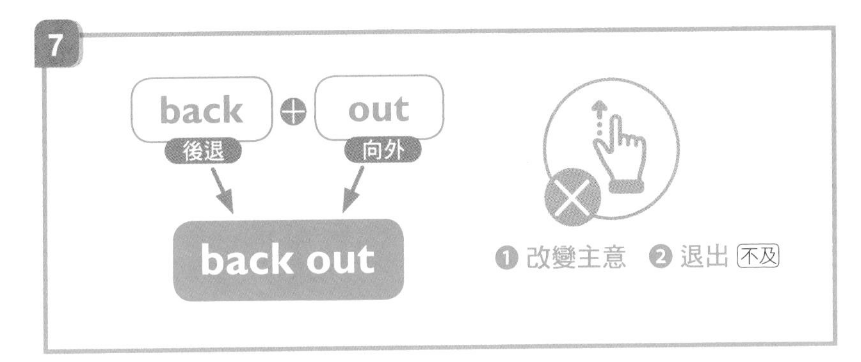

❶ Although Bryan had agreed to buy Tracy an espresso machine, he **backed out** and gave her a new purse instead. 雖然布萊恩答應買一台咖啡機給崔西，但他**改變主意**買了一個新皮包給她。

❷ Laura **backed out** of her work contract and quit. 蘿拉**中止**工作合約後便辭職了。

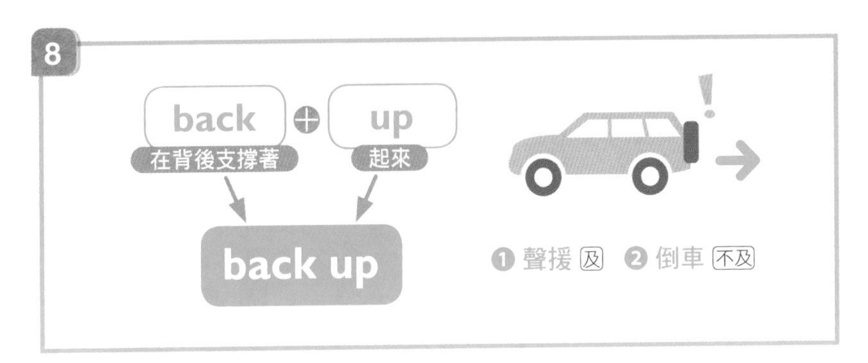

❶ The central idea of your research paper is very interesting, but you need to **back** it **up** with some evidence. 你的研究報告的論點非常吸引人，不過你需要一些證據來**支持**這個論點。

❶ A good theory is **backed up** with observations and data. 完整的學說會**以**觀測資料**作為支援**。

❷ The taxi driver passed by my apartment, so he had to **back up**. 計程車司機駛過了我家公寓，所以他必須**倒車**。

116

9

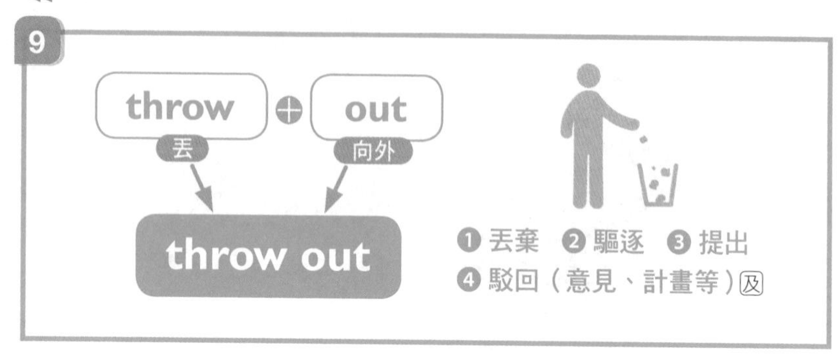

❶ Those shoes are really old; it's time to **throw** them **out**.
這些鞋子真的很舊了；該**丟**了。

❷ Tim got **thrown out** of the club because he tried to start a fight with some people.
提姆因為險些釀成打群架而被**趕出**俱樂部。

❸ Let me **throw** this concept **out** to you and see if you like it. 請讓我**提出**我的想法，再看看你是否喜歡。

❹ The lawsuit was **thrown out** of court because there wasn't enough evidence.
這件訴訟案因證據不足而被法院**駁回**了。

10

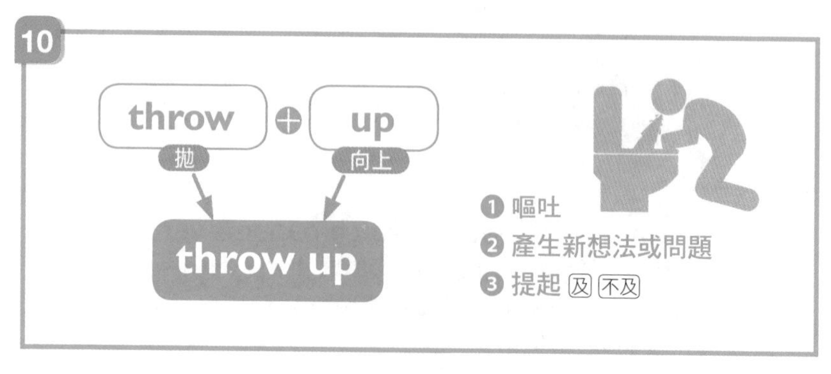

❶ Diane had a stomachache and **threw up** on the school bus. 黛安胃痛，於是在校車上**吐**了。

❷ The discussion group **threw up** some great ideas.
這個討論小組**想出**了一些很棒的方法。（英式用法）

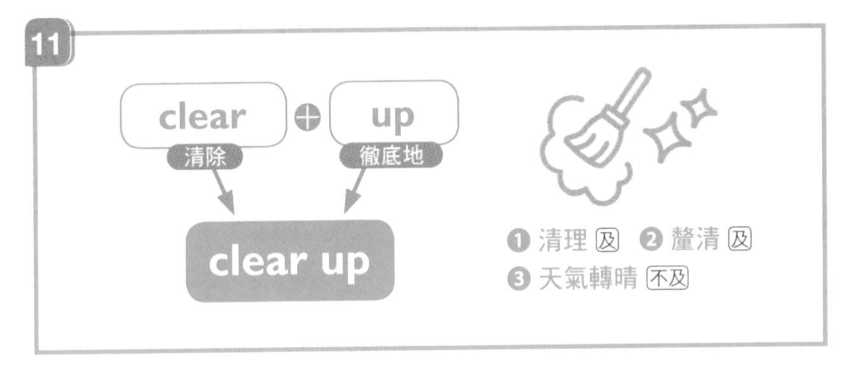

11
clear
清除
up
徹底地
clear up
❶ 清理 及 ❷ 釐清 及
❸ 天氣轉晴 不及

❷ Joanne's doctor **cleared up** any questions about her worsening health.
瓊安的醫生**釐清**了她健康每況愈下的因素。

❷ Wade asked his tutor to help **clear up** his confusion about the English homework.
偉德請家庭老師幫忙**釐清**他做英文作業時遇到的難題。

❸ The sky began to **clear up** in the afternoon, so football practice wasn't canceled after all.
下午天空開始**放晴**，所以足球練習並沒有取消。

The Ruined Cake
毀掉的蛋糕

Suzie and Emory are chatting about a ruined cake.
蘇西和艾墨利在聊一個毀掉的蛋糕。

117

Suzie: I'm so upset! The cake I made last night is ruined! Oh boy, I worked so hard on it . . .

Emory: Don't **beat around the bush**[1]! Just tell me what happened.

Suzie: Someone left it uncovered in the fridge, and it **dried out**[2]. It looks like someone took a bite out of it as well! It looks terrible.

Emory: I bet your roommate was just **fooling around**[3]. He probably did it as a joke.

Suzie: No, I think he did it to **get even with**[4] me. He's trying to **stir up**[5] a fight!

Emory: **Slow down**[6]! you're talking too fast. Do you really think he **is up to something**[7]?

Suzie: There's no question. He's still mad at me for **putting an end to**[8] his dream of becoming a famous architect by accidentally spilling coffee all over his designs.

Emory: Aha! Well, that explains things . . .

蘇西：　我好生氣！我昨晚做的蛋糕全毀了！天啊，我可是費盡心力耶……。

艾墨利：　**講話**別**兜圈子**了！快告訴我怎麼回事。

蘇西：　有人沒把蛋糕蓋上盒蓋就放入冰箱，整個蛋糕都**乾掉**了，好像還有人偷吃了一口！真糟糕。

艾墨利：　我賭是妳室友**搞的鬼**。他可能只是開個玩笑。

蘇西：　不，我認為他是在**報復**我。他只是想要**激怒**我，和我吵一架！

艾墨利：　說**慢一點**，妳講太快了。妳真的認為他在**盤算**些什麼嗎？

蘇西：　沒錯。他還在氣我不小心把咖啡灑在他的設計圖上，害他**結束**了成為名建築師的夢想。

艾墨利：　啊哈！喏，這不就解釋了一切……。

118

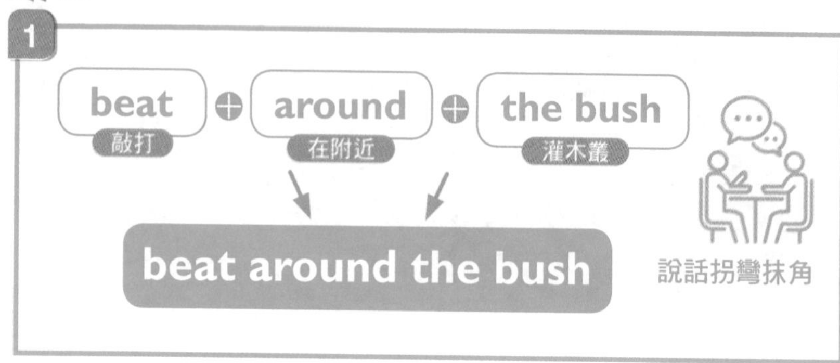

- Kyle was embarrassed to tell his boss that he was quitting, so he **beat around the bush** for a while.
  凱爾不好意思告訴老闆他要辭職，所以他講話一直**兜圈子**。
- Lyle **beat around the bush** before he asked Jenna to the prom. 萊爾在邀請珍娜參加舞會前，講話一直**拐彎抹角**。
- Quit **beating around the bush** and tell me what you really think about my idea.
  別**拐彎抹角**了，告訴我你覺得我的意見如何。
- Don't **beat around the bush**—get to the point!
  別**拐彎抹角**了，有話就直說吧！

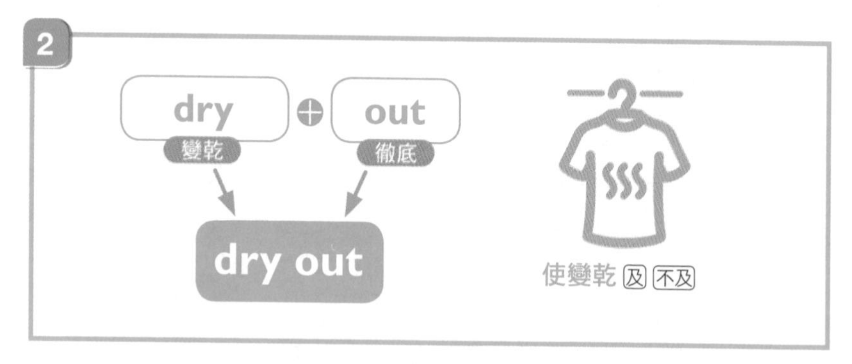

- The potatoes I left in the sun **dried out** and became hard. 我放在太陽底下**曬乾**的馬鈴薯變硬了。
- In the countryside, people sometimes hang meat in the sun so it **dries out**. 鄉下人有時會把肉掛在太陽底下**曬乾**。

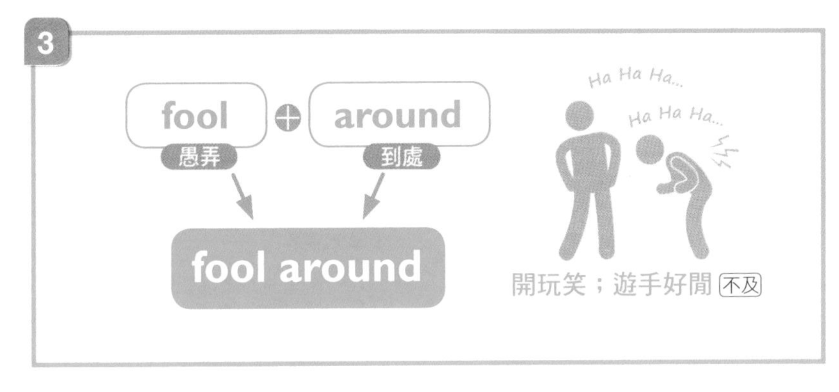

- Ed **fooled around** all weekend and didn't do any work.
  艾迪週末都在**鬼混**沒寫作業。
- Don't **fool around** in class, or the teacher will call your parents! 上課別**打混**，否則老師會打電話給你的父母！
- Jimmy is always getting in trouble for **fooling around** in class. 吉米老是因為上課**打混**而惹上麻煩。

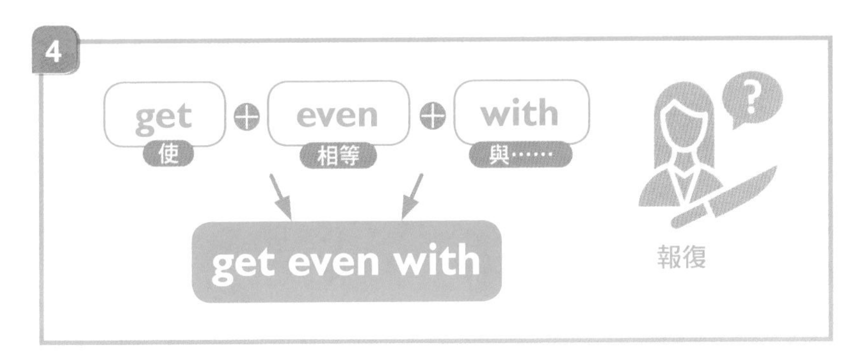

- Jackie decided to **get even with** Mohammed for teasing her in front of her friends.
  穆罕默德在賈姬朋友的面前取笑她，所以賈姬決定**報復**他。
- How do you plan to **get even with** Juliana for ruining your party? 茱莉安娜破壞了你的派對，你要如何**報復**她？
- I want to **get even with** the guy who hit me with the ball. 我想**報復**用球打我的人。

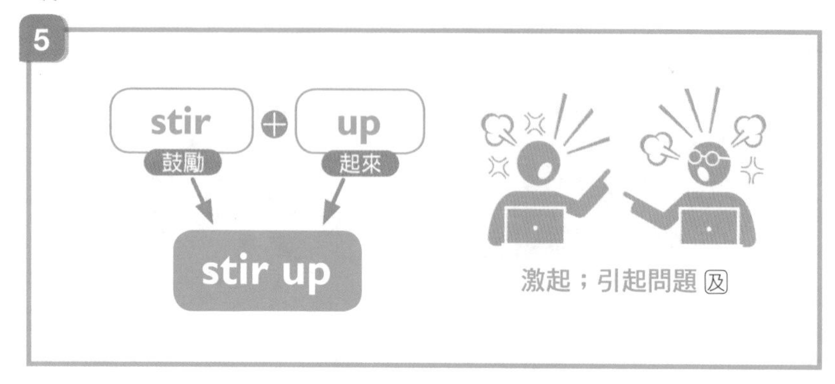

- Looking at her high school yearbook **stirred up** some sad memories for poor Tina.
  可憐的緹娜在看高中畢業紀念冊時，**激起**了許多不愉快的回憶。
- The fight between the two boys **stirred** the problem **up** even more.
  這兩個男孩之間的爭吵**引起**了更嚴重的紛爭。

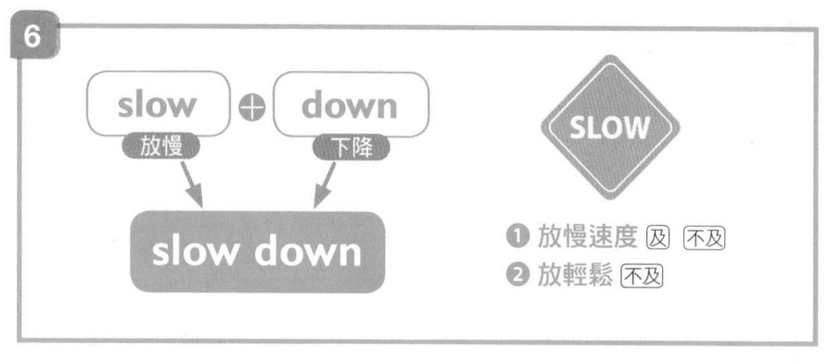

❶ You're driving close to a school; please **slow down**.
你開到學校附近了，請**開慢**一點。

❶ I wish the driver would **slow** the bus **down**; he's driving dangerously fast!
我希望有人能讓公車司機**開慢**一點，開這麼快很危險！

❷ The doctor told him to **slow down** or he'll have a heart attack. 醫生要他**放輕鬆**，否則會得心臟病。

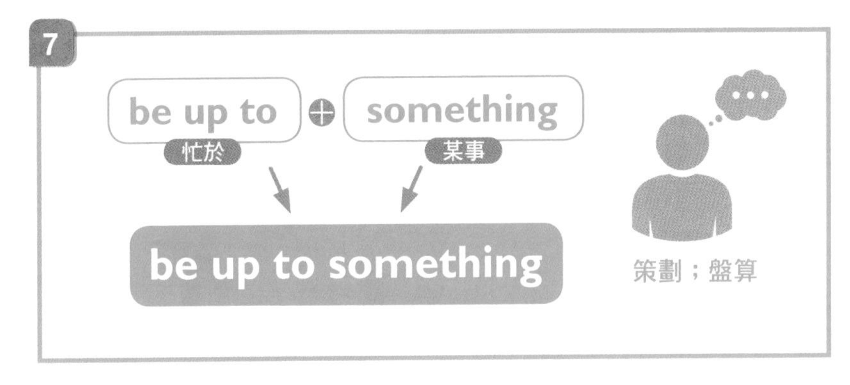

- Eli is acting pretty strange; I think he **is up to something**.
  依萊最近舉止怪異，我想他在**暗中盤算些什麼**。
- It seems as if Carl **is up to something**—he's probably planning a surprise party.
  卡爾看來在**策劃些什麼**，他可能打算辦一場驚喜派對。

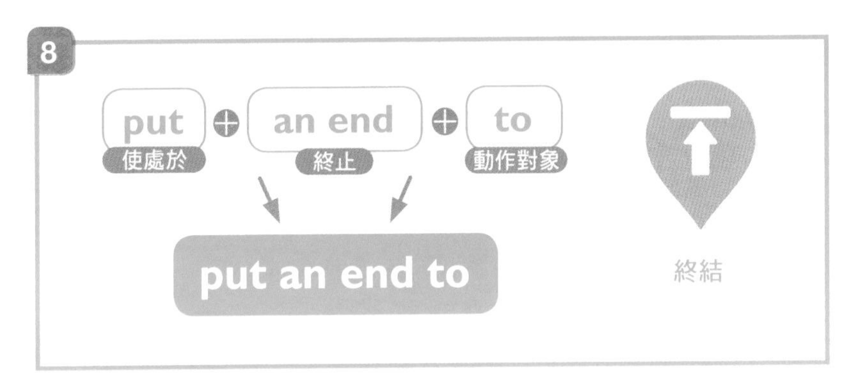

- The ringing phone **put an end to** our private conversation. 我們的私下談話因為電話聲響起而**結束**。
- A terrible rainstorm **put an end to** our day at the beach.
  一場暴風雨來襲，**結束**了我們在海邊的行程。

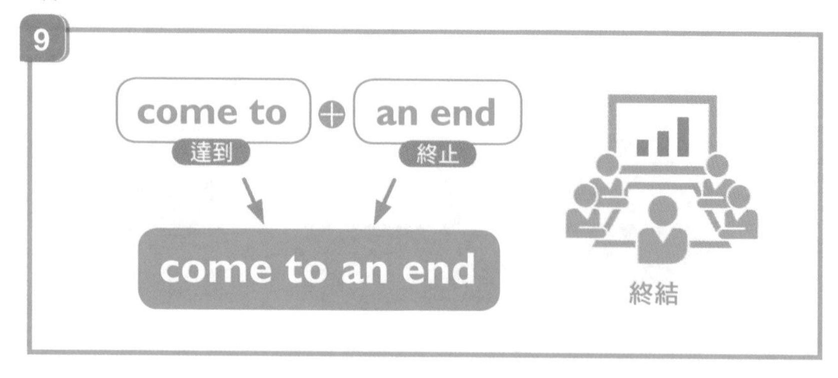

- There is an English idiom that says "All good things must **come to an end.**"
  「天下無不**散**的筵席」是一句英文諺語。
- When my boss asked for our opinions, I thought the meeting would never **come to an end**.
  當老闆問起我們的意見，我感覺這個會議永遠不會**結束**。

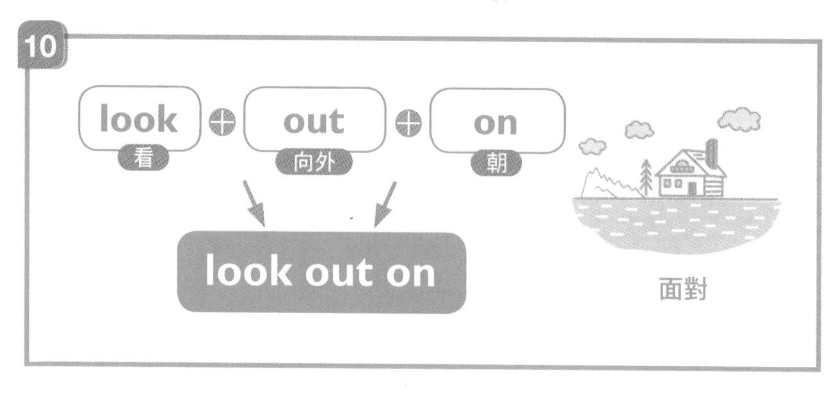

- Sam's new apartment **looks out on** the Brooklyn Bridge. 山姆的新公寓**正對**著布魯克林大橋。
- The five-star hotel **looks out on** the ocean.
  這間五星級飯店**面對**著大海。

❶ Gwen was very interested in the class, so she **took in** everything the professor said.
關對這門課非常有興趣，所以她把所有教授說的話都**記住**了。

❷ The old lady was **taken in** by the used car salesman, who convinced her to buy a car she didn't want.
這位老太太被賣二手車的推銷員**騙**了，他說服她買了一台她不想要的車。

❸ During their first night in Paris, the happy couple walked around and **took in** the sights.
在抵達巴黎的第一個夜晚，這對幸福的夫妻四處**拜訪**了許多名勝。

❹ I'll have to **take** this dress **in** at the waist. It's too big.
我必須把這件洋裝的腰圍**改小**，它太大了。

Unit 31

Moving Away From Home 離家

Emma asks Marcus what his family thinks of his plan to move to Nebraska. 艾瑪詢問馬克斯關於他的家人對他計劃搬到內布拉斯加州的看法。

121

Emma: How did your dad take the news that you've decided to move to Nebraska?

Marcus: Actually, he really **kept his head**[1]. At first, he thought I was **putting** him **on**[2].

Emma: And when he found out you were serious?

Marcus: Well, **it goes without saying**[3] that he'd prefer me to stay at home, but I guess he isn't as narrow-minded as I thought.

Emma: And how about your mom? Did she **lose her head**[4]?

Marcus: Yeah, my mom's different. As soon as I began to tell her the news, she **cut** me **short**[5] and told me I was **wasting my breath**[6].

Emma: Boy! You must really be **on edge**[7] now!

艾瑪： 你爸對於你要搬到內布拉斯加州的看法如何？

馬克司： 事實上，他還挺**冷靜**的。他起初以為我在**騙**他。

艾瑪： 那他發現你是認真後的反應是？

馬克司： 唔，**那還用說**，他當然希望我待在家裡，但他不像我想像中的不開明。

艾瑪： 那你媽覺得如何呢？她有**慌了手腳**嗎？

馬克司： 是啊，我媽的反應就不同了。我才一提起這件事情，她便**打斷**了我的話，還說我在**白費唇舌**。

艾瑪： 天啊，那你現在一定**坐立難安**！

keep one's head 保持冷靜
lose one's head 失去理智

122

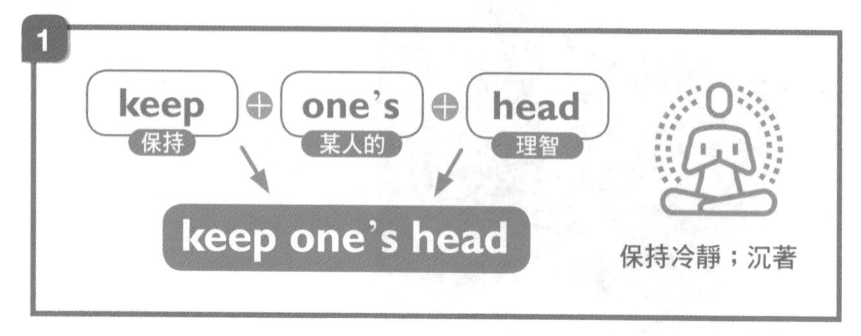

- One of Juliet's best qualities is her ability to **keep her head** when things seem totally crazy. 即便事情失控，茱麗葉也能夠**保持冷靜**，這就是她的個人特質之一。
- Calm down and **keep your head**; there's no reason to get stressed out.
  冷靜下來，**保持鎮定**，沒必要那麼緊張。

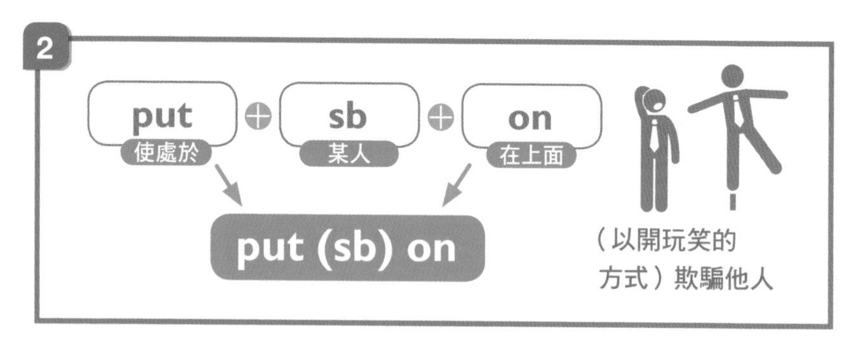

- You told me that you were going to study, and now I see you at the movies; it looks like you were **putting me on**.
  你說要去唸書，但我現在發現你在看電影，看來你是在**騙我**。
- I didn't really win a sailboat; I was just **putting you on**.
  我並沒有贏得一艘帆船，我只是**騙你**的。

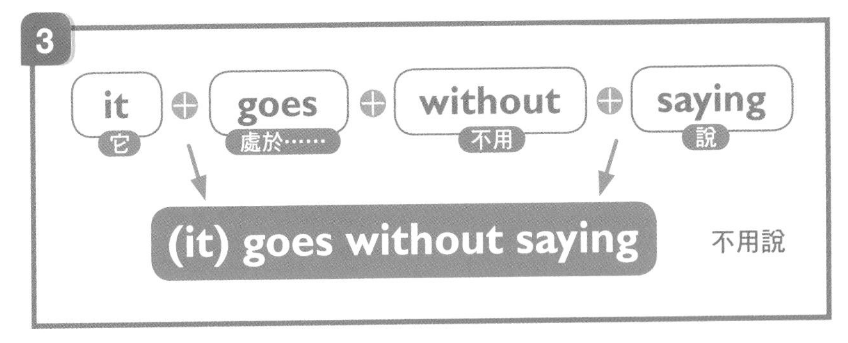

- **It goes without saying** that in today's world, time is money. 在現今的社會，**不用說**，時間就是金錢。

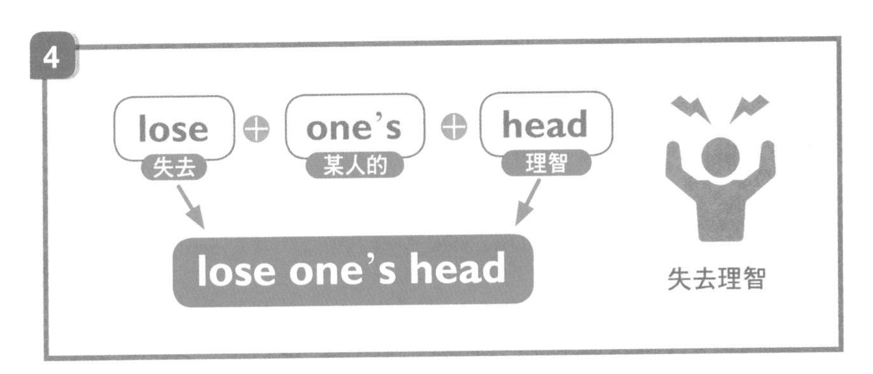

- I was so frightened that I **lost my head** completely. 我很害怕到完全**失去理智**了。
- Although Tim is usually calm in class, for some reason he really **lost his head** today. 提姆上課通常都很安靜，但他今天為了一些因素而**失控**了。
- Erin **lost her head** in the meeting this afternoon, and our boss fired her. 艾琳今天下午開會時**情緒失控**，所以老闆把她解僱了。
- I usually stay quite calm in meetings, but this time I just **lost my head**. 我開會時通常很冷靜，但這次我**失去理智**了。

123

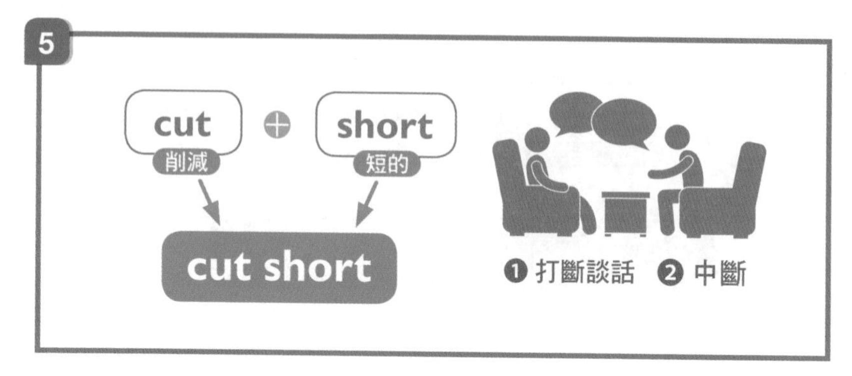

❶ While Wanda was telling Chris a boring story about her day at work, he **cut** her **short** and turned on the TV.
當汪達在告訴克里斯辦公室發生的無趣瑣事時，他**打斷**了她，並把電視打開。

❶ Just as Alfredo was getting to the funny part of the joke, his cell phone rang and **cut** him **short**.
當阿爾弗雷多正要進入笑話最精采的部分時，手機鈴聲**打斷**了他。

❶ I started to explain, but she **cut** me **short**, saying she had to catch a bus.
我開始解釋時，她**打斷**了我的**話**，說她必須去趕公車了。

❷ James **cut** his workday **short** to go home early.
詹姆斯**結束**工作，提早回家。

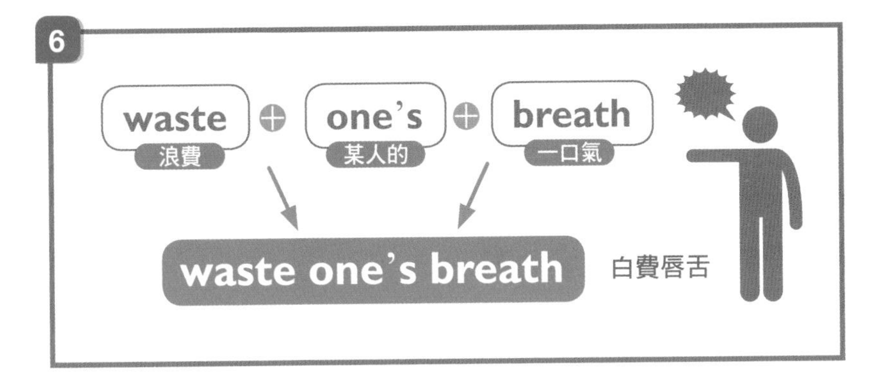

- Don't **waste your breath**—I've already asked him to help, and he said no.
  別**白費唇舌**了，我已經請他幫忙了，但他不願意。
- Phillip is so stubborn; don't **waste your breath** making suggestions. 菲力普很固執，別**浪費唇舌**提供他意見。
- Eddy lectured his sister on how dangerous it is to go out alone in the city at night. However, he was just **wasting his breath** because she wasn't listening.
  艾迪告訴妹妹晚上獨自到市區很危險，但他只是在**白費唇舌**而已，她根本沒在聽。
- Honestly, you're **wasting your breath**—she doesn't want to hear what anyone else has to say.
  老實說你在**白費唇舌**，她並不想要聽其他人的看法。

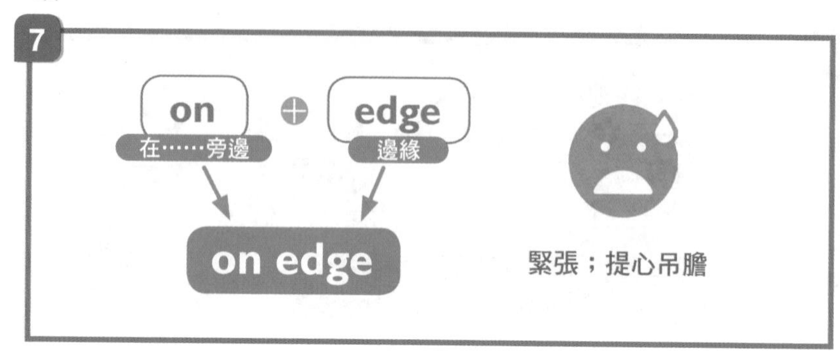

- My sisters and I were **on edge** while we waited to hear whether our flight was delayed.
  在等待飛機是否會延誤的消息時，我姊妹和我很**緊張**。
- It was the night before her first day of college, and Mel was **on edge**. 梅兒上大學的前一個晚上非常**緊張**。
- Is something wrong? You seem a bit **on edge** this morning. 怎麼了嗎？你今天早上看起來有點**不安**。
- You're always **on edge** waiting for an important call because you don't know when the phone will ring.
  你在等重要電話的時候總是很**不安**，因為你無法得知電話何時會響。

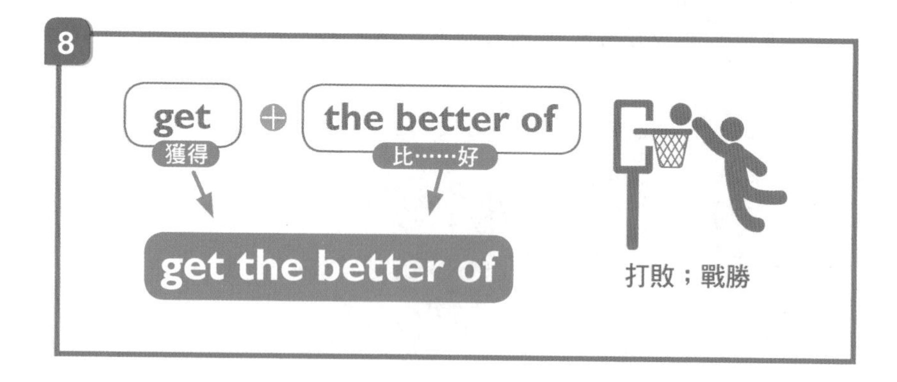

- Although my teammates and I played our best, the other team **got the better of** us.
雖然我們球隊打得很好，但我們還是被別支球隊**打敗**了。

- My brother **got the better of** his asthma and rarely gets sick anymore.
自從我哥哥的氣喘病**治癒**了後，他便很少生病了。

- Her curiosity **got the better of** her, and she opened the letter. 她在好奇心的驅使下，打開了信。

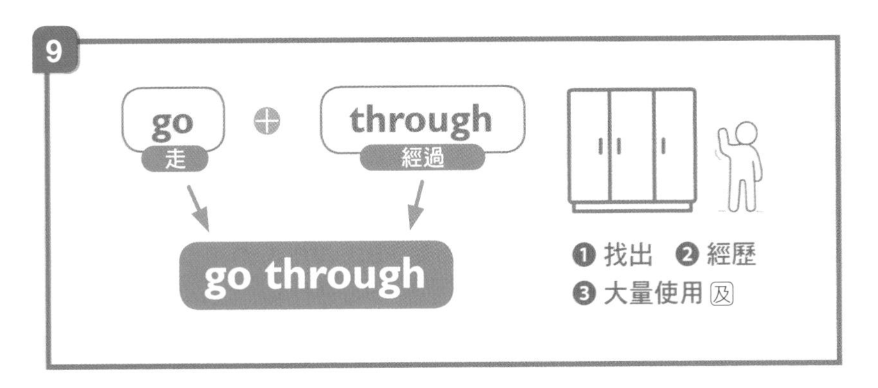

❶ Olivia is **going through** her closet to find some clothes to donate to charity.
奧立薇亞**翻遍**了衣櫃，找出一些衣服捐給慈善機構。

❷ We'd better let Seth relax; he **went through** a terrible situation at school today.
我們最好讓塞斯休息一下，他今天在學校**經歷**了很不愉快的事情。

❸ My Italian friend **goes through** so much pasta because she eats it for lunch and dinner every day.
我的義大利朋友**吃了很多**義大利麵，每天中餐和晚餐都會吃。

125

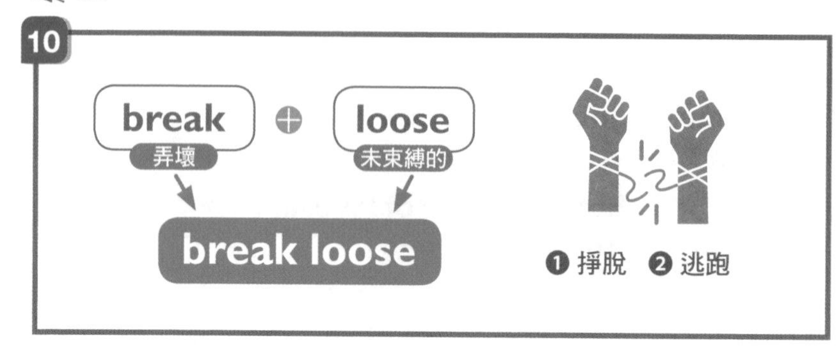

❶ We saw a movie where the hero is tied to a chair but he manages to **break loose**. 我們看了一部電影，劇中的男主角被綁在椅子上，但他後來設法**掙脫**了。

❷ During the thunderstorm, all three horses **broke loose** from the barn and ran into the forest because they were scared. 暴風雨來襲時，這三匹馬因害怕而從馬廄**逃**了出來，跑進了森林裡面。

❷ People worry that they will be unsafe if that tiger ever **breaks loose**. 人們很擔心那隻老虎要是**逃跑**了，他們會有危險。

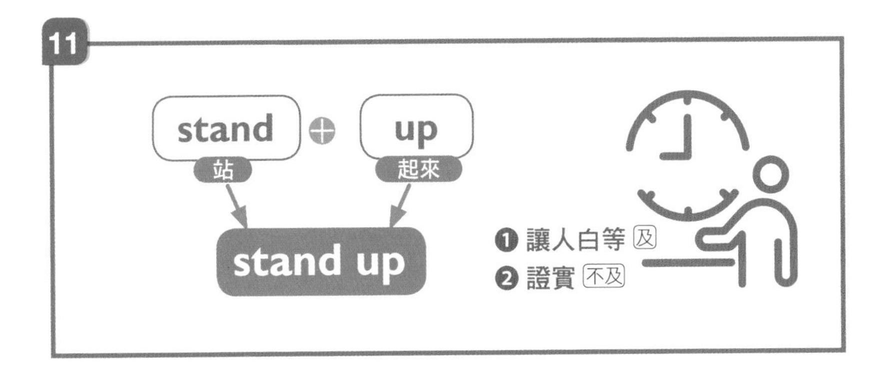

❶ I had planned to take Martin out for dinner, but he **stood** me **up** and never showed up.
我原本打算帶馬汀出去吃晚餐，但他**放我鴿子**，沒有出現。

❷ The information Joel used in his report will never **stand up** to critical review.
喬爾報告中的資料無法**證實**這篇評論。

❷ Their evidence will never **stand up** in court.
他們的證據在法庭上永遠無法**證實**。

Being Kicked Out of School 被退學

Amy tells Arthur about getting kicked out of the university. 愛咪告訴亞瑟有關她被退學的事情。

126

Arthur: What did your mom say when you told her that you were kicked out of the university?

Amy: She really **went off the deep end**[1].

Arthur: Well, I suppose that's understandable. After all, you did copy some texts in your report; you really did **goof up**[2].

Amy: But it's not fair! I didn't know doing this would be such a big problem! I never knew that copying texts would **screw up**[3] my life so much. And nothing I do helps. I've been **kissing up to**[4] the teacher of that class, but she doesn't care.

Arthur: Kissing up isn't the best way to deal with this problem. You've really **lost your touch**[5], Amy. You used to be a model student, **more or less**[6]. Now you have to **step down**[7] from your position on the debate team and from your role in the honor society.

Amy: What a disaster!

亞瑟： 妳媽知道你被學校退學後有說什麼嗎？

愛咪： 她**大發雷霆**。

亞瑟： 嗯，我想那是可以理解的。畢竟，妳真的抄襲了別人的文章。妳真的是**大錯特錯**。

愛咪： 可是太不公平了！我不知道這樣做會引起這麼大的麻煩！我又不曉得抄襲他人的文章會**搞砸**我的人生。我後來想要補救，但是都沒有用。我一直想去**討好**該科老師，但她都不理我。

亞瑟： 討好老師不是處理這個問題的最佳方式。愛咪，妳真是太**沒有經驗**了。**好歹**妳以前也是模範生。現在妳得**退出**辯論社和榮譽學會了。

愛咪： 真是糟透了！

go off the deep end 大發雷霆

screw up 搞砸

🔊 127

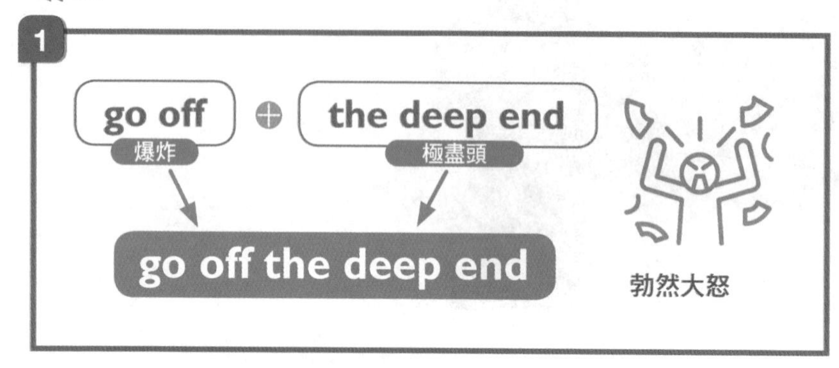

- Alan was a great guy until he **went off the deep end** and started gambling all the time.
  艾倫在**脾氣變差**、開始賭博前，一直是個好好先生。
- When Daphne told her father that she had crashed his car, he was so mad that he **went off the deep end**.
  當達芙妮告訴父親她把他的車撞壞時，他**勃然大怒**。

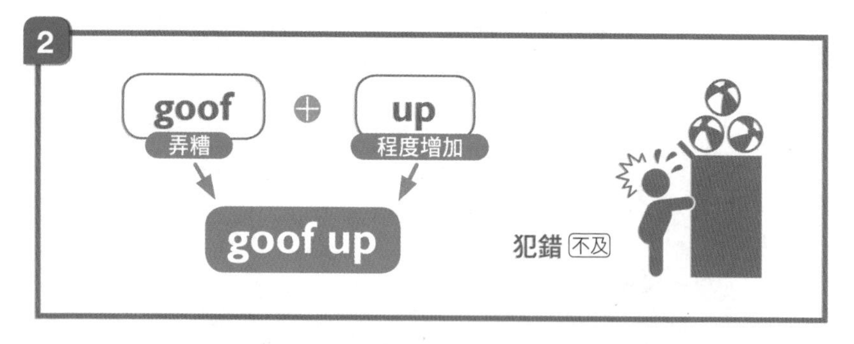

- Valerie **goofed up** and showed up at the university on Saturday. 薇樂麗**搞錯**日子了，她星期六還跑去學校。
- If I go near a skateboard, I'm sure I will **goof up** and fall off. 我若是站在滑板上，肯定會**玩不好**摔下來。

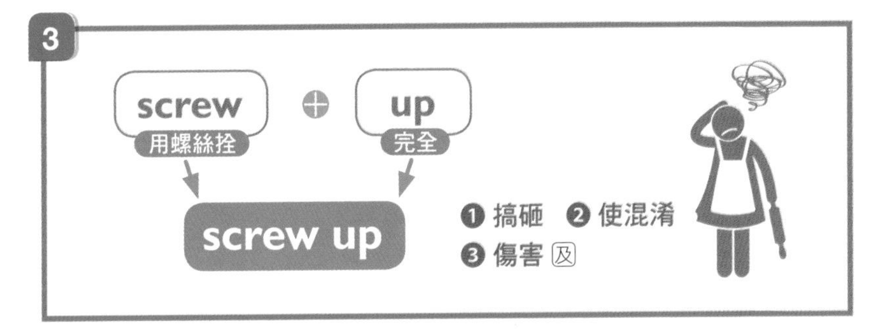

❷ The waiter **screwed** Mira's order **up** and brought her mashed potatoes instead of French fries.
服務生**弄錯**了米拉的餐點，他應該要送薯條過來，而不是馬鈴薯泥。

❸ Nicole really **screwed** Sam **up** when she left him.
妮可離開山姆時真的**把**他**傷得很重**。

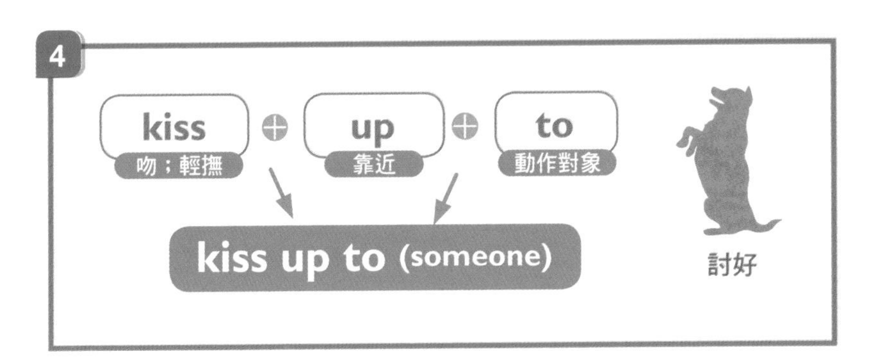

- Amanda always **kisses up to** her boss when she wants to take a day off.
  每當亞曼達想休假時，她都會**討好**老闆。

- Kyle **kisses up to** our soccer coach because he thinks it will help him get promoted to team captain.
  凱爾老是在**討好**足球隊教練，因為他認為這樣做就能成為隊長。

128

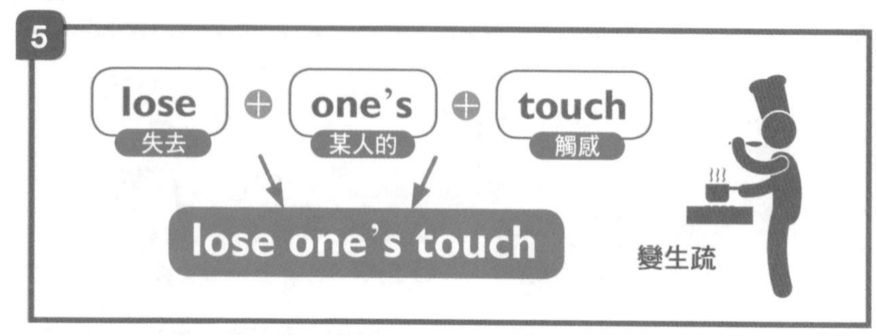

- Although Gene's first book was a bestseller, it seems he **lost his touch**—his second book is not so good. 金的第一本書很暢銷，但他顯然**退步不少**，第二本書就沒賣那麼好了。
- When I watched my favorite actress in her newest movie, I saw that she still hasn't **lost her touch**.
我最愛的演員在最新的電影中，演技可是一點都沒**退步**。
- The goalkeeper's performance in the game shows he is not **losing his touch**.
守門員在這場競賽的表現一點也沒有**變生疏**。

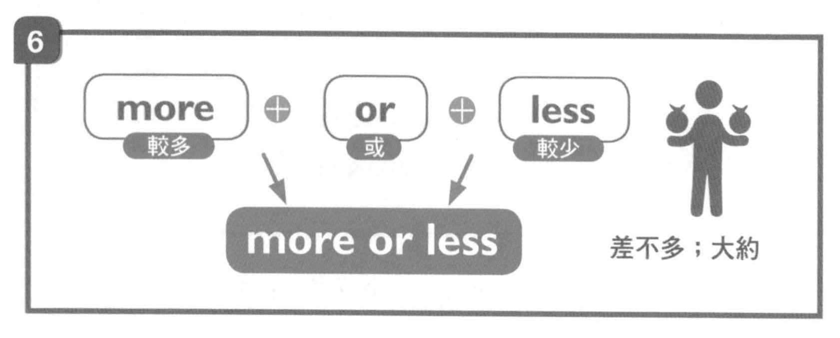

- Going on vacation was **more or less** worthwhile; the only problem was that it rained the entire time.
這假期**大致上來說**都很好，唯一的問題是一直在下雨。
- This bag weighs 20 pounds, **more or less**.
這袋東西**大約**重 20 磅。
- The project was **more or less** a success.
這項企畫**大致上來說**是成功的。

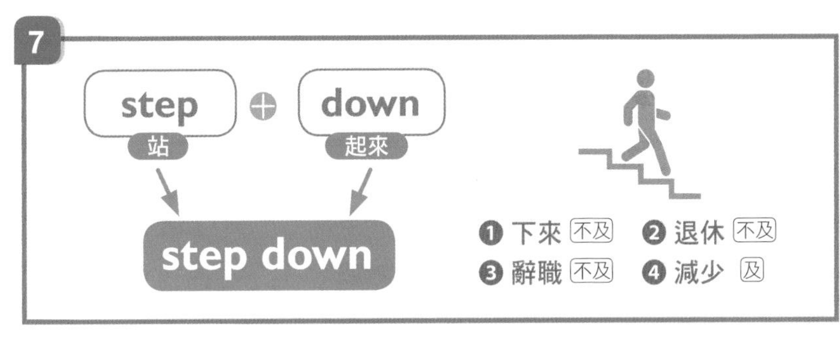

❶ Biff **stepped down** from the ladder and shook Hank's hand. 比夫從梯子上**下來**與漢克握手。

❷ We need to hire a new manager at our company because the last one just **stepped down**.
我們公司需要聘請一位新的經理，上任經理才剛**退休**。

❸ After Ronny got in trouble for taking too long of a vacation, his boss asked him to **step down**.
朗尼因休假太長而造成困擾，老闆要求他自動**請辭**。

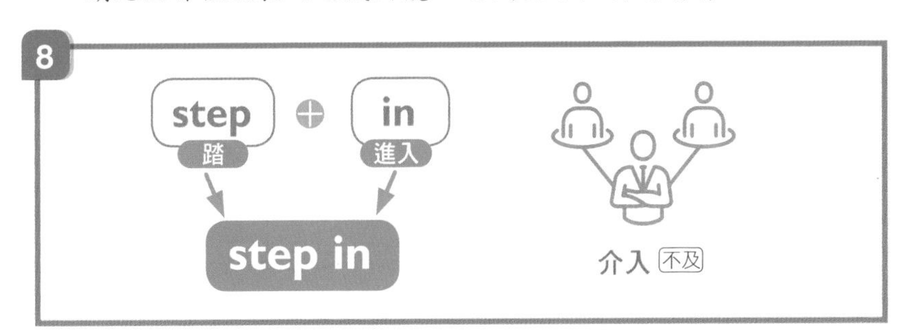

- When Luke saw his sisters arguing, he **stepped in** and helped them reach an agreement.
路克**介入**了他兩位姊姊的爭吵之中，幫助他們達成協議。
- I know you haven't asked for my advice, but please let me **step in**. 我知道你沒有問我的意見，但請容我**插句話**。
- When Isabelle couldn't teach the class, her sister **stepped in** and gave the lesson.
伊莎貝爾無法授課時，她姊姊就會到學校**代**她上課。
- After the leading actress broke her leg, Jane **stepped in** and played the role. 女主角摔斷了腿後，珍**加入**演出這個角色。

129

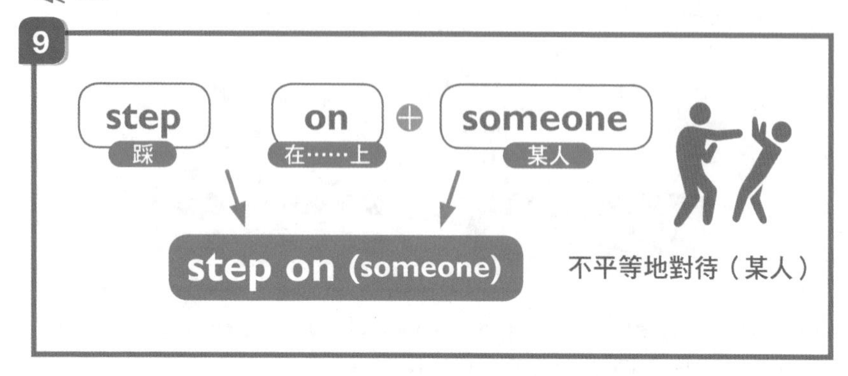

- Sometimes the nicest people get **stepped on** the most.
  心地善良的人有時是最會受**欺負**的。
- You should be more confident and stop letting people **step on** you. 你要對自己要有點信心，不要再讓別人**欺負**了。

- Regarding the matter **in hand**, I suggest we cancel the next meeting.
  就**目前**這件事情而論，我認為應該取消下次會議。
- Because Elaine's birthday is next week, the preparations for the party should be well **in hand** by now.
  伊蓮的生日就在下星期，派對現在應該都準備好了。

11

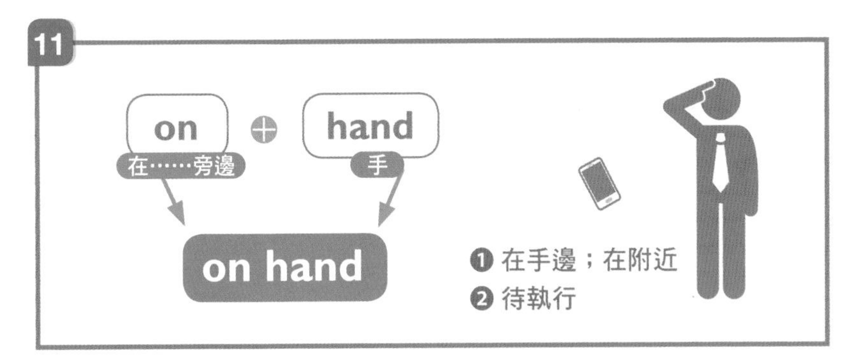

❶ If you don't have a calculator **on hand**, please ask to use your partner's.
如果你**手邊**沒有計算機，請向組員借。

❶ I need to make a phone call; do you have your cell phone **on hand**? 我需要打通電話，你**身上**有手機嗎？

12

- I can't believe you found a computer for only $100—what **a steal**!
我不敢相信你買了一台才 100 塊錢的電腦，真是**太超值**了！

- I bought this used cell phone at a good price; it was **a real steal**!
我用很便宜的價格買到這支中古手機，真是**賺到**了！

Kicking the Habit
戒掉惡習

Ronald tells Wendy about his new plan.
羅納德把新計畫告訴溫蒂。

130

Wendy: Why are you smiling? Something must be **looking up**[1] for you.

Ronald: You got it! I'm in a good mood because I've been **kicking around**[2] an interesting idea .

Wendy: What's the idea? Tell me!

Ronald: Well, I noticed yesterday that I had gained five more pounds, and that's the **last straw**[3]. I watch too much TV, and I'm too fat. It's time for me to **kick the habit**[4] of eating junk food and being lazy.

Wendy: Sounds like you**'re** really **on the ball**[5] with this idea. But what are you going to do?

Ronald: A group of friends and I will **put together**[6] a basketball team, and we'll practice three times a week. This way, we'll all have a good time. I can lose some weight, and when my girlfriend sees how good I look, maybe she'll want to **make up with**[7] me. So, you want to join us?

Wendy: No thanks. I'm going home to watch a movie and eat some pizza—but have fun!

溫蒂： 你為何笑得這麼開心呢？一定是有什麼**好**事。

羅納德： 沒錯！我的心情很好，因為我一直在**思考**一項有趣的計畫。

溫蒂： 什麼計畫？快告訴我！

羅納德： 唔，我昨天發現體重增加了五磅，我**不能再這樣下去**了。我看太多電視，吃太多東西了。我該**戒掉**吃垃圾食物和懶惰的**壞習慣**了。

溫蒂： 看來你已經很**清楚**你的想法了，但你要怎麼做呢？

羅納德： 我會和一群朋友**組成**一支籃球隊，每個星期練三次球。這樣一來我們可以玩得很愉快，而我的體重也會減輕。等我女朋友看到我帥氣的模樣時，她也許會想和我**重修舊好**。所以，妳想不想加入我們呢？

溫蒂： 不，謝了。我想回家看電影，吃披薩，反正你開心就好！

kick around 考慮

kick the habit 戒掉壞習慣

131

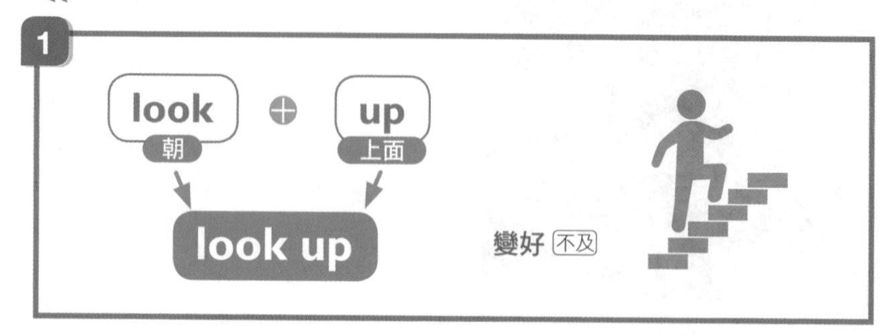

- Ever since Jasmine got a raise at work, things have been **looking up**. 潔絲敏加薪後，一切都**變得很美好**。
- Things are really **looking up** this semester, and I'm getting excellent grades.
  這學期一切都**變得很順利**，而我的成績也很優異。
- I hope things will start to **look up** in the new year.
  我希望在新的一年事情會**變得很順利**。

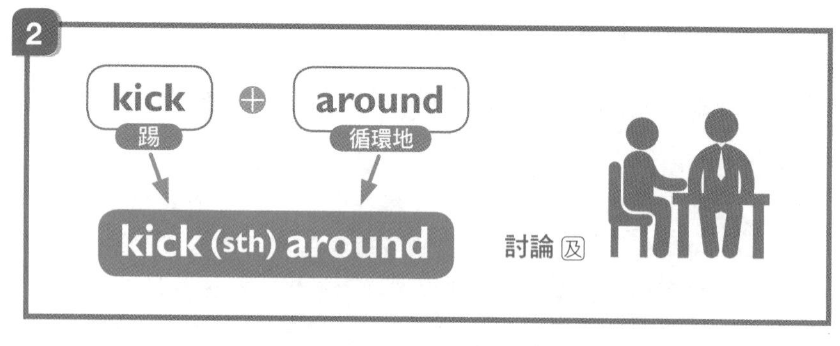

- We **kicked around** the plan of going on vacation in Spain, but in the end we never went.
  我們一直在**討論**西班牙之旅的計畫，但我們最後並沒有去成。
- Agatha **kicked around** the idea of studying psychology, but in the end, she decided not to.
  雅嘉薩**考慮**過是否要修心理學這門課，但她最後還是決定放棄。
- I need to get everyone together so we can **kick** a few ideas **around**. 我必須把所有人聚集在一起，**討論**一些想法。

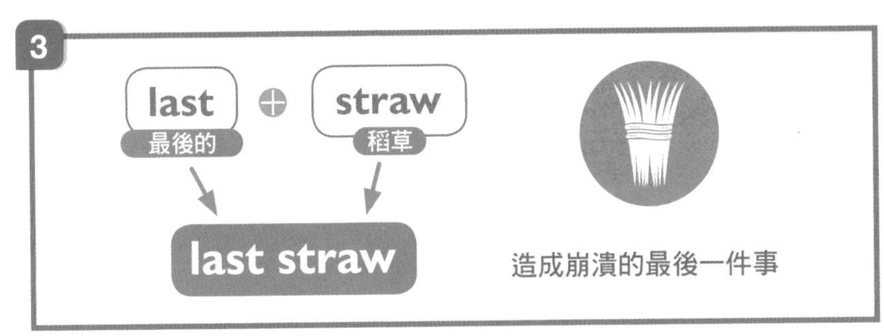

- There's a well-known English proverb that says it's "the **last straw** that breaks the camel's back."
  「壓垮駱駝的**最後一根稻草**」是一句著名的英文諺語。
- Saul's car breaking down on the way to work was pretty bad, but when it broke down again on the way home, that was the **last straw**. 索爾的車在上班途中壞掉已經很不幸了，然而車子又在回家路上拋錨，真是衰到了極點。
- Paula has always been rude to me, but it was the **last straw** when she started insulting my mother. 寶拉對我一直很沒有禮貌，但令人忍無可忍的是她開始羞辱我的母親。

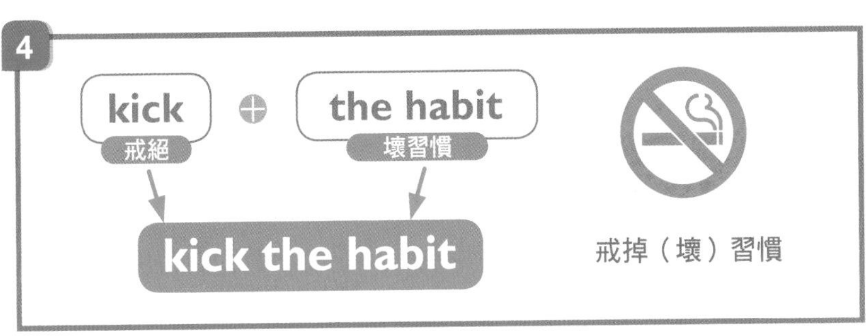

- Steven used to be a heavy smoker, but he **kicked the habit** last year. 史帝芬曾經是個老菸槍，但他去年**戒**菸了。
- Ike finally **kicked his bad habit** of biting his fingernails.
  艾克最後終於**戒掉**咬手指頭的**壞習慣**了。
- Researchers said smokers who **kick the habit** have less chance of developing cancer.
  研究人員表示，已**戒**菸的人罹患癌症的機率會較低。

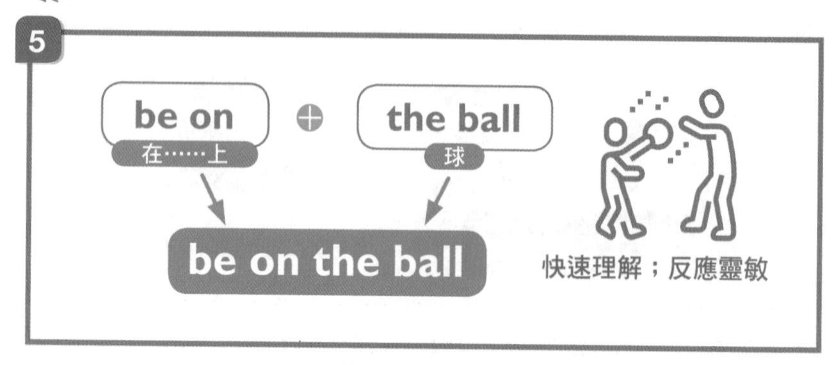

- After his third cup of coffee, Harry **was** really **on the ball**. 哈利在喝了三杯咖啡之後，終於**清醒**了。
- After getting little sleep the night before, Corey **was** not **on the ball**. 柯瑞昨晚沒什麼睡，所以**頭腦不清楚**。

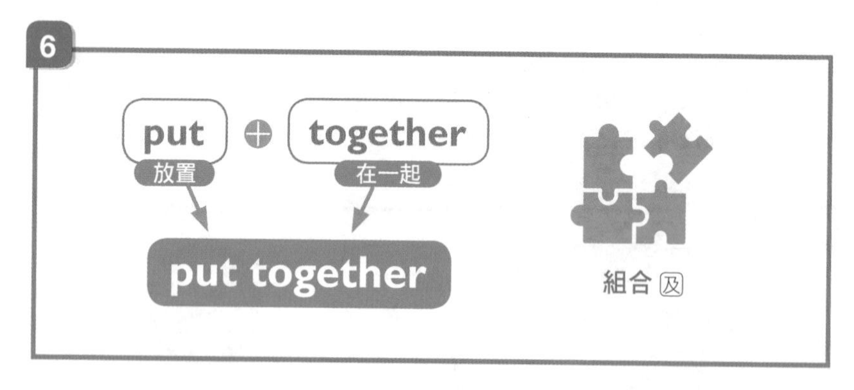

- Taylor really knows a lot about motorcycles. If you give him all the parts, he can **put** one **together**! 泰勒真的很懂摩托車。只要給他所有的零件，他就可以**組裝好**！
- Model airplanes come in pieces that have to be **put together**. 模型飛機是一片片的，必須**組裝**起來。

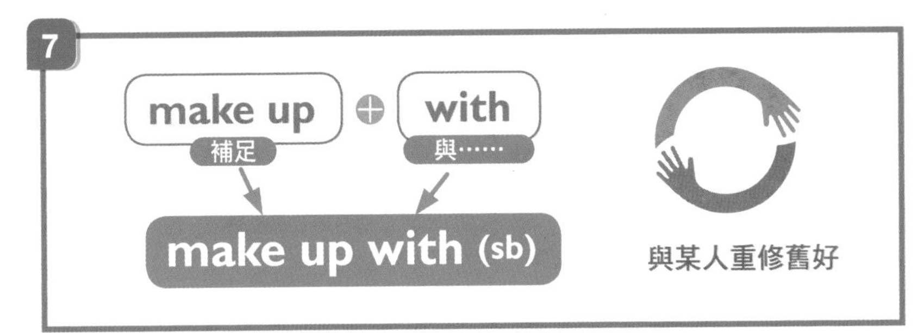

- After the argument, Taylor **made up with** Rachel by giving her some flowers.
  爭吵過後，泰勒送花給瑞秋，和她**重修舊好**。
- Joel and Alice had a big fight, and I'm not sure if they'll ever **make up with** one another.
  喬爾和艾莉絲大吵了一架，我不確定他們是否還會**合好如初**。

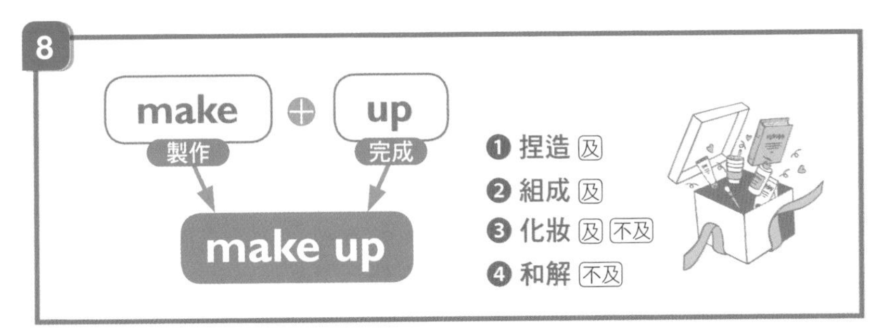

❶ Because Ron didn't want to go to the party, he **made** an excuse **up** about having to write a report.
因為朗不想參加派對，所以他用寫報告**作為**藉口。

❶ Kate **made up** a great story about a princess, which she told her daughter at bedtime.
凱特在女兒睡前念了一個她**編**的公主故事。

❷ Two halves **make up** a whole. 兩個一半**合起來**就成一個。

❸ The fashion model was all **made up** for the photo shoot. 時尚模特兒已完**妝**準備照片拍攝的工作。

❹ They kissed and **made up**, as usual.
他們親吻對方，然後**合好**，一如往常。

133

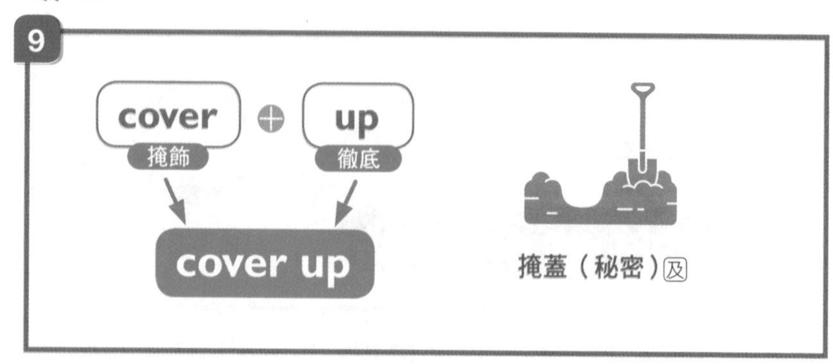

- Will tried to **cover up** the fact that he was caught cheating, but everyone found out about it.
  威爾企圖**掩飾**他考試作弊被抓的事實，但大家都發現了。
- If you are caught doing something illegal, it may not be a good idea to **cover** it **up**.
  做違法的事情如果被抓到，最好不要企圖**隱瞞**。
- The company tried to **cover up** its employment of illegal immigrants. 公司企圖**掩蓋**僱用非法移民的事實。
- I was amazed that the building contractors we hired tried to **cover up** the problems they had. 我很意外我們所聘用的建築承包商，竟然企圖**掩飾**他們所遇到的問題。

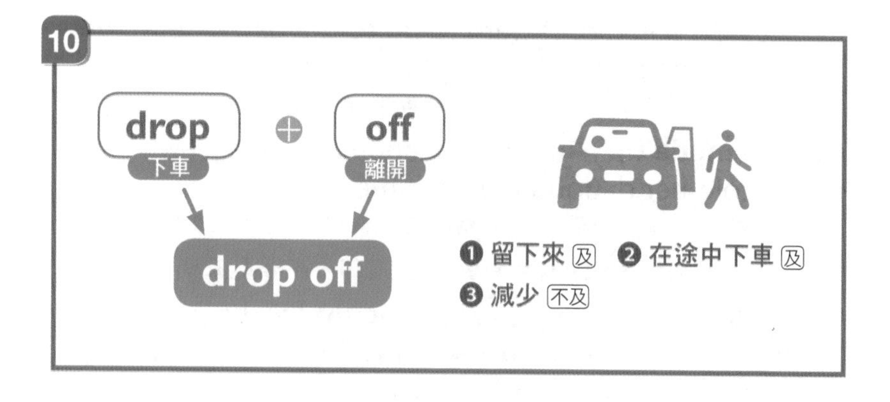

❶ Melissa **dropped off** her passport at the hotel and then went off to explore Paris.
瑪莉莎將護照**留在**飯店後，便開始在巴黎觀光。

❷ Jordan **dropped off** her sister at the park and then went to the movies.
喬登**讓**妹妹在公園**下車**後，便去看電影。

❸ The price of plane tickets to California always **drops off** after the summer.
夏天過後，飛往加州的機票總是會**降**價。

❸ The demand for mobile phones shows no signs of **dropping off**.
人們對於手機的需求一點也沒有**減少**的現象。

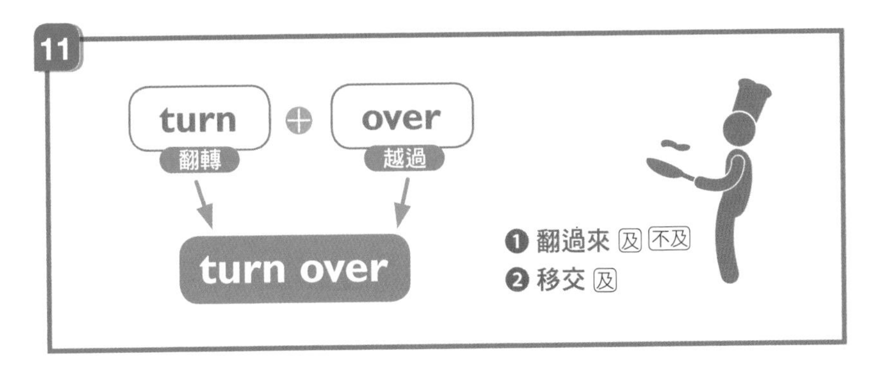

❶ In the middle of the night, Nancy **turned over** and slept on her back.
南西在半夜**翻了個身**，變成仰躺。

❷ Before leaving her job, Dolores **turned over** her tasks to a coworker.
辭職前，桃樂絲把工作**交付**給同事。

Unit 34

Getting Married
結婚

Cleo tells Felix about her uncertainty about marriage.
克莉歐將她對婚姻的遲疑告訴了菲力斯。

134

Felix: So are you really getting married tomorrow?

Cleo: Actually, I think I'm **getting cold feet**[1], but I could never tell that to my fiancé **face-to-face**[2].

Felix: Are you serious? What's happening? Come on, you have to **fill** me **in**[3]!

Cleo: Well, there's no question that I've really **fallen for**[4] him, but I'm just not sure that I want to **be with him**[5] forever.

Felix: I think that's perfectly normal. However, you're right—once you get married, it isn't as if you can **trade in**[6] one husband for another! **It figures**[7] that you would be nervous. I guess you really should think carefully about what you want.

fall for 愛上

菲力斯：看來妳明天真的要結婚了？

克莉歐：事實上，我有點**害怕**，但我不會把這件事情**當面**告訴我的未婚夫。

菲力斯：妳是說真的嗎？怎麼了？說吧，**告訴**我吧！

克莉歐：嗯，我真的非常**愛**他，但我不確定我是否想要和他**共度**一生。

菲力斯：我想這很正常，不過妳說的沒錯，一旦結了婚，老公就不能**換**人了！妳會緊張是**理所當然**的。我想妳應該好好想想自己想要什麼。

get cold feet 害怕

face-to-face 面對面

fill in 告訴

135

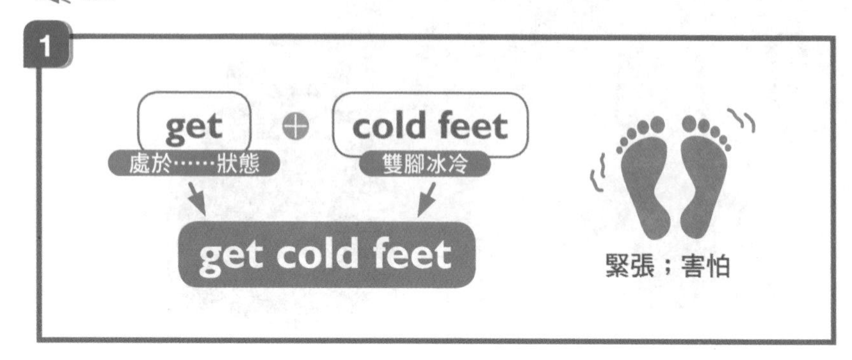

- Ten minutes before the wedding, Francis **got cold feet** and ran off.
  婚禮前 10 分鐘，法蘭西斯**太緊張**所以臨陣脫逃了。
- You have always wanted to go bungee jumping, so don't **get cold feet** now!
  我知道你一直都想要嘗試高空彈跳，所以別**緊張**嘛！

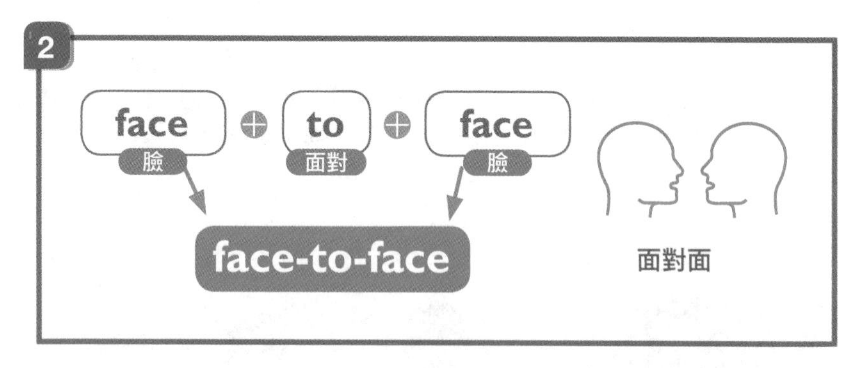

- Nate had spoken with Jeb a few times on the phone, but they had never met **face-to-face**.
  奈特和傑伯通過幾次電話，但他們從未見過**面**。
- She has refused a **face-to-face** interview, but she has agreed to answer my questions in a letter.
  她拒絕**面對面**會談，但同意在信中回覆我提到的問題。

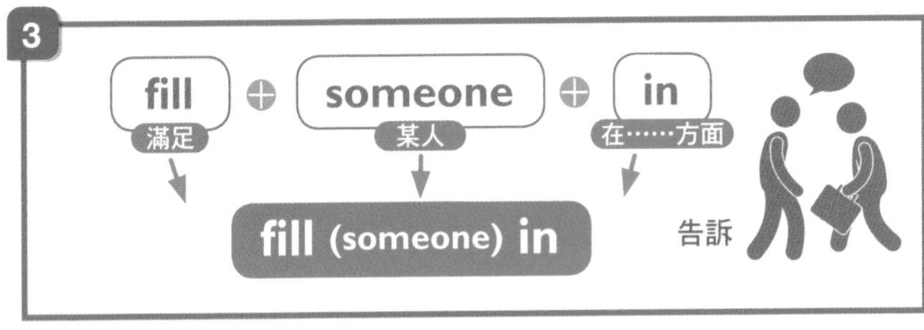

- Anne **filled** the class **in** on her trip to Canada.
  安把加拿大之旅的事情**告訴**全班。
- After Clarence was **filled in** by Tyrone, the two guys got to work. 泰倫**告訴**克萊倫斯該怎麼做後，兩人便開始行動。

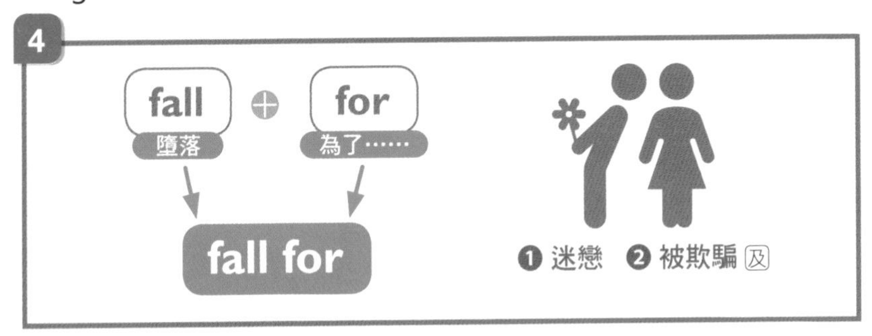

❶ Poor Kim! She **fell for** a married man.
可憐的金！她**愛上**了有婦之夫。

❶ Barry married the first woman he **fell for**.
拜瑞和初**戀**女友結婚了。

❶ I always **fall for** unsuitable men. 我總是**愛上**不該愛的男人。

❶ They met at a friend's party and **fell for** each other immediately. 他們在朋友的派對上相遇，迅速地**陷入熱戀**。

❷ I stupidly **fell for** her story until someone told me she was already married.
在別人告訴我她已婚之前，我一直傻傻**相信**她說的話。

❷ Our teacher **fell for** Dylan's story about being sick yesterday; actually, he was at the beach.
狄倫**騙**老師說他昨天生病，其實他昨天去了海邊。

❷ He told me he owned a castle in Spain, and I **fell for** it.
他說他在西班牙擁有一座城堡，而我真的**相信**了。

136

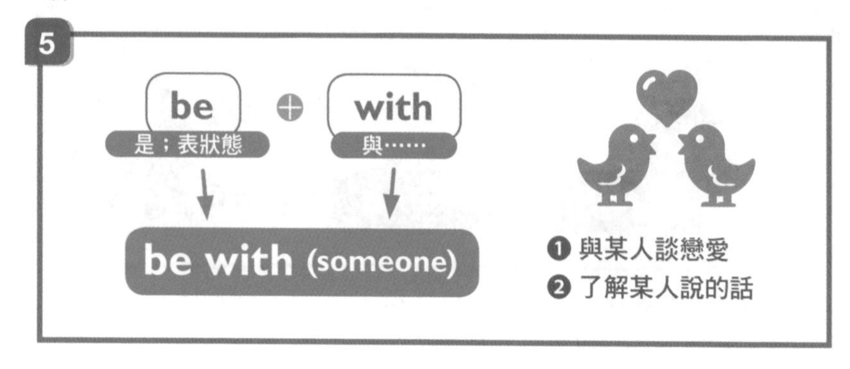

❶ **Are** you **with** Patty, or are you still single?
你**和**派蒂**在交往**嗎？還是你依然單身呢？

❷ You look puzzled—**are** you **with** me?
你看起來很困惑，你**了解我說的話**嗎？

- Erin got the price of the new car down when she offered to **trade in** her old SUV.
艾琳新買的車子不貴，因為她用舊的 SUV **折抵**。
- If I **trade in** this TV, will you lower the price of the new one? 如果我用這台電視來**折抵**，你願意算我便宜一點嗎？

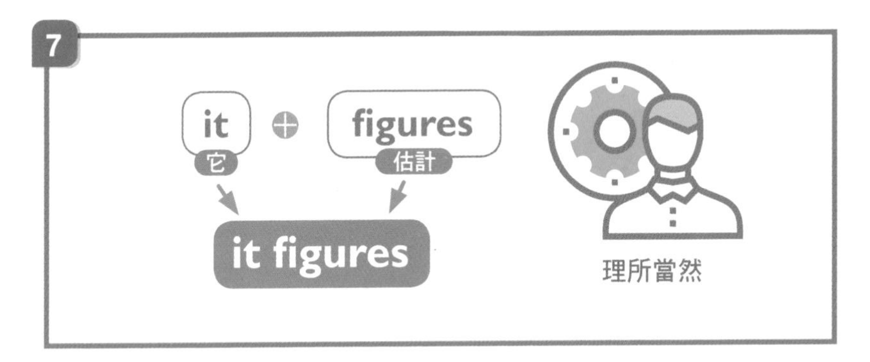

- **It figures** that it rained on my only day off of work this week. 在我這星期唯一不用上班的這天，**果然**下雨了。
- **It figures** that you woke up late since you were at that party till 3 a.m. 你狂歡到半夜三點，今天**當然**會很晚起床。

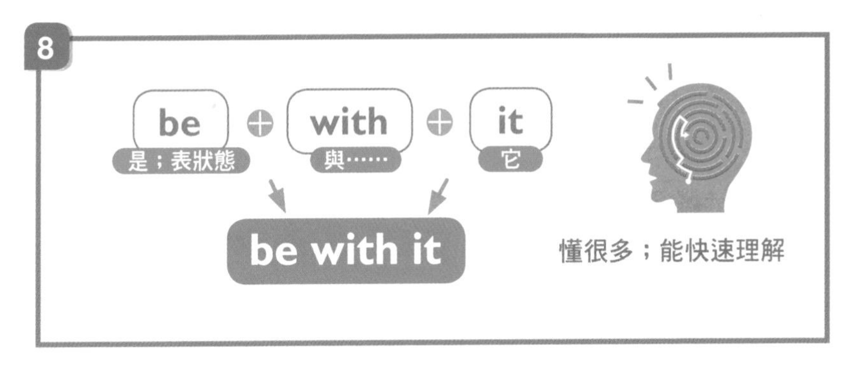

- Although my parents are not young people, they'**re** really **with it**.
  雖然我的父母年紀不小，但他們**理解力**真的**很強**。
- If you want to **be with it**, you'd better start paying more attention.
  如果你真的想要**把它搞懂**，最好專心一點。
- After a long night out, Jenna **wasn't** really **with it** at work the next day.
  珍娜昨晚在外面瘋了一整夜，隔天上班效率很差。

137

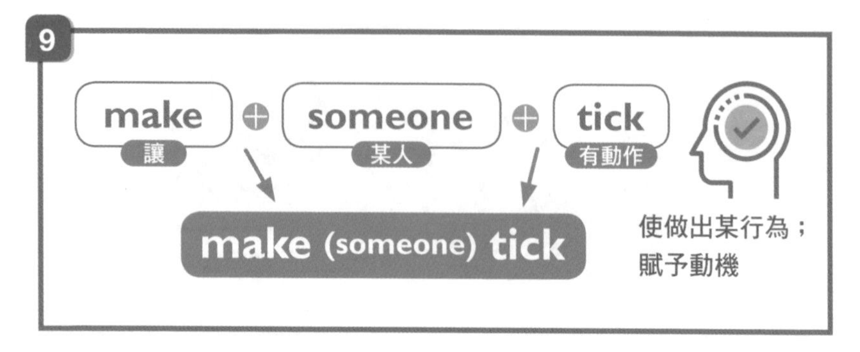

- Lance is a strange guy; I really don't know what **makes** him **tick**. 藍斯是個怪人，真不知道他為何要**做出**這些事情。
- I always wondered what **makes** the president **tick**.
  我一直在想是什麼**讓**總裁**行動**了。

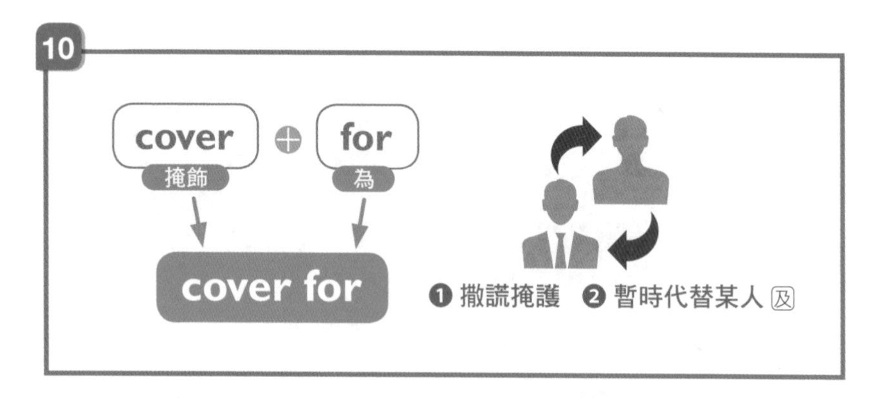

❶ Although he knew his brother had eaten all the cookies, Dale **covered for** him.
戴爾雖然知道弟弟吃了所有的餅乾，但還是**幫**他**隱瞞**。

❷ Please **cover for** Donna; she's sick this week.
唐娜這星期請病假，請**暫代**她的職位。

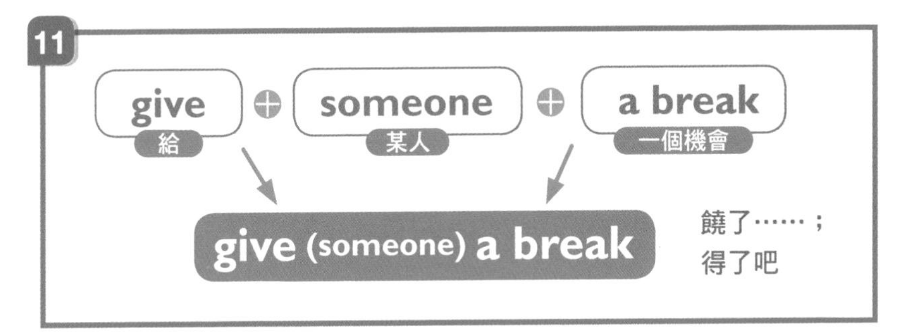

- I know that Ruth is not doing her job well, but **give** her **a break**—it's her first day here!
  我知道茹絲的工作表現不理想，但**饒了**她吧，她才第一天上班！
- I know you're disappointed about your low test score, but **give** yourself **a break**. It was a very hard test, and no one did well! 我知道你因為考試成績不好很失望，但**放過**自己吧，這次的考試很難，大家都考不好！

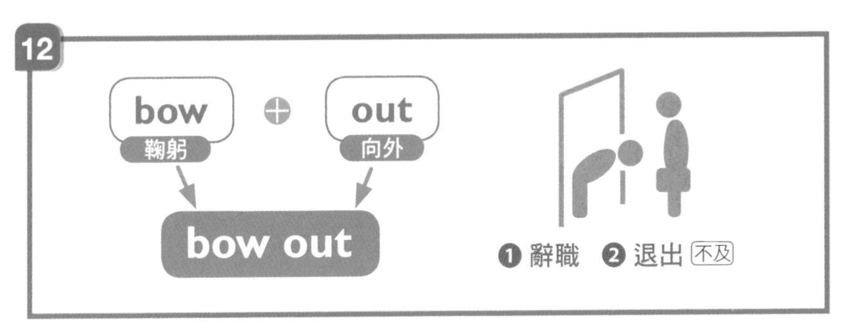

❶ Mark plans to **bow out** in six weeks, after having spent 20 years with the company.
馬克在公司服務了 20 年之後，打算在六個星期後**退休**。

❶ After working as a senator for just a few months, Ms. Luther **bowed out** to accept a different job.
在當了幾個月的參議員後，路瑟女士決定**卸任**，接受別份工作。

❷ An accident forced Jennifer to **bow out** of the show just before the first performance.
一場意外讓珍妮佛在首演之前被迫**退出**。

The Missing iPod
失竊的 iPod

Gina and Mick talk about Dilbert.
吉娜和米克在談論狄伯特。

138

Mick: Do you know where Dilbert is?

Gina: **Search me**[1]! I haven't seen him for a few days.

Mick: Are you trying to **get a rise out of**[2] me? I just saw you speaking with him a few hours ago.

Gina: Okay, okay. Let me **get something off my chest**[3]. I'll be honest with you. I have seen Dilbert, but he doesn't want to talk to you.

Mick: But I have to talk to him. He's trying to **pin** the blame **on**[4] me for stealing his iPod—but I didn't do it.

Gina: I see. Fine, **stick around**[5] here, and I'll go get Dilbert. **By the way**[6], I don't think he'll **let** this **slide**[7] until he finds that MP3 player or someone pays for a new one.

Mick: I don't blame him, but there's no way I'll **pick up the tab**[8] for a new one. I didn't take it!

米克： 你知道狄伯特在哪嗎？

吉娜： **不知道**！我好幾天沒看到他了。

米克： 妳想**惹火**我嗎？我幾個小時前才看到妳和他在聊天。

吉娜： 好吧，那我就**實話實說**了。老實說，我是有看到狄伯特，但他不想和你說話。

米克： 可是我有事情要告訴他。他想要把 iPod 被偷的事情**怪罪**到我身上來，但又不是我做的。

吉娜： 我知道了。好吧，在這裡**耐心等一下**，我去找狄伯特過來。噢，**對了**，在他找回 MP3，或有人買新的給他之前，我想他不會對這件事情**充耳不聞**的。

米克： 我不怪他，但我不會**付錢**買新的給他。又不是我偷的！

stick around 耐心等待

pick up the tab 付帳

139

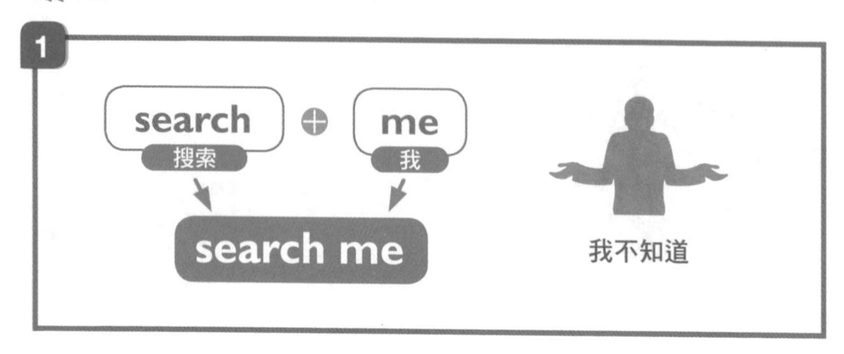

- **Search me**! I have no idea where Fourth Avenue is.
  不知道！我完全不知道第四大道在哪裡。

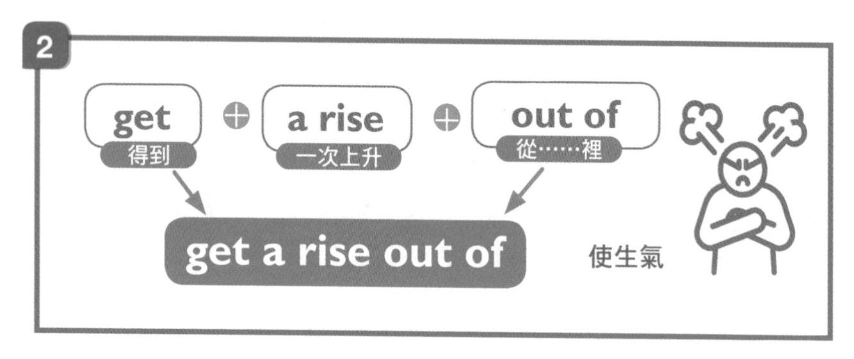

- Arnold **got a rise out of** Gerald with his insulting comments.
  阿諾無禮的批評令傑拉爾德很**生氣**。
- Donny's teasing always **gets a rise out of** Mildred.
  唐尼的揶揄總是令米卓瑞德非常**生氣**。

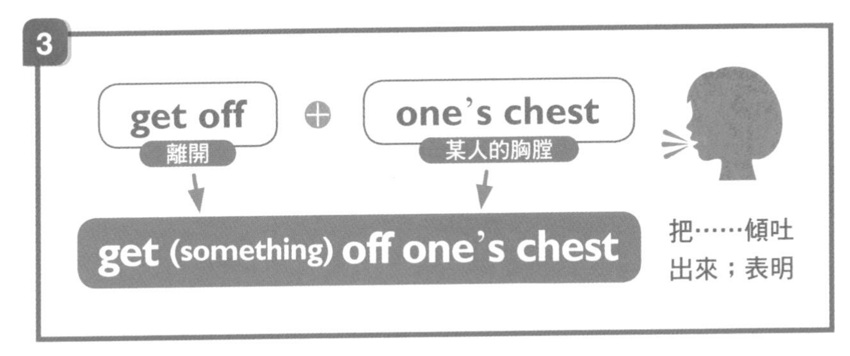

- After Justin told Hailey his secret, he said it felt good to **get** it **off his chest**.
  賈斯汀把秘密告訴荷莉之後，他覺得**說出來**心情變好了許多。
- We listened as Brooke **got** her worries **off her chest**.
  我們在聽布洛克**說**她的困擾。
- I had spent six months worrying about it, and I was glad to **get** it **off my chest**.
  我已經為這件事情煩惱了六個月，很高興終於能夠把它**說**出來了。

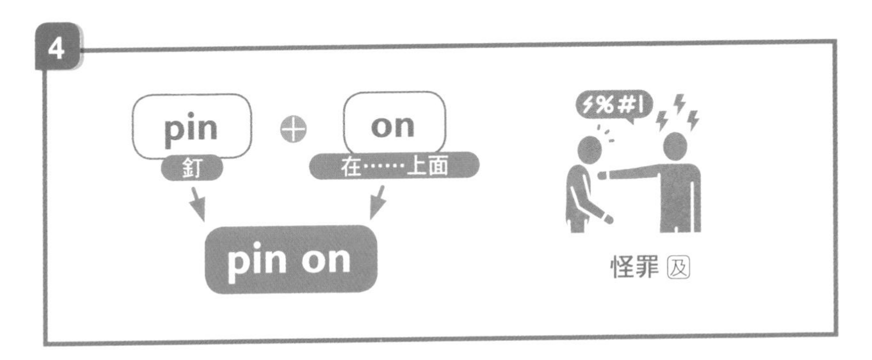

- The police tried to **pin** the blame **on** Vanessa even though she wasn't there.
  雖然凡妮莎當時不在場，但警察還是企圖**讓**她**背黑鍋**。
- Gustavo **pinned** the crime **on** his neighbor.
  葛斯塔佛**怪罪**到鄰居身上。

140

- Please don't **stick around** here anymore; go home.
  請不要在這裡**等**了，回家去吧。
- Although they didn't have any money to spend, the teenagers **stuck around** the mall all day.
  這些年輕人即使沒有錢可花，但還是在購物中心**待**了一整天。

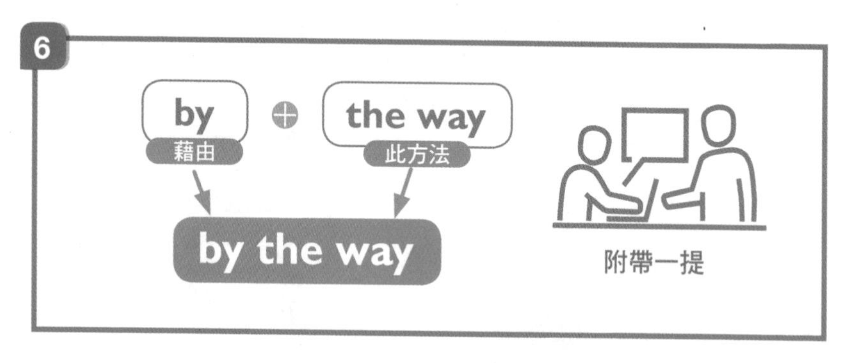

- It's nice meeting you; **by the way**, I'm Rick.
  很高興認識你，**對了**，我叫瑞克。
- It sure has been a busy day at the office! **By the way**, what are you doing this weekend?
  今天上班真的很忙，**對了**！你週末有什麼計畫嗎？
- I think we've discussed everything we need to. **By the way**, what time is it?
  我想所有需要討論的事情我們已經談完了。**對了**，現在幾點了？

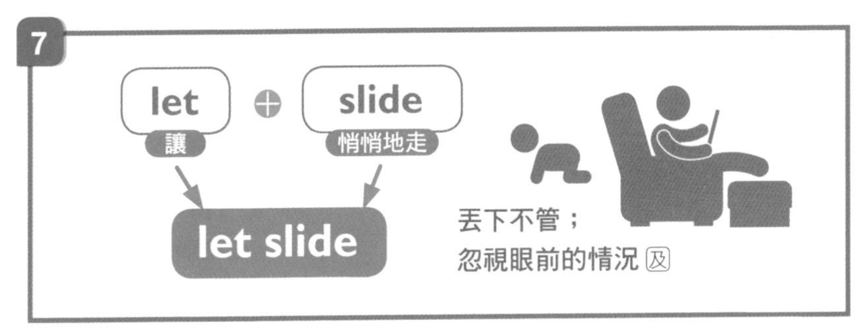

- It's important to not **let** your responsibilities **slide**.
  千萬別**忽視**了你應負的責任。
- Alexis **let** her research paper **slide** and, in the end, never finished it. 艾莉克絲**忽略**了研究報告，她最終沒有完成。
- I was doing really well with my diet, but I'm afraid I've **let** it **slide** recently.
  我的節食計畫原本進展得很順利，但恐怕我最近有點**疏忽**了。
- It's easy to **let** exercise **slide** when you feel bad, but that's when you need it the most.
  身體不舒服時最需要運動，但人們常會**忽略**這點。

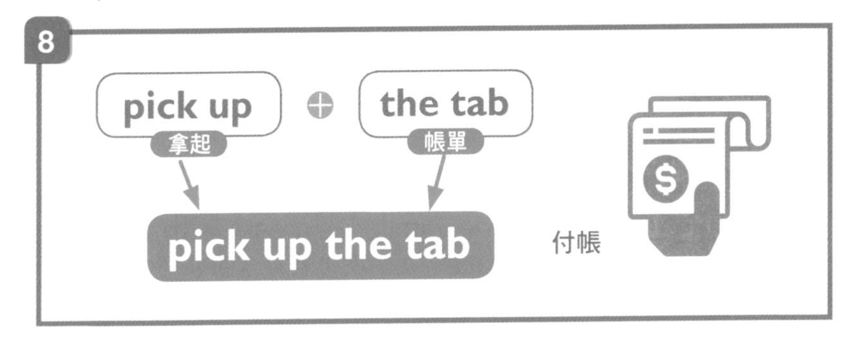

- Don't worry if you don't have any money. Andrea will **pick up the tab**. 沒帶錢沒關係。安德麗雅會**付錢**的。
- Because I was the only one with a credit card, my friends asked me to **pick up the tab**. As usual, they didn't have enough money. 朋友身上的錢一如往常地不夠，由於我是唯一擁有信用卡的人，所以朋友要我先**付帳**。

141

- Ella and Connor **lived it up** for a weekend in Las Vegas.
艾拉和康諾在拉斯維加斯度過了一個**奢華**的週末。
- The couple **lived it up** during their honeymoon in Hawaii. 這對夫妻到夏威夷度過了一個非常**奢華**的蜜月。
- She's alive and well and **living it up** in the Bahamas.
她在巴哈馬的生活過得很好也很**奢華**。

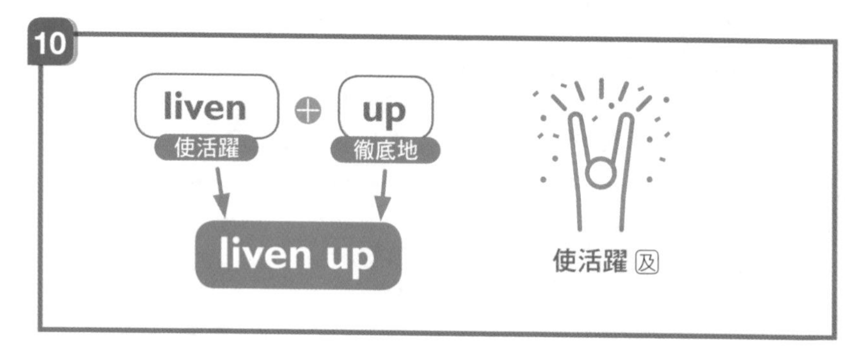

- The chef **livened up** the vanilla ice cream with fresh fruit and chocolate sauce. 在主廚用新鮮水果和巧克力醬的裝飾下，香草冰淇淋變得非常可口動人。
- The meeting **livened up** when the CEO started telling some funny jokes.
在執行長說了一些笑話後，這個會議**變得活潑**許多。
- A colored shirt can certainly **liven up** an outfit.
色彩鮮明的襯衫絕對能夠**讓**穿搭**活**起來。

❶ You can go out to eat anywhere you like, but don't **go to town** and spend all your money on one meal.
你可以到任何你喜歡的餐廳吃飯，但別**太過頭**而把所有的錢都花在一頓飯上面。

❷ Tom and Nicole have really **gone to town** on their wedding. 湯姆和妮可**全心全意地投入**籌備婚禮。

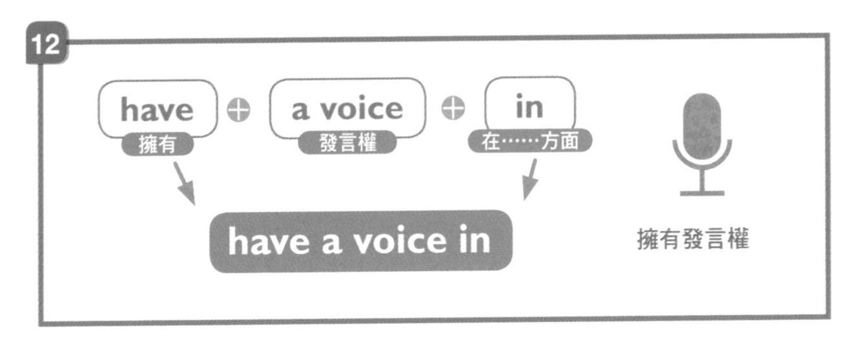

- In a true democracy, everyone **has a voice in** what the government does.
  在真正的民主國家中，人民都**擁有發言權**。

- Whenever my company has an open position, the boss lets everyone **have a voice in** choosing the new employee. 每當我們公司要聘請新員工時，老闆讓所有人**都擁有**選擇新同事**的權利**。

Checking In
辦理住宿登記

Joanne checks into a hotel.
瓊安在飯店登記住宿。

142

Clerk: Good evening, ma'am. Would you like to **check in**[1]?

Joanne: Yes, I would. Are there still nonsmoking rooms available?

Clerk: Don't worry. You haven't **missed the boat**[2]. There are plenty.

Joanne: That's good news; if there were no nonsmoking rooms here, I'm afraid I'd **lose my cool**[3]. My husband and I have been looking for a hotel all day! How much is one night here?

Clerk: A double room is $95 a night. I'll just need to see some ID.

Joanne: That's a great price. Oh, no! I think I left my ID with my husband. Can I show it to you later?

Clerk: No problem. I'll **take you at your word**[4] for now—but please remember to stop by with it later.

Joanne: Of course. I won't **cop out**[5].

Clerk: Here's your key. Remember you must **check out**[6] by 10:30 tomorrow morning.

Joanne: Is it possible to **leave open**[7] tomorrow night, too? We may stay two nights if this hotel **serves our purpose**[8].

Clerk: That's fine.

服務員： 晚安，女士。您要**辦理住宿登記**了嗎？

瓊安： 是的。請問一下，禁菸樓層還有空房間嗎？

服務員： 別擔心，您並沒有**錯過**。我們還有許多空房間呢。

瓊安： 太好了；若是沒有禁菸房間的話，我可能會**不知所措**。我和我先生整天都在找飯店投宿！請問住宿一晚的費用是多少錢？

服務員： 雙人房每晚是 95 元。我需要查看您的身分證。

瓊安： 價錢很合理。噢，不會吧！我想我的身分證在我先生那裡我能夠等一下再給你看嗎？

服務員： 沒關係，我**相信**您，但稍後請務必拿過來。

瓊安： 放心，我不會**逃避責任**的。

服務員： 這是您的鑰匙。請您記得明天早上 10 點 30 分前要**辦理退房**。

瓊安： 我們可以明天晚上**才決定**嗎？如果這裡**符合**我們的需求，我們可能會待兩個晚上。

服務員： 好的。

143

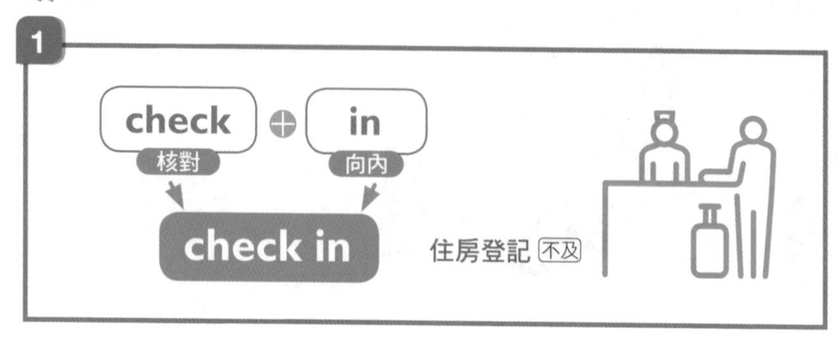

- Before you can stay at this hotel, it is necessary to **check in** at the front desk.
  入住飯店前，要先到櫃檯**辦理住宿登記**。
- Is it possible to **check in** at the hotel after midnight?
  我可以在半夜**登記住宿**嗎？

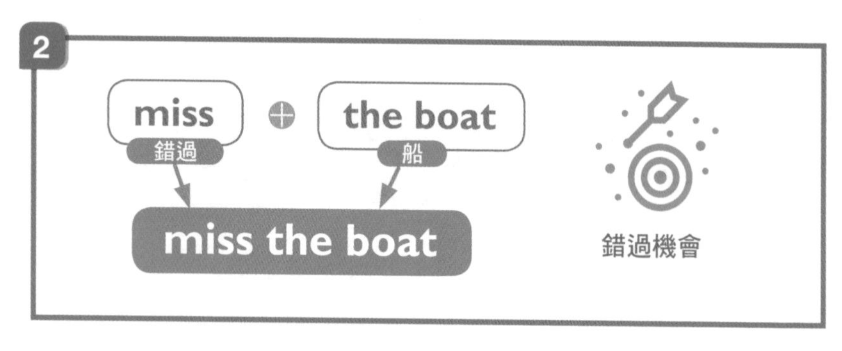

- We could have bought cheap tickets to L.A. yesterday, but we **missed the boat** by thinking about it too much, and now they're all gone.
  我們昨天本來可以買到飛往洛杉磯的便宜機票，但我們因為考慮了太多而**錯失機會**，票現在都賣完了。
- This is your last chance to accept this job; if you are still unsure, I'm afraid you'll have **missed the boat**.
  這是你最後接受這份工作的機會，如果你還是無法決定，恐怕會**錯過機會**。

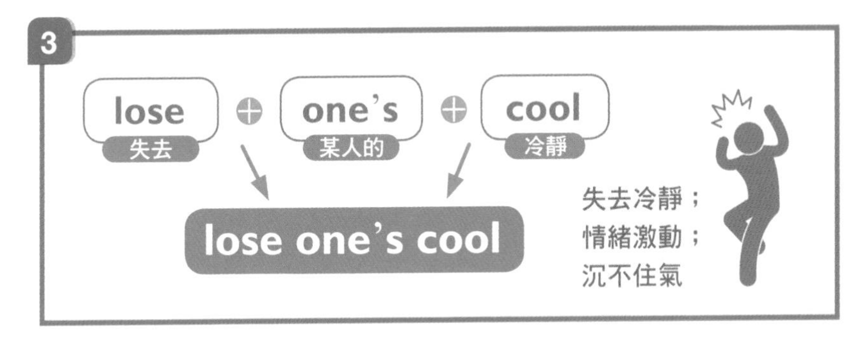

- When Aaron heard that he had failed the class, he **lost his cool** and started crying like a child. 亞倫知道他這科的成績不及格後，**情緒很激動**，接著哭得像個孩子。

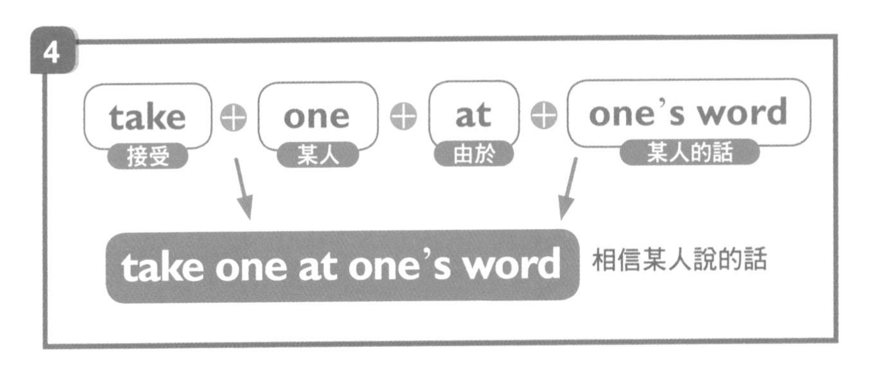

- Although Aiden didn't have a written agreement, he **took his boss at his word** and started working the next day. 雖然艾登沒有接到書面通知，但他**相信老闆說的話**，並且隔天就開始上班。
- Joel is an honest guy. You can definitely **take him at his word**. 喬爾絕對是個老實人，你可以完全**相信他說的話**。

144

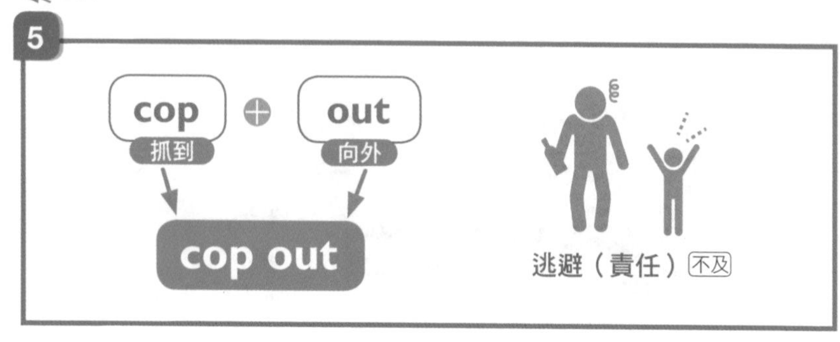

- Go talk to that pretty girl; don't **cop out** now!
  去和那個漂亮女孩說話吧，別再**逃避**了！
- Just as the group was about to go mountain climbing, Diane **copped out** and said she was too nervous.
  就在登山隊準備出發時，黛安因為太緊張，所以**放棄**了。
- Martin **copped out** of the parachute jump at the last minute with some feeble excuse.
  馬汀在最後一刻因為一些牽強的理由而**放棄**了跳傘。

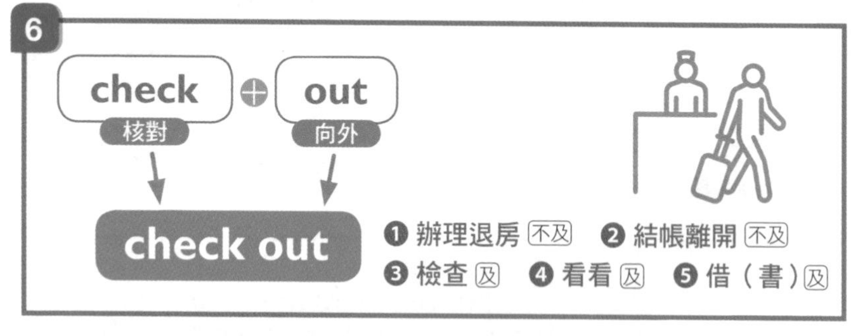

❶ Be sure to **check out** before noon tomorrow.
明天中午前一定要**辦理退房**。

❸ If you have time today, could you please **check out** the weather forecast for this week?
你今天有時間的話，可以請你**查**一下這週的天氣預報嗎？

❹ I'm going to **check out** that new club.
我要去**看看**那家新開的俱樂部。

❺ I **checked** three books **out** of the library this afternoon.
我今天下午向圖書館**借**了三本書。

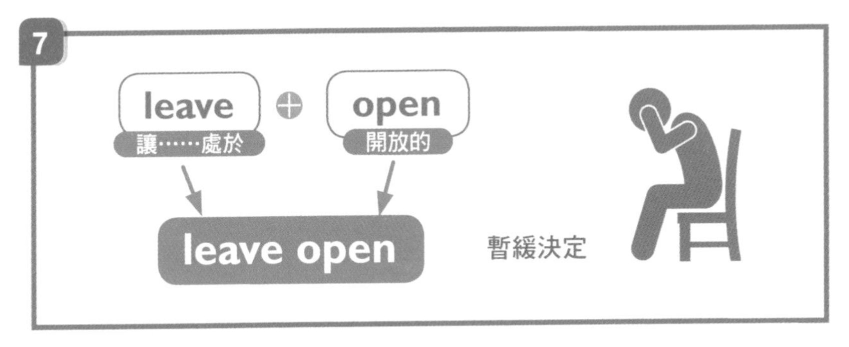

- Danielle **left open** the possibility that she could drive me to school, but she said she wasn't sure yet.
  丹妮葉拉**暫時還沒決定**是否要載我去學校，她還不確定。
- Brenda **left** the weekend **open** just in case her boyfriend invited her to the party.
  布蘭達**先**把週末**空下來**，免得男朋友邀請她參加派對。

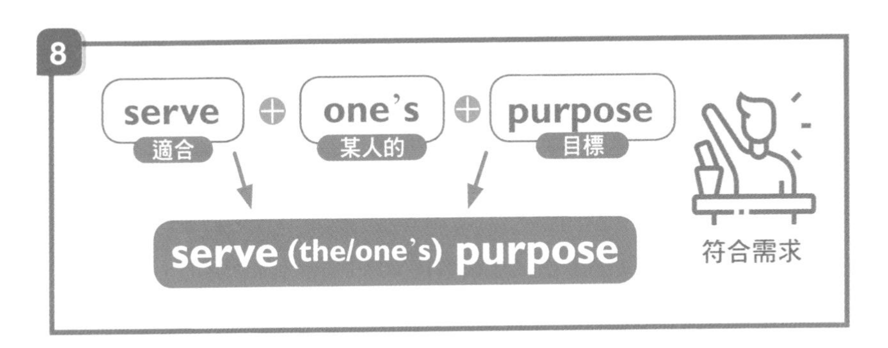

- Before you spend a lot of money on those programs, you should be sure they will **serve your purpose**.
  你在投入資金前，應該要先確定這些案子是否**符合你的需求**。
- This new laptop will surely **serve the purpose**.
  這台新的筆記型電腦肯定能**符合需求**。

145

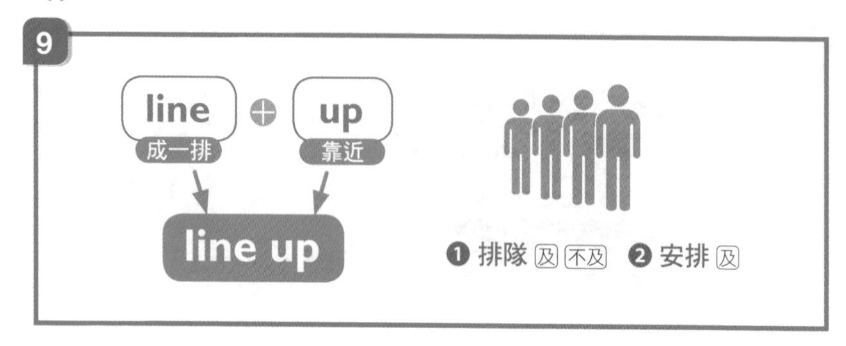

❶ The security guards made us **line up** to get into the club.
安全人員要我們**排隊**進入俱樂部。

❶ The little boy **lined up** all his toy cars so he could see each one. 小男孩把所有的玩具車都**排成一列**，以便看到每台車。

❶ Your grade in this class **turns on** how well you do on the final paper.
你的期末報告**決定**了你在班上的成績。

❷ The dog **turned on** Lola and tried to bite her.
那隻狗**對**蘿娜**產生敵意**，而且還企圖咬她。

❷ Suddenly, Vicky just **turned on** me and accused me of undermining her.
維琪突然**對**我**產生敵意**並且指責我暗中說她壞話。

❸ What **turns** kids **on** these days? 現在的孩子**喜歡**些什麼？

- Jasmine wants to live in Texas **in the worst way**.
  潔絲敏**非常**想要住在德州。
- Phil wanted to buy that video game **in the worst way**, but he didn't have enough cash.
  菲爾**非常**想要買那台電動玩具，但他的錢不夠。
- After a day in the hot sun, I needed a shower **in the worst way**. 在大太陽底下待了一天，我**非常地**想要沖澡。

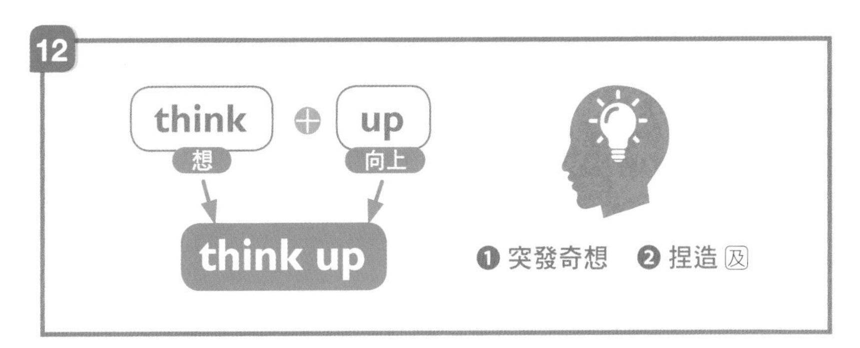

❶ Harriet **thought up** a great topic for her thesis.
哈莉葉**突然想到**一個很棒的論文主題。

❶ Paul **thought up** his own chicken soup recipe.
保羅**想出**了獨家的雞湯食譜。

❷ I don't want to go tonight, but I can't **think up** a good excuse. 我今晚不想去，但我**想**不**到**好的理由拒絕。

Showing Off
炫燿賣弄

Bob shows Angie his new mobile phone.
鮑伯把新手機拿給安姬看。

146

Bob: Take a look at my new cell phone! It is also a camera and an MP3 player, and it can even go online. It can also do a lot of other cool stuff, but I'm still **learning the ropes**[1].

Angie: Hmm . . . that's interesting. When someone calls you, does it have a special ring?

Bob: That's the best part! Whenever I get a call, it makes the sound of a cow. That's sure to **make waves**[2].

Angie: I'm sure. You know, it is a cool phone, but you shouldn't **show off**[3] so much. Where did you buy it, anyway?

Bob: This phone **was up for grabs**[4] in a hot dog-eating competition, and I won! Those competitions are a great way to win prizes. There's another one next month, and the winner gets a flat screen TV. You want to compete, too?

Angie: No way, man. **Not on your life**[5]!

Bob: Okay. Well, **keep your fingers crossed**[6] for me.

鮑伯：　妳看我的新手機！它也是相機、MP3 播放器，還可以上網。我想它還有許多很新的功能，但我還在**摸索**當中。

安姬：　嗯，聽起來不錯。那有人打電話給你時，有什麼特別的鈴聲嗎？

鮑伯：　這就是這支手機最棒的地方！只要有人打電話給我，手機就會發出牛叫聲。許多人肯定會**非常驚訝**。

安姬：　我也覺得。這支手機很棒，但你不應該到處**炫燿**。總之，你在哪裡買的呢？

鮑伯：　**每位**參加吃熱狗大賽的人**都有機會贏得**這支手機，所以手機是我贏來的！參加比賽是贏得獎品很好的方式。下個月還有一場比賽，贏的人可以得到液晶電視。妳也想參加比賽嗎？

安姬：　才沒有。**想都別想**！

鮑伯：　好吧。那就為我**祈禱**吧。

show off 炫耀

keep one's fingers crossed 祈求

147

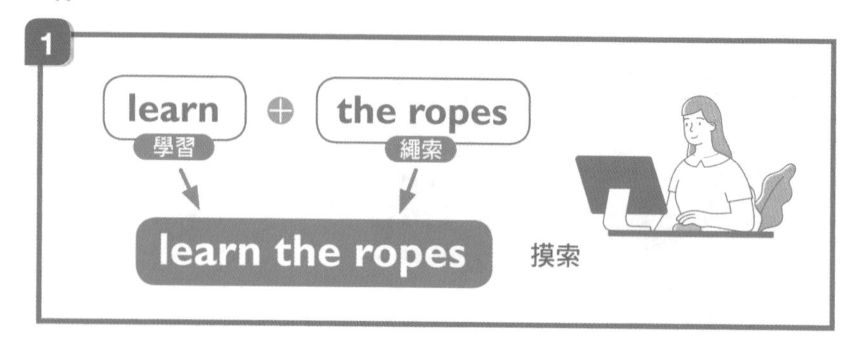

- It's my first day working here, so I still need to **learn the ropes**. 今天是我第一天上班，所以我還在**摸索**當中。
- No one will expect you to do much around the office until you are trained and have **learned the ropes**.
在你完成培訓並**抓到要領**前，公司是不會派給你太多任務的。
- It'll take time for the new receptionist to **learn the ropes**. 新來的接待員要花一些時間來**摸索工作內容**。

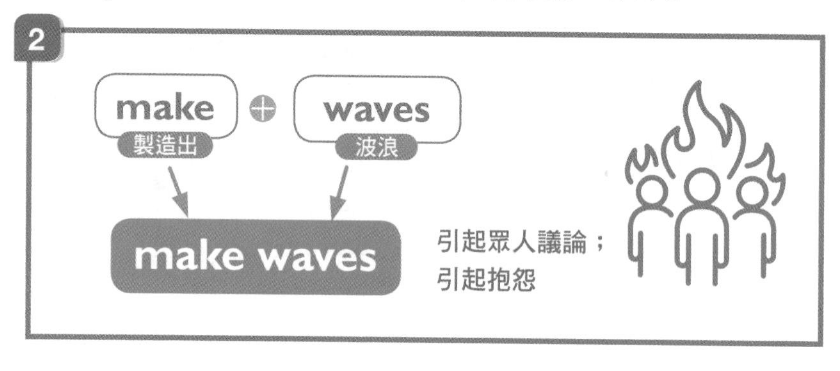

- Pam got fired from her job because she was always **making waves** during important meetings.
潘老是在重要會議中**挑起事端**，所以她被解僱了。
- The key to working well with a team is to not **make** too many **waves**. 團隊合作的關鍵就是不要**興風作浪**。
- Our culture encourages us to fit the norm and avoid **making waves**.
我們的文化鼓勵我們行為舉止要合乎規範，不要**興風作浪**。

- Don can be really annoying. Whenever there are pretty girls around, he always tries to **show off** his physical strength. 唐有時很討人厭，只要有漂亮女生在旁邊，他總會想要**炫燿**他那壯碩的身材。
- I think Melissa could be a good basketball player if she stopped **showing off** and was more of a team player. 只要梅麗莎別再**炫燿**，多點團隊精神，我認為她會成為一名優秀的籃球員。

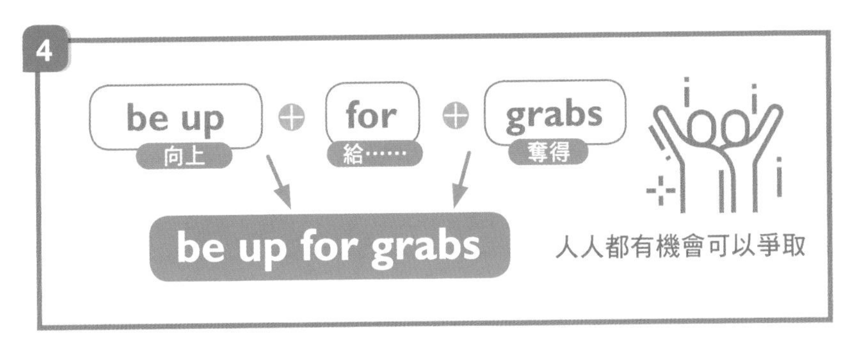

- The new car **is up for grabs** in the marathon! 贏得馬拉松比賽的人可以**得到**這台新車！
- The math teacher's job **is up for grabs** because he's quitting. 他要辭職了，所以數學老師一職**空了出來**。

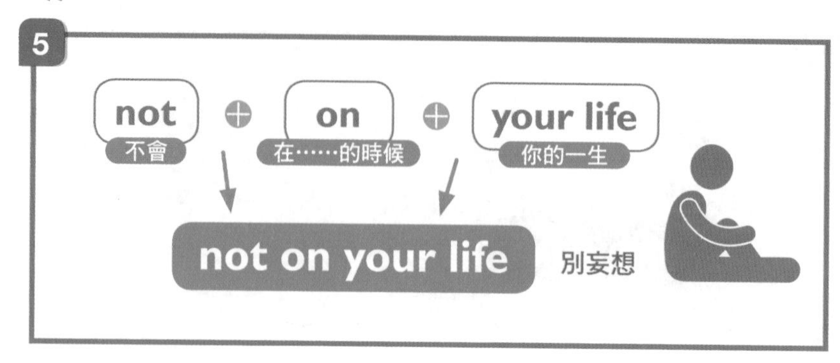

- You think I'll let you go to New York by yourself? **Not on your life**!
  你以為我會讓你獨自去紐約嗎？**想都別想**！

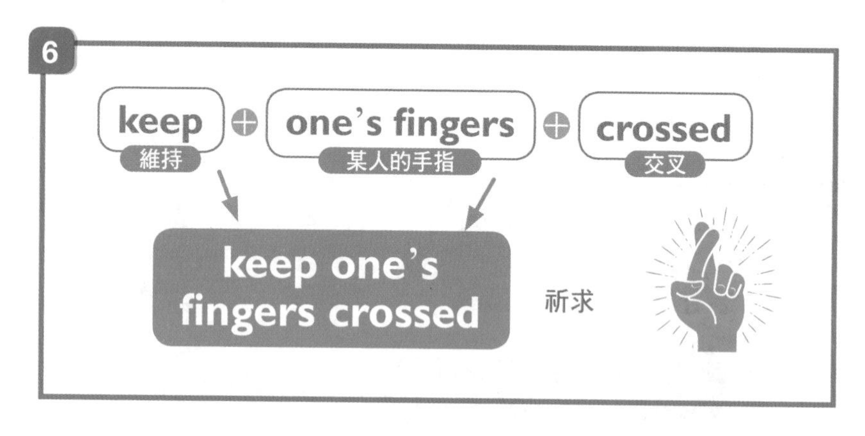

- Your little sister has a big test today, so **keep your fingers crossed** for her.
  你妹妹今天有重要考試，所以為她**祈禱**吧。
- **Keep your fingers crossed**! I have a job interview this afternoon.
  我今天下午有工作面談，替我**祈禱**吧！

❶ The little kids **carried on** all night because they had eaten too much candy.
孩子們整個晚上**吵個不停**，因為他們吃了太多的糖果了。

❷ As soon as the movie was over, Caroline **carried on** with her homework.
電影一演完，卡若琳便**繼續**做功課。

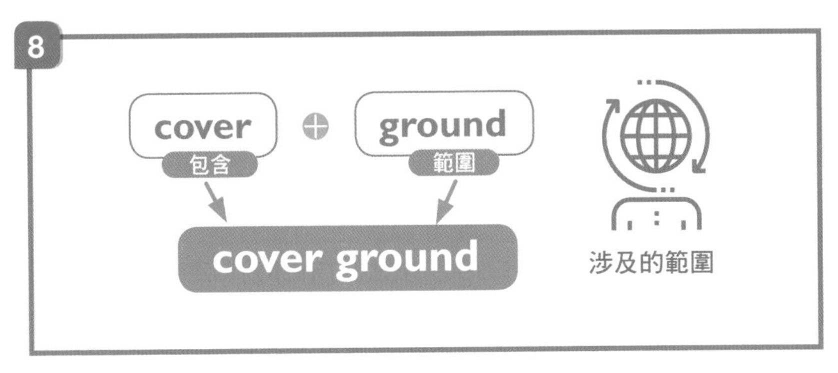

- The big research project is due soon, so we tried to **cover** a lot of **ground** before Monday. 這份報告再不久就要送出，我們必須趕在星期一之前**完成**所有的**細節**。
- The students **covered ground** on all the issues during their discussion. 學生的討論**涉及**了所有的議題。

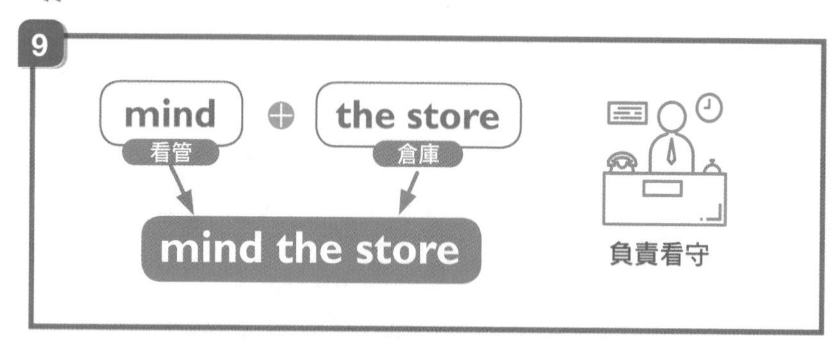

- While Mr. Richardson was away from the office, Jack **minded the store**.
  理查森先生不在辦公室時，是由傑克暫時**打理一切**。
- Who's going to be **minding the store** while your manager's away? 經理不在時，是由誰**負責管理**的？

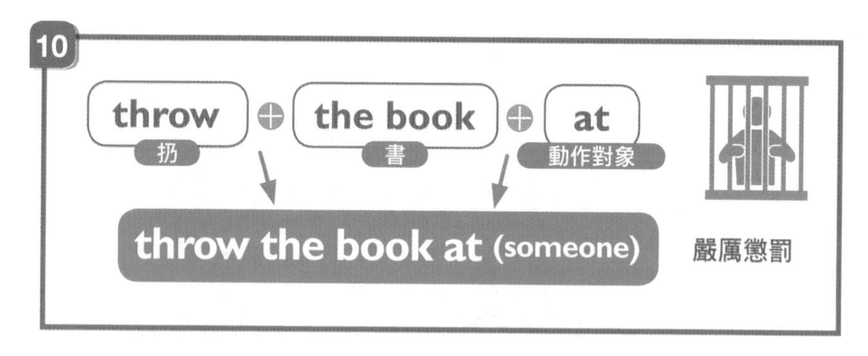

- When Julia was first caught by the police officers, they didn't punish her too much; the second time, however, they **threw the book at** her.
  警察第一次抓到茱莉亞時，並沒有很嚴厲地懲罰她。然而他們第二次抓到她時，便對她**施以嚴懲**。
- After several arrests for drunken driving, the judge finally **threw the book at** Jack. 傑克好幾次被抓到酒醉駕車，法官終於對他**做出嚴厲的判決**。

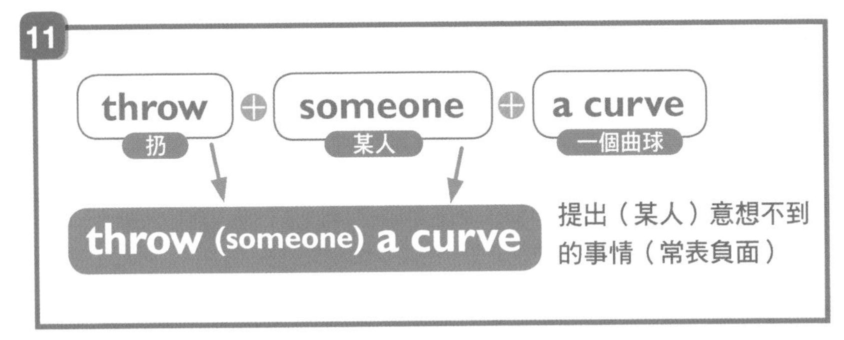

- Victoria's dad really **threw** her **a curve** when he said she couldn't do anything special for her birthday—the fact was, he had planned a surprise party. 維多莉亞的爸爸**騙**她沒有準備特別的生日計畫。事實上，他策劃了一場驚喜派對。
- Lisa **threw** me **a curve** by asking me to go to the theater instead of the mall.
  莉莎**意想不到地**約我去看電影，而不是去逛街。
- Jerry really **threw** me **a curve** when he asked me a personal question at work.
  傑瑞上班時**問了一個令我意想不到的**私人問題。

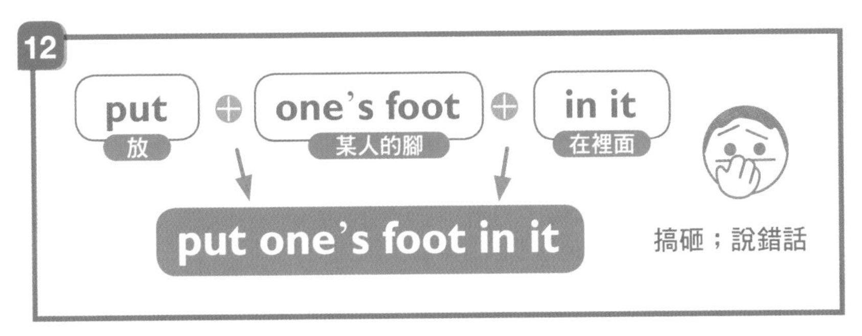

- I really **put my foot in it** yesterday when the boss overheard me making fun of her.
  老闆昨天無意中聽到我在開她玩笑，我想我真的**搞砸**了。
- I really **put my foot in it** with Diane. I didn't realize she was a vegetarian.
  我真的**搞砸**了與黛安之間**的關係**。我並不知道她吃素。

The First Week at College
大學生活的第一個星期

Samantha talks to Al about her first week at college.
莎曼莎跟艾爾說起她第一個星期的大學生活。

150

Al: How was your first week at college?

Samantha: Well, it was hard! In the beginning, I felt like I **was over my head**[1].

Al: Why do you say that?

Samantha: I needed help all the time. Luckily, I had the best tutor a student could **ask for**[2], but I knew things weren't supposed to be that tough.

Al: So what happened?

Samantha: I had to **take the bull by the horns**[3] and really study harder. College **is a far cry from**[4] high school, and although my professors are happy to **give me a hand**[5] sometimes, I had to learn how to be a better student.

Al: So now you can deal with what your professors **dish out**[6]?

Samantha: **By all means**[7]! There's no doubt.

Al: It sure sounds like you **landed on your feet**[8] after those early difficulties. Congratulations!

艾爾：　妳在大學的第一個星期過得如何呢？

莎曼莎：唉，很難熬！我一開學就**忙得一個頭兩個大**。

艾爾：　怎麼說？

莎曼莎：我總是需要別人的幫助。幸好我有一位可以**求助**的好助教，可是我覺得事情應該沒那麼困難才對。

艾爾：　發生了什麼事情嗎？

莎曼莎：我得**不畏艱難**，並且更用功唸書；大學**和**高中**不同**，雖然有時教授很樂意**幫助**我，但我必須要學會如何成為好學生。

艾爾：　所以妳現在能夠應付教授**指派**的作業了嗎？

莎曼莎：**那當然**！別懷疑。

艾爾：　看來妳已經從之前所遇到的困難中，**重新振作起來**了。恭喜妳！

151

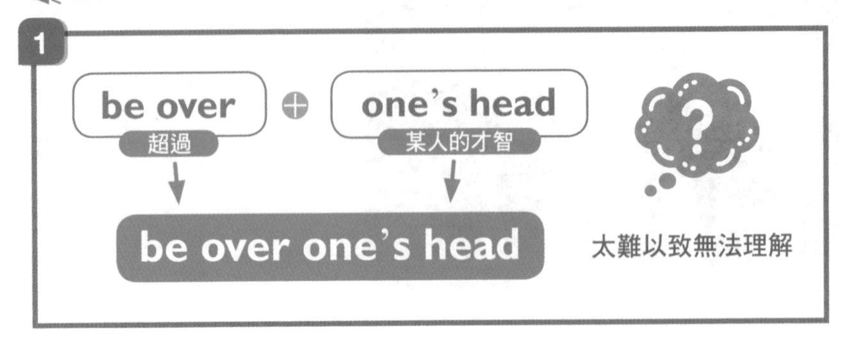

- Jonny is pretty young, so a lot of the jokes that the older boys were telling **were over his head**. 強尼年紀很輕，那些較年長的男孩所開的玩笑，**超出了他所能理解的範圍**。
- Everything Aiden heard in the class was really interesting, but a lot of it **was over his head**. 艾登在課堂上所學到的東西都很有趣，但有些**超出他所能理解的範圍**。
- The math homework was really tough. It **was** way **over my head**. 數學作業真的很難，已經遠**超出我所能理解的範圍**。

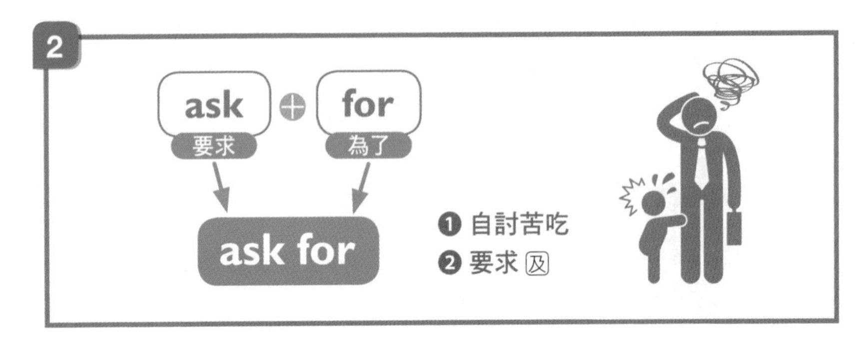

❶ You are **asking for** it if you don't clean up your room like mom ordered.
如果你不照媽媽要求打掃房間，就是**自討苦吃**了。

❷ Dr. O'Maley is the best dentist anyone could **ask for**; he's professional, friendly, and kind. 歐邁利醫生是最優秀的牙醫，每個人都**想**給他看診。他很專業、友善和親切。

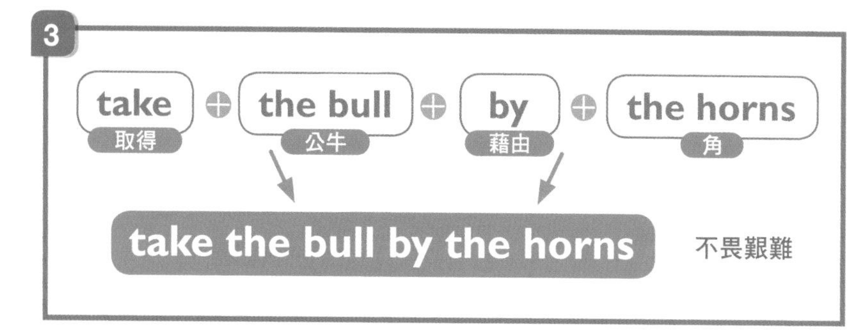

- Roland didn't want Alison at his party, but he was too shy to **take the bull by the horns** and tell her to leave.
  羅蘭不想要艾莉森參加他的派對，但他太膽小而**不敢**開口要她離開。
- If you are unhappy with your life, it may be time to **take the bull by the horns** and try something new.
  如果你對生活不滿意，應該要**不畏艱難**去嘗試新事物。

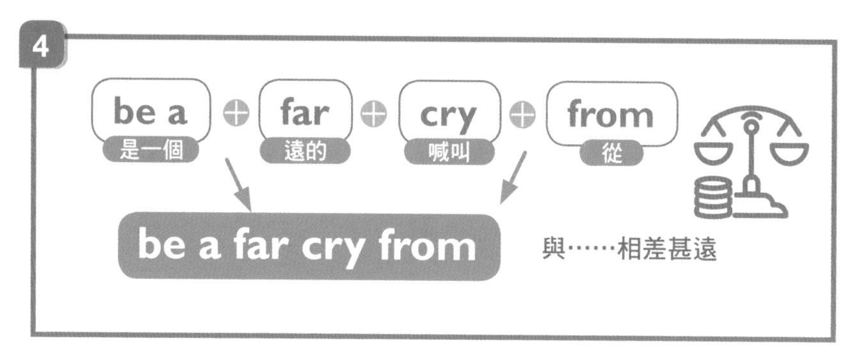

- New York **is** really **a far cry from** the little village where I was born.
  紐約和我所出生的小村落真的**有很大的差異**。
- This little stream **is a far cry from** the Mississippi River.
  這條小溪和密西西比河相比，簡直就是**天壤之別**。

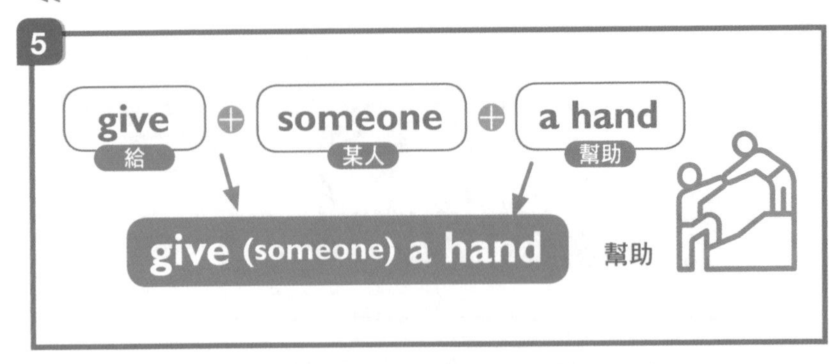

- Will someone please **give** me **a hand** moving these boxes? 有人可以**幫**我搬這些箱子嗎？
- Ivan **gave** Muriel **a hand** with her work because she needed help. 穆芮需要幫忙，艾文便**幫**她做功課。

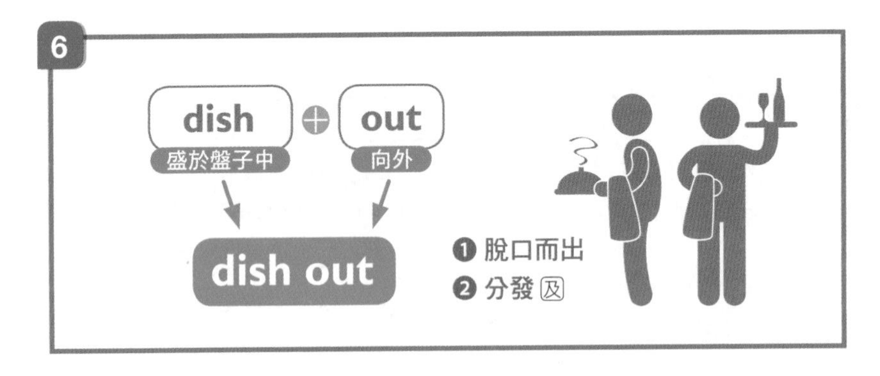

❶ Mira was in a great mood, and she **dished out** compliments to everyone
she saw. 米拉心情很好，她**不假思索地**稱讚每個她見到的人。

❷ The waiter **dished out** soup to everyone at our table.
服務生**送**湯給在座的每個人。

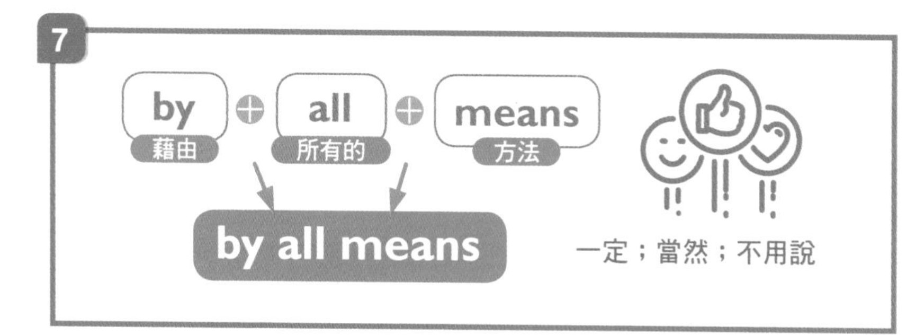

- **By all means**, feel free to use my apartment when I'm on vacation. 我去度假時，你**當然可以**隨意使用我的公寓。
- Well, there's still an extra seat available in the car, so come along with us, **by all means**.
  嗯，車子還有空位，你**當然可以**和我們坐同台車。
- "May I borrow this pen?" "**By all means**."
  「可以借我這支原子筆嗎？」「**當然**。」

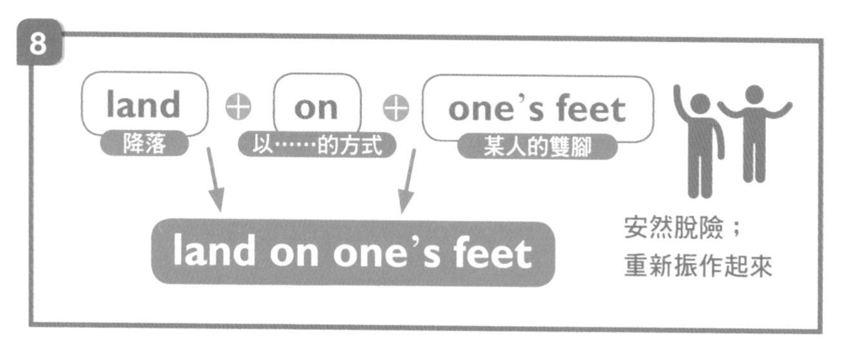

- No matter what crazy things happen to Tiffany, she always **lands on her feet**; she's a very smart woman.
  蒂芬妮遇到什麼事都能夠**安然脫險**；她是一個很聰明的女人。
- Bobby really **landed on his feet** with that raise at work.
  巴比靠著工作加薪而**重新振作**起來。
- It may take a few months to get a job, but I'm sure you'll **land on your feet**.
  找工作可能會花上好幾個月，但我相信你一定會**重新振作**起來的。

153

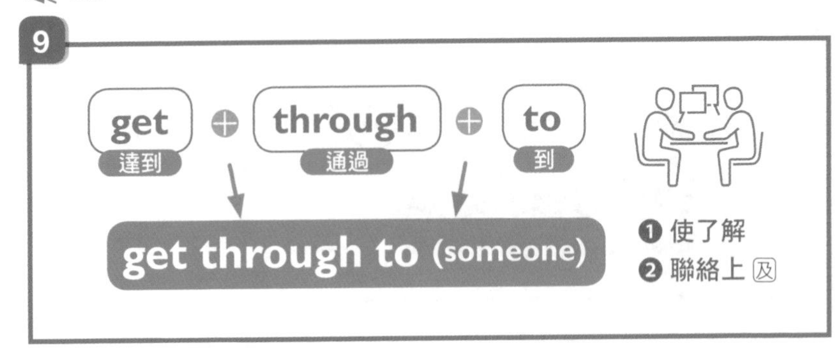

❶ Despite the best efforts of Jeff's friends and family, no one could **get through to** him and convince him to stay in college. 除了傑夫的朋友和家人，沒有人能夠與傑夫**溝通**，並且說服他繼續就學。

❶ Barney finally **got through to** his girlfriend about exercising more. 巴尼終於**讓**女朋友**了解**到她必須多運動了。

❶ We can't **get through to** the government just how serious the problem is! 我們無法**讓**政府**理解**問題的嚴重性！

❶ Pictures can sometimes help you **get through to** people more effectively than writing can.
圖片有時候比文字更容易幫助人們**理解**。

❷ I **got through to** the wrong department.
我**聯絡**錯部門了。

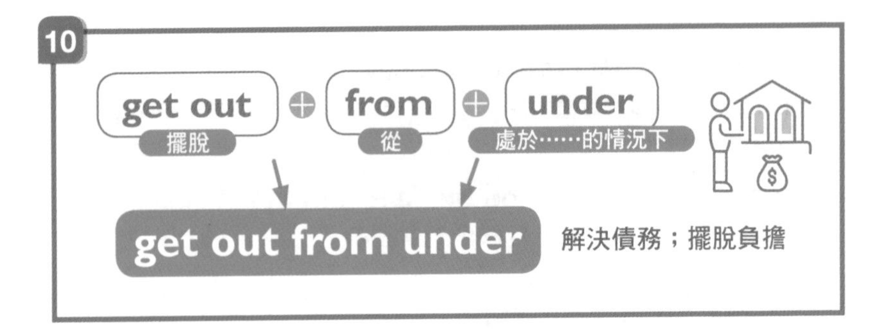

- Ron wasn't sure how to **get out from under** his credit card debt, so he started looking for a second job.
  朗不知道要如何**解決**卡債，所以他開始找兼職工作。

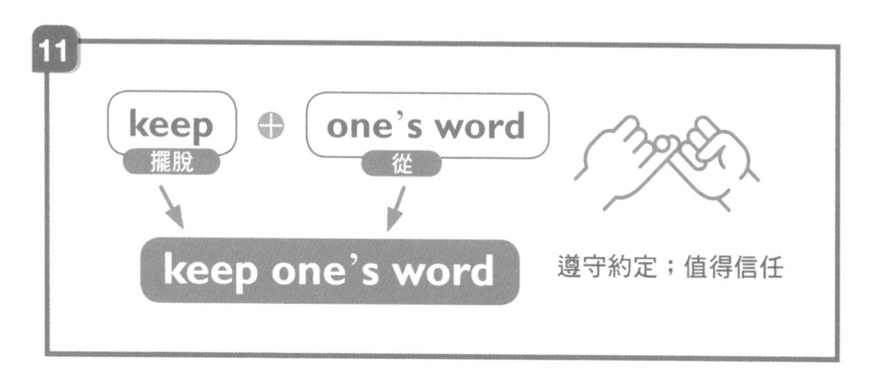

- You can really count on Dan—he's the kind of guy who **keeps his word**.
  你可以相信丹——他是個**說話算話**的人。
- I hope I can trust you to **keep your word**.
  我希望你能夠**遵守約定**。
- I said I'd visit him, and I shall **keep my word**.
  我說過會去拜訪他，而我應該**遵守約定**。
- Jeff is someone who **keeps his word**—you can rely on that. 傑夫是個**說話算話**的人，很可靠。

Getting Home Late
晚回家

Ernie calls his mom to tell her he got in trouble at school and will be home late. 爾尼打電話告訴媽媽他在學校惹上麻煩，所以會晚點回家。

154

Ernie: Hi, Mom? I won't **be in**[1] until late today. I have to stay after school.

Mom: Why? What did you do?

Ernie: It was all Ms. Butterworth's fault. She's the one who is making me stay late.

Mom: Were you **goofing off**[2]?

Ernie: Well, yeah, a little. Also, when Ms. Butterworth asked where my report was, I **talked back to**[3] her.

Mom: Why did you do that?

Ernie: She was **keeping after**[4] me to finish my report . . . I was in a bad mood.

Mom: I guess that's where she **drew the line**[5]. Anyway, if I **were in her shoes**[6], I'd probably do the same thing. You were really **getting out of line**[7].

Ernie: Can I still go to the dance this weekend?

Mom: Hmm, I'm not sure. Let's **play it by ear**[8].

Ernie: Oh, Mom!

爾尼： 嗨，老媽？我今天會晚點**回家**。我放學後必須留下來。

媽媽： 為什麼？你做了什麼好事？

爾尼： 都是巴特沃斯老師的錯，是她要我留那麼晚的。

媽媽： 你又**偷懶**了嗎？

爾尼： 嗯，算是吧。還有，巴特沃斯女士問我報告交了沒時，我和她**頂嘴**。

媽媽： 你為何要那麼做？

爾尼： 她一直**嘮嘮叨叨**，要我寫完報告……而我當時心情不太好。

媽媽： 我想這就是她**無法接受**的原因了。總之，如果我**是她**的話，我可能也會這麼做。你真是太**沒規矩**了。

爾尼： 那我這星期還可以去參加舞會嗎？

媽媽： 嗯，我還不確定。**要看你的表現**囉。

爾尼： 噢，老媽！

155

❶ What time will you **be in** tomorrow? 你明天幾點會**在家**？

❷ I'm sorry, but the doctor **is** not **in** today.
很抱歉，醫生今天休診。

❸ I heard that colorful sandals **are in** this summer.
我聽說今年**流行**顏色鮮豔的涼鞋。

- Jan **goofed off** last weekend and went camping when she should have been painting the house.
  珍上週末本來應該要油漆房子，但她**偷懶**跑去露營。

- The reason you're getting a bad grade in this class is because you **goofed off** when you should have been doing your homework.
  該做功課時，你卻在**摸魚**，這就是你在班上成績不好的原因。

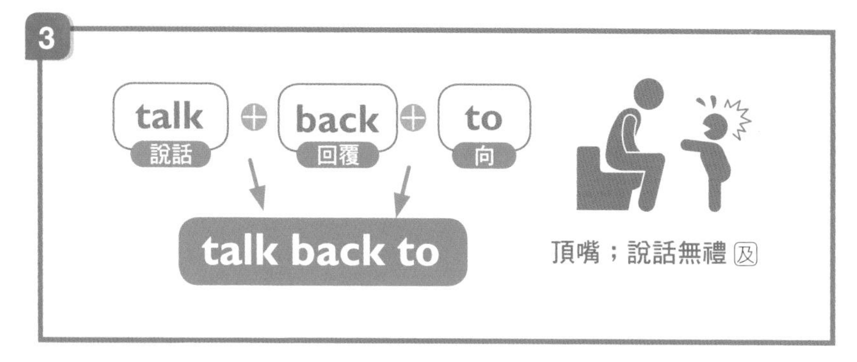

- Grandpa was mad when my little sister **talked back to** him. 爺爺對我妹妹和他**頂嘴**感到很生氣。
- Don't you ever **talk back to** me again! 你還敢**頂嘴**！

- The teacher **kept after** Art until he finished his report.
老師**一直嘮嘮叨叨**直到亞特寫完報告。
- I **kept after** Lucas to let me borrow his car for the weekend, and in the end, he agreed.
我**一直問**盧卡斯週末是否可以把車借給我，他最後終於同意了。

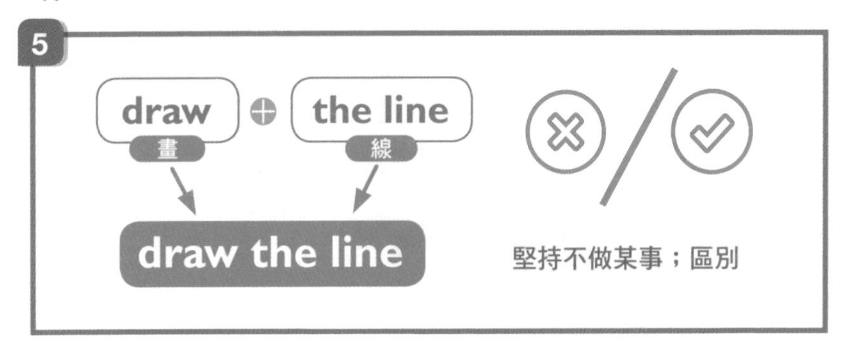

- Although Phil sometimes has a piece of chocolate or two, he **draws the line** at cake because he is trying to lose weight.
  雖然菲爾有時會吃一、兩塊巧克力，但他為了減肥**拒**吃蛋糕。
- My parents told me I have to be home by midnight; although they don't mind if I'm a little late, they **draw the line** at 12:30. 我父母要我在午夜前回家，雖然我覺得晚點到家無所謂，但他們**堅持不**超過 12 點 30 分。

- Oh, boy! I wouldn't like to **be in** your **shoes** when you tell your dad that you locked the keys in the car!
  噢，天啊！**如果我是**你，就不會把你是如何把鑰匙留在車內的事情告訴你爸！
- What would you do if you **were in** my **shoes**?
  如果你**是**我的**話**，會怎麼做呢？

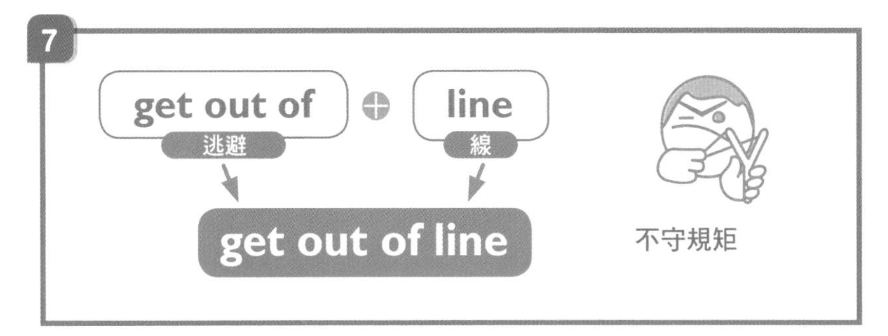

- Please behave when we visit my aunt and don't **get out of line**.
  到我阿姨家拜訪時，要注意你的行為舉止，不可以**不守規矩**。
- The teacher told Amanda that if she **gets out of line** one more time, he'll have to kick her out of class.
  老師告訴亞曼達要是再**不守規矩**，他就只好把她趕出教室了。

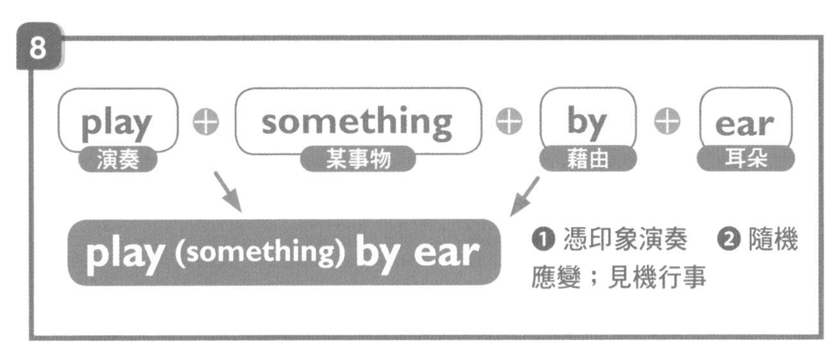

❶ Maggie can **play** anything on the piano **by ear**.
瑪姬只要聽過一遍旋律，便可以用鋼琴彈奏出來。

❷ For now, John is a math major in college. He has decided to **play** it **by ear** as to whether he'll get a degree in physics instead. 約翰目前在大學主修數學，但他決定要**見機行事**，看能否轉為主修物理。

❷ I'm not sure if we'll go to the park this weekend; let's **play** it **by ear**. 我不確定這週末是否要去公園；**看情況吧**。

157

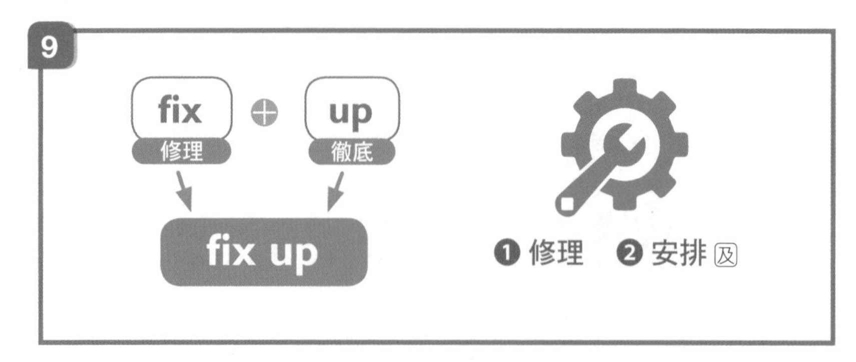

❶ The teenagers spent the weekend **fixing up** the old truck. By Sunday night, it was working like new!
一群年輕人利用週末**修理**卡車，他們在星期日傍晚前就讓卡車變得像新的一樣！

- Although Sandra thought she had practiced playing the flute enough, she made some mistakes during the **dry run** and realized that she needed to practice a lot more before the performance.
  雖然珊卓拉認為她的長笛已經吹得非常熟練，但她在**排練**時犯了一些錯，她覺得在表演前需要再多練習一下。
- In the weeks before he went onstage with his monologue, Brian did a **dry run** every night.
  在演出的好幾個星期前，布萊恩每天晚上都在為獨角戲**排練**。

- They decided to do a **dry run** at the church the day before the wedding.
  他們決定婚禮前在教堂做一次**預演**。

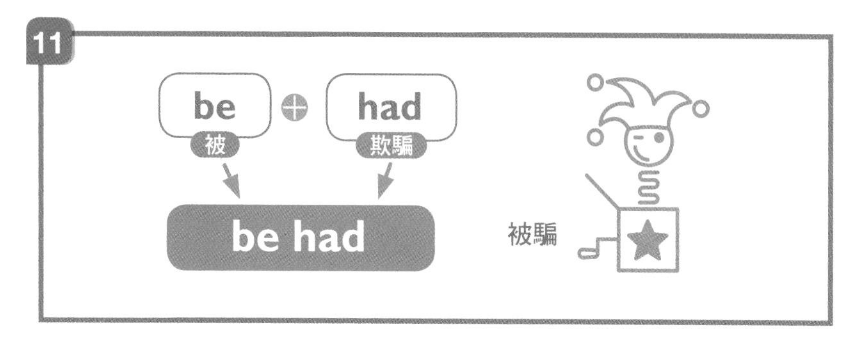

- When you go shopping for a new computer, it's a good idea to bring along an expert so you don't end up **being had**.
  買新電腦時，最好找內行人陪你去，才不會**被騙**。
- I'm sorry to tell you this, but if you just spent $1,200 on this stereo, you **were had**.
  很遺憾地告訴你，如果你是花 1,200 元買這個音響，你就是**被騙**了。
- If you paid much for this car, you've **been had**!
  如果這台車花了你很多錢，那你肯定是**被騙**了！

Step by Step! 背誦版

圖解狄克生片語

一本學會470個關鍵日常英文片語

作者	Matt Coler
審訂	Judy M. Majewsky
翻譯	李盈瑩
編輯	王采翎／丁宥暄
主編	丁宥暄
內文排版	劉秋筑／林書玉／黃恆香
封面設計	林書玉
圖片	Shutterstock
製程管理	洪巧玲
發行人	黃朝萍
出版者	寂天文化事業股份有限公司
電話	02-2365-9739
傳真	02-2365-9835
網址	www.icosmos.com.tw
讀者服務	onlineservice@icosmos.com.tw
出版日期	2022 年 12 月 初版一刷

國家圖書館出版品預行編目(CIP)資料

Step by Step圖解狄克生片語：一本學會470個關鍵日常英文片語(背誦版)(寂天雲隨身聽APP版)/Matt Coler著；李盈瑩譯. -- 初版. -- [臺北市]：寂天文化事業股份有限公司, 2022.12　面；　公分

ISBN 978-626-300-173-2 (25K平裝)

1.CST: 英語　2.CST: 慣用語

805.123　　111020543

- 郵撥帳號 1998620-0
  寂天文化事業股份有限公司
- 訂書金額未滿1000元
  請外加運費100元
- 若有破損　請寄回更換